THE DEAD BELL

QUID MIRUM PRESS

an imprint of The Publishing Circle

THE DEAD BELL / REID WINSLOW
FIRST EDITION
ISBN 978-1-955018-09-8 (paperback)
       978-1-955018-19-7 (hardcover)
       978-1-955018-16-6 (large print)
       978-1-955018-13-5 (eBook)

Book design by Michele Uplinger

DEDICATION

This book is dedicated with love to my wife Jane,
to my children Eleanor and William,
and to my friends Bill and Bob.

The DEAD BELL

REID WINSLOW

QUID MIRUM PRESS

Dead bell or **deid bell** (Scots/Gaelic), also called "death", "passing bell" or "skellet bell"—a hand bell rung in medieval Scotland and England. Bells were often baptised and, once baptised, were believed to possess the power to ward off evil spells and spirits. At the death bed they were rung in the fervent belief evil spirits, standing ready to grab the soul in its passage, were kept away—the soul gaining the head start.

Sunt lacrimae rērum
et mentem mortālia tangunt

Here are the tears of things.
Mortality touches the heart.

—VIRGIL—

MEMBERS OF THE JURY, if you believe that a witness testified falsely as to a part of his or her testimony, you may choose to disbelieve other parts of his or her testimony, or the whole of it, but you are not required to do so. You should bear in mind that inconsistencies and contradictions within a witness's testimony or between that testimony and other evidence do not necessarily mean that the witness is lying. Failures of memory may be the reason for some inconsistencies and contradictions; also, it is not uncommon for two honest people to witness the same event yet perceive or recall things differently. Yet, if you find that a witness has testified falsely as to an issue, you should of course take that into account in assessing the credibility of the remainder of his or her testimony.

UNIFORM JURY INSTRUCTION—(Witness False in Part)

PROLOGUE

SUMMER 1972
Springfield, Illinois

THAT YEAR, THE GHOSTS ARRIVED. As far back as I can remember, the hot months of summer were spent in large rubber rings suspended in the cool clear water of Springfield Lake. Stuffed into tubes, I and my best friends, Bobby Dolan and Gerry Obersheimer, drifted through lazy days which seemed to last forever, a time marked only by sun and water.

As we floated, Bobby droned on about the new video game called Space Invaders. Now just thirteen, Bobby spent every waking hour and most of his money at the video arcade. When he was picked up at the arcade for truancy, his mother sent him to the lake, believing the fresh air would be good for him.

Obersheimer, the only son of industrious first-generation Germans, carried the weight of his complicated, unwieldy surname with stoicism. He had not complained when his name had inevitably devolved into the handy nickname, Kraut. Kraut's parents worked during the day and left him in the care of his significantly older sister, Greta Obersheimer. Greta, the purported summer chaperone, also bore the weighty soubriquet Great A, given in homage to her greatest natural asset.

Hoping to free herself of the odious responsibility of looking after her brother, Great A instead offered Kraut money—in her words, to dig a hole and bury himself in it. When these instructions failed, Great A—typically an indifferent sibling at the best of times and with a false bonhomie bordering on the grotesque—would urgently press an additional ten dollars into Kraut's sweaty hand. Inherently distrustful by nature, and blessed with a wholesome entrepreneurial spirit, Kraut immediately suspected his sister's motives and investigated. He was not disappointed. He recounted his exploits to our delight. He told us he'd crawled (I had no trouble imagining him as a latter-day commando) through the underbrush, over vines and brambles, to the back window on the first floor of his house. Once in place, he lifted his head in time to hear the throes of Great A's carnal awakening, courtesy of Ricky, her boyfriend. In keeping with his genuine free-market spirit, Kraut leveraged his silence into a steady flow of cash from Ricky and Greta.

That summer, we'd all turned thirteen, and only Ben Edison, my older brother at fifteen, had access to illicit contraband: cigarettes, beer, and girlie mags. Although two years older, Ben's talent at procuring the "good stuff" meant he was included in our group without question. What he got from hanging out with a group of thirteen-year-olds I could never figure out. That summer in Eden, the Serpent hadn't appeared yet. Life was good. It got even better when, for reasons never entirely clear, the local Jaycees, with the blessings of the city, placed a raft in the lake. Rudimentary and purpose-built, the raft was comprised of fifteen 2x6s fastened with bolts to four large fifty-gallon drums. The float was barely wide enough for the four of us, even when stacked like cordwood. Secured to the lake floor, a chain fell away into the green darkness. The raft was our refuge, the slow *tak tak tak* of the water beating the rhythm of the summer as damselflies danced over the shimmering surface of the lake.

The western end of Springfield Lake consisted of a large lagoon, formed by two spits of land on opposite sides, which extended like jaws, north and south. Inside the lagoon, the lake opened up again for a half a mile until it met a narrow dam at the end that spilled into a small creek below the lake. A railroad bridge stood guard over the dam.

In early July, our group grew with the addition of Jimmy Newsome. Jimmy simply appeared at the lake one day and, with the effortless tenacity of a burr, affixed himself to our group's fabric. Despite our age differences, Jimmy seemed to fit naturally. Even at eleven, he was an adept mimic, and could imitate teachers, girls, and movie characters with equal ease. In turn, he seemed unfazed by our gushing, vulgar, inane, and misinformed drivel, always remaining silent.

The middle of August arrived during the Summer of the Raft, as we called it later. Throughout the dog days, the sun shone bright and clear, and I could imagine myself flying straight up and reaching Mars.

After almost a full day on the raft, Kraut and Bobby drifted fitfully between sleep and snacking, while Ben and Jimmy pitched potato chips in the water, luring the sunfish to rise. Deep in thought, I peered into the dark shadows, straining to follow the chain as it descended to the lake floor.

Six weeks earlier, we'd invented a game, the rules and

goals of which were amorphous and flexible. The simple challenge was to see who could follow the chain to the bottom, where the lake was probably over fifty feet deep. Now, well into August, none of us had succeeded in coming anywhere near touching the muddy lake bottom. In 1931, the lake was formed when Spaulding Dam was strung across Sugar Creek. Eyes fixed on the green deep, I often wondered whether there were trees, houses, and rocks that covered the bottom . . . a silent world preserved in dark water.

At first no louder than the singing buzz of the dragonfly hovering next to our raft, the sound grew a few seconds later into a distant whine—a vacuum cleaner maybe, muffled, insistent, and mechanical. The whine droned for several seconds until it was cut by a trenchant *thunk*, which we all saw came from a speedboat passing the entrance to the lagoon as it hit a wave, its bow pointing dangerously into the air.

Alerted and nettled by the sudden intrusion into the afternoon, we watched the boat as it quickly neared. Sitting upright, in a moment he would later tell me he regretted, Ben flashed the boat the finger.

The twin Mercs screamed at full throttle as the boat veered towards us. Now a football field away, the boat tore towards us, and I could make out three grinning males. Looking half man, half boy, the trio was clearly drunk with the joy of terrifying pissant kids who'd had the balls to flip them off. Standing at the wheel, the largest one, his greasy long hair flying behind him in the wind, screamed a war whoop, his mouth a knotted rictus. The other two man-boys, faces red and angry, howled in a chorus as—closing in on forty feet—a collision was impending.

The boat lurched suddenly to the right, engines snarling as the props popped out of the lake and threw a wall of six-feet-high water onto the raft. The wake peeled our platform off the surface like a chisel shaving, pitching one end high into the air. As the fifty-gallon drums jutted several feet out of the water, the anchor chain squealed as the raft reached the full extent of its swing. Pulled to its limit, the line finally gave, snapping the raft over like a mousetrap on its back, hurling us into the water.

Beneath the water, all I could see was turbid green, and the vegetation ripped from the bottom of the raft. I could vaguely make out the flashing white of arms and feet flailing around me. Peering into the darkness below, I heard the roar of a boat motor above, beating thunderously, then quickly receding to a high whisper like the rasping of cricket wings.

Lungs aching and heart pounding I began to surface, the boat engine sounding an angry hiss as it retreated. Rising toward the surface, I heard echoing calls like seagulls, which I soon understood were voices screaming through the water.

Breaking the surface, I took a deep breath and, looking around, saw Ben and Bobby clinging to the slimy overturned drums that jutted into the air. The broken chain was wrapped around the raft. Several yards away I could see Kraut swimming towards shore. Ben gestured for me to swim over. Recalling Ben's futile gesture of defiance, after reaching the rocking drums, I turned to my brother.

"Nice going, asshole," I said, taking hold of the slick raft.

Ben stared at the receding boat, stunned bewilderment plastered to his face. After a few seconds he looked over at me, finally processing what I'd said. "Shut the fuck up, Tom. Help me get this thing turned over."

In less than a minute, the platform splashed with a deep thud, settling upright. I noticed a small piece of orange T-shirt caught on the edge of the raft. I could feel my pulse quicken as I looked for Jimmy. Not seeing him, I yelled at the others to look for him. The other three were already searching, clearly panicked. Several seconds later, Bobby screamed for help, pointing at the spotted orange-red of Jimmy's shirt that floated thirty feet away. Bobby swam the distance in seconds. I could see Jimmy wasn't moving. Swimming as fast as I could, I reached Bobby and took Jimmy from him. I got my arms around Jimmy's little chest. Holding the boy, I was struck by how white the skin on his back was and how his arms drooped like kelp in the water. With Bobby's help, I turned Jimmy over. A deep red gash in Jimmy's forehead rose to an ominous dark blue welt. Jimmy wasn't breathing. Together, Bobby and I towed Jimmy towards the raft. Ben and Bobby pulled him onto the slippery surface.

"Jesus, you're cut!" Ben said, pointing to my face. I touched the area above my right eye and was mildly surprised, in a disoriented way, to see my fingers red with slick blood. Although I felt light-headed, the wound itself didn't seem to hurt much.

Kraut, having swum like crazy, finally reached the beach and dashed for the area of the beach where the woods lined the lake. He returned a minute later, accompanied by two teenagers. Soon, a small crowd gathered at the edge of the lake. Finally, a man in his early twenties, dressed in a telltale lifeguard-red T-shirt, ran into the lake with a life preserver and swam to the raft.

The lifeguard flipped Jimmy over and pumped his small chest. Finally, giving a halfhearted wretch and vomiting a thick ball of mucus and water, Jimmy moved. Seconds later, two other men dragged a neon-colored dinghy to the water. They fired up the small attached outboard and reached the raft in seconds, pulling Jimmy, who still lay unconscious, into the dinghy. They transferred Jimmy to a waiting pickup which—with a shower of sand and leaves— disappeared, leaving stunned beachgoers behind.

Shortly after, we made it back to the beach, where, as an afterthought, one of the lifeguards bandaged my forehead, telling me to get it looked at. When I finally got home, I resisted my mother's interrogation, telling her I'd fallen. It was only the next morning, when the pain woke me, that I allowed my mom to take me to the emergency room, where I received ten stitches. The wound was slow to heal and left a raised ridge of white scar tissue above my right eye.

Not that I needed a physical reminder of that day.

The police questioned us for hours about the particulars. Each of us recalled only the boat and a general description of the boys. All of us omitted disclosing Ben's universal gesture of defiance. A few days later, a speedboat was found abandoned in a cove at the other end of the lake at Sanctuary Park Road, the ignition jammed with a screwdriver. Several wet cigarette butts littered the vinyl seat covers.

In the investigation that followed, the city tacitly admitted the raft may have been poorly secured to the bottom and later quietly removed it.

None of us saw Jimmy Newsome again. We learned he was in the hospital and, later, learned he was getting therapy . . . although none of us knew what that meant.

Jimmy didn't return to school and his family moved. All that remained of Jimmy Newsome was a torn swath of orange-red fabric, which I folded neatly and stuck in the top drawer of my dresser.

It wasn't until I was in advanced CPR at the police academy many years later that I learned about near-drowning. After several minutes without oxygen, the brain sustains damage beyond repair. In frigid water, the time is longer before hypoxia, as it's called, kills brains cells by the millions and, like rain on a watercolor, washes the canvas into blurred and muddy splotches. The ability of different persons to tolerate hypoxia depends on a variety of factors, including age, previous health, water temperature, and the promptness and effectiveness of the resuscitation efforts. Irreversible damage from hypoxia can begin in as little as five minutes. In a warm summer lake, six minutes without oxygen might mean reviving a person who'd then live in a persistent vegetative state. More time than that, and there is no point.

Time stood still that afternoon; for thirteen-year-olds, seconds, minutes, and hours morph and stretch like figures in a funhouse mirror. I could never be sure how long Jimmy was under. For years, I tried to bracket, to put a framework on what happened to Jimmy and what the outcome was likely to have been. I'd played the rescue like a film loop, reviewing the data until, like worn fabric, it shredded in my head. I calculated in water temperature and the arrival of the first responders, but I couldn't be sure how long Jimmy was under. Accessing the peculiar timetable of my childhood, the nearest I came to figuring Jimmy's time down was that it lasted the duration of a *Roadrunner* episode.

SPRING, SUMMER, AND FALL

DECADES LATER

CHAPTER ONE

MAYBE THIS TIME I CAN MAKE IT HAPPEN.

I study my feet as they grip the tiled concrete edge of the pool stretching out in front of me. Large and white, my toes are fringed with brown hair and armored with clipped nails. The smooth green water reflects fluorescent lights and black lines, wavering between fat and thin.

I draw air deep into my lungs and hurl myself onto the glassy surface, which breaks to receive me, muffling my ears and cocooning me from the outside. With each stroke, my head rises and I can hear the brassy sound of slapping water bouncing off the tiled walls. With the downstroke, the sound deadens again.

At the other end, where the pool sinks far below, my feet dangle, and I stop to listen. I can hear only my breath and the throaty *gluck gluck* of the rippling water hitting the drain. When I left the apartment this morning, the sunrise, its early light fragile and clean, painted the street with promise. I'd arrived at five-thirty on this beautiful Saturday morning and, as I'd hoped, the pool was empty. I'd come for the silence and the solitude.

I manage to put in thirty lengths before resting again. My breath comes hard as I perch at the deep end, hanging onto the concrete edge of the pool. The cavernous room is still empty, the lights buzzing steadily. Drawing three quick deep breaths and releasing the edge, I drift, eyes open, to the bottom. I land on the flat, hard plane and sit there, legs folded, arms extended, as though bestowing a blessing on the pool. My breath silent, I perceive only the muffled hum and *click click* of the pool's mechanical heart, and the warm water holding me a few inches above the tile floor. After a bit, I open my eyes and see the dark green shades and dim glaze of ceramic squares in the corners, barely discernible through fluid astigmatism.

Suspended still, inert as a bubble in oil, I will myself to stay submerged. After sixty seconds, my lungs begin to ache. I release a small burst of air through my nose and settle firmly on the bottom of the pool. After ninety seconds, my vision narrows. With a violent, autonomic twitch, I expel the last of my air. My chest convulses, and my throat clenches tight as a knot, the dark cool green now lit with electric red and black. Finally, like blades of a spring knife, my legs shoot me to the surface and into the silence of the lights and the empty room.

My hungry lungs wrestle chlorine-filled air with each gasp. I lurch towards the edge of the pool and hug the cold, wet surface, my arms extended like wings, and sprawl until my pulse slows and the vivid reds and blacks recede. Finally, I pull myself up and out of the water.

Fighting the urge to vomit, I make my way to the shiny

metal bench to secure a towel. Sensing the first gray, heavy notes of a headache, I put my head between my knees. I sit for several minutes before gathering the strength to make the trip to the locker room. I carefully navigate the slippery deck, yet still slide on a small patch of wet grime, driving my elbow into the unforgiving cinderblock wall.

Once inside the locker room, I need to sit down again, so I weave toward the wooden bench near my locker. The smell of strong disinfectant wafting from the showers magnifies my headache. The pain in my elbow thrums, hot and loud. Seated in front of my open locker, I see the clock on the wall reads six-thirty. Holding my arm, something else edges out the throbbing. Starting sharp and thin, like an insect sting, it spreads as I try to put a name to it. The new feeling, now more of a solid ache, is shame and anger. This same feeling assaulted me earlier, along with the din of the garbage crew hurling metal garbage cans with symphonic gonging, waking me from half-sleep. Stirring, I'd sent an exploratory leg under the covers, only to find the bed empty. I dragged myself to the kitchen, where I'd found a note affixed to the fridge by a magnetic Tabasco sauce bottle.

Written in Trina's distinctive cursive, the note informed me she'd be staying with her sister overnight. This was hardly a surprise, given the several days' conflict which had erupted between us. Relying on the peculiar logic of conflict, as I'd left the apartment that morning, I'd managed to transform Trina's departure—by all rights a small tragedy—into feelings of relief; there'd be no boxing match that night. Even if it meant being alone, I'd felt resolved, if not entirely content.

I have reached a stage in my existence where I can

claim enough self-awareness to articulate what I hope to gain from life. Recently, I was startled to realize I am too far along, too anchored, to change my course towards that elusive destination: contentment. I seem to be perpetually entangled and confused, my perspective smeared with a dark brown stain of frustration. Something has been making me irritable, discontented, and swinging at everything with all my might. But, like trying to punch something underwater, I haven't been able to land a blow, and I feel out of control and useless. I have to admit I've taken this out on Trina.

The small mobile phone setting on the locker's utensil tray springs to life, startling me. I answer, "Edison."

The monotone voice on the other end responds with, "Article nine off Moffett", providing an address. I acknowledge the call and hang up.

By sheer force of will and perseverance, I have reached the rank of investigating detective, appointed to Major Case Task Force for Lake County Illinois. Lake County is in the northeastern corner of Illinois, along the shores of Lake Michigan. It is the third-most populous county in Illinois after nearby Cook and DuPage counties. Its county seat is Waukegan, which is referred to locally as one of the collar counties of Chicago. Lake County is also the second most wealthy county in Illinois and one of the wealthiest counties in the nation. The lakefront communities of Lake Forest, Lake Bluff, and Highland Park are part of what is known as Lake Michigan's Gold Coast.

I am on rotation, and it is my turn to pull the call. I've worked Lake County for over eight years—long enough to know Moffett is in Lake Forest where tall hedges, iron gates, and security cameras preserve privacy and keep out the masses.

Reaching into the locker, I pull out my clothes, dress quickly, then shut the locker with a solid metal clunk. I pause for a moment to consider my situation. After a few seconds, I come to the grudging conclusion, if only to myself, that I've been a shithead.

I leave the athletic club, waving to Tyler, the club manager, as I depart. I climb into my red Audi TT. The Beast, as I privately call it, giving in to the juvenile urge some men have to name their cars and weenies, is a vanity I allow myself. That I drive a car like the TT, even if it is pre-owned, has raised a few eyebrows at Division. I live in a tidy prewar railroad apartment in Waukegan, which provides shelter to the strong, muscular, and loud working-engine of North Chicago. The car is a symbol of a time when I'd hoped for something larger, a place in the order of things that resonated with purpose—a goal.

On weekends, I used to watch from my fourth-floor window as my neighbors dutifully mowed their tiny lawns and polished bumpers on cars for which they paid the bank every month while they drank beer and dreamed of something more. The TT, bought with the proceeds from the sale of my parents' house in Springfield, is my contribution to the counterrevolution, my rolling middle finger to the forces pushing to keep my face planted to the mat.

After half an hour, I see the signs for Lake Forest and turn down a parkway lined with pink dogwoods. The trees arch over the road in frothy shades of white, rose, and purple. Spring has come late to Illinois, but it made a showy entrance. Even so, after so many false starts, most locals, like jilted lovers, are skeptical of Mother Nature's first gesture of generosity and accept the sunny weather with healthy mistrust.

Giving Mother the benefit of the doubt, I roll back the convertible top and feel the breeze as it rolls wet and fragrant down the street, pushing dogwood blossoms in waves across the asphalt. I almost feel happy. Scanning the passing signs, I finally find the small green sign marked simply *Moffett*, framed by tall emerald green thuja hedges. Had I blinked, I might have missed the sign entirely. Half a mile down, as I near the address, I see police cars lined up like so many stacked dominos along a tall brick wall. A location van stands open in front of the driveway. Blue lights tick quietly on a large paramedic unit backed into the driveway. Even in the early weekend morning, a small knot of people edge against the yellow police tape for a better look.

Passing the entrance, I park in the first available spot, carefully leaving distance between the TT and the adjacent thrashed '97 Pontiac Firebird, which seems out of place with the clean street and late model European sedans dotting the driveways and cul-de-sac. A breeze caresses the parkway surface, whipping light green seed spores from the flowering trees into lazy curling patterns that swirl down the immaculate asphalt.

The house, if you could call it that, is a four-story brick and stone structure with two-story windows running the length of the front. Surrounded by a tall brick wall topped with wicked foot-long spikes, the entrance is dominated by stone steps that rise to black doors saddled with brass fixtures that gleam with new polish.

At the gate, the uniform points me to a path which

follows the brick wall, finally opening out into the garden. The brick wall, which I estimate is over twelve feet, extends the length of the garden. At the end of the lawn, half a football field away, the wall makes a sharp turn and extends another fifty yards until it turns left again. Rows of carefully tended rose plants and shrubs cascade upwards towards the back of the house. A white stone pergola dominates the center of the garden, which is, in turn, framed by a large, circular, dry fountain.

Fifty yards out, at the end of the lawn, the cluster in the far corner might pass as an intimate congregation gathered to celebrate a wedding or bar mitzvah. The mound of bright yellow plastic tarp on the ground pegs it as the Article Nine of the Illinois Criminal Code *Homicides and Crimes Against the Person* called in by the dispatcher. The tarp, the emergency responders' orange uniforms, and the intercom squawks, serve as a jarring contrast to the green peace of the morning. I can see the techs in the far corner, looking for footprints.

Striding the lawn, I nod to obligatory *hellos* and *how ya doin's*, recognizing auxiliary crime techs I've worked with before. Over near the corner, I see Lou Watson, the senior forensic tech and owner of the thrashed Firebird. I feel a frisson of relief that I've parked a few feet away. Watson, who grew up on the dangerous streets of Riverdale, is the first Black lab tech in Lake county. He possesses an encyclopedic knowledge of jazz, which is our only point of common interest . . . aside from violent death. I sometimes find myself drawn into lively and heated conversation with him, often over truly arcane issues like pre- and post-Camarillo Parker. This time, however, I am not in the mood to talk and, even less, to pass niceties. I look around, noticing two cameras pointing into the center of the garden. I gesture to one of the techs.

"Surveillance?"

The cop shrugs. "Yup. No data."

"None?"

The cop raises his shoulders in resignation. "They been having problems with da system. Can't tell if it was turned off or flushed."

I make my way towards the tarp. As I cross the lawn, the sun breaks over the tops of the trees. The air, heavy with spores and pollen, carries the light chirp of a woman's laughter. I halt, looking quickly to my left to find the sound. A short blonde woman in a tech uniform quickly averts her face.

I stand still, my neck aching, suddenly tired. Recalling Trina's laughter, I realize it has been months since I've heard her light music. Startled out of my reverie by a blue jay across the garden, I edge towards the far border of the garden. A small group of techs and one cop ring the tarp. They part to allow me room. I steel myself as I stride forward. The laughing woman moves to one side as I crouch to peel back the plastic. Grey, matted hair drapes over the broad shoulders of the corpse, which lies encased in a yellow rain jacket. Under the jacket, the victim wears a white terry robe, its collar stained the color of rust. Adjusting my feet to get a better view, I hear a spongy noise under my shoes. I see the woman's hair is wet, as is the robe, jacket, and the surrounding ground. Tugging at her left shoulder, I meet the fleshy face of an older woman, her blue-grey eyes gazing without light, the chalky skin of her cheek smeared with dirt and leaves.

Watson joins the circle. I turn to him. "Why's she wet?"

Lou ignores me. Walking his crab-like walk, he nudges techs and cops aside with his considerable size as he circles the body. Working with an urgent athleticism, he swings a Nikon D7100 camera, adjusting the focus. I turn to the female uniform who stands several feet away.

"She got a name?"

"Faith Wesley."

The dark jitters, which have plagued me since early morning, become impossible to ignore, rising undeniably, inexorably, and as urgent as a spastic colon. I want only refuge to purge them in private. "That it?" I shoot at the woman.

"Well, they've got money, I'd say," she volleys back.

I scan the faces around me, certain my condition is as obvious as if it was written on the back of my jacket. Realizing the choice is either to gather myself or call in someone else, I take a breath, will away morbid reflection, and begin organizing the crime in my mind.

Over the years, I've responded to hundreds of felonies. Most crime is easily sorted and as predictable as an *I Love Lucy* rerun. Typical crime is comfortable, a Fred and Ethel domestic shooting, say, or a drug deal gone south, and usually constitutes a few days' work.

I kneel next to Lou as he inspects the ground next to the body. He retracts the yellow sheet and touches Faith Wesley's head, muttering comments as much to himself as to anyone else. Doing my own internal calculus, and ignoring Lou as best I can, I start a mental ledger: means, motive, and opportunity. I mentally sift through the scenarios—sexual assault, burglary, lover's quarrel—and for each make a mental note. I'll need to follow up with the ME's office for a rape kit and make sure to have the brick wall periphery completely searched for signs of entry and exit.

Lou finally points to indentations on the edge of the lawn in the spot where he'd been standing earlier. "Sprinklers," he says, his exhale whistling through his nostrils. "You hear they're releasing the complete Art Tatum catalog next week? Remastered." He rises to his feet and adjusts the waist of his pants. I am certain that if Lou doesn't start taking care of himself I'll be looking at him under the yellow sheet before too long.

I shake my head, responding to Lou's attempt to engage me, then nod towards the mound. "Hadn't heard. Can we turn her all the way over?" I see the female uniform roll her eyes and shake her head in disgusted disbelief. I find myself angry at the woman and defensive of Lou.

With Faith Wesley on her back, Lou continues to catalog and mutter. The human remains of Lake County are a wrecking yard, and Lou seems immune to the carnage. I've never gotten used to it.

What I see is a gash the color of crushed pomegranates cut deep into the pale flesh of Faith Wesley's neck. Her tongue sticks out in perpetual disdain.

Lou coughs once. "Yup. And in August they're supposed to reissue most of Bud Powell's stuff on Verve."

"What about the sprinklers?" I ask, becoming annoyed at Lou's prattle.

"The system fires up at 6:45. The ground under her is damp but not soaked. Morning dew is my bet. She got here between 4:00 and 6:45."

"Fucking shit," I say, placing the tarp over the woman's unseeing eyes.

Lou raises his big shoulders in resignation. "That's

life," he says, placing his clipboard in his bag—a gesture so Gallic and laden with ennui I fully expect to see him fire up a Gauloise and sigh through a column of smoke, ". . . *et puis je fume.*"

"How bad for forensics?"

As if on cue, Lou pulls out a pack of Marlboro Lights and motions to the tall brick wall fifteen yards away. "Well," he says, once we've stopped at the wall, where Lou bends to light the cigarette, "we won't get any transfer prints, and the chance of decent fiber material is shitty. Best we can hope for is footprints and maybe some DNA material under the fingernails." Now that we are standing next to the brick wall, it strikes me how truly high it reaches. Shaking his head, Lou pushes the blue plume out of his nose and gestures towards the scene. "This looks pretty clean. The other team is looking over by the far end of the wall."

After taking another drag, he says, "Quite a scene. Weird." He pitches the butt over the wall and out onto the street, ignoring the standing order against smoking on site.

I nod. I watch Faith Wesley being loaded onto a gurney and rolled across the lawn. I've come to understand this part of the job I do is as much the province of a village witch-doctor as a trained forensic investigator. Despite the technology and the precise mathematics of violence, police procedure is still riddled with traditions and superstitions.

As I stand in silence, my thoughts inevitably turn to Trina, remembering a period when the stars aligned and I'd believed in our future. Recently, the best either of us have been able to muster is a dark détente, tense blue and grey periods that streak our lives like rain down a window. I never seem to see the ugly parts coming. Like nausea or the flu, the darkness flares up, then passes with time. But over time, the return to intimacy—not physical and driven by hunger—but trust, the true currency of love, flows sluggishly. We've been spending as fast as we earn.

My cell phone rings, pulling me back to the present.

As so often happens, when naming a ghost, it appears.

I peer at the screen, not particularly surprised to see Trina's name. Debating whether to answer the call, my resolve finally collapses with a groan and a splash like a decrepit wooden bridge. I answer, finding a safe spot several yards away in a small hedge next to a bed of roses.

"Hello?" My answer gives nothing.

Her voice sounds brittle and clipped. "D'you get my note?" she asks.

"Yup. You staying up there with Sophie 'til Monday?" The question is as much a challenge as a request for information. Within the few seconds between us, we are back to the form of lovers' brinksmanship known as "Who Cares Less."

"I'll call you and let you know when I'm coming down," Trina says, moving a step closer to the edge of no return, the point where neither of us can take back what we've said.

Despair, shame, and spite thump loudly against my insides like wet wash on a spin cycle. Looking to land a preemptive strike, I offer, "I'm working a new case, just called in."

"All weekend?" Trina says, revealing her disappointment and, perhaps, hope.

"So far. Looks like it." I kick at a tuft of grass.

"Where's Liam?"

"With his mom," I answer, dislodging the piece of sod and kicking it towards the hedge.

She exhales deeply. Almost in a whisper, she says, "I

wish you'd take a different tack on the cat."

This is everything I need to know. Looking behind me to make sure I am out of earshot of the staff, I drill into the phone, "I thought I was pretty clear."

"Tom, you're not being fair."

"You lied to me about the fucking cat," I growl.

Trina comes back swinging. "I knew you'd overreact. I was right on the money. You can be right, Tom, and you can be alone."

I yell into the phone, "You lied to me because you know I told you we—and that means Sophie too—are not going to have a fucking pet." Realizing I've screamed, I turn to see the team looking over. I worry about reports of my outburst getting back to Delahunt.

"I gotta go," I say, my voice softer, still hoping to salvage some reentry into the conversation, but the line is dead.

CHAPTER TWO

A T FIFTY-ONE, I CONSIDER MYSELF A GOOD specimen of the male of the species. I work hard to keep in shape, and quietly judge my colleagues, whose academy photos could not with any certainty be used to identify them. As they grouse and fret over the obstacle course during the qualification physicals, I try, without much success, to hide my schadenfreude when the results are posted and a handful of officers are offered the choice of either getting fit or facing early retirement. The office became more serious when a senior inspector collapsed on the rope wall and later died.

I've never held any pretense of having classic good looks. I inherited my pleasant, if not chiseled, face from my father. I am thankful the hair on my head is full and cut close. One time, I was asked during a party game to describe the actor I most resembled. I chose Jeff Daniels, not Brad Pitt—classic American, but not American classic. As I approach my mid-fifties, the skin at the corners of my eyes has become finely etched, and creases mark the edges of my mouth. My eyes are deep set and give me what I've been told is a brooding look. The distinctive white scar above my right eye dashes any remote chance of magazine good looks. The width of a bead of caulking, and the length of a cutworm, the scar is the product of an accident in my teens and serves to toughen a face which I think might otherwise tend to the boyish. I have also been told I can look menacing, and that my blank stare can be like reading Sanskrit. Trina once said I had the face of a killer but the heart of a poet, to which, laughing, I'd replied, "That is a damn sight better than the reverse."

That, of course, was before the train went off the rails, before I decided to take my stand with Trina. In the right circumstances, I can be domineering. I don't think of myself as a bully, but with Trina, I have to admit it often comes down to a simple conflict of wills. If one or the other of us could gracefully withdraw, if only for a little while, I am sure we'd have less conflict. But, almost in the same instant I have this thought, the small voice in my head asks whether, when the accounts are settled, if it is really worth going through the daily adjustments and compromises. I wonder if being alone isn't a better solution.

Staring at my cell, I entertain the idea of calling Trina back and, weighing the required ownership of my conduct against the discomfort of solitude, I drop my phone in my pocket.

One of the uniformed officers standing at the back of the garden tells me the place is called Walsingham. I push the intercom. While I'm standing there, the cop, obviously impressed, tells me the place got its name from the doors which came from England, weigh a thousand pounds apiece, and are sixteen-feet high and four-and-a-half-inches thick.

Moments later, the famous doors open, admitting me to the front hall, which is dominated by a crystal chandelier suspended from a soaring three-story skylight. The air is heavy with furniture polish and the cool citrus fragrance of wealth. I savor the quiet and order—the greatest gift granted to the wealthy—the illusion of freedom from loud anarchy, sudden noise, and the ugly.

I have always harbored a streak of anarchy, fueled no doubt by my blue-collar upbringing and a vestige of college philosophy. I also believe the foundations supporting the cloisters of privilege contain faults that lie beneath. When the revolution inevitably comes for those who firmly hold the belief life is beautiful and scheduled, reality will be visited with the startling speed and ferocity of an African savannah feeding frenzy. The delicate web of complex golf-course courtesies and arcane yacht club mannerisms will flap uselessly in the raging winds of change.

I follow one of the uniforms who's been assigned the house until we finally reach a room at the back that overlooks the gardens. A blonde woman stands alone, facing away, towards the windows.

The officer next to me clears her throat. "Ms. Edwards, this is Detective Tom Edison. He's here to see you."

The woman turns to face me. I can immediately detect the same aquiline features as those of her mother. Thin lips are set under a strong nose. She gives me a look, her steely blue eyes with their dark irises and shiny clear surfaces, unblinking. Her skin is polished and smooth. She wears a light grey tailored jacket over a silk blouse, and light grey wool slacks, which are, I think, maybe a size too small. She stands there, arms crossed, and remains in the middle of the room. "Linda Edwards," she says, turning to me but making no move to shake my hand. "My father's getting dressed and will be down shortly."

She stands there, arms folded, asserting distance and an implied intent to invoke status. Rather than attribute her demeanor to shyness, insecurity, or simply a reaction to her recently dead mother, I assume she is acting to establish standing.

"Over here, if you will." Linda gestures to a large couch. I walk further into the room but remain standing. Coming to a stop, she turns to me and tells me she's lived at the house with her parents and her daughter since her divorce. The previous night, she claims, she'd been at a gallery opening in Chicago and then had eaten dinner in Lake Forest with Nora Summers, one of her best friends. It was late, she says, and they'd had too much to drink. She'd dropped Nora at her house and when she'd returned, looked in on her daughter, Emma, then went straight to bed. The first she'd learned of her mother's death was when her father came and woke her and told her to get the police.

"When were you up this morning?" I ask.

"At about seven-thirty."

"Can you tell me why the surveillance system has been erased?"

Linda shakes her head. "I don't think it was erased. The system has had problems for months."

"Didn't anybody think to get it fixed?"

Linda's face darkens. "We didn't think something like this was going to happen."

"Well, we're going to want to get a look at the recorder."

"Help yourself."

"Where is it?"

Linda's cheeks color and her eyes narrow. Taking a deep breath, she says, "Look, I have a ten-year-old who has soccer this morning."

"Your daughter—Emma, is it? She's here?"

Linda hesitates, seeming a little surprised, then she nods. "Yes, upstairs in her room."

"Does your ex live here in Lake Forest?"

Linda shakes her head. "In Chicago, but I don't see what that has to do with my mother."

"Name?" I ask, enjoying the fact she clearly dislikes sharing.

"Lenten Edwards."

I looked at her, puzzled. She manages another thin smile, which almost looks pretty on her.

"His family's related to Jonathan Edwards. 'Sinners in the hands of an angry God', Yale, Aaron Burr and all that . . ." she looks towards the door. "He's also a lawyer." As if this final statement is itself the best evidence of the fact he's a scoundrel.

"Anyone besides you and your parents and Emma living here?"

"The housekeeper, Frances Reynolds. But she's been in England with her family for the last several weeks. Jesus Morales maintains the grounds and has access to the house. His wife, Alma, does menial work and helps Frances with the cooking when she needs it. She's been sick lately."

She pauses and rises to her feet. "If you'll just excuse me one min—"

At the far end of the room, the door opens, revealing a slim man in his early seventies. I am struck immediately by the man's lined, narrow face and clipped gray hair.

Unflinching blue eyes, lined with dark heavy pouches, stare back at me. A small dusting of silver stubble shades the man's cheeks.

Clearly relieved, Linda takes her father by the arm. "Daddy, this is Detective Tom Edison."

Charles Wesley extends a hand. "Linda, it's cold in here. Will you adjust the heat?"

I take Wesley's hand. The man's grip feels cool and strong. Charles bows slightly, in a continental fashion, gesturing for me to sit down. I move towards the couch and sit.

"Mr. Wesley, I'd—"

"Daddy, Mr. Edison—"

I shoot a glance at Linda. "I was just starting with Ms. Edwards when you came in, so we haven't gotten far."

Wesley shrugs, then takes a seat on a long brocade couch. He turns his attention to a small table next to the couch where a small crystal bird lays on its side. He carefully rights it. Next, he selects a piece of porcelain, holding it to the light.

After several seconds, the old man closes his eyes, as if seeing the events unfold in his own private movie. "I don't share my wife's taste for the garden," he says. "I believe in cutting to the chase, Detective Edison, if you'll forgive the cliché. I'm fairly sure you'll hear some unflattering things about Faith, but I'd ask you to bear in mind, like most people, she was complex. Faith was raised on a farm in Iowa and was a brilliant student. She got a scholarship to Yale in classics, which is where I met her." He pauses for a couple of seconds to place the porcelain on the table to his left. "She had a quick mind and was financially very capable. Faith was also a fierce championship tournament bridge player."

"She sounds like a formidable woman."

Charles smiles. "Formidable, yes. A good word, like a fortress. We had our differences. I often thought Faith too direct. She wasn't gifted with subtlety and she had a strong sense of loyalty, which was easily betrayed. I might have said in certain instances she lacked compassion. For those she cared for, however, she would move heaven and earth."

"Do you have any idea who might have done this, Mr. Wesley?"

"None whatsoever."

I shift, looking over at Linda. "There's something troubling in all of this. Your wife was killed in a—" I struggle, trying to be delicate "—particularly brutal way. We've got a couple of theories we're gonna look at."

"How dreadful," Charles says.

I don't want to tell them as part of standard police protocol we will need to rule out contract murder, and that, eventually, we will have a rape kit done as part of the workup. "Do you have any idea why anyone would want Mrs. Wesley dead?"

"*De mortuis nil nisi bonum*," Linda mutters, looking at her father.

"Well, goddamn it," Charles says, turning to his daughter, visibly angry.

Linda doesn't apologize.

"Did she have enemies?"

Charles closes his eyes. "Enemies," he says, weighing the word slowly. "Faith didn't really care what others thought of her, but I can't believe anyone would want to murder her."

"Do you have any guns?"

"Several, but since Emma's been here, we've locked them up. They seem a bit pointless now," he says, shaking his head.

"Can you tell me about the surveillance system?"

Charles' eyes shift. "I don't pay attention to that stupid thing. I have no idea . . ." he mumbles, trailing off.

For several seconds the only sound is the quiet whir of the ventilation system coming to life. I wait for Charles to finish whatever thought he had until it becomes obvious he's done talking. The old man rises and walks to a grand piano at the far end of the room. Gently opening the lid, he sits and begins to play a tune, quietly at first, then a little louder. A slow, melodic theme. Four single slow notes, followed by an ascending triad, with a minor interval at the end.

Without hesitation, I say, "Schubert."

Wesley looks over, surprised. "Just so. Do you play?" He continues the melody.

"Not really. I took a couple of music-history classes at Northwestern," I admit reluctantly. Wesley stops playing. He suddenly looks very old.

"*Der Tod und das Mädchen*," he says, as if offering the answer to a classroom.

I reply, "Death and the Maiden."

Charles smiles briefly. "Very good." He nods at me. "The song is a dialogue between the maiden and Death as he comes to claim her."

Charles plays the next phrase. "She tells him, 'I'm too young . . . don't touch me.'"

The tempo increases. "Death replies, 'I'm a friend and you will sleep softly in my arms . . .'" The music stops. Charles closes the lid and gazes towards the window. I wonder if the bizarre vignette Charles just enacted is a way of expressing his grief or some kind of test to measure my intelligence.

"I found Faith when I walked outside at about seven-fifteen. It was about five minutes after seven, and she'd not yet returned to the kitchen from the garden. She would start coffee, or if Frances was here, she'd have coffee ready and read the paper. It was late, so I put on my robe and went downstairs. Seeing no one in the dining room or kitchen, I went out."

Charles returns to the couch, tapping the porcelain, and examining its structure. Even from where I sit, I can see fine blue designs on its translucent surface. Linda, who's been standing at the other end of the room, moves next to her father, sits, and takes his arm. I'm jaded enough to wonder if this is a genuine display of affection or a small piece of theater for my benefit.

"Were any of the staff here?"

Linda jumps in. "Jesus doesn't come in until eight-thirty. When Alma comes on Saturdays, she comes with him."

I ignore her. "When you went out, what did you do?"

Charles shifts in his seat, staring into a place surely gone in time but alive in his memory. "I walked out along the path. It was wet because the sprinkler system was on. When I got to the rose garden, I found her, face down." He begins to shake, making no sound, then clutches Linda's hand and holds it tight. I can see the sudden display genuinely catches her off guard.

After a few seconds, I clear my throat. "The coroner's office will verify cause of death. Crime scene technicians will be around the house for most of today. It can be disturbing, so if there is somewhere you can go, I suggest you do. They will ask you for some of Mrs. Wesley's things to get DNA and rule out prints. Fairly standard stuff."

"Can I go now?" Linda asks, releasing her father's hand and getting up from the couch. She looks peeved. I walk over to her and hand her my card.

"You can text me to let me know when I can talk to Emma," I say. "My cellphone number is on the back."

She nods, moving to the door, leaving her father alone with me as she skirts a uniform entering the room to report the scene has been processed.

Once the uniform is gone, Wesley makes his way to a tall mahogany sideboard and pulls a stopper out of a crystal decanter. The stopper releases with a solid clink. "Will you take a drink?" the old man asks, pouring three fingers into a heavy-looking crystal glass.

I shake my head. Charles sits down again. He takes a long, single pull from the glass. He looks into the bottom and swirls the contents, then finishes it off. We sit there for a few seconds as Charles apparently gathers his thoughts.

Taking the silence as an opportunity, I ask if Mrs. Wesley had any close friends she kept in touch with. Mustering something close to a smile, Charles answers, "The Hookers."

I look at him, bewildered.

"Her crochet friends," Charles rises again to refill his empty glass at the decanter, this time making sure the glass is a stout four fingers.

"I'll need the contact information for those people and information about her bank accounts and finances—"

"Just a second there," Wesley sputters. With effort, he puts the glass on the side table, his eyes narrowing and a slight flush darkening the wattle of his throat. "The bank accounts and finances—is that really necessary? I mean, for God's sake, who's being investigated here?"

I realize I've kicked up a hornet's nest and move quickly to explain. "In a homicide of this kind, Mr. Wesley, we need to know if there's anything unusual about the family finances. Is there an accountant or financial advisor I can speak to, to avoid disturbing you?"

Wesley moves unsteadily to a carved side desk and extracts a small notecard. "Fred Atwater," he says, handing me the paper. The veneer of civility is cracking.

"Are either Mr. or Mrs. Morales here? I'd like to speak with them."

"Let me see," Charles says, walking to the door, leaving me to look around.

I make my way over to the glass case containing antique samurai war armor and, according to the engraved placard, a katana-samurai sword made by Masamune. The placard identifies the sword as the legendary *Honjō Masamune,* the ceremonial sword of the Tokugawa period, passed down from one shōgun to another for two-hundred-and-fifty years.

I hear the door click. "A family heirloom," Charles says, joining me in front of the case. "During the US occupation of Japan, the *Honjō Masamune* was found by US GIs and taken to a police station in Mejiro. In January 1946, for reasons which still aren't clear, the Mejiro police gave the sword to a man identified in the police records as Sgt. Coldy Bimore."

Charles walks over to the sideboard and pours himself another three fingers. "It turns out there was no Sgt. Coldy Bimore. My father acquired the sword at considerable cost and under complicated circumstances." He shuffles to the couch again and sits, careful not to spill the drink. I can't really fault him for taking a few drinks on a day like this. "It's too valuable to give away and too dirty to sell," he says, taking a drink.

"What about the Moraleses?" I ask, leaving open the question of the sword's provenance.

Charles shakes his head and takes another pull from the glass. "Apparently they've not arrived yet."

"Can I have an address?"

"You may," Charles says, leaving me to guess whether he'd intended the subtle grammar correction as a rebuff. He reaches out to hand me another small notecard, already made out. "The number for Jesus and Alma. A couple of the hookers are on there, too."

Wesley extends his hand, a sign it is time to leave. I take it, more out of politeness than a concession it is time to terminate the interview. Wesley gazes at me, smiling sadly. "I know you'll do what you have to Tom—may I call you Tom?"

I nod tentatively, wondering whether I've unwittingly ceded some privilege of rank. Wesley quickly says, "Good. You may call me Charles," although he offers the courtesy in a way that invites neither closeness nor friendship.

He sighs deeply and wavers slightly, clearly feeling the effect of the ten fingers of whiskey. "Please excuse my lack of decorum as an old man who's had too much to drink. I'd appreciate it if you could use some . . ." he pauses, apparently searching for the right word, "discretion," he finally mumbles, then grips my arm.

"We'll be as careful as we can," I assure him.

"Thank you." Charles pats me on the shoulder. "We've

been through a lot."

As I walk down the driveway to where my car is parked out on Moffet, I see the emergency vehicles are gone and, mercifully, Lou's Firebird is gone as well. I again catch a glimpse of the lake through the trees. The sun, full in the sky, shimmers on the lake's surface. I can hear the woodcocks, warblers, mergansers, and chorus frogs, and feel the day brimming with life.

At the end of the drive, as I wait for the gates to open, I survey the house behind me, marveling at its tall walls and vaulted windows, secured with the tight and orderly webbing of privilege and convention. I'd been raised in chaos and disorder, and knew that order, perhaps an illusion, maybe even a myth, brings the promise of comfort—a promise of the honey-warm porch light across a dark field to guide one home.

The gate opens, and once I get the Beast started, I head down the road to Waukegan.

CHAPTER THREE

COMING INTO SPRING, I'D HOPED TRINA AND I might have a renewal of sorts. I'd suggested biking trips and a weekend junket to New Orleans for Mardi Gras, neither of which had happened.

I'd been married and divorced. Following which, I'd bounced around in what a friend of mine referred to as a Post-Divorce Fornication Frenzy until, ignoring office protocol, I'd managed to get the name of the new intake clerk over at Central Command in Waukegan. Katrina Sophia Wilkerson, or Trina, as she was known to her friends. Trina's stunning good looks are the product of her mother, a classic Russian beauty and her father, a dead ringer for Sidney Poitier. In 1975, after scaling the Berlin Wall in a hail of bullets and spotlights, her mother, Tatiana, was debriefed by Lieutenant Donald Wilkerson. Her father's striking dark features left her with a flawless café au lait complexion and a smile that lights up her face.

Some years later, I came to see the iron will in her daughter that Tatiana used to brave the Soviet gauntlet.

After jockeying with four other hopefuls, I'd finally gotten her to agree to dinner. We'd settled on Hanoi Pearl, Vietnamese dining in Waukegan being something to ponder in its own right. Over hot noodle hue soup, and bun—delicious noodles—we'd laughed about office politics and found a common interest in psychology. I'd watched her smiling eyes and was amazed at her infectious laugh. After dinner, she'd astounded me with the suggestion that we go back to my house and hang out. Given our respective ages and histories, I had good reason to believe "hanging out" didn't mean going back to play Parcheesi. I'd noticed she had tea with dinner and water at the bar, so there would be no discounting whatever lay ahead as a misguided drunken pitch. My playbook usually followed the same basic pattern: pick up, pre-dinner drink, dinner, some form of entertainment, and then, if everything went according to plan, sex—the latter performed at the date's house. Late night exit and, if it went well, a promise to see each other soon. No weird breakfasts or awkward morning tooth brushing. All clean and calculated.

Maybe it was because I was caught off guard, but I'd agreed to go back to my apartment. This was risky, if for no other reason than the dismal condition of the place. After the divorce, the lion's share of the furniture went with Katie. I'd been content with a television, a couch, and an armchair—the essential elements needed for entertainment. The couch could easily accommodate the small group of friends who might feasibly need to crash, and the armchair was handy for pizza boxes.

When I opened the door, I feigned a wince, but Trina

didn't seem to care. After touring the apartment, we came together and made vigorous love. In the small space between us, as we lay in the darkness, she'd asked me about my provenance—where I came from. Reaching into myself, astounded at my amazing good fortune and feeling open and unguarded, I'd obliged and told her about Springfield, Jimmy Newsome, and my childhood.

When I finished talking, wondering to myself what prompted me to share the story, Trina touched the nape of my neck, and said, "How sad. You never saw him again?"

Completely entranced with the sweet, sleek hamadryad landed in my bed, I simply replied, "Other than Ben and me, none of us really saw each other at all after that. Bobby's parents moved to Milwaukee the next fall, and Krau—Gerry fell in with another crowd. Ben and I always called it The Summer of the Raft."

"What a tragedy," she said. The room fell quiet.

Tragedy, true and more so. There was more that remained unsaid, which I would never tell her, because at an early age I'd learned there were things that should never be shared, never be exposed. Dark Knowledge had to be guarded, protected like a cracked rib, shielded like an abscess. Over time, with any luck, the natural capacity to heal would harden like the fibrous scar on my head. Eventually, the splinter would be safely entombed in tissue. I put great faith in my inherent capacity for adaptation. I was a man who did not trust, certain that with time any trauma would eventually be absorbed.

Later that night, Trina made herself at home walking around the apartment. I resigned myself to let her form whatever conclusions she might. We'd made love again, and in the early morning, she'd pulled a volume of W. B. Yeats from the shelf, which fell open to a section I knew well. Slowly she read:

> *How many loved your moments of glad grace*
> *And loved your beauty with love false or true,*
> *But one man loved the pilgrim soul in you,*
> *And loved the sorrows of your changing face.*

"*When You Are Old,*" I'd said, pleasantly surprised.

Trina's face darkened like a cloud bank reaching a beach. "Let me ask you a question." She looked at me as if I was someone who'd arrived fifteen minutes late to a movie and was trying to catch up with the action.

"Shoot," I said, putting my arms around her warm shoulders.

"You're a cop with an empty apartment and piles and piles of books?" she asked, more a question than a statement. Her expression eased into a smile, and I realized she was teasing me.

"The empty apartment is because I live alone, which is a long story."

"They always are." She chuckled, shaking her head, but the smile remained.

"The books," I said, "are because at one point in my life I want to do something a little more cerebral."

She laughed lightly. "I like books. Poetry, too."

I could tell she was revealing something about herself. I'd shown her a glimpse of myself and she was reciprocating, extending a tentative feeler.

"I wanted to go to school and then maybe travel and write," she said. "We never seemed to have the money for either, so I ended up in the Department. What I know about all this," she said, gesturing at the bookshelf, "I taught myself."

Trina was that most unusual breed of people—a dreamer. "You need to do what you want, Trina," I said, realizing as soon as I'd said it, it sounded like mansplaining.

Her face flushed, and her brows pulled tight together. "Well, sometimes the things we want just don't come. We can't help what we don't have." She turned and looked at the books, again avoiding my glance. I'd touched a nerve. She sat down next to me, turning to look straight in my eyes, her expression struggling somewhere between skepticism and preparing to give me a knuckle sandwich.

I saw that, with a few poorly chosen words, I'd reversed what looked like my first truly successful connection with a woman in months, if not years. Scrambling to find firm ground, I offered, "You know, if you want something, you should do it, and never let anyone tell you it can't be done."

She smiled again, the squall blown out as fast it had come in. "I know. Thank you." She nibbled my earlobe, laughing and whispering a wonderfully obscene suggestion in my ear. We made love again several times over the weekend, and by Monday the sudden Sou'wester was long forgotten.

As we'd made love, I'd noticed three small Chinese characters tattooed on the firm ridge of Trina's lower back and asked her what the symbols meant.

"Moo shu pork," she'd laughed.

"Seriously."

"It's the last two characters of a poem by Li Po, a Chinese poet from the eighth century. She recited:

Before my bed,
There's bright moonlight
So that it seems

Like frost on the ground.
Lifting my head
I watch the bright moon;
Lowering my head
I dream that I'm home

Trying to be light and off the cuff this time, I said, "Don't you have a home?"

Her eyes widened, searching my face. "A home is a place you build with someone. I'm still in the moonlight."

Something in the way she'd said this made it seem as pure and honest an observation about the places of the heart as I'd ever heard.

Eventually, we moved in together. In the beginning, Trina voiced her reservations about having her daughter, Sophie, move in with us. When we moved into an apartment in Waukegan, my son, Liam, stayed with us as well. Over time, Liam came to accept Trina and Sophie as natural extensions of our family. We'd seemed to fall together without effort.

Neither of us raised the subject of marriage that first year. We were a modern couple and didn't need traditional labels. Trina's marriage to Sophie's father was filled with drama and ended badly. We both had baggage and we might have been a little skittish, but we would never have admitted it out loud. The days seemed to flow effortlessly, one into the next. There didn't seem to be any reason to change. I honestly believed we were both content with the arrangement. We were just floating. What we'd built together felt effortless, warm, busy, and necessary. There was nothing tying us. There was also precious little binding us together.

CHAPTER FOUR

A FTER FILING PRELIMINARY NOTES IN THE EARLY afternoon, I check my cellphone. One message. "Hi. I'm coming back tomorrow afternoon, and you should plan on having dinner with me. I'll see you then. Bye."

I pick up the office phone, hitting speed dial. A few seconds later, a male voice answers with the texture of bark dust. "Yeah?"

"Larry, can you come in? We pulled a murder in LF." The voice on the other end grunts and hangs up.

Forty-five years earlier, in Amarillo, Texas, in the maternity ward of St Anthony's Hospital, Ernest and Phyllis Welk named their newborn in honor of their favorite entertainer. Family legend had it the singer was a distant cousin, though no hard evidence ever surfaced to support the claim. In a simple act of sincere and sentimental homage, Larry Welk's parents branded him with an immortal moniker, believing in the magic inherent in an auspicious name, much like naming your child Napoleon or Caesar, hoping whatever forces meted out fortune and luck might, in the off chance, see fit to throw a little on Ernie and Phyllis's kid. But, as happens, over time the nation's cultural DNA mutated, and LW's fame faded into the grey and sepia tones of champagne music. By the time he was in high school, Larry carried the dubious soubriquet "And A One." When he turned eighteen, he'd told me he'd actually explored changing his name, but, learning of his intent, his mother was crestfallen. When, at last, both his parents and The Great Entertainer were all dead, he was so deeply connected, if not attached to the name, he resigned himself to bearing the burden, but said he'd sworn never to inflict anything like that on his own progeny. Any hope the association would fade into obscurity was dashed when, in his thirties, the show renewed for a third round of reruns.

My relationship with Larry has been, from the outset, a complicated one. I can certainly commiserate as someone whose own parents had the same misguided belief in the magic of nomenclature. My brother Ben was named for Ben Franklin. Searching around for a name for their second son, my parents could certainly have chosen a less weighty moniker than the one I share with the Genius of Menlo Park. Once, I looked in the phone directory for Greater Metropolitan Chicago under the name Edison, just to see what other parents with the surname had done to their kids. There were the old favorites, Edward Edison, George Edison, Charles, and of course Anne Edison, and west in Naperville there was even a Charlotte. As I scoured other directories, I saw some less lucky kids had parents who favored the Old Testament. There were two Adam

Edisons, three Sarah Edisons, one Ezekiel, and a Ruth. But, I think child welfare should have been called in for the poor boys in Pinckneyville whose parents, digging deep into the Old Testament, had the cruelty to name their boys Habakkuk and Shadrach Edison.

Wearing my name is doubtless less of a burden than the weight borne by Larry Welk. Nonetheless, it could provide a bridge, a shared experience, to build a friendship. But Larry is not a normal case.

His recent arrival in Chicago, and his tenure as my assistant, are the result of a chance meeting with a buddy. A brilliant and successful criminal defense lawyer in Texas, Larry was forced to resign from the bar for reasons which, depending who you talked to, ran from sleeping with the wife of a senior appellate court judge, to drunkenly showing his male appendage at a dinner in honor of the retiring Lieutenant Governor. I had no trouble believing either story, and was certain that, in either case, Larry was cast out from Texas into the Land of Nod—in Larry's circumstance, Chicago—to fend for himself.

Leaving the smoking ruins of his life in Texas behind him, Larry managed to snag an interview in Lake County for a clerical position. This was a courtesy from one of the State's attorneys who'd gone to school with him. By the time Larry blew into town, I had been shorthanded for six months. I was asked to sit in on the interview, which I attended with cautious optimism, hoping, with help, I could dig out of the tailings pile that had accumulated in my office.

At Larry's interview it was clear the bureau chief, Ed Delahunt, immediately disliked him, his thick panhandle accent, and his bolo tie. Delahunt, who was what some might call humorless, called me into the hall and made it clear he viewed Larry Welk as a loser. Believing we'd spent enough time on what was clearly not a good fit, I made small talk after Delahunt left, mostly for the appearance of courtesy. I shared the details of a credit card scam I was working. Larry observed that the mortgage banker thieves he'd defended in Texas, were, in his words, "cutting a piece off a fat hog's ass." The comment made me laugh out loud, and I began to rethink Larry. I asked him several questions about financial fraud, only to find out Larry possessed vast knowledge of banking practices. He also had a good working knowledge of forensic science, and after I scanned the legal brief he pulled out of his bag, I could see he was a good legal writer. If anything, he was overqualified. A half an hour later, and I was sure Larry was a gem in the rough and pushed Delahunt to hire him. The obligatory background check turned up nothing more heinous than two prior divorces and evidence of poor social judgment. Larry was assigned a small inside office and stacks of backlogged cases.

As it turned out, I was right. In the first few weeks we worked together, Larry proved not only to be a capable file jockey but also showed uncanny skill at uprooting information and locating pieces of data carefully buried in the dirt.

With only three weeks on the job, when I asked him to look into a string of used car dealerships that were being used to launder money, Larry traced the money to a drug outfit and, in the process, also located a second set of hidden accounts. When we got the records for the accounts, they contained two-and-one-half-million dollars, or as Larry called it, a "shit-ton of cash."

Over time, details of his story would filter out like small ingots. Whether the details were true or not was anyone's guess. One thing was clear: Larry fled Texas for a reason. His evil temper, added to his late arrivals following a hard night, made it clear I needed to give Larry his distance until the effects of coffee and aspirin smoothed his demeanor. I also learned to accept the good with the bad. Calling Larry on a weekend, I'd have to take what I found, weighing the need for data on possible serial killers against dealing with Larry during a mid-weekend drunk.

Watching the clock until Larry's arrival, I sift through the list of names from the crochet club. I call several numbers and get no answer, leaving messages to call Larry. My luck starts to change towards the end of the list. The first woman to answer says she is shocked to hear of Faith's death, but puts me off, offering, "It would be a waste of time. We were never close."

The second woman, Delia Ostergaard, is also shocked, but she agrees to meet the following day. After confirming the appointment, I check the release lists on Corrections' database.

I make it through the files for three counties when the clop of Larry's boot heels on linoleum cut the quiet of the office. I look up to see the meaty face of a man whose round head is topped with strands of blond hair turning silver, laid thinly across his scalp in a style once ungenerously called "the pullover." Framing the sockets of his red eyes, thin wisps of eyebrow dangle over heavy lids with long blond lashes. His cheeks are shaded with silver and grey from a day's growth, and his mouth is drawn down into a sour knot.

"This'd better be fucking good," Larry says, plopping

himself in my armchair.

In a concession to midwestern style, Larry has lost the bolo tie, but the shiny pointed-toe cowboy boots are still as out of place as the short-sleeved shirt in April, which stretches like a tarp and is battened down with a bright snakeskin belt across his middle. I don't say anything, resigned to the fact that summoning Larry to the office on a weekend is basically de-caving a hibernating badger. Larry nurses a coffee cup, which I suspect contains a little of the hair of the dog.

Larry nods his head and closes his eyes, seeming to wait for my explanation. He breathes heavily, slowly rubbing his hand over the bristle on his cheek. He's clearly suffering, so I nod to the coffee pot, but he declines, waving his hand. Recounting the facts of my visit to the Wesley place, I omit my crisis with Trina, and the fact my life seems to be unraveling. I describe the crime scene, the murder victim, and the Wesley family. Finally, I tell him I've just started going through the release files for sex offenders. Larry shakes his head.

"Nope. Perverts use household stuff. Laundry line, newspaper cord, electrical wire—whatever's handy. DVs," he says, referring to domestic violence perps, "manual strangulation. I'd go murder-for-hire before sex."

We spend the next several hours, each combing the major Midwest files, looking for potential leads. Larry asks about security.

"Any video? These places usually have a small army working for them."

"That's what's strange. The surveillance wasn't working, and none of the family seemed to care. The other thing, Wesley Senior keeps guns locked in a cabinet, but doesn't use them. This doesn't look like a B&E or a sexual assault."

Pending a return on the kit from the ME's office, we agree to put off reviewing the sex-offender list. If it turns out Faith was raped, we'll reopen the search. I begin to feel fatigue like a plastic bag around my head. I've been going since four-thirty this morning—over fifteen hours.

Surveying the remains of his cold meatball sub and four empty pop cans, Larry shakes his head. "Well, I don't know whether to scratch my watch or wind my butt. Could be a contract job, or—"

"Are we ruling out the family?"

"That dog don't hunt," Larry says, shaking his head.

"What?"

Larry begins loading the sandwich paper and potato chip wrappers into the lunch delivery bag. "It don't add up," he says, his voice loaded with molasses. I've noticed the Amarillo blackstrap is thickest when Larry is tired or hungover. Larry can turn off the Texas cornpone and sound like a Nebraska insurance salesman when he wants to. "You think any of them social register bluenoses got the cojones to do this old lady?"

I have to concede the point. "They wouldn't want to get their hands dirty." I rub the back of my neck. "Follow the contract angle. Who might take a contract out on Faith Wesley?"

Larry tosses the stuffed delivery bag into the trash can, setting his eyes on his computer screen. "Somebody had to know she was going to be out there—somebody who knew her routine."

"What about the house staff, the Morales?"

Larry laughs. "Jesus, Tom. Blaming the Mexicans?

That's almost Texan."

"Well, they'd know her schedule. Track them down and at least find out what they know."

"I'll bring 'em in," Larry says, miming a pistol with his finger.

"Seriously, Larry, they may know something."

Larry shrugs, grabbing his rumpled jacket. "Maybe she was collateral damage. Maybe she stumbled into something."

"The killer wanted somebody else in the house?"

"Who else was there?"

"The daughter, the granddaughter, and the husband, Charles."

"Maybe Charles or the daughter was the intended victim, and she just got in the way. You said the daughter was a real be-autch. Charles do something that'd get him killed?"

"Oppress the masses?" I feel my eyes start to droop. I need to go home.

"I think we look at that, too. Former employees. Environmental nuts."

We agree to reconvene at the office early the following morning, after which I will head over to the ME's office for the autopsy.

When I reach the parking lot, I produce a single sheet of paper with Nora Summers' number, which I'd folded neatly and placed in my pocket earlier. I dial the number as I climb into the Beast. The phone rings several times and I am prepared to hang up when a female voice finally answers. I tell her I am calling to meet with her about Faith Wesley and apologize for the lateness of the hour. She agrees to meet with me in two days.

When I get to my apartment, I reheat two hotdogs and a bowl of Boston Beans. I've been going for seventeen hours. Despite feeling tired, I know attempting sleep will be pointless.

After putting the dish in the sink, I get my gym bag and drive to the athletic club. No one is on duty except Tyler, the assistant manager. I wave as I head down to the locker room.

The pool is empty again. I jump in the clear water and swim thirty laps, finishing at the deep end. Taking a deep breath, I let myself drop ten feet to the bottom. Sitting cross-legged, I watch the bubbles drift to the top of the pool and the lights glimmer off the surface of the water, hearing the soft hum of the pump. After about forty seconds, I release the air and rise to the surface. The only sound is the *thap thap thap* of the water against the sides. The air is overly warm and the chlorine stings my eyes, which stream with tears. I remember the name of the kid driving the boat—the kid with the cigarette and long hair. Paulie. I'd known his name then, but never told the cops.

CHAPTER FIVE

THE LAKE COUNTY CORONER'S OFFICE SITS IN an unassuming building on MLK Blvd in Waukegan.

Two levels down, MOPEC KA 501 three bay, two-tier, refrigeration units hold the recently deceased of Lake County. Next door are examination rooms, each equipped with a MOPEC CE 100 autopsy pedestal table, complete with downdraft ventilation, irrigation, and fluid collection.

I'm here to witness Faith Wesley's postmortem, conducted by Dr. Joyce Hong, Senior Lake County Coroner. Anyone who's ever visited a coroner's office in full swing will tell you the sights aren't what get you. There's a top note, the strong astringent odor of formaldehyde. This is followed by the sharp pine fragrance of disinfectant. Finally, a darker base note resonates somewhere between last week's chicken giblets and the garbage disposal.

I always use a dab of eucalyptus in my nose before

heading in.

As I enter the examination room, despite my precautions, I have to fight a small gag reflex. I suit up and put on my mask, joining Hong, who is already masked and gowned and standing next to the human remains of Faith Wesley. Draped under a green county sheet, she lies face up. Hong motions to the table where she's about to start the inventory. Approaching the table, she uncovers the body and begins cataloging the physical history of Faith Wesley's biological end.

Lying naked under the bright surgical lights, stripped of vanity, pretense, or modesty, Faith Wesley is no more than the sum of her parts. In the end, what distinguishes her are a caesarian scar, varicose veins, and her weight. I look away as Joyce examines Faith's genitals, which she notes show no sign of trauma or sexual assault. "The rape kit came back clean," she says, replacing the drape.

Moving down the length of the table, she pushes back the cover, revealing Faith's legs and lower torso. She then moves to the top of the table, opening Faith's eyelids and mouth, shining a light up into the nasal cavity. Next, she extends her gloved finger slowly along the sharp line of the wound in Faith's neck. Joyce reaches for the microphone dangling over the table and begins to dictate.

"Examination of the head and neck area reveals massive trauma to the neck in the peritracheal and esophageal areas. There is petechial hemorrhaging in the sclera of the eyes. The ligature has severely compressed the carotid artery and has partially severed the cricothyroid artery. There are hematomas and evidence of bruising at the root of the tongue. Moderate exsanguination is evident, which, although not the primary cause of death, contributed, along with rapid onset hypoxia, to shock, unconsciousness, and, ultimately, death." She pauses.

Taking advantage of the lull, I say, "Exsanguination?"

Joyce smiles. "Bleeding . . . she bled out, but shock and the lack of oxygen to her brain is what killed her."

Pulling back the fleshy folds of Faith's neck, Joyce peers inside the wound, gesturing for me to take a look. I comply, fighting a strong revulsion rising in my throat. Pointing at the neck wound, she continues to dictate.

"Close inspection of the wound reveals the esophagus is abraded and torn, consistent with rapid compression." Joyce waves her hand and points again, directing me to look at the wound, displayed in Technicolor clarity by the high-powered surgical lights.

"Inspection of the back of the neck in the cervical 3-4 area reveals a laceration indicative of a pinching action, again consistent with a rapidly constricting small-gauge high-tensile ligature. Further inspection reveals the articulations of the cervical spine are visible but not exposed."

She pauses, turning off the Dictaphone.

"What's with the wound?" I ask, hoping to get out of the room before the worst part.

She pulls down her mask, revealing a strong face and dark, intelligent eyes. In the eight years I've known her, she's never missed a day's work, and her reports are detailed, thorough, and insightful. A few years ago, she was offered a bundle to teach Marshall University's post-doctoral program but turned the opportunity down.

She eyes me, pausing to adjust her steel-rimmed glasses. "Well, a couple of things. First, a strangulation with a cut reaching as far back as the articulations of the spine—

whoever did this put his heart into it."

A cell phone rings to the tune of *Brick House*.

"Excuse me," she says, reaching into her pocket. "Hong here. No, I haven't looked at the tox screens yet on the girl—I'll get back to you." She hangs up and shrugs. "Backlog. You know the Feds are busy investigating the clowns in Cook County, and there are several investigations into the National DNA labs. What a fucking mess."

She opens a binder on the table and makes several notes. "I understand Mrs. Wesley was sitting in the sprinklers for at least forty-five minutes. She died from strangulation, but I'm willing to bet there was a lot more blood before the sprinklers washed it away."

"Yeah, I'm struggling with why she was killed this way."

Joyce puts her mask back on and leans close to Faith Wesley's neck, pulling her glasses up and staring. After a bit, she stands up.

"High-tensile wire. Execution. Terrorists, military, even the mob."

"Can you tell just by looking at the wound?"

Joyce looks up, appearing irritated. "The depth of the wound, the strength of the material, are all consistent with high-tensile-strength carbon wire, like a garrote."

"A garrote?"

She nods. "An instrument of assassination, and in some countries, like Spain, a method of execution—two pieces of wood with a hole drilled through them," she says, mimicking the grip for me. She pulls back sharply. "The wire is passed through a hole in the wood and then wrapped or tied. When you pull, the leverage is extraordinary. The reason assassins like it is because a garrote is small and easily concealed. If it isn't made out of metal, it can pass through a metal detector." She moves to the other side of the table. "The mob uses this technique regularly. It's efficient and virtually impossible to trace. Easy there," she says, pointing at my hand, which has been absentmindedly playing with the lever on the examining table. "You'll dump her on the ground if you're not careful."

I step away. "Contract killing?"

Joyce shrugs. "Could be. A hit is definitely a possibility, but motive is your job, Tom," she says, walking over to a small white cabinet several feet away. "This case is interesting, though." She opens the cabinet and pulls out something that looks like an oversized Dremel with a wicked blue blade fixture on the end. She gives it a gun, and it springs to life, whirring with a deep whisper. "No facial wounds, no blunt force trauma or stabbing, more like an execution, as I said." Noticing my reaction to the saw, she smiles. "Like it?" she asks, giving it another gun. "It's the new MOPEC 5000. Even works under water."

Sensing my fading resolve, she puts the saw down. "You want to miss this part? I don't think we're going to get much more than we have, but I have to follow protocol."

I nod quickly. I know an examination of the brain is routine in a homicide investigation. "Thanks, Joyce, I do," I say, with genuine appreciation.

She nods. "We'll be finished in about another eighteen hours, after the lab tests are back, then we're going to release the remains." She pauses, holding the saw like a baton. "You know, I've seen Faith Wesley's name on the society pages. It just seems senseless." She guns the motor and gestures for me to leave.

I have to agree. Senseless is right. But there is never much sense down in the dark water.

■ ■ ■

Leaving the ME's office, I place a call to Executive Assistant State's Attorney Frank Steinman, the lead prosecutor for the task force. After a couple of minutes, I am put through.

"Hi Frank, it's Tom."

"Tommy! I heard you pulled a nasty homicide down there in Garden Party Land."

At one time, as an ambitious young lawyer, Steinman had been known to arrive at five in the morning to review the weekly case assignment sheet setting on the chief's desk, cherry-picking the promising cases. His initiative served him well. By the age of thirty-five he was the Senior Assistant Felony State's Attorney, which meant that every case, except for homicides and rapes, went through his office. Possessing the political ethics and moral conscience of a Borgia, the stairwells of the Justice Center are littered with the corpses of colleagues who, invited to a friendly dinner with Frank, hadn't tested the wine before drinking.

It was only a matter of time before he was elevated to Lead Prosecutor for Major Crimes. By then, he'd earned the justified fear and mistrust of his colleagues. He cherry-picked his team, just as he had the files, and soon it was recognized that a place on Steinman's team meant promotion and publicity.

Eventually, as a hardened political operator of the first order, Steinman started an exercise on every new major felony case, which had become an institution in the department—the Check-In With Frank. Every murder, rape, aggravated assault, or high-profile case requires a phone conference with him.

I recount the essential facts, asking for support on

warrants and court orders. Over the years, as much as I can without risking insubordination, I've resisted bringing Frank completely into my cases. Choosing my facts carefully, I omit the run-in with Linda Edwards, the meeting scheduled with Nora Summers, and my episode on the lawn.

"The Wesleys are pretty big hitters," Steinman observes.

"I've already gotten some resistance from them about turning over financial stuff," I reply reluctantly.

"Why do you need financials, Tommy?" Steinman asks. I haven't been called Tommy by anyone since I was twelve.

Struggling to hide my aggravation, I say, "It's obvious. We think this is potentially a hit, whether it's against Faith Wesley or Charles Wesley isn't clear. If it is a hit, it is probably either financial or political. In either case, the financials could establish motive. Money moving in or out, insurance policies, stock accounts or real estate, anything that would give anyone a reason to have Faith Wesley whacked."

Frank sighs audibly. "They're going to lawyer-up pretty fast, especially if they think there's a chance the stuff could put them in an unsympathetic light."

I smile to myself. Unsympathetic is a big word for Frank.

"It's confidential, and right now getting anything from them is like nailing Jell-O to a tree. Can you help me out or not?"

"Understood, Tommy. We got your back," Steinman says, clearing his throat and backing off. "I'll get Shahbaz on it," he says, trying to sound accommodating.

I like Tony Shahbaz well enough, but Frank's false

courtesy and deference don't fool me. Tony is Steinman's number two, meaning there is no choice but to agree to the assignment.

"Actually, you can call and tell him I assigned you," Steinman says. Frank likes to preserve the image he is too busy and important to be bothered with the administerial task of making assignments. Things aren't ordered in Frank's department, they are ordained.

Shahbaz is different than Steinman's other henchmen. Intelligent and independent, Tony is Steinman's hand-picked lieutenant. This is despite his well-known refusal to pay unceasing homage to his boss. I suspect Steinman chose Shahbaz for just those qualities. Tony is protected because Steinman recognizes Tony will tell him what he needs to know, not just what he wants to hear. But I know telling Truth to Power is an art, and serving as court jester is a dangerous occupation.

The last case Tony and I worked together involved a homeless man savagely beaten to death in Waukegan. Steinman saw the case as a nuisance and complained that Tony and I were wasting time and resources. We'd assigned two investigators and canvassed the streets for weeks. In the end, we netted four teenagers who later confessed they'd done it to "see what it felt like", nailing the two who'd swung the crowbars for twenty years each. The other two walked on a plea deal. Ironically, the state prosecutor received a civic justice award. Tony and I always take the opportunity to share our disdain privately.

Tony is happy to hear from me. I ask him to set up a file, summarize the case for him, requesting search warrants for Fred Atwater, the Wesley's accountant.

Tony chuckles darkly. "Frank give you a hard time?"

Still entirely unsure of Shahbaz, I settle on, "Frank was unhappy with the fact that we're looking for financials and background from the Wesleys."

Shahbaz mutters a quick "uh-huh" followed by, "Always taking the long view, Frank."

Even after all that, I am never entirely sure where Tony's allegiance lies. If I could be certain my opinions aren't going to get back to Steinman, I might urge him to be more cautious, pointing to Tony's predecessors who were once Favored Sons and have failed to mark the turning tide of preference.

"Whatever," I reply.

Tony promises Atwater's warrants will be ready for signature within the next seventy-two hours and hangs up.

CHAPTER SIX

T HE NIGHT BEFORE MY VISIT TO THE MORGUE, I'd dined with Trina. We'd sat apart, staring at unfinished salads, pushing the greasy leaves across our plates. As the minutes passed with small talk, broken by long silences, the reason for the meeting loomed larger between us. Finally, Trina stopped maneuvering the spinach on her plate and leaned forward.

"Tom, you know I love you."

"I love you, too," I said, struggling to conjure the emotion described by those words. Trina and I lived a modern life with a modern relationship: married without being married—a harried life, communal, cluttered, and intense, littered with unfulfilled intentions, with projects begun and left uncompleted. Yet for all that, we'd held each other in the dark, promising in whispers that we were happy, and each finding something unique in the other. Sitting across from her, I sensed a shift that signaled that however unique or special she'd felt about what we'd had, it was not enough to hold us in place.

Her eyes fixed on me, and she shook her head. "I love you, but I can't live with you. You've been different the last several months and I can't understand why you seem so angry." Putting down the fork she'd been using to twirl the remains of her salad, she sighed and said, "I'm moving up to my sister's for a few weeks while I try to figure out what to do."

Her face distant, her eyes dark and shaded, she seemed to recede, a Kirlian image, like the silvery aura of a severed leaf, the outline of our lives together fading into shadows until the last black photo plate.

"It's about a cat, Trina," I said, struggling to hide my desperation.

"We both know it's about much more than Bumpers."

"Is that its name?" I said, my voice suddenly tight and dry.

"It doesn't matter," she said, pushing the salad plate away from her. "I'm going to be at the apartment tomorrow morning. I'd appreciate it if we didn't have a scene."

She rose and patted me on the shoulder, the tender gesture of a sibling, leaving me to pay the bill.

Driving back to the apartment, I reached into the glove compartment to find a CD Lou had told me about several weeks before. After a few seconds, I heard David Gray's voice, pure and true:

Well, we had to grab on to something
So, we're pulling at the threads
And now the world's unraveling
Inside our very heads

The Audi whipped silently down the highway. I turned

up the volume.

All this talk can hypnotize you and
We can ill afford
To give ourselves to sentiment
When our time is oh so short
Had to draw the line.

■ ■ ■

"Hello, Emma, I'm Detective Edison."

I know I've made a mistake almost as soon as I sit down across from Emma. Distracted, she pokes her cheek with her index finger, legs dangling restlessly under the table. As I was leaving the office, Larry told me getting information out of the girl would be "like tryin' to scratch your ear with your elbow." Confronted with the fact the interview is likely a complete waste of time, I have to acknowledge the main reason I've pushed hard for it is to prove to Linda I can do it, even if it is a pyrrhic victory if ever there was one. Emma stares at me, lips hermetically sealed, and I can feel a warm flush rise under my collar. I take a deep breath and smile, trying to relate to her as I would when speaking to Liam.

"I know who you are," she says. Her eyes, clear blue like her mother's, scan me with distrust.

"Did your mother tell you why I want to talk to you?"

"Mom said you'd be talking to me about Grandma." I can feel her feet swinging slowly under the table.

"Can you remember anything from the morning your grandma was hurt?"

The girl shrugs, staring at the floor. "I was really sleepy. Mommy had to wake me up three times."

"Did your grandma ever say she might be afraid, or sad?"

Emma shakes her head, swinging her legs faster, brushing my shin under the table. She stares out the window for several seconds, apparently weighing the repercussions. I motion to Linda to step outside. She rises as Emma watches, slowly following me to the door where she stands, her arms rigid by her side.

"What's the problem?" she asks, her jaw tightly clenched.

"I need a couple of minutes alone with Emma."

She exhales quickly. I can smell alcohol on her breath. "We agreed this was only going to take a couple of minutes."

I lean closer, now certain she's been drinking. In a voice just above a growl I say, "I can bring Emma to the office for examination with a shrink and make her testify before the grand jury. You won't be around then. Or, you can give me a few minutes with her to see if she's got anything else to add."

She shoots me a look Larry would describe as "friendly as fire ants."

"Three minutes—that's it," she says, turning briskly and marching down the hall.

When she's gone, I turn to the girl.

"Did you have something you wanted to tell me, Emma?"

Emma stares at the door and after several seconds slumps in her chair and says, staring at the floor, "Grandma told me things about my dad. Like he has dirty pictures, and he's mean."

"Do you believe those things about your dad?"

"I asked my daddy. He got mad and said they were

lies."

"Has your daddy been mean to you?"

"Well . . . he," she stammers, "he just gets mad sometimes," she blurts, pushing her finger into her cheek again. "Not at me, but at stuff."

"Does he hit you?"

"Oh, no . . . he never hits me," she says, almost in tears.

As I watch her, I detest myself. I imagine myself conducting the interview with Liam, who is a few months younger, and it makes me want to puke.

Almost as an act of penance, I reveal a little of myself to her. "You know Emma, I have a little boy about your age."

"Is he in school?" she asks, looking up at me.

"Yup."

"Where?"

"He goes to school by his mom's house in Westinghouse."

"He lives with his mom?" Her face folds with confusion.

I feel a momentary twinge of sadness at the simplicity of the girl's question and the simple truth. "Yes, he does."

"My dad wants me to live with him, but I can't."

The door swings open and Linda marches over to Emma.

"Three minutes," she says, edging out a smile.

I thank Emma and shake her little hand, which is warm and wet. Turning to Linda, I say, "Can I talk to you for a second?" I pick up my things and walk out.

I turn to her in the cavernous entryway.

"Emma's grandmother told her stuff about your ex-husband. Shitty personal stuff."

Linda sighs, shrugs, and nods her head slowly. "My mother detested Lent, but I didn't know she was spreading that to Emma." She nods towards the front door. "I think you said you had to go."

Instead of fighting her, I walk beside her as she escorts me out.

When I am standing outside, I face her directly. "If I find out there's more you're not telling me, I don't care how well-connected your family is, I am coming for you."

"Fuck you, Tom," she says as she slams the door behind me.

CHAPTER SEVEN

AFTER MY MEETING WITH EMMA, I GO TO SEE Nora Summers.

Nora Summers lives a half-mile from the Wesley house in Lake Forest, in a yellow-framed colonial set back from the street by a long path and a garden in the front. Approaching the house, I can see through a stand of flowering azaleas to the other side, where a grass field littered with volunteer daisies, dandelion, and sorrel, stretches down to a far fence overtaken by honeysuckle vines.

A trim brown-haired woman opens the door. I already know from Linda Edwards that Nora and she have been friends since early childhood, which would place Nora in her mid-forties. When I identify myself, she gestures me inside. The first thing I notice about her are piercing blue eyes, set deep into her face. She's wearing a thin Lycra running shirt and loose athletic pants, and her hair is pulled back with a scrunchy. She wears no jewelry except a small gold pendant. I can see Nora Summers possesses the rare gift, without the need to state it or point to it, of being a natural beauty. The architecture of her face, her subtle gestures—even the way she walks—suggest she is different. What my father used to call a thoroughbred.

"Would you like some tea?" Her full mouth breaks quickly into a smile. "I understand your meeting with Linda didn't go well."

Before I can craft a clever retort to cover for the botched interview, she points through the doors at the back of the kitchen.

"Why don't you go back onto the porch? I'll be there in a minute."

In the few seconds we've chatted, she's managed to convey she doesn't care what Linda thinks and is able to think for herself. I like her already. Watching her walk with a slight limp towards the kitchen, I have to admit she's seems pretty clever.

Enclosed within tall windows, the porch runs the length of the house and opens onto the garden. The weather has turned warm and two of the windows are open, carrying the scent of fresh-cut grass. I scan the porch, which is more of a dayroom. Two large daybeds and a large plantation chair surround a long teak table. Against the side wall, a large white bookshelf holds a framed black-and-white photograph, the whites turning the color of cream and the blacks and grays dimmed from time. The picture is of a couple in their mid-forties with a small child. The man holds a young girl. His face is smiling as he looks directly at the camera. The girl's face is lit by an open smile as she clings to her father's neck. The woman standing next to the man seems to be looking to the right, away from the photograph, towards something or someone who has caught her attention. Her face bears the same enigmatic expression Nora wore a few minutes earlier when she answered the door. Like Nora, the woman's hair is full and shiny, her nose chiseled and straight.

The quick rattle of the tea tray being placed on the table behind me breaks my thoughts. When Nora comes up behind me, I notice she smells faintly of lavender.

"Your parents?" I ask, nodding at the photograph.

She nods, staring at the frame.

"Yes, that was taken when I was very young."

She looks down at the floor, then at me. I see again that her eyes are quick, intelligent, and sad.

"They died a long time ago. Car accident."

I search for an appropriate response. "I'm so sorry," I say finally.

The room is filled with silence, broken only by the sound of Nora working intently at arranging the cups and sugar. I watch as she pours tea. Finally, with a gesture, she directs me to sit in the plantation chair and she sits across from me on the daybed, legs crossed, Indian style. She takes her cup in both hands, which I notice have long, sturdy fingers without polish, like a woman used to the outdoors, or an athlete. "When I was about ten, a few years after that picture was taken, my parents were involved in a car accident driving back from Chicago. They'd been dear friends of Charles and Faith, and I didn't have any close living relatives, so they took me in and eventually became my guardians."

She takes a long sip of her tea. I watch as her expression darkens. "They raised me as one of their own until I was in my mid-teens and went away to school."

From the other room, the persistent mechanical cheep of a phone sounds. "Excuse me a minute," she says, rising to her feet. I watch her walk into the next room, again marking her slight limp. She closes the door, although I can hear the indistinct cool alto of her voice through the panels.

Admitting to myself a more than casual interest in the answer, I search for signs of a male presence. The photos on the porch seem only to be of Nora and her family. There are no pictures of children or happy couples on vacation. The porch and daybeds suggest no one else is living in the house. Nora continues to talk in the other room. I hear her laugh twice, then lower her voice.

I wait a couple of minutes. Growing impatient, I rise and open the porch door, moving into the spacious living room. The room is ringed with bookshelves and monographs, antique copies of *Plutarch's Lives*, Vasari's *Lives of the Artists*, and a multi-volume set of Aristotle's writings. At the far end of the room, on a shelf recessed into the wall, sets a dark, shiny cone, more than a foot in height, topped with a sturdy square handle. I go over to take a closer look. The date, 1509, is embossed on its side. I reach for the dome and it feels cool and smooth. Taking it in both hands, I turn it, still balancing it on the shelf. The other side bears a coat of arms with a tree and fish, set in the same relief as the date. I lift it with both hands. The weight surprises me, causing my grip to slip, and for a second, I almost drop it, making the heavy bronze bell sound a deep baritone, somber moan. Embarrassed, I quickly return the bell to the shelf and turn to find Nora at the door.

"I'm sorry," I say, color rising in my face.

She grins. "You know about curiosity and the cat,

Tom." Until that point she's addressed me as "detective."

"Well, I was interested . . ."

"It's a Deid Bell, used at funerals," she says, gesturing back towards the porch. "It's Scottish. It's been in my family for five-hundred years—the first Summers is recorded in Scotland in the twelfth century. I'm the last Summers in my line and it passed to me when my parents died. It's a little morbid, but the bell is special."

"It's certainly heavy," I say, smiling.

Nora laughs lightly.

I can feel myself drawn to her, wanting to like her. It does not occur to me that part of my feelings may be tied to my recent rejection by Trina and my bruised ego. I don't even pause to consider my newfound attraction is less than forty-eight hours after separating from my live-in partner. If anything, I feel justified. We stand for an awkward moment in the middle of the room, neither of us certain where to go, or what to do. Finally, taking her earlier lead, I head towards the porch.

Once seated in the plantation chair again, I ask, "Why did you leave the Wesleys?"

Nora shrugs. "I wanted to go away to school. After school, I went to live in Europe."

"What about Faith?"

The side of her mouth turns up slightly, and she eyes me as if I'm trying to work a con. "C'mon Tom. By now you must know Faith didn't get on with anyone."

I shake my head. "You're not answering my question."

Ignoring her tea, she rises and picks up a small mister and begins to spray a group of orchids clustered by the window, methodically wetting the tops of each and inspecting the leaves.

"I tried to give Faith a wide berth. Until I came back, I didn't think much about her at all." Pulling several spent flowers off the plants, she sighs. "As far as Faith was concerned, I introduced Linda to cigarettes, beer, and, ultimately, freedom."

"Where did you go in Europe?"

"You name it. Eventually I landed in Spain. Madrid. I saw myself as some kind of artist and activist. I lost track of the Wesleys for years." She returns the mister to its shelf. The sun catches the side of her face, highlighting the contours of her cheeks. I catch myself staring at her mouth. She looks over at me and raises an eyebrow.

"When did you see the Wesleys again?" I ask, trying to sound official.

She frowns, but her eyes twinkle, making it clear I'm not doing a very good job of investigating. She waves her hand idly at me. "Linda was just separating from Lent. We ended up spending time together."

"What about Lent Edwards?"

Nora gives a subdued grunt. "I never knew what Linda saw in the sonofabitch. He's a Neanderthal clown. Although there's not much laughable about the fact he hit her."

"He hit her?"

Pulling twigs off a beleaguered begonia, she sighs again. "Linda would show up with unexplained bruises and say she bumped into furniture."

"Could he have killed Faith?"

She drops the handful of crumpled plant litter into the wastebasket by the door and shakes her head. "Maybe a few years back, during the divorce, but not now." I watch as she makes her way to a tall Schefflera that sets in a large, blue-glazed floor pot.

"What about last night?"

"You mean me?" She looks back at me.

"You and Linda."

"I had tickets to see a show in Chicago and I invited her. We went out to The Stone Pillar for drinks afterward. We got back to Lake Forest at eleven-thirty."

"What time was the dinner over?"

"I think it ended at ten."

"Did you stay at the Wesley house?"

"No, we'd had a few lemon drops, but Linda insisted on driving me home. Are you going to arrest us for driving impaired?" She laughs and tosses the additional dead leaves into the small wastebasket.

Despite myself, I laugh as well. "We're really struggling with why Faith was killed in such a brutal way."

"Was it that bad?" she says, her mouth pulling into a small knot.

I nod. "What about Charles? We're also thinking Charles might have been the intended target."

"What about Charles, indeed," she says, picking up her cup from the tray and taking a long sip of cold tea. "Leave Charles to music and poetry—everything else gets done by Faith." She puts the cup down.

"You don't think he might have people who want to kill him?"

Nora shakes her head. "The Wesleys made their money in the late eighteen-hundreds in textiles and steel. Charles' father sold off the majority interest in the last company just before he died in 1950. It's been pretty much shrewd financial management since then, and Faith has been the public face for decades."

The room falls silent, and I search for something to continue the conversation. Trying to appear artless, and probably failing, I casually ask, "So, what about you? Are you married?"

She stares out the window, seeming to drift somewhere else. The room falls quiet, and all I can hear are the birds outside the porch. Her face, like the surface of the lake, gives nothing. The silence grows uncomfortable. Finally, she looks directly at me.

"Why do you need to know?"

"Because . . ." my words teeter as I sift through my emotions, fearing a terrible miscalculation, wondering honestly whether I am just trying to connect to another human being.

"Because," I finally say, at a loss for anything else, "I like you."

Her face brightens, and the corners of her eyes frame a smile. "Nice. I like you, too. And, no, I'm not married, not ever. No children as far as I know either." She chuckles.

Relieved I haven't completely misjudged her, I know what attracts me to her is that I know so little about her. In my room of possibilities, I imagine outcomes, avoiding any vision of professional disgrace and censure. Finally, I say, "I don't know you."

She sits down across from me on the daybed. "Knowing is one thing, understanding is another. We may not know each other, but I think we understand each other perfectly."

We spend two more hours talking and I'm drunk with it. I'm awed by her, and I quickly see she possesses a vision of life that only deep sorrow or tragedy can give. The sudden death of her parents has made her see life as something to be grabbed and lived. By the end of the

afternoon, my conflict with Trina is far away, replaced by a
new fascination—a desire to understand Nora.

On the outskirts of Waukegan, as I head north,
Jimmy Newsome comes to me again, floating face down.
The bright orange T-shirt with the missing piece, the
abandoned boat, and Paulie. Like sun off the water, some
things are too bright to look at. I turn the corner, gliding
the Beast into the garage under the apartment. My mind
drifts from Lake Springfield to other water, bright blue and
chlorinated, then screams and a Mariachi band . . . then
silence. Sitting in my car, I especially remember the long,
strained silence.

CHAPTER EIGHT

THE NEXT MORNING, LARRY MEETS ME AT THE door to my office, reporting his efforts with contacts in Chicago PD have been fruitless, or in his words, "tighter than bark on a tree." I can't be sure, but I think I smell the faint odor of alcohol on his breath . . . although it could just as easily be oozing from his pores. Whichever it is, Larry is clean-shaven and looks grey and pale, but he is upbeat, so I decide to let it pass.

"Believe me, I'm gonna remember when CPD comes looking for a favor up here," he says, throwing himself into my armchair.

I recount what Dr. Hong said about sexual assault, so we give ourselves a pass on searching sexual offenders. We also agree that with nothing coming in that points to a mob contract, we'll focus on interviewing friends and acquaintances to see if we can stir up a lead.

"I'm going to meet some of the hookers today," I volunteer.

Larry leers at me. "There's hooers?" he asks, using the time-honored soubriquet.

I shake my head and share Charles Wesleys' little joke.

Larry is unimpressed, rolling his eyes. "Figures."

The Lake Forest Crochet Club meets at each other's homes every other Thursday afternoon. Delia Van Ostergaard—of the Shaker Heights Van Ostergaards, mind you—cheerfully ushers me into her home, explaining the mission had been to produce blankets and scarves for sale at auctions and charity events. But if Delia is any indication, the hookers haven't produced anything in years, and if margaritas, lemon drops, vitriol, and slow poison were crochet stitches, the towns along western Lake Michigan would be awash in socks, sweaters, and scarves.

Highlighted, shaped, and tinted hair frames Delia's fleshy face. Her dress, too tight and short for her age, pulls at her waist. Her eyelids, tugged sharply back towards her ears, produce a look of perpetual surprise.

Launching herself onto the couch, she says, in a voice of ground glass, "Shocked, absolutely shocked." Then she points at a chair, indicating I should sit.

"This'll be a huge blow to Charles, poor darling—and to Linda, of course. The group won't ever be the same without Faith." She attempts to knit her eyebrows into a show of concern, maneuvering her expression to show sorrow. Unable to manage the gymnastics required of her tightened face, she settles on a grotesquerie somewhere between elation and terror. I almost have to look away.

I ask whether Faith had any enemies she can think of.

Delia ponders for a minute, reaching for a cigarette box on the coffee table. Her face lights up in a small show of recognition. "Well, she tracked down her deadbeat brother for thirty grand he'd borrowed from her. She chased him over three states for fifteen years to collect on the judgment, even got it renewed when it expired in South Dakota."

"Do you think he had anything to do with it?"

Delia laughs, which rolls smoothly into a deep cough. Recovering, she says, "I should think it highly unlikely." She looks around for a lighter.

"Why's that?" I ask, working hard to suppress the irritation rising in my chest.

Leaning over, she opens the drawer to the table next to the couch. Pausing, she sneers for effect. "Because he died penniless in Oklahoma two years ago."

I feel the dull red glow of impatience. "Anyone else you can think of?"

Perhaps sensing my growing lack of interest, she lights the cigarette and sits back into the couch. The place smells faintly like a tavern.

"Well, Faith was certainly known to have a point of view. She kept active in the Lake Forest Historic Preservation Committee and went after several people for violations. There was a lawsuit, but Lent managed to get her out of it."

"Lawsuit?"

Delia takes a drag and smiles, or something like it, shaking her head. "At the Spring Gala of the LFHPC, she'd had a couple of drinks, mind you, and . . . you're not Jewish are you?" She eyes me with suspicion, searching for a lurking Zionist. I respond I'm not. Satisfied, she continues.

"Faith said Milt Waldstein was . . . I think the phrase was 'a thieving Jew bastard.' The historic preservation people were fighting with Milt over his plans to put a mall in over by the college. They eventually settled out of court." Delia shrugs, rolling her eyes. "Entirely blown out of proportion, if you ask me."

"Had she made comments like that before?"

She drops her voice into a conspiratorial whisper the consistency of steel wool. "Well, you remember OJ Simpson? When they were about to announce the verdict, she said—remember she'd had a couple of Long Island iced teas—'I hope they fry the nigger.' You could have knocked me over with a feather." She laughs loudly.

I'm quickly coming to the conclusion Delia is a waste of time. Closing my iPad and trying to hide my disgust, I get to my feet. "She certainly had a lot of opinions."

"Faith cared about and protected her family," Delia says, taking another drag of the cigarette, tapping the ash into the tray in front of her. "She wasn't like what you're trying to make her out to be."

"I'm not trying to make her to be anything," I say. Changing my tack, I ask, "Do you know Nora Summers?"

Delia nods. "They raised her like their own for years. She seemed to do nothing but bring them grief. Finally, they sent her off to school and then she went to Europe where she became some kind of degenerate hippy."

She opens the cigarette box on the table, finding it empty. Shaking her head, she says, "Her parents were killed one night coming back from a party in Chicago. The police investigated the accident and never found out why it happened. Brand new car, as I understand. They interviewed everyone at the party, who swore they were both sober as judges when they left. Closed the investigation down after a couple of weeks, just like that."

She rises, slowly fighting inertia, and moves over to a

small table where she opens a drawer. Unable to find what she's looking for, she closes it, returning to the couch.

"After they died, Charles and Faith brought her up. Faith thought the girls' relationship wasn't healthy."

"Why?" I ask, trying to hide my heightened curiosity.

Preoccupied, Delia doesn't seem to sense my interest. She scans the room again, finally settling on a long table at the far end. Grunting, she pulls herself off the couch again and waddles over to the table, opening a side drawer. With a small "aha" she retrieves a fresh pack of cigarettes.

"Do you mind if I smoke?" she asks, pulling out another cigarette.

I shake my head. "Tell me about the girls."

She lights up before carefully filling the silver case with the newfound pack of smokes. Taking a deep drag, she leans closer, exhaling a large gray cloud in my face. She remains standing, evidently wanting to avoid the athletics of pulling herself out of the couch again.

"She thought Nora wasn't a good influence—boys, cigarettes." She takes another pull on hers. "You know, she was always protective of Linda, right up through," she pauses, blowing another plume of smoke, this time into the air, "the divorce. Lent almost destroyed that family and that darling little girl." Finally, she sits down in an armchair a few feet away. "It didn't get really ugly until the whole business about pornography came up."

Lowering her voice again, she confides in a hoarse whisper, "Lent had online pornography and Linda produced some of the Internet files. I don't know much about that kind of thing. Apparently there were buckets of it. Some of it pretty strange. Whips and leather." She looks at me to gauge my reaction. Seeing nothing, she adds,

"The expert savaged him."

"Who was the evaluator?"

"A Dr. Slack or Stack or something like that," she says, stubbing the cigarette into the ashtray.

"Did you ever hear that Edwards beat Linda?"

Delia reaches for the small silver box, flipping the lid to retrieve another smoke. "Well, they settled out of court, but they spent huge amounts of money on attorneys."

"That wasn't my question. Did you ever hear he hit her?"

"Faith always thought he did. Linda denied it, but if someone was capable of that, it'd be him," she says, quickly blowing smoke into the air. The thick cloud hangs between us.

"Where's he now?"

Delia chirps, her voice light with schadenfreude, "In Chicago. He was a partner with some big firm, but now he's picking garbage downtown."

"Literally?"

"Oh no," she says, blowing another plume out of her nose. "He has a small practice somewhere downtown. Not what his practice used to be, as I understand."

"How often does he see Emma?"

"I really don't know. Once a month, something like that. The evaluator—Dr. Stark, that's his name—recommended supervised visitation."

I leave Delia at the door. Walking to my car, it strikes me I've just spent a half an hour with a woman professing to be one of Faith Wesley's closest friends, a woman who didn't shed a tear or express grief at the loss. I call Larry from the car and ask him to get on the interviews, especially those with Alma and Jesus Morales. Larry clears his throat. "Ya know, I tried them at the number you got from Wesley. They ain't called back yet." Before I can say anything, he hangs up.

In addition to Larry's crappy attitude, the interview with Delia has me irritated. All of it leaves me feeling chafed. The man graduated top of his law school class and the hominy grits and molasses tone is wearing thin, especially in view of his increasingly frequent absences. If Larry doesn't pull out of the nosedive soon, I'm going to give him the boot.

I start down Delia's driveway, barely missing a cat.

■ ■ ■

The Beast hums deeply, whipping up I-94 to Waukegan. I turn over Trina's comment this morning as she stepped into the station wagon that towed the U-Haul trailer crammed heavy with her stuff. "*Merde de chien*, Tom." She'd slammed the door, and gunned the gas, jerking the load behind her. *Merde de chien* is French for dog shit—our code for perspective.

After her father died suddenly of a heart attack, Trina was raised by her uncle, who was twelve years older than her father. We always called her uncle Papa Rich.

Over the years, we'd spent several holidays with Papa Rich. It was a family tradition to go around the table and share reasons for gratitude. Rich was a talker, and one Thanksgiving after a couple of cocktails, he stood and recounted how, on June 9, 1944, he was part of the 320th Barrage Balloon Battalion which flew over occupied France on D-day. The 320th was an African American Army unit that flew hydrogen balloons to protect soldiers landing on the beaches from strafing German airplanes. Later they moved from Omaha Beach to the City of Cherbourg. General Eisenhower gave them special commendations for "courage and determination."

I got hit by a strafing German plane, and the rain, which had hung in the air most of the summer, drenched my face and gear. Through the roar of wind and the sound of the surrounding aircraft, I could feel shock waves hit my chest as flak shells exploded.

Papa Rich fancied himself an "auteur" and Trina told me when she was growing up he'd said he wanted to work for a newspaper. Life and raising his brother's kids got in the way of his dream. He ended up in auto parts. Giving Papa a chance to wax lyrical after a couple of beers at Thanksgiving was a sign of respect. No one, even the smaller cousins, was bored or restless.

I heard the lethal fragments whiz by, and in the grey morning light I watched them hit my friends' legs, chests, testicles, and groins, and I heard them scream as they fell to earth. Some, maybe the lucky ones, were dead before they hit the ground.

I hit the ground at twenty miles an hour, rolling hard to break the fall. The chute dragged me onto my knees and across a farmyard. I stopped when I hit a fence rail that forced the wind from my lungs. The solid crossmember caught me in the solar plexus.

Counting myself lucky, I got to my feet and looked around. Across the yard, I saw a small farmhouse, its windows dark. Fighting the urge to puke, I pulled in my chute, rolling it as I went. Finally, gathering the stringers, I smelled the repulsive stench, pungent and intestinal—unmistakably—of shit. I realized I'd been dragged headlong through a large, yellow, wet pile of shit.

I'd laughed reflexively, thinking that was hilarious. Rich had glared at me and said, "Given my choices, I prefer to assume it came from a dog." He then continued.

Stretching mid-thigh to my boots, a thick, oily, adhesive yellow paste ran the length of my right leg. I quickly tried to scrape off the evil-smelling lacquer, cursing the dog and the beleaguered French people for not cleaning the shit up around there.

As if, I remember thinking, in the middle of Nazi oppression and torture, the French should've at least had the decency to keep their yards shit-free for their liberators. Rich kept on his roll.

I made some headway in removing the tarry paste, but then the sound of nearby gunfire startled me. I grabbed my weapon and ran to join my unit.

As he told it, over the next two days, he would try several times to remove the hardened crust from the cracks in his boots and pants. Despite his efforts, it stuck to him as effectively as commercial adhesive.

On the third day, my platoon entered a town called Carentan, in what came to be known as the Battle of Bloody Gulch.

*The Nazis had left it in ruins, their departure marked by a particular viciousness. I'd already heard stories about booby-trapped toilets and pear orchards rigged with grenades. As I walked up the main road, I saw burning churches, mutilated bodies, and—*Rich started to tremble. *And—*he paused, and I could see the image remained fresh these decades later—*children's corpses.*

Rich took a long pull of his beer and continued. *When I reached the center of town, we were given orders to disperse and clear the town. Accompanied by a corporal in my platoon,*

I walked down a small side street and entered the first two-story house on the right. Entering through the kitchen, I started up the stairs, while the corporal proceeded to search the first floor. On the landing, the hall opened into three small bedrooms, each with two beds. The first was empty, its contents overturned and broken. I crossed the hallway to the second bedroom.

A flash of dull gray steel was all I saw as a Nazi soldier lunged, throwing me to the floor. The wicked steel point of a bayonet sank deep into the wood. With a splintering twist, the soldier pulled the bayonet clear, scratching my face. He lunged again, this time driving for my chest. He over-committed, giving me enough time to jump to my feet.

We stood apart, each measuring the other. I saw a face that will stay with me until I die. He couldn't have been more than eighteen. His hair was grimy and acne covered his face. His eyes were bright with fear. The sound of his heavy breath seemed to fill the room. I followed his eyes to the far corner.

Sprawled like a marionette, a girl lay on her back, blue eyes staring, unseeing, at the ceiling. Her dark blue farm dress was up around her chest, shredded. Her knickers had been surgically sliced, exposing her privates. One small white breast emerged from her dress. Her face was bruised and her arm was bent in an unnatural position. She couldn't have been much more than fourteen.

The man shook his head quickly. "Ich war ihr gehilfen," he said, watching me draw the obvious conclusion. "Nein! Ich habe half ihr," he said, shaking his head, and looking again to the corner. I drove a sidekick into his solar plexus. He retched, but regained his balance, rushing at me with the point of the bayonet. I dropped to the floor, sweeping the soldier's legs and, grabbing his own knife, thrust its fourteen-inch length into his chest.

"Sheiss," was all he said.

I walked over to the girl's body, covered her up, and placed a lace doily from the dresser over her face. I walked downstairs, expecting to find the corporal. After several minutes, I wandered to the shed in the back of the house. The door was closed. I was about to walk away when I noticed a trickle of blood flowing under the door. Drawing my weapon, I pulled open the door to find the corporal leaning against the wall of the shed, his eyes unseeing and a large slit in his throat.

Three and a half days in, I finally got a chance to wash and clean my pants. I asked my lieutenant for a translation of the German's words. "I was helping her," the officer said.

I never knew if the Nazi was telling the truth. It was possible the same animal who had slit the corporal's throat had gotten to the girl first. That wasn't the point. Whether the kid was guilty or not wasn't the point. The point was, dog shit is God's way of providing perspective. Perspective and gratitude. I stank for three days but lived to come home.

Rich had survived and married, raised a family, and started a small but successful automotive parts store in Cleveland. French dog shit is the daily unpleasant, sticky stuff. The real problems, the Carentans of life, well there is nothing much you can do to prepare for those. Prepare for the worst and be grateful for what you get.

To Trina, the fight about the cat is French dog shit.

■ ■ ■

Turning into the parking area under my building, I narrowly miss a pylon. Despite repeated requests from me and my neighbors, the fluorescent lights in the subterranean cavern are out, and large dark areas cloak the garage in blackness. I pull into my numbered space, considering my predicament.

I've returned to Nora's house every day since our first meeting on the porch. In the stolen afternoons and evenings, curled together, we've shared pieces of ourselves. I told her about my sudden departure from college, my divorce from Katie, and my relationship with my son, Liam. I confided to her about growing up in Springfield, and the comedy of errors that was my childhood.

For her part, Nora has lived in a world as foreign to me as the mountains of Nepal—fantastic, hidden, and remote. She told me about going to boarding school in Switzerland; summers spent at camps fragrant with pine needles, nestled in the lakes of the Adirondacks; her travels as a young woman around Europe; and how she eventually settled in Spain. She'd had dreams of becoming a professional photographer and had apprenticed in Barcelona with a famous portraitist. She'd lived in Spain for years. She never married, had no children, and has been living a life drifting from one interest to another.

Yet, even as we've passed the afternoons, or have lain together in the evenings, I have been struck by her reluctance to reveal more of her feelings; never a frank refusal to share, but rather an imbalance in what we've laid bare. When I ask about her family, she teases me about investigating her and, bridling, I always feel defensive, so I've stopped asking.

For all her questions, I've also chosen to be selective about what I divulge. I haven't come clean about Trina. She's gone and what we had together has gradually faded into a collection of images, reaching a point where I can review the collage and say to myself, "This was my life with

Trina." Like many other things, I bury any regret, hoping it will finally calcify and, like bone, weave stronger.

The day Trina left, towing the U-Haul, she'd taken most of her imprint on the place: photographs, music, and a box of letters. I reason to myself the collapse is the inevitable end to a failed relationship. The break, which at first was painful, tinged with ambiguity and the specter of possible reconciliation, has slowly hardened with time. I read somewhere there is a process called confirmation bias where each new fact or event seems to confirm what one believes is true. Whether true or not, we see links and patterns that we use to justify our belief that our lives have a story and follow a plan, fostering the illusion we have some control over our destiny.

I feel no need to share any of this with Nora. In fact, given the terms of our deal, it seems fine to leave a lot of things unsaid. The few times I've pushed her for more, she's withdrawn, and I've resigned myself to thinking that what isn't given freely shouldn't be asked for, contenting myself with the physical gifts she gives me.

■ ■ ■

Sitting alone in the car in the dark, I stare at the blank cinder-block wall, considering the shadows.

Every two to three months I run a sex offender check for my ex-wife Katie's neighborhood in Hyde Park. My experience as a detective brings with it the deep-seated belief evil can be setting in the doorway of an apartment building or buying cigarettes at the local store. There is never a sign or flashing light that says, "Hey, watch out." Being safe, I'm convinced, is a matter of being aware. I believe to some extent being a victim is Darwinian. The antelopes who don't watch out at the river's edge are the ones the crocodiles get. Recently, I ran a check, and it came up with a hit for a Ronald Erland, who's just been released after serving sixteen years for thirteen counts of Forcible Sodomy of a Minor. I call Katie and tell her about it. She replies, "Okay, thanks," and quickly moves to another topic.

"I'm serious, Katie, you need to pay attention."

"I understand, Tom. I'm not an idiot."

It is useless to lecture her, so I hang up.

■ ■ ■

La Festiva Resort in Cancun was like many Mexican resort destinations. Simple bungalows, a pool, tennis courts, and access to the beach. Katie and I had agreed taking a vacation to the Mexican resort with Liam would be a welcome change. We hadn't been physically close in months, and I'd recently stopped drinking. Katie was clearly feeling that between her child and a sober husband, the wild Mexican fiesta was passing her by.

We'd been at the resort three days. Days on the beach and time at the restaurants and tennis court were fun. But, despite all that, Katie grew increasingly irritable. Finally, she told me she was going down to the cantina to get a margarita, and she asked me to watch Liam. My boy, who was then five, trotted aimlessly around the condo in his swim shorts.

At first I refused, feeling a surge of resentment. Later, Katie pushed again, and I folded. Gathering up her room keys, she sighed and left for the cantina. The clock read

12:30.

I pushed reheated leftovers at Liam. The veranda outside was bathed in sun, and a gentle breeze brushed the curtains. The tinny sound of mariachi music drifted in from the speakers outside.

Lunch, instead of putting Liam to sleep as I'd hoped, seemed to rejuvenate him. "Dad, can we go out?"

"Maybe later, Liam," I replied. Unlike my son, the leftover pizza made me sleepy. I watched my son drift into the bedroom to watch cartoons.

Later, Liam touched my arm. "Where's Mom?"

I raised my head to check the clock—2:30 PM—two fucking hours. She said one drink, I thought to myself, fighting fatigue and resentment, finally nodding off again.

A few minutes later, Liam was at me again. "Dad, can we go to the pool?"

"Sure thing, chief," I said, turning on the couch.

Later, I started up, scanning the room and then the clock: 2:55. I'd been fully asleep for about twenty minutes.

"Liam?"

No response. The door to the condo was open. I found my cell phone and, dialing, cursed when Kathy's phone emitted a dull buzz in the drawer next to the bed.

"Liam?" I said, a little louder. If Liam answered, I was up for whatever demands the boy could muster. The condo remained silent. My heart raced, a cold sliver of fear stirring my guts.

I ran to the entryway downstairs. The afternoon sun struck me in the face. A bougainvillea-draped trellis spanning the entrance cut the light into triangles. As I ran down the path, several lizards scampered under the bushes. The hot terracotta walkway burned my bare feet, yet I raced all the way to the bottom of the drive where the entrance met the highway. Fearing the worst, I scanned the highway that separated the condos from the beach. Passing cars veered noisily by as I stood a few feet from the entry gate.

I strained to see if I could find Liam on the beach. After several seconds, I ran uphill, small pebbles cutting my soles, sun beating on my head and the back of my neck. Reaching the pool veranda, I threw open the latched gate onto the shaded patio, alive with mariachi music and splashing water.

At the far end, Katie sat, glass in hand, at the cantina. Laughter pealed as she engaged with an older couple.

I searched the pool, which was roiling with frenetic activity. Several screaming kids were jumping into the deep end, and three large teenagers hung on the edge of the pool, their backs to the crowd. After several seconds, I located Liam in the middle of the pool, jumping on his toes, struggling to keep his head above water. In the space of a few seconds, Liam submerged, then reemerged, choking, and went under again.

At the cantina bar, Katie laughed again, oblivious to the fact our son was drowning.

I jumped in the pool, fully clothed, a tidal wave of water parting before me. I caught Liam, who grabbed me with tight little hands, and pulled the boy to safety. I sat my son on the pool edge and watched Liam cough for several seconds as he caught his breath. The boy's T-shirt and pants were soaked. When he finally regained his breath, he sputtered and started to cry.

"I'm sorry, Dad! I'm sorry!"

Angry at my son, truly angry, probably for the first time

in my son's life, I pulled him closer to me. "Goddammit, Liam, how did you get down here?" I was also angry at myself.

"I'm sorry," Liam said, sobbing.

The commotion caught the attention of the cantina crowd. It took a minute, but Katie made her way over. Her eyes did not come immediately into focus and she wavered on her feet. Clearly drunk, she bent down. Looking at Liam, she took a few seconds to understand what had just occurred.

"Jesus Christ, what happened here?" she said, kneeling beside Liam. Drunk though she was, she could quickly tell Liam's being at the pool, wet and in distress, implicated her as his mother. She could also see I was angry. Through her haze, she also knew she'd far outspent any tacit agreement we'd had about her furlough that afternoon. She reached clumsily for Liam, but I kept my grip on him. There was an awkward moment as we both struggled for control of our son. Several people looked away.

What Katie decided to say, and how she handled the awkward mess the three of us had landed in would determine the next decade of our lives. Had she chosen to voice relief that Liam was okay and apologized for not coming back sooner, tacitly accepting accountability for this terrible collision of circumstances, we might have been able to repair some of the damage.

"What did you just say?" I asked, as if to frame the moment.

She stared at me through her sunglasses, her face set and flushed red with sunshine and alcohol. She turned to Liam, shaking her head. "Jesus, Tom, how did Liam get over here? Weren't you watching him?" She turned back to eye me with angry defiance.

We spent the next seven hours arguing about who was responsible for Liam's near-drowning. I pointed out that if she wasn't drunk and hadn't left for longer than she said she would, Liam wouldn't have gone out unattended. She countered that if I hadn't fallen asleep on the job, it wouldn't have happened either. Both of these things were true, however, neither of us expressed an ounce of accountability or, the most important thing, gratitude Liam was still alive.

A deep and cold resentment descended on us both; resentment at what we'd become and a sad realization we were now so different from what we'd been, or thought we were. The truth was, we'd never really known each other.

Returning to Illinois from Mexico, I moved into the guest bedroom. Within eight weeks Katie moved out, taking Liam with her, leaving me with my books and a few sad sticks of furniture. Within a few months, we divorced.

■ ■ ■

It is still difficult, years later, sitting in the darkness of the garage, to give words to the emotions that ran through me. First was anger at Katie, whose drinking was a personal betrayal to me and to Liam. The second emotion was my own shame and guilt over allowing my son to escape the condo while under my watch. I felt unmanly, unworthy of being a father, like one of the parents Katie and I read about in the Sunday paper who left their children in cars to die in the summer heat.

If Larry knew Yiddish, he might tell me *mentsch tracht, Gott lacht*—man plans, God laughs. All prior planning is, in other words, futile, and the future can lie in the balance of a few seconds or a few words.

The parking lights in the car time out, leaving me in complete darkness. I extend a hand to the passenger side, looking for my cell phone. When I locate it, it lights up, illuminating my face. Dialing Trina's number, I feel a sudden stab of regret, realizing, for the first time since we'd had the dinner and I'd returned to find the apartment emptied of most of her belongings, Trina is truly gone. All my self-talk and plans come falling down, and I am filled with an acute need to talk to her.

After several rings, an automated female voice informs me that at the request of the subscriber the service has been turned off. I feel tired. Ending the call, I get out of the car, slowly walking over to the narrow staircase that leads up to the lobby.

CHAPTER NINE

WHEN I INTERVIEWED LINDA EDWARDS, among the things she told me about her ex was he could trace his family back to Aaron Burr, and his famous grandfather, Jonathan Edwards, a co-founder of Princeton. Burr famously put a bullet into Alexander Hamilton and lived in infamy. *Sinners In The Hands Of An Angry God* was the name of Jonathan Edwards' famous sermon promising eternal agony dangling by a hair over the fires of hell to those not in favor with The Almighty. In college, I'd been struck enough by the sermon to look up the preacher. The portrait in an American survey book reflected a small, pinched mouth and a vulpine nose lying beneath shadowed, deep-lidded eyes. A face that could express disdain or derision with equal ease.

Sitting in Edwards' waiting area, I sift through the tattered heap on the coffee table. Old *TV Guides*, and *People* magazines from when Bush Senior was president are mixed in with a *National Geographic*, which, when I pick it up, falls open to a piece on the Masai women. At the far end of the coffee table, a laminated newspaper ad asks,

Have you been RAPED, BEATEN, ASSAULTED, THE VICTIM OF A CRIME?!!! Preventable crimes may entitle you to a CASH AWARD!!!

Call O'Connor and Mozen today!

We can help!

I put the tattered *National Geographic* on the table and reach for a small, heavily-thumbed leaflet that bears the title, *Getting a Divorce: What You Should Know.* I scan the contents and turn to the first section.

DECIDING CUSTODY

Custody goes to the parent the court makes the determination is in the "best interests" of the child. This is based on factors which the court believes will foster a healthy, normal childhood for the child, given the circumstances.

Often the court needs assistance making this difficult decision. To help the court, there is a custody evaluator, usually a psychologist, or a doctor who can assist the court in making this decision. The evaluator is required to meet with the family and make recommendations. The American Psychiatric Association requires the evaluator be fair and impartial and refrain from bias or undue influence of one parent or the family.

I remember when Katie and I went through the process of deciding custody. Looking back at my own childhood and realizing Liam would thrive best by being with his mother, Katie and I successfully avoided the nightmare that was a custody battle in court. I make a mental note to have Larry track down Dr. Stark, the evaluator in the Edwards' case. If what Delia said about Edwards is true, he is likely to have an opinion about Edwards.

I look at my watch. Fifteen minutes have passed.

As I wait, fighting a slowly rising tide of resentment, I settle on Nora and the day we'd grappled like college wrestlers on the back porch of her house. I remember running my hand over the smooth slope of her abdomen, over her full breast, coming to rest on the warm ascent of her buttocks. I'd caressed the cool, firm apple of her right cheek, moving down her thigh until my palm felt rough, dry texture—a bandage.

"What's this?" I'd asked.

She'd smiled, pulling my hand away.

"You're not supposed to ask," she'd said, her face drawn into a mock pout. "I had a mole removed. Now all the mystery is gone." I'd laughed, bending down to place a warm, lingering kiss on the ripe curve of her behind. Again, I'd let silence fill in what she'd left unrevealed.

Much as I am nettled by Nora's opacity, I feel soothed when she reveals a glimpse of her secret world.

A few days after the episode with the bandage, we were lying on the porch when, as if deciding I'd passed some test, she shifted to look at me.

"I had a baby brother," she said, her voice barely a whisper.

"Had?"

"He died when I was six. He was barely three years old."

Casting about for something meaningful to say, the

best I could produce was, "How awful."

She nodded, her gaze unfocused as she searched the past. "He fell down the stairs." Charles and Faith were over for dinner, and my parents blamed the nanny for not watching him."

"I'm so sorry," I said.

She shrugged and shook her head. "Don't be. But the cookies seemed to point up everything to me. I made them when things were normal and safe. They were the last thing I ever made for my parents. They sat around for a couple of weeks because I didn't want to throw them out. Finally, someone, probably Faith Wesley, got rid of them."

I'd stroked her hair, searching for something to say. "You must have been devastated. Did Faith try to help?" I'd asked.

She'd shaken her head. "Not really. That wasn't like her at all. The thing was, they could never figure out why the accident happened. My parents weren't drinkers, and while it was winter, the roads were clear. The investigation was closed. After a few months, I was in a new school and living with the Wesleys. Charles stepped in and saw to it that I was happy. My parents became memories in my head. Like this photograph over here," she'd said, handing me the picture I'd looked at when I first met her.

A cloud had drifted across the sky, painting the porch in shadow. I'd glanced at her and could see the sparkling traces of tears on her face. If I had not looked carefully, I might have missed them.

"God, Nora, I—"

She'd smiled and reached over to brush the side of my face, then changed the subject and asked me if I thought what I did actually served some type of purpose. I'd thought about it, finally answering, "It depends on what you think justice is."

She'd brushed her fingers lightly over my lips. "Now you're being coy. I thought that was my job." She'd smiled. "Justice—setting things right—resetting the balance sheet."

I'd laughed. "A lot of what I spend my time doing is being a kindergarten teacher."

Nora sat up. "You don't believe in any of that 'satisfaction of the public outrage' stuff?"

I'd reached out, stroking the underside of her full breast, tracing the pouting outline of the areola with my finger. The bud stiffened under my thumb. "I don't know. After you've seen the same skells year after year, it seems like kindergarten, and not some grand scheme of justice."

Nora's eyes had narrowed as she brushed my hand away from her swelling nipple. "That sounds pretty facile, Tom. Everybody sits around bitching about how the bad old world is going to hell, but they're not interested in doing anything to fix it themselves."

I'd reached over for her again and pulled her to me. "I get it. If you simply forget and give in, let the law of the jungle win, you'll end up with savagery."

"They spent thirty-three years chasing after Mengele, you know."

I'd chuckled. "As far as I know, Josef Mengele wasn't hiding in Lake County, Illinois."

"Laugh if you want, but you know what I mean," she'd said, her voice clipped. I'd sensed she was getting annoyed.

"I do. You mean that part of our obligation as humans is to keep track of what debases us. The issue isn't keeping track, the problem is what you do with the debasers."

I'd kissed her mouth and felt her skin, warmed in the

afternoon sun, as she pushed her backside against me. Our discourse on justice had stopped when she'd leaned back and whispered in my ear, "Let's fuck."

What started as an infatuation quickly became something deeper, but in the process I feel trapped between memory and desire. I am living in a gray world of morbid reflection. In the time we've spent together, I've wanted to open myself to her, tell her everything. Each missed chance feels like sand drifting to the bottom of a riverbed, hardening, only to be covered by the next layer.

■ ■ ■

Finally, Lent Edwards stands in front of me, black shoes shined to perfection, his sharp face unmarked by levity or laughter. He extends a perfunctory apology, muttering something about being caught on a call. Edwards wears a tailored sports coat over a neatly pressed shirt adorned with a brightly colored, hand-painted Italian tie. The hands at the end of the cuffs are large and tan, with clean, manicured nails. I can instantly see the semblance to his famous forbears. His deep-set eyes and tight mouth carry the same expression of disapproval.

As we walk towards the back of the office, Edwards trails me. "I moved here a little over two years ago. I was a partner at Lattimer Wardwell."

"Former chair of the real estate practice."

"You've been doing your homework," Edwards says, seeming mildly surprised. He directs me to an office at the end of the hallway.

Wanting to keep Edwards off balance, I launch in. "To be honest, I've heard some nasty things about you."

Edwards gives me a look. "Why am I not surprised?"

In contrast to the chaos outside, Edwards' office is meticulous, with files placed in organized stacks, and deal files bound on the shelves behind the desk. The walls are lined with photographs of him and Emma and, just behind the desk, a picture shows him with several well-groomed men holding golf clubs. Edwards holds a silver cup in one hand. The rest of the wall space is taken up with awards from the Illinois State Bar Association, the Greater Chicago Chamber of Commerce, and the Chicago River Development Association for his help in spearheading the redevelopment of Ogden Slip in Chicago.

I decide to press again. "Can you tell me where you were Saturday morning?"

Taking a seat behind his desk, he nods slowly. "Sleeping one off in my apartment."

"Were you alone?"

His eyes narrow. Edwards is a lawyer, and I can tell he's not going to cooperate. He shakes his head and runs a hand through his hair. "I don't see that's any of your business."

"Mr. Edwards, you agreed to meet with me. If this is a waste of—"

Edwards' lips tighten into a knot. "I agreed to help, not to an interrogation."

Undeterred, I continue. "I know you were in the military—I think it was the Rangers. OCS and Eighty-Second Airborne, Desert Storm. DSM—Distinguished Service Medal. Impressive."

I pause to gauge his response. "I also know you were in a nasty divorce and that one of the main charges leveled was you abused your wife."

His eyes blink slowly. He takes a breath to start talking,

and checks himself, folding his hands in his lap.

"I'm here, in this office," he says, "because Faith Wesley had more pull with the senior partners at Lattimer than I did." His voice rises. "I left Lattimer as an abusive pervert, abandoning my wife and a small girl—a liability to the firm," he says, then checks himself again.

"All the more reason for you to want Faith Wesley dead."

Edwards shakes his head. "No . . . good try, though. I spent every dime I had to go to court to get time with Emma, but that's done. It's been done for years."

"Okay then, what about Friday?"

Edwards' mouth pulls into a tight pout of refusal. "I told you, I'm not going there." He moves to the window, where pigeons swoop in the air current, settling in the crevices under the fire escape. A solitary piece of newspaper floats in the updraft, which is lit by a beam of afternoon sun that stretches through a space between buildings. It strikes me as oddly beautiful.

"I can bring you in for a polygraph."

Edwards throws his hands up in disbelief. "I spent Friday night with a woman I met at a bar downtown. She left early Saturday morning."

"I'll need the name."

He grunts and then sneers at me, as if I am some kind of deviant. "She said her name was Stacey, which is probably true. I met her at Carnahan's on Lake Street. That's all I can tell you about her, other than she wasn't a real blonde, or a professional girl, or if she was, she'd be starving to death."

"What about your custody case?"

The sneer quickly fades, and his eyes narrow. "What

about it? Linda hired Lori Erlich. What does that have to do with Faith being murdered?"

"I heard you beat Linda."

His face flushes. "You ever been divorced?"

"None of your fucking business," I snap.

Edwards grins, seeing he's hit pay dirt. "What shit did they say about you in yours?" He rises abruptly. "If you want to talk to me again, it'll have to be through my lawyer. Please leave." He points to the door.

As I head to my car, I call Tony Shahbaz, demanding a warrant for Edwards' office, car, and apartment.

"Tom, the guy's a lawyer. They're never going to let us just go through his drawers. Get reasonable."

"Do what you can," I reply, and hang up.

■ ■ ■

Sporting a small halo of mustard on his right sleeve, Larry greets me as I walk into my office. The metallic odor of alcohol hits my nose.

"We get anything from the Morales couple?"

"Chicago PD uniforms went to check the apartment. The neighbors haven't seen them in over two weeks. The mail was uncollected."

"Doesn't sound good."

"It ain't. Both of 'em dead. Shot point-blank in the head." Larry clears his throat with a deep cough. "Manny Gorak's the detective handling it for Chicago PD. Treatin' it as a drug killing. Speaking of which," he says, picking at the yellow spot on his sleeve, "Your jazz buddy, Lou Watson, called to say they found blood and a piece of fabric—black polyester—on one of the iron posts outside the hedge. They're processing it through CODIS." CODIS refers to the FBI's Combined DNA Index System. "They're trying to get an ID on the blood."

"What did the fabric look like?" I ask, searching my desk for a restaurant coupon.

"Black, silk-poly blend. About three millimeters square. Ripped."

"Poly blend?"

"Yeah, like a pair of exercise pants."

Larry clears his throat again. Not just a polite *ahem*, but a guttural scraping of the tonsils. It's a habit I really don't like. "The other thing. I called Wesley's abacus jockey. No financials without a court order."

I tell Larry I've already lined up a warrant with Shahbaz. Larry tells me he checked up on the restaurant Linda and Nora Summers went to and confirmed with the maître d' they each had two glasses of wine and were out by 10:30.

"What about the Edwards' divorce file?"

"It's sealed," Larry says, continuing to finger the mustard stain.

"Call Shahbaz and get it unsealed." Almost as an afterthought I add, "While you're at it, pull the investigation file on the Summers' car crash in 1968."

Larry looks up. "That's going to be in archives." Meaning the file is going to come from Springfield, a pain in the ass under any circumstances. "You think there's an angle on all this?"

"Just get it, Larry, please."

Doing my best to camouflage my motives with a plausible reason, I say, "Nora Summers lived with the Wesleys. I just want to do some background."

Larry shrugs and walks out, our debrief apparently over. I call Manny Gorak and, as Larry said, the detective is an asshole. Gorak makes no pretense of professional courtesy, letting me know my call is an inconvenience. After some jockeying, he finally agrees to meet me at the Morales' apartment.

When in Chicago, I often treat myself to Staropolska. To devotees of Polish sausage, Staropolska is what Turin is to religious relics. Once seated, I order Polish pancakes, plums wrapped in bacon, and of course, a large Polish sausage. After the meal, sated like an anaconda, I doze in the TT until the phone rings. I look to see if it is Trina's number.

It's Nora. I answer, and she quickly offers two tickets to see Cirque du Soleil this weekend.

"I thought you might like to take Liam," she adds.

"That's very generous." The tickets are impossible to come by. "Really, I—"

"Please, Tom, I get free tickets all the time, I have several, and I hate to see them go to waste. Take them." With the offer, Nora is bringing Liam into a situation I'm still uncertain about, adding another sharp moving part. I feel uneasy. But, after a few seconds, I convince myself Liam's excitement and the prospect of disappointing Nora outweigh any potential harm. "Thanks. That's really nice of you." I pause again. "What do I owe you?"

She sighs loudly. "Nothing. Should I drop them at your office? "

If I've had any doubts about whether what I am doing with Nora might be a problem with the Department, the quick stab of conscience resolves any questions. I tell her I'll pick them up at her house later in the day.

. . .

The Morales family lives in a five-story walk-up stained with rust and reeking of stale urine. I reckon the trip from the projects in New City to Lake Forest is thirty miles, one way. If you drive, which Jesus would need to do for landscape work, it takes a little over an hour in good traffic. If you take public transportation, it's a two-hour trip. Each way. Jesus and Alma have been making the trip, as far as I know, for over thirty years, at least twice a week.

I climb three flights of stairs lit by flickering fluorescent bulbs. A baby's cries echo down the airshaft. On the third-floor landing, I strain to see down the dark hallway. A woman wearing a housecoat and hairnet, a cigarette dangling from her mouth, comes out of one of the apartments, carrying a bag of trash. She stares at me and starts down the stairs. I can see the apartment marked with police tape at the far end.

My dealings with Chicago PD have never been good. Most of the time, crime in Lake County is local. Cook County has its own coroner, its own major crime unit. When, occasionally, cases bleed over, Chicago PD is always too busy and important to help. I've never gotten the feeling it is an intentional snub; it is more like having to deal with your snotty cousin from the city.

I knock on the door, and a uniformed officer lets me in. Inside the apartment, the air is thick with rose-scented perfume. On the living room wall, a pastel Jesus, hands outspread, welcomes all comers. I wonder idly where He was when the Morales family was being dispatched to meet Him.

In the corner, a heavyset man with dark hair stares at a

blurred and fading family photograph on the wall.

"Detective Gorak?" I ask, trying to get off to a good start.

I join him at the photo on the wall. I extend a hand, which he ignores, leaving me to put my hand in my pocket. The faded portrait, color bled out to shades of green and yellow, is of a man and a woman, both smiling. They are in traditional Mexican dress, the image taken decades earlier. The couple is surrounded by several other people, including an older woman and much older man, both staring, unsmiling, into the camera. They are the parents, I surmise. Behind them, two younger men also stare defiantly. They have on clean plaid shirts and bolo ties and hold cowboy hats. The only people smiling in the picture are the young couple holding each other, dressed for what is clearly their wedding portrait.

Manny Gorak turns, his tight white short-sleeved shirt pulling at the shoulders, the armpits stained with sweat. Up to this point, I'm not certain if the deal with the handshake is simply an oversight or an insult.

"That's me. Edison, right?"

"Edison," I say, "but you can call me Tom."

Gorak assesses me like an aging tuna sandwich. "Division said you'd be down."

Ignoring the snub, I offer, "They worked for a woman murdered in Lake Forest last month."

"Yeah—the Wesley case," he says, unbuttoning his shirt. "It's fuckin' stuffy in here."

"We've been trying to get an interview with them for three weeks."

"Looks like that ain't going to happen," he says, pointing towards the table where photographs are spread out.

"The Moraleses have already been transported?"

Gorak nods, inviting me to leaf through the photos. The place has already been processed and is only a few hours from being released to the landlord and a cleanup crew.

I scan the pictures. In the first one, Alma and Jesus sit on the couch, looking every bit as if they are preparing for a follow-up portrait to the picture on the wall, except they are older. Looking at photos that were taken closer up, I see Alma and Jesus have circular holes in the center of their foreheads. In a second close-up, a section of Alma's nose, right cheek, and a portion of her ear look as if they were chewed off.

"Dead over ten days," Gorak says. "That's why we got 'em out of here."

"What's with the nose and ear?"

"The cat. Starving. Disgusting animals, if you ask me," Gorak ventures.

"No argument from me."

Apparently, my dislike of cats proves to Manny I'm not a complete idiot.

"If it hadn't been for the yowling, the neighbors would've waited another week until the smell started to make it through the walls. Even so, it was pretty ripe in here. Animal control took the cat."

"What d'you have on them?"

Gorak checks his notes. "Alma Morales and Jesus Morales. She was fifty-seven, he was sixty. They're cholos, living here with no green cards for thirty years. Jesus Christ, it's a freakin' oven in here." He wipes his forehead. The stains under his arms are spreading down his shirt.

"Children?"

"None, like I said. No other family that we can tell right now. If I had to guess, I'd say the shooter used a small-caliber handgun with hollow-tipped rounds. My guess is nine mil or twenty-two," he says, then points over to a rusty fire escape. "No sign of forced entry. They knew the shooter. No sign of a struggle. Executed. Drugs." It's clear that as far as he's concerned, to paraphrase Ethel Barrymore, "That's all there was. There wasn't any more."

"Anything from the rest of the house? Cash? Paraphernalia? Scales?" I ask, tacitly acknowledging what at least sounds like a viable working hypothesis.

"They crossed the wrong people—know what I mean?" Manny shakes his head.

Figuring there's nothing left to see, I give him my card and start to leave. Gorak catches me at the door. "You gonna open a file on any of this?"

"You mean, add this in with Faith Wesley?"

He sighs deeply. "Sure."

The implication is clear. Close this file, so he can add it to the statistics. Leave it open, and it is a project— something he'll have to deal with. I shake my head. "Probably not." I make for the stairwell, certain Manny's case will be closed by the end of the day. As I head down the stairs I yell back, "Your jurisdiction, your case."

"You got it," he yells in return as he slams the door.

■ ■ ■

Larry left me a note saying State Archives in Springfield called and said they'd pulled the Summers' file. I step into his office, waving the pink sheet.

"Thanks a lot. What about the fabric and the blood from the crime scene?"

He shifts in his chair. Larry seems to have changed his shirt, and he looks like he might have had a complete night's sleep. "They're backlogged too, and Cook County lab is behind on CODIS. It's like that all over the fuckin' place."

"Push it, will you?" I've started to wonder if Larry's drinking is affecting his ability to get simple things done—like lab tests.

I consider sending Larry to have the file copied, but decide that would raise too many questions. The trip to Springfield will take me just under four hours. It will take the entire day to look at the file and get back. After cleaning out my parent's house, I haven't been back in several years. Once I'd buried Ben, there's been no reason to visit. Driven by the inevitable force of my own life—my son, my job—all tying me to the present, I've left Springfield in the past. As I drive its streets on my way to the government complex buildings, it rushes to meet me.

As I drive up Clear Lake Avenue, the businesses, the houses, all look smaller, as if propped up like an empty movie set. The fragrance of white pine, tulip, and Kentucky coffee trees hangs heavy in the air. Several of the giant American beeches that once shaded the park are gone.

Illinois keeps its institutional memory in an imposing granite building on the Capitol Complex. At over fifty-three-thousand cubic feet of records, its stone hallways extend, cool and shaded, in each direction. Echoing voices bounce around the rotunda on smooth marble floors. At the reception desk, a fresh-faced intern directs me down the corridor and tells me to wait.

Twenty minutes later, the clerk resurfaces, pushing a squealing metal cart, and asks to see my badge. He then points to a section of metal-topped tables where he begins unloading. The dusty manila folders emit a boggy odor of deteriorating paper and ink, the fragrance of time. On the outside, each folder bears a faded label: Summers - LK Cty Case 2388656 (Vehicular INV). He arranges them on the table, one through five.

The first jacket contains color photographs dimmed by time, the greens washed to yellow and reds bleeding to rust. They'd been taken in the early days when the Department first shifted from black and white pictures of accident and crime scenes to the grisly palette of color. Nothing is left to the imagination. I count seven yellowed envelopes of eight-by-ten photographs. The first picture shows a chained blue Cadillac Deville as it's being pulled out of a lagoon, water cascading off the chassis. In the next picture, grim-faced uniforms surround the car as it is hoisted onto a wrecker, its right front panel crushed into a flat plane almost parallel to the windshield.

Turning to the next folder, I brace myself for the next set of photos. Inside the car, two bodies, those of a man and a woman, are sprawled across the front seat. The woman is wearing a black evening dress, torn open and revealing a full, white breast. Despite the poor quality of the picture, I see a thin film of muck and dirt covers her pale skin. With her eyes closed, dark hair falling flatly to one side, she appears to be asleep. Even through the grey shades of time, I can see Nora in her mother.

The man is draped over the front seat, the left side of his face visible through a partially open window. I recognize him from the photo in Nora's house. Even after all these years, the picture is jarring. There's a large concave dent in the middle of his forehead, and the eyes stare lifelessly out the window. The man wears a dark suit and thin tie, and his white shirt is stained deep red, turned rusty orange with time.

I'm unprepared for the third group of pictures, which are close-ups of the woman's hands, the fingers ripped open and fingernails broken. More pictures display the inside door handle and the window toggles. The vinyl is torn, and the window switches have been ripped out of the door handle on the inside.

Taking a deep breath, I sit back for a moment, overcome, struggling with sadness and revulsion. I can't possibly tell Nora her mother drowned slowly as she tried to claw her way out of the sinking car. The truth of the accident, if she were to know, is more horrible than anything I can share, and simply reaffirms what she already knows: her parents died tragically in a violent and senseless accident. Telling Nora her mother suffered would add nothing but grief.

I scan the report for the name of the investigating officer. Detective Peter Strauss, Lake County Sheriff's office. The crime predated the Major Crimes Task Force. Investigations back then were handled by the sheriff or the Illinois State Police. Opening the fourth folder, I see Strauss' summary report typed out, with a neat signature at the bottom.

At approximately 1117 hrs on November 15th, 1977
- Model 1964 Cadillac Deville 64-63L lost control
on the northbound Skokie highway next to Skokie
Lagoon. The vehicle traversed the far-right median
and landed in the lagoon which at that point is 16

*feet in depth. Once in the water, the power windows
became inoperable, and the vehicle flooded and the
occupants, identified as Mary Louise and Edward
Summers of Lake Forest, were trapped in the vehicle.
Mr. Summers sustained a severe head trauma from the
vehicle's initial impact with the concrete median and
appears to have died instantaneously. Mrs. Summers
appears to have died from causes related to drowning.*

*Brake malfunction has been ruled out as a cause of the
accident.*

I search all five folders for a mechanical report, which
would have been standard procedure. Two staples on the
third folder hold telltale shreds of paper. The report is
missing. The fifth folder holds a closing summary: Case
closed 2/12/68. P. Strauss LCSD #56-05.

Returning the file, I ask the clerk about the missing
report.

The clerk shrugs, shaking his head. "In a file that old,
things go missing. It may be a long shot, but sometimes
duplicates are kept by a separate department. If it was the
investigating officer's summary or file, you're screwed."

As I leave Springfield, disappointment gnaws at me.
The fact I've wasted a complete day is salvaged only by
the one piece of new information I've come away with: the
name of the lead investigator, Pete Strauss. Typically, the
identity of an investigating officer forty years gone means
nothing. But in this case, I unearthed a piece of local
legend. Before Major Crimes Task Force, there was only
the Lake County Sheriff's Department, where Strauss was
assigned . . . where he was known simply as "Dirty Pete."

CHAPTER TEN

I N THE WEEKS FOLLOWING FAITH WESLEY'S MURDER, time seems to slow. We finish interviewing Faith's hooker friends, each one less helpful than the one before. There is still no hit on the DNA sample, and I begin to blame the stalled case on Larry's incompetence. Already prickly about his drinking, Larry has grown even less congenial. For my part, I can't shake the sense he's somehow tumbled to my special interest in the Summers' case.

To make things worse, the Wesleys have gotten their lawyers involved. What's surprised me most is the number of people on the legal staff protecting the Wesleys' interests. A lawyer from Stanhope Thornton placed me on notice that they are the "liaison" to the investigation and insist all further contact be made through the "team." Larry prefers the soubriquet "weasel dicks."

The strain with Larry finally gives when he reports, for the third time, the lab told him they are processing the sample and will get back to him as soon as possible. I slam my fist on the desk. "Goddammit, Larry, what is the fucking problem over there?"

"Call 'em your goddam self if you don't believe me," he snaps, marching out of the room.

Ronald Reagan's famous appropriation of the old Russian proverb "trust but verify" always made good sense to me, so I call the lab director. I'm placed on hold through a flavorless rendition of *Bridge Over Troubled Water*, all of *Can We Still Be Friends*, and the first two minutes of *Every Kind of People* before a female voice comes on the line. She identifies herself as the Law Enforcement Services Coordinator. She quickly explains, in a patently rehearsed speech, that a backlog since spring has resulted in new protocols for sample handling. I get the feeling I'm being worked.

"Do you know where the Wesley sample is now?" I ask, struggling to suppress the rising irritation in my voice.

There is a brief pause, and I can hear her shuffle paperwork. "Yes, well, it's in line. We had some trouble locating it."

"Locating it?" I'm not sure I fully understand what the coordinator is telling me. "Are you saying you misplaced it?"

"Lost track temporarily," she replies briskly, making it clear mine isn't the first call of its kind she's fielded recently. I think she might qualify as one of Larry's weasel dicks.

"Lost track?"

"An administrative mix-up." She sighs loudly. "Look, there's no problem with chain of custody," she says crisply.

I know she has me by the snarglies. If I piss her off, she'll bury the sample until the next solar eclipse. I settle on false bonhomie. "Good. What is your name again?"

She exhales loudly. "Mrs. Grant. We're working twenty-four shifts to get them done."

"Thank you, Mrs. Grant. When can I expect the results?" I ask again.

"Within the next few days."

"Fuck," I mutter.

"No need to use profanity, Detective Edison," she barks, hanging up the phone.

Replacing the receiver, I see Mrs. Grant has skillfully put me on the defensive, shifting the blame, when the problem is exclusively the fault of her department. Despite my disappointment, I'm relieved the process at least seems to be moving forward. I also grudgingly acknowledge, if only to myself, this problem doesn't seem to belong to Larry.

I've tried, without success, to call Trina at her work, only to be politely informed she isn't in the office and I'm then put through to voicemail. Finally, I leave a halting message in which I ask her to call me. I realize I'm not sure what I would say if she had answered.

Waiting for the labs, I focus on other files, among them an arson ring. Several local grocery stores in one section of Waukegan have been torched in six weeks' time. The case so far has been treated as typical extortion . . . until one of the grocery stores hired a night watchman who died in the latest fire. Now it is murder.

I've closed two grand-theft larceny cases and testified in an assault and kidnapping case against a pimp named Dexter Withers, also known as Sonny T. Sonny runs a chain of tanning salons, preying on bored, confused, vain teenage girls. In exchange for looking good at reception, they get free tanning, Ecstasy, coke, and sex. He's parlayed this resource into an extra service at the salon for some of his discerning male clients. Eventually, movies were made. Several girls from Waukegan had the temerity to complain to Sonny. For their ingratitude, they received a severe beating with a sock full of coins, after which they were dumped in the Almond Marsh Forest Preserve to find their way home. After their bruises healed and the swelling subsided, those lucky enough to recover their lives were not of a mind to talk about Sonny. A couple of girls had simply vanished, but no one could pin that on Sonny.

Finally, one of the girls survived with a fractured face and missing teeth, but she held on to enough will to confront the animal who'd destroyed her life. Sonny received fifteen years in Menard for aggravated assault. I made sure my contact at Corrections knew someone in Menard who would give Sonny the sock treatment.

Gorak's report on the Morales's finally crosses my desk. Not one to disappoint, Manny concludes the homicides are the result of "local drug-related activity", closing the investigation. There are no family or friends to object and the file is outside my jurisdiction, so it has joined the millions of other cases where the truth is known only to God. Meanwhile, I wait on the DNA and mark time until I can get the financial stuff from the accountants, which is working its way through the State Attorney's office.

I'm in my office when the phone rings. The caller ID says it's Steinman. I let it ring through to voicemail. About three minutes later, Larry comes to the door.

"Steinman's on the phone and says it's urgent, that he knows you're avoiding his calls."

Fighting the urge to tell Larry to lie, I pick up the

receiver. "Frank," I say, without inflection.

"Holy shit, Tom." Frank likes to start a conversation with a declaration. "I got Stanhope Thornton on the phone, howling about the accountants. What's so important about the fucking financials?"

"It's a routine request, Frank, that's been completely blown out of proportion. I've been dealing with the Stanhope team for almost a month. Tracing the money is just standard procedure in a homicide case. You know that."

"You're chasing your own dick. You should be going after Lent Edwards."

"Did they say that, Frank? That I'm chasing my dick?"

"Look, they're frustrated with the pace of the investigation. It's been weeks since the murder, the CODIS stuff isn't in yet, and you haven't made progress on Edwards."

If Frank wants to get me riled, he's succeeded. "We don't have anything that even puts Edwards at the scene. We have a lot of innuendoes and circumstantial stuff. Plus two dead witnesses in Chicago."

"Drug murders."

"And as for CODIS, Frank, that's out of my hands," I say, recounting the substance of my conversation with the lab.

"Misplaced?" Steinman interrupts when I get to the part of my conversation with the lab. For all his political thuggery, Frank's success is in part due to his early championing of efforts in the late 80s to get DNA accepted as valuable evidence. He's fought several hard-won court battles, establishing protocol for chain of custody and scientific certainty.

"I don't know what's going on over there, Frank, but if you have any pull, please use it."

Steinman grunts. I think he's going to hang up, but he says, "One other thing. The Summers' accident. Don't these people have enough shit to go through without digging all that up?"

Steinman has caught me off balance. I immediately suspect Larry. "I was just trying to fill in background on one of the witnesses—the Summers woman."

Steinman snorts. "Look, you're the investigator, but it sure looks like you're spinning your wheels from here," he says, at last hanging up.

I stare at the phone, wondering if Larry's betrayed me, skillfully executing a first strike, complaining to Steinman or Shahbaz that I've been wasting my time. As angry as I am with Larry, I just can't bring myself to believe he has that much treachery in him. It runs against his character— or at least what I think it is.

I turn to place my weekly call to Katie to coordinate Liam's pick up. The process is something I dread with a gray sense of foreboding, like a trip to the dentist, or renewing my car registration: mandatory, tedious, and unpleasant. Katie answers on the second ring. We quickly compare schedules and confirm the arrangements, then I ask her, "Did you look at the link for that guy I told you about? Ronald Erland?"

"I told Liam to be extra careful."

"Can you pick him up from school instead of letting him take the bus? Please look at the link so you know what Erland looks like."

"Tom, he'll be fine on the bus. I have a really busy work schedule for the next two weeks."

"If I could, I'd pick him up myself . . ."

"No need to do that, Tom. I've got it covered. I'll talk to you later," she says, hanging up.

After the episode with Liam in Mexico, we have never been able to recover. It was entirely foreseeable that Katie would try to find comfort with someone else—and she did. Her boss, Lenny, an architect at her firm, and at least ten years her senior, is still a shelter from the storm. During the divorce, I complained to my lawyer about Lenny being at the house. The lawyer bluntly replied the way to win a divorce is to show the other person is morally bankrupt, a pervert, a drunk, and a slut—a danger to the children. From where I stood, the court didn't seem the best way to unravel the snarled fish line our lives had become.

You would think with my experience watching my disintegrating marriage with Katie, I would've been aware enough to see the warning signs with Trina. But our end had come on like a storm, without warning—the result of a cat. The kitten appeared on scene one Friday afternoon when Trina's daughter, Sophie, unloaded it on us. Sophie's father, wanting to be the bigshot, promised a cat, allowing Sophie to get one at the pound. After a couple of loud nights with the kitten, which was infested with worms and ear mites, he backed out. I've never liked Andy, Trina's ex, but this one really burned my ass.

To boot, pets are a hot spot for me. I had denied Liam a puppy several months earlier. Our lives are too busy to work in animals. But here was Sophie with a kitten she loved and was pushing to keep. With the kitten, I resisted and was assured by Trina the cat would only stay a couple of days until other arrangements could be made—maybe a return to the pound. In the middle of it all, Liam renewed his campaign for a dog. It was a shitshow.

During all the drama, I suddenly remembered Trina spent Thursday night cleaning the tiny closet we called an office. At the time, she'd blamed the sudden effort on an obsessive need to keep the small space organized. The next day, she'd come home late, explaining she'd had to "pick up a few things." With the cat's arrival, I saw Trina had planned ahead. Feeling betrayed, I confronted her the first day Sophie was gone, just the way Mike and Carol Brady would've done it.

"You lied to me about the cat," I said over coffee.

"I didn't lie. I didn't know the cat was coming," she replied unconvincingly. When she saw I wasn't buying, she added, "Sophie called and told me the cat would only need to stay here a few—"

"That's not the point," I said, pointing at her with my coffee spoon. "You knew for two days the cat was coming."

"God, Tom, can't you just let it go? You're so focused on being right all the fucking time that you can't see what you look like." She rose, depositing her cup in the sink.

"That cat's not staying."

"You should see yourself right now, tied up with anger," she said, shaking her head, which only served to make me angrier.

"I am angry, very angry, and you're trying to avoid the fact you hid something from me and tried to work me." My emotions slipped under me like scree down a hillside. It finally struck me what hurt me wasn't the cat, annoying as it was. It was Trina's betrayal, which, however small, was like a nick in the paint job of a new car: the end of perfection.

We'd argued for several hours. Finally, Trina packed

herself and the cat in the car and went to her sister's house, leaving me the note under the Tabasco magnet.

■ ■ ■

About a week after the trip to Springfield, I tell Nora about the file and its missing contents. I expect her to be happy, even grateful for my efforts. In fact, I'm so sure the trip to Springfield is an offering of my affection for her, I am unprepared for her reaction.

"You pulled my parents' file?"

Lying sprawled over one another on the sunporch, the hot, lazy summer afternoon drifts by. Nora lies topless, the light polishing her breasts in yellow and amber, highlighting the fine down on her arms, painting her nipples a deep rose. She pulls away from me, sitting upright. "Why did you do that?"

"You said the case was closed without a complete investigation. I wanted to see what I could find out," I say, rushing to explain myself.

She searches my face, her dark eyes looking for a motive, her mouth finally broadening slowly into something like a smile.

"I suppose I should thank you." She shakes her head slowly, running her hand along her arm, her eyes impenetrable. I'm not sure if I detect a note of sarcasm.

"I thought you'd want to know. The file raised more questions than it answered." I tell her about the missing mechanical report, but think better of telling her about the pictures of her parents and her mother's desperate struggle to save herself.

"What's in a mechanical report?" she asks, rolling to

face me.

"The inspection of the car."

"Does it really make a difference after all these years?"

"It might say why the car failed. Don't you want some closure?"

"That's just it, Tom. I thought I had closure."

A light breeze blows through the porch window, ruffling the pages of a newspaper lying on the floor. The stillness is broken by the caw-caw of a murder of crows in the trees outside. Nora stares out into the garden. I reach to touch her leg. She doesn't move it.

"I'm not sure I want to know anything more than what I've known all these years."

It hadn't occurred to me that Nora might have made peace with what she knows and doesn't want to know anything more.

"I won't do anything more if you don't want me to."

"I don't think finding out how the car failed is going to make me feel any better about how my parents died. I've lived all these years knowing they died in a terrible car accident and that was enough." She rolls on her back.

Her rejection of my simple offering is depressing. I burned up an entire day to recover some small nugget to present to her, and she's rebuffed my efforts.

Sensing my shifting mood, she moves closer and brings her lips to my ear.

"Thank you," she whispers. "I know why you did it. I just don't want to know anything more." She reaches between my legs and gives me a purposeful squeeze.

CHAPTER ELEVEN

T HE LAKE COUNTY COURTHOUSE IS TWO BLOCKS from my office. I walk over to the imposing modern structure. Small slits for windows are set into the monolithic sand-colored façade. The civil filing clerk's office is nestled deep in the bowels of the building.

Divorce records are sealed to preserve the privacy of the parties. A lawyer friend of mine says divorce law is all about good people behaving badly, and criminal law is all about bad people trying to behave well. Sealing divorce records ensures some measure of privacy for normally decent people who are treated like serial killers.

Shahbaz got me a signed order from Judge Wardman for Edwards' divorce records. I give the case slip and warrant to the clerk, who produces two gorged folders, each bearing large black lettering, stating "SEALED." I tote the files to a table at the far end of the room and split the red tape, the contents of the files spilling on the table like fish guts.

I search quickly through the file, knowing what I want. I find an order appointing William Stark, M.D., PhD. In the next folder I find the objections to Dr. Stark filed by Lent's attorney, citing the fact Stark did the evaluation in the judge's own messy divorce and is clearly prejudiced.

Stepping into the hallway, I tap the number into my phone and am quickly connected to David Schumer, Edwards' divorce lawyer.

Schumer comes straight to the point. "Look, Lent said you might call. I'm not trying to be difficult, but I can't and won't talk to you, Detective."

I'm hoping I can overcome his natural sense of mistrust. "I've got a couple of questions and they might actually help Lent."

"That would be a first."

"I'm looking at the divorce file. How did Stark's name get suggested?"

I hear a long exhale and a pause. "Usually the attorneys try to agree. Lori Erlich uses Stark a lot, and I didn't want him."

"Why?"

"Because he'd given the judge custody of his own kids, and it was a zero-sum game. The judge was going to follow any recommendation he made. If he went against us, he'd be unbeatable. I didn't want to bet everything on black."

"So, you objected?"

He lets out a long breath. "We had no choice—not if we were going to represent Lent the right way. I knew it would piss off the judge, but I objected anyway because Lent was being shafted." He pauses. "Just to give you an idea of how hard it was to go against the judge, I've got about seven cases in front of Ainsworth right now."

"Was the judge angry you made the motion?"

"He told me another motion like that and I'd find myself in front of a professional ethics committee."

"So, you left it at that?"

"It's a bad day when you take a shot at the king and miss." He chuckles darkly. "Besides, Stark still comes in handy with some of my cases."

"You still use him?" I ask, unable to hide my disbelief.

Schumer sighs loudly into the phone, making it clear I'm reaching the end of the goodwill train. "Stark's got amazing academic credentials and there isn't a committee or public task force he isn't on. He's done work for Cook County Mental Health, and he's on the State Department of Corrections' Psychiatric Services Advisory Board. On the stand, he's like your friendly neighbor Bill, come to tell you the facts over the fence. He's devastating. Good luck."

Schumer makes a quick goodbye and hangs up.

Returning to the file room, I open Stark's report letter. The report summarizes the family's social history, education, the background of the parents, and describes meetings with Emma and interviews with her parents. Stark paraphrases letters and communications received by "knowledgeable" friends and acquaintances, including Delia van Ostergaard, who described Lent as "controlling and angry."

On Lent's side of the ledger, Edward Lattimer, a partner at Lattimer Wardwell, points out Lent served his country with distinction, was a good father, and was supportive of his child in every way. A pretty strong case.

Stark sets down his verdict at the bottom of the report, in succinct and precise medical terminology:

Although the psychological testing would suggest the father has a normal presentation, the testing results are altogether inconclusive. By history, the father is a strong-willed and controlling person, with severe anger management problems. Conversely, the mother is portrayed universally as caring and competent. I can only conclude custody be awarded to the mother, with supervised visitation to father on an initial basis to establish a baseline for his emotional issues. If I can be of any further assistance to the court, please don't hesitate to let me know.

Very truly yours,
William Stark, M.D. PsyD.

Schumer was right. Lent never had a chance.

■ ■ ■

Every day since I started the force, except for Christmas, I've picked up coffee at Gregory's, a local Greek diner. Leaving the restaurant, my cell phone rings. Clutching a bagel and coffee, I fumble to answer it without dropping the butter-coated paper in my hands. Finally, turning the phone where I can see the screen, I see it's Tony Shahbaz.

"What's up?" I ask, dodging a large yellow dollop of butter that falls to the pavement, narrowly missing my shoe.

Tony chuckles. "Don't sound so happy to hear from me. Wardman signed the warrants for Edwards' car and his apartment, but not his office . . . too much privileged material. Frankly, I didn't think we were going to get anything." He pauses, then adds, "Steinman asked this morning what we are doing on this case."

I sigh. "He called me yesterday. It wasn't good."

Shahbaz snickers. "Don't worry. It's simply that they want you to get everything you can on Edwards. Frank says stop digging around in their shit—including the Summers' accident—and the bank accounts."

I flinch when Tony mentions the Summers' case.

"Thanks for the heads up, Tony."

"No problem. But you'd better do something about Edwards. At least make it look like you think he's a suspect." Tony laughs. "This fucking place has the social dynamic of a barrier reef."

Several hours later, Shahbaz emails the signed warrants for Edwards' trunk and glove compartment.

The next morning, Larry strides manfully into my office. I look up, expecting a gray, puffy face and wrinkled shirt, surprised instead to see him in a white shirt, neatly pressed suit, his hair carefully parted and freshly cut.

"Jeez, Larry. What's the occasion?"

At an uncharacteristic loss for words, he stammers, "I have visitors coming from out of town." His face flushes dark pink. After several seconds of silence, he adds, "Going to lunch."

"Really?" Deciding Larry's recent conduct warrants twisting his tail, I persist. "What visitors?"

"Family," he mumbles. The cornpone is gone, and his expression is set in defiance.

I shrug. "Family. Good, I guess. I didn't know you had a family. You don't talk about them much."

"My daughter."

"You have a daughter?"

Larry's face breaks into an open smile. "Sharon. She's

getting married. Thinks I don't know, but I found out. She's coming up to tell me about it and get my okay."

"You know anything about the guy?"

"Comes from a good Houston family. Money. Nice kid from what I hear."

"Well, good luck getting through all the wedding planning."

Larry laughs. "Least I can say is I'm grateful they ain't eaten supper before they said grace."

"Pardon me?"

"They're not living in sin. His family is very conservative."

"Did you have something else?"

He grins. "I ran an IJIN search on the Wesley family," referring to the Illinois Justice Information Network.

"You did? Why?"

"Never assume that just 'cause they're rich, they haven't been in trouble. Faith, Charles, and even Edwards—all clean. But . . ." He pauses for effect, letting me catch up.

"Linda?"

"The very same." He spreads the IJIN sheet on the desk.

"Arrested and convicted when she was twenty-one for a 12-4."

"Aggravated Domestic Assault? Are you kidding me?"

"Guess who the complainant was?"

"Charles?"

"Faith. She tried to strangle her own mother. Can you believe it?"

■   ■   ■

The summer after the ghosts arrived, when I was fourteen, I was shipped off to a church-sponsored summer camp. My parents blamed my mother's deteriorating health and, along with it, the fact the summers at the lake were coming to an end. Camp Four Winds promoted personal growth through prayer, rigorous exercise, fellowship, and outdoor living.

It also boasted a chaplain. But, as I learned from the counsellors, fully qualified ordained clergy were expensive and in short supply, so the camp settled for an accountant who'd finished three terms in divinity school. The ersatz cleric presided over mealtime grace and morning prayers. As far as the camp was concerned, this was the full extent of his job description, believing it a fair exchange for five weeks in the woods and free room and board.

Up to that point, my exposure to religion was limited to serving as an altar boy at Saint Agnes, the local Catholic church. Saint A was a tired brick building several blocks from my house that stood on a hill right next to the high school playing field. As a modest parish, Saint A brimmed with the love of God, but lacked the coffers for indoor air conditioning. The diocese directed its firehose of money to the more prominent parishes. So, for several weeks in late spring and in the early fall, worship was served in cassocks and surplice in the oppressive heat. Assisted by loud fans at the back of the sanctuary, Father Rourke kept the church windows open in hope that the heat would not deter the faithful. Father R. always said God had a sense of humor. God was certainly laughing in late spring and in early fall when the Regis High School Marching Band took the field for afternoon practice.

As Father Rourke began the consecration, intoning

the Jubilate Deo, invoking angels, archangels, and all the company of Heaven, the *Stars and Stripes* roared through the church. As he shouted the Parce Domine, "Spare, Lord, spare your people: Be not angry with us forever", he eyed the open window with dismay while *The Gladiator* rang through the church. After communion, we would complete the service to the strains of *The Liberty Bell*. So, my spiritual development by the time I got to Four Winds consisted of Sousa marches and stolen communion port. Until camp, I'd had no cause to consider the larger questions of redemption and forgiveness. When I'd abandoned my place as altar boy, no one, least of all Father Rourke, seemed the least bit interested in learning why.

At Four Winds, I felt moved to unburden myself. Wracked with conflicting feelings and looking for answers, and if not answers, at least guidance, I decided to attempt a confession of sorts. Who better than the sort-of-chaplain to receive it? Other than his duties as grace giver at meals, he seemed to spend most of his time in his tent. So, one afternoon I found the accountant-cum-confessor sitting on a three-legged stool, wearing his bush hat artfully tilted in a show of studied outdoorsiness.

He invited me to sit down. When seated, I looked around, waiting for several awkward seconds for some cue, some direction, to begin the process. We stared at each other, as the quasi-minister seemed to realize I might have some reason other than crushing boredom, or the need to hide, which typically drove the boys to his tent. He straightened his spine and placed his hands on my knees, leaning towards me in a gesture of pastoral concern. Lowering his voice, he asked if there was something he could help with.

Whether it was some sixth sense, or something in his false bonhomie, I could tell immediately I'd made a mistake. In an instant, I knew the erstwhile padre would provide nothing like clarity or forgiveness. Perhaps sensing my fading resolve, he tightened his grip on my knee, coming further forward.

"Is there something you wanted to share, Tom?"

Sensing his desperate need to counsel, to sharpen his pastoral skills on something more sturdy than cigarettes and teenage self-abuse, I saw he was not to be trusted. I faltered, trapped. The grip on my knee tightened further.

To escape my predicament, I knew I'd have to find a satisfactory sin, one of sufficient moral turpitude, one that would carry minimal consequences. I quickly ran the calculus, finally stammering, "If . . . if you knew something someone did and didn't tell anyone, is that bad?"

I could see him running through his inventory of a thousand natural shocks that flesh is heir to, from sexual deviance to frank homicide. After several seconds, he finally said, "Not telling would be lying by omission, Tom. That's a sin unto itself." He placed his free hand on my other knee, bringing his face close enough that I could see the yellowed sclera of his eyes and the broken capillaries lacing his nose. "You don't want to sin, do you, Tom?"

"No sir," I said forcefully, pulling one of my knees from the man's grip.

The pastor released the other knee and adjusted a suspender holding up his camp shorts.

Needing to procure currency of sufficient value to pay the ferry master, I sorted every transgression except the very thing which had brought me there. Finally I said, "I smoked a couple of cigarettes."

Eyeing me with suspicion, he was clearly disappointed. "Are you sure that's all it is?"

"Yessir," I replied, nodding earnestly.

Tugging at his suspender, he asked, "How did you get the cigarettes?"

I stared at the dirt floor of the tent, which was littered with candy wrappers. "I stole them from my mother."

He shook his head, doubting my story. All our bags were searched on arrival. He seemed sure I was holding back and hoped to unearth something more troubling— liquor, or sodomy perhaps. Padre stared at me for several seconds, until I finally added, "And I drank two cans of beer."

Alcohol was a sin of greater worth than choking on a couple of cigarettes. He sat back in satisfaction. "How did you smuggle it in?"

"In my bag. I'm really sorry. I needed to get this off my chest."

He sighed and, seemingly satisfied with my explanation, overlooked the obvious problem of how I could have smuggled cans of beer in with my bags. He leaned close again, his face inches from mine. I could smell cigarettes and halitosis. "It's okay . . ." he said, struggling to remember my name, "Tim. We all have urges and temptations every now and then." He winked knowingly.

Rising quickly and stepping into the sunshine before the chaplain could stop me, I said, "I need to go to archery. I really appreciate the chance to talk to you."

"Wait, Tim," the chaplain said, jumping to his feet, bowling over the campstool. "Let's talk more about this." I bolted towards the archery range, which wasn't open for another hour and a half. If I had to, I'd cop to the half-lies

I'd told, the cigarettes and beer, and receive a consequence. At worst, the beer might get me sent home.

But the accountant/chaplain never violated his oath, whatever that was. I never returned to the tent confessional. Ironically, the absence of consequences, or absolution— any action by the chaplain—made me lose my faith in more than just the camp. It smashed my belief that a Higher Power could or would help me or right the wrongs in my life.

■ ■ ■

After the episode with Jimmy Newsome, my relationship with my brother, Ben, also changed in subtle and irreversible ways. After the accident, we'd stopped going to the lake during the summers and spent less time together. I had always done well in school, and after the accident I buried myself in books. Ben, always a mediocre student, began to skip classes and was perpetually on academic probation. Our parents tried to bribe Ben with money, privileges, and praise; at best, his response was apathetic.

More troubling, at least to me, was that Ben seemed to adopt a new philosophy. "Difference does it make?" he'd say, shrugging, as if, at seventeen he was resigned to the "fuckedupness" of things. I avoided the house and, in particular, Ben, formulating my big plans for getting out.

As we drifted apart, any chance we had to sort out our respective lives was lost. Had Ben asked, I might've told him about the guys in the boat and why they'd come. But my brother hadn't asked, and I hadn't told him, because it was easier to be angry at Ben than to talk to him.

CHAPTER TWELVE

I'D SHARED THE IJIN HIT WITH THE TEAM AT Stanhope, Thornton and Webb. Several hours later, Satterman called, asking for a meeting at the house. Because the lawyers were going to be in attendance, I asked Shahbaz to come along, and told him at the first sign of games we'd leave and meet down at the station.

I sit down across from Linda Wesley, her father, and an immaculately groomed man I assume is another weasel dick. Mr. GQ is perfectly tanned and has on a tailored silk shirt and sports jacket, a sign of seniority in a firm where, Tony tells me, grey suits are still mandatory, even for partners. Mr. GQ extends a large brown hand and introduces himself as Cranston Webb, of Stanhope, Thornton and Webb.

After the niceties, Webb's smile drops. "Detective, do you have some questions for my client?"

I shake my head. "You asked for the meeting." I glance at Linda. She is busy staring at the table. I lean towards her. "You didn't tell me you tried to strangle your mother."

Webb's palm shoots into the air, directing Linda to hold her answer. "Look, I know it may seem to you that you've actually got something on Ms. Wesley, but you're completely out of line." Webb looks from me to Shahbaz, daring us to take him on, and then, waving his hand, signals Linda she can speak.

Linda starts slowly. "When I was a teenager, my mother and I had a lot of conflict. I was drinking a lot and running with a crowd she didn't like, including Nora. We both had too much to drink and we got into a fight here at the house." She shoots a glance at her father, whose face is blank.

I push the incident file in her direction. Webb leans over to inspect the contents.

"You were twenty-one, not a teenager, and you were charged with aggravated domestic assault. That's more than a family squabble."

"I had Mother on her back, trying to pin her. She told the police I attempted to strangle her. She wanted to teach me a lesson, so she filed charges. It was a sad and awful family drama which, thankfully, is ancient history." She looks over at Webb.

Webb clears his throat. "If you think an altercation that occurred over twenty-five years ago has relevance, I'd like to know why."

"It shows aggravated violence directed at her mother."

Webb smiles, shakes his head, and looks unimpressed. "Linda said you had a poor interview a few days ago. It's clear you have an agenda." Webb exhales, taking another tack. "Look, the reason we asked for the meeting is to clear up any misconceptions. From where I stand, trying to dig up dirt on members of the family who are the victims of a brutal homicide is . . ." He seems to struggle to find the words. "Well, I'll just leave it there."

"That's it? That's all you're going to say about this?" I ask, pointing to the IJIN record.

Webb gets to his feet. From where I'm sitting, he towers over me. Even at seventy, he's an impressive specimen of the species.

He shrugs. "I don't see there is anything more to say. If you'll excuse us, we're busy dealing with other issues created by your office." He nods to Charles and Linda, who both get to their feet. He places a protective arm around Linda and they head to the door.

"One more thing," Webb says, turning back to us. "Tony, tell Spyro I'll see him at the first hole on Saturday." He turns and leaves.

I can see this has been a carefully staged piece of theater to deflect any serious stock we might put into the assault. Ironically, for me at least, it has the opposite effect. The fact they went to the trouble of calling a meeting with Cranston Webb tells me they don't see it as just ancient history. The reference to Spyro is an extra.

I look at Tony, who shrugs. Spyro Spouros is the State's Attorney for Lake County.

Tony shakes his head. "Cranston Webb's the only living name-partner at Stanhope and one of the most expensive legal talents in America. He's telling us that if we aren't careful, he'll shove a nine iron up our asses. You've scared the Wesleys, Tom. Be careful."

Later that day, I stand in the parking lot outside Edwards' office as the sun beats down on the pavement. I'm accompanied by a uniformed officer. We searched

Edwards' apartment yesterday, finding it spartan and clean, utilitarian, and furnished in gleaming Scandinavian chrome and leather. The main concession to décor were several photographs of Emma and framed seventeenth-century etchings.

With lunchtime approaching, I can see a line forming outside a Mexican mobile taqueria. A neon sign points down to a small step and a storefront boasting, "Numbers Game! Breakfast!"

I've arrived to execute the warrant on the car, which is parked outside the offices. Because he is unrepresented, I gave Lent a courtesy call five minutes ago. For all his claims of poverty, Lent drives a late model Series 700 BMW with all the bells and whistles. I'm about to have the uniform jimmy the trunk when Edwards arrives. He tells me he's retained a lawyer and hands his cellphone to me. His lawyer, Mike Obrien, says he's on his way and to wait. Already irritated, I glare at Edwards in the heat of the day, which carries the odor of fried food and decaying garbage. We stand there, saying nothing for several minutes, until a S600 Model Mercedes with tinted windows slides to a stop. A tall, bald man with reflector Oakleys steps out. O'Brien was with the States Attorneys' Office where he earned a reputation for winning cases and being a hard-nosed asshole. At one point, he'd been a protégé of Steinman's, but being smart and ambitious, decided to jump over to the other side.

I hand the warrant to Mike O'Brien. He quickly scans it. Edwards is red-faced and sweating in the midday sun.

"Go to it," O'Brien says.

Edwards' grey BMW 735i sets in a secluded spot reserved for residents of the building. O'Brien hands me the keys and I open the back of the car. The trunk hatch lifts effortlessly to reveal a cardboard box, golf shoes, an athletic bag stuffed with clothing and, in the corner of the trunk, a small shoebox.

Snapping on latex gloves, I reach for the shoebox, which feels heavy. I pull it open to find a clean Colt Defender 7000D.45 caliber pistol, a precision handgun manufactured for defense contractors. Its stainless-steel finish gleams in the sunlight.

Glaring at O'Brien, I check the weapon. It holds seven rounds. The shoe box also contains a small box of ammunition and a cleaning rag. I eject one round from the chamber and it tumbles into the trunk.

Turning to O'Brien, I say, "You shouldn't leave a live round in the chamber. I hope this is registered. We might have to take it."

"It is," Edwards says, bristling.

"Shut up, Lent," O'Brien tells him, eyeing his client.

I return to the trunk and pull the personal effects. In the back corner under a throw blanket is a soiled banana box heaped high with loose papers. The top layer is grimy and several pages are torn. It looks like Lent threw the stuff in the back of his car and forgot about it. Lifting the box, I walk over and put it in the front seat of my car.

When I return, O'Brien steps closer, trying to use his size to passively intimidate me. "What you gonna do with the carton?"

"I'm impounding it. Back the fuck off." Looking at him, I can feel the ferret jumping around in the sack, just looking for a way to get out. O'Brien is a big guy, and I'm sure in the right situation he knows how to handle himself.

"What if it contains privileged documents?" he asks,

trying to appear conciliatory.

"If Mr. Edwards was my lawyer, I would certainly hope he didn't store my files in a carton in the back of his car." I click the electronic door lock to the Beemer and hand the keys to Edwards.

■ ■ ■

I've been in the office for an hour when the phone rings. The caller ID says it is Steinman. A call I'm expecting.

"I just came from a meeting with Spouros. He wants to see you in an hour."

"What about?"

"You brought this on yourself, Tommy," Frank says, and hangs up.

The Lake County State's Attorney's offices are graced with a wood-paneled conference room. Steinman, and the current State's Attorney, Anthony Spouros, known as Spyro to his friends, are sitting at the conference table. Next to them is my supervisor, Ed Delahunt.

Delahunt hasn't said anything to me about the investigation or Spouros.

"Sit down, Tom," Spouros says, gesturing to a seat across the table from the three of them. It is to be an inquisition.

Spouros holds an unlit cigar and taps it against the back of his hand. "Tom, we want to know how close you are to making an arrest in the Wesley case." The son of Greek immigrants, Spouros is intelligent and put himself through law school working as a repo man. He's genial, funny, and quick. He also has hands like jackhammers and has been known to break chairs when angry.

"I've got several leads I need to follow up. We've had delays in processing the physical evidence because of a bottleneck with the crime lab."

Steinman shakes his head. "Yeah, we all know about that," he says, leaning forward, "but this seems pretty easy. Edwards has a history of smacking his wife and he hated the Wesley woman."

I bristle, checking myself. "What about Linda Wesley's sheet for DV? She tried to strangle her mother."

"Blaming the victim, Tommy? Jesus." Steinman throws his hands up, turns to Spouros and Delahunt and shrugs, as if to say this comment alone should justify my removal from the case.

I glance at Delahunt, who nods slowly.

"If I can get some help on the lab work, we could wrap this up, one way or the other."

Spouros rises. Behind him hang the portraits of the last seven State's Attorneys, a silent jury. Easily six-feet-four, weighing in at somewhere around 240, Spouros' shirt is crisply pressed but pulls tightly against his middle, which hangs ponderously over his alligator belt. Leaning across the table, he says, "Tom, the guy doesn't have an alibi, has a history of mental instability, and has a deep hatred of the victim. Do we need to visit the idea of having someone else handle the case?"

Irritation eddies and swirls around me. "First of all, Spyro," I say, using the State's Attorney's nickname, a familiarity I've yet to be given, "the psych tests in Edwards' case were all within normal limits. The only indication of an anger problem comes from Dr. Stark and the family, who are all biased." I pause, waiting for him to react. When he doesn't, I continue.

"The daughter, Emma, seems pretty conflicted about her father. We're trying to track down the woman Edwards claims to have slept with on the night before the murder. The search of his apartment was negative. We've got a lot of innuendo, but nothing firm to nail him. Acting too soon could be as much a mistake, if not a bigger mistake, than waiting. We know where he is. He's not going anywhere."

Delahunt shifts. He has on a dark blue blazer and grey slacks and an unassuming red-and-blue striped tie—government issue all the way. Removing his glasses, he cleans the lenses with a handkerchief procured from his breast pocket, glances at Spouros, and ignores Steinman.

"Spyro, Tom's doing the best he can with what we have," he says, placing the handkerchief carefully back in his pocket.

I've known Ed Delahunt for eight years, working directly under him the prior three years. Delahunt is quiet and smaller than many of the men under his command. It might be easy to underestimate him or take his understated style for weakness. I'd been in Division for less than three weeks when I heard a story that while in the Academy, and a newly minted cadet, Delahunt was cornered in a bar by two drunk bikers who'd decided to pick a fight. Quietly drinking his beer, Delahunt warned them to leave him alone. When the larger of the two swung at him, he'd ducked, springing back with an elbow to the bridge of the guy's nose. When the other one didn't take a hint, coming at Delahunt with a barstool, he hit him in the mouth with the butt of a pool cue, knocking his teeth out. He calmly finished his beer and walked out. No charges or reprimands were ever filed. I've always shown him deference.

"We've given this case our top priority," Delahunt says,

eyeing Steinman, "and gotten a lot of resistance for what I consider routine stuff like financials and access to the family for interviews."

I'm surprised, and not a little grateful to Delahunt for having my back.

Steinman snorts. "That's all well and good, Ed, but we've been at this investigation for over three months. I guess I'm wondering why we don't just pop Edwards."

There is a lull in the conversation. With nothing left to say, Delahunt nods, signaling for me to leave. As I walk to the door, Spouros says, "Let's not make this another Winters."

Winters is shorthand for policing disasters. Otis Winters did time in Joliet for drug trafficking and aggravated assault. He believed his girlfriend was cheating on him. When he got out, he waited in the darkened hallway of her apartment building and cut her with a straight razor before dousing her with lighter fluid and setting her on fire. She'd managed to make it to the apartment of a neighbor or he would have finished the job. Otis's lawyer plead the charges down from Attempted Murder to Assault Four—domestic abuse—and Winters served six months of a suspended sentence.

Once he was out, he stayed with his brother, Gerry, and Gerry's family, where he got into a fight with him. Gerry's wife called 911, screaming that Otis was going to kill them.

That night, Otis shot and killed his brother in the living room. Realizing his sister-in-law, nieces, and nephews—who had all been innocently watching TV—were witnesses, he shot and killed all of them. After a five-day, three-state manhunt, he was finally cornered in a Kmart parking lot in Kenosha, Wisconsin. He wedged a shotgun in his mouth and pulled the trigger. The precinct intake sheets for the sister-in-law's call were never found. When the 911 tapes were eventually located during the protracted civil-rights suit brought by the family, you could hear Otis screaming in the background.

■ ■ ■

I wait for Delahunt by the elevator. Descending to the first floor, Delahunt is quiet, his lean face folding into a narrow frown. When we enter the parking lot, he turns to me.

"Tom, I know you're working hard on this, but we're messing around with dangerous people here. Career-enders. I've read the file reports. I agree we don't have enough yet, but for God's sake get something soon."

"Can you pressure the lab to get the CODIS stuff put through?"

Delahunt nods. "I'll see what I can do. You're putting a lot of stock in the labs," he says, exhaling as we reach a blue 2007 Buick LeSabre. Despite the ninety-degree heat, Delahunt opens the door and climbs in. "Jesus, what a mess."

Delahunt starts the Buick and rolls down the windows. He blasts the AC and pulls the seatbelt across his lap, reaching to fasten the buckle.

Standing next to the car, I ask, "Do you remember a detective named Pete Strauss?"

Delahunt's face darkens. "I sure do. Why?" Delahunt looks up at me, assessing the question. "Is this something you've dug up as part of your investigation?"

"I'm looking into a vehicular death he investigated."

"What in God's name for?" Delahunt says, his eyes

narrowing and jaw tightening as he fidgets with the seatbelt.

"One of the Wesley's family friends, Nora Summers, lost her parents to the accident. I'm curious about the circumstances of the accident. Strauss ran the investigation."

Delahunt puts his arm out the window and points to the ground. "Drop it, Tom."

"It's more for background, than—"

Delahunt gives the engine a small gun. "Leave it. Strauss is dead. He died in Vegas twenty-three years ago and there's nothing in that file that would help here," he says, revving the engine to accentuate his point. He puts the car into reverse.

As he backs out, I say, "I thought maybe knowing about the circumstances of Nora Summers' . . ."

"I said, drop it. Strauss was a lousy cop and nothing but trouble." He pulls the car out of the space, stops and puts his head out the window. "I don't want to hear you've been digging around in cold files. You heard those two in there. Right?"

"Yessir."

The window glides up as he makes a U-turn and slowly pulls out of the lot.

■ ■ ■

Later that night, sitting in what passes for my living room, I brood on my meeting with Spouros. The air conditioner, an early investment purchased with Trina and deceptively named the Zentron Arctic 5000, is quickly losing the last of whatever five thousand it once had, until it finally gasps its last breath. The open windows face onto the street and children's voices, high and clear, ring in the evening air. The shades sway in the feeble breeze as laughter erupts, and in the distance a siren sounds. Glancing out the window, the tenement stoops recede down the street in parallel rows, extending like an Escher print into the next block, then the next, until finally coming together in the dark. The streetlamps, islands of light, float like isolated galaxies where moths and flycatchers dance around their feeble suns. Several blocks away, an ice-cream truck's sing-song transforms the night into a makeshift carnival. After several minutes in the darkness of the apartment, I decide to go for a swim.

The pool closes at ten. After swimming laps, I cross my legs and sink to the deep. Enveloped in silence, I hold my breath until dark black spots dot my vision and, fighting the urge to vomit, I heave myself onto the tiled surface. In these few moments, I'm somewhere else, alone and at peace. There are no children's voices on the beach. There's no boat, there's no raft, there's no Paulie.

Back home, I fall sound asleep until I'm jolted awake by my cell phone. Groping for the phone, I see the screen reads: *3:15 AM - caller ID blocked.* My heart quickens, thinking it might be Trina.

"Hello?"

Silence.

"Who is this?"

After a few seconds, the line goes dead. I drift back to sleep.

The phone rings again; this time I can see it's 3:45. Again, the ID is blocked. Under normal circumstances, I would turn the phone off, but Department rules require me to keep it on. The hair on the back of my neck prickles as I push the answer button.

"Who is this?"

The caller hangs up.

CHAPTER THIRTEEN

T HE BIG BOX IN THE TRUNK OF EDWARDS' CAR turns out to be filled with hate.

Battling Kate for custody of Liam, I was amazed at the number of groups that sprang up in the fertile shitty pastures of American domestic relations. Everyone, it seemed, had an opinion or agenda on topics as diverse as family law reform to overthrowing the constitution.

As I scour the contents of the box, it's clear not much has changed. The same problems seem to exist, and little has been done to fix the system that inflicts very real damage on the people who are forced to participate in it. An outfit calling itself Alliance for Non-Custodial Parents Rights convincingly argues that visitation laws, child custody, and support enforcement all violate the constitutional rights of non-custodial parents. Other groups contend the "best interest of the child" means equal access to both parents and presumes shared custody.

Further down in the box I find a pamphlet comparing the plight of men in divorce to the Jews' treatment at the hands of Nazis. It calls on men to "drain the feminist swamp."

Towards the middle of the carton I find Edwards' handwritten notes on parental alienation syndrome. This tragedy happens when a child aligns with one parent, becoming obsessed with hating the other parent without any feelings of guilt or responsibility. It's actually similar to a cult experience in that there's no room for doubt. Eventually, the child's bond with the rejected parent is completely destroyed.

My last meeting with Edwards and O'Brien was antagonistic enough that I figure we can dispense with pretenses. This time, we sit at the large steel table in the interview room at headquarters, its surface etched with years of boredom, despair, and fear. I put the box in front of Edwards and begin pulling out piles of divorce rights' stuff and a folder from a group calling itself Parents and Children Together, PACT, with some handwritten notes.

Glancing at the notes, Edwards leans back in his chair with a smirk on his face, unfazed. I know he thrives on being in control, high on his need to be right. O'Brien sits tensely next to his client.

I open, my tone conciliatory and matter of fact. "The parental advocacy stuff was pretty typical. I actually looked at some of those groups myself during my divorce."

I turn to O'Brien. "You haven't been divorced, right, Mike? Ronnie still puts up with you?"

He just shrugs.

I turn to face Edwards. "But the fight isn't over, is it

Lent? The fight for Emma is still going—"

O'Brien raises a hand in front of his client. "Don't say anything, Lent. Tom, if this is the best you've got, then I think—"

I continue, ignoring O'Brien. "She may spend her weekends with you, but she doesn't like you, know you, or love—"

"Edison!" O'Brien is on his feet, and leans over the table, bringing his face within inches of mine. The fluorescent light shines off his bald head.

"Tell me, Lent, about how Emma doesn't want to know you. Tell me Faith Wesley wasn't the cause of that."

Edwards shoots to his feet, his face twisted into a red mask of hate. "You fucker, I'll—"

O'Brien turns away from me and thrusts his mass in his client's face. "I'm going to caution my client to remain silent. Sit down!" he yells at Edwards. Reaching for his briefcase, he says, "Edison, unless you've got enough to arrest, we're leaving."

I gesture towards the door.

O'Brien signals to Edwards to leave. After the door closes on his client, he says quietly, "You and I go back a while, but I forget what a prick you can be."

I raise my hands in surrender.

"Your fucking client's a dirty smug bastard," I say, gesturing towards the hall. "He still has reason to want Faith Wesley dead."

O'Brien picks up his bag. "Tell it to a jury," he says, slamming the door behind him.

I consider O'Brien a cordial acquaintance, maybe even a friend, and know this little scene will take months to repair. But I've gotten what I came for. There's a chink in the armor—enough to make me think Steinman might actually be right. It isn't the money, or the disgrace heaped on him by the Wesleys. The motive is Emma.

■ ■ ■

I return to my office, looking to pull the copies of the Edwards' divorce file, and in particular the write-up by Stark. The investigation file is a mess. Figuring Larry would know where Stark's report is, I walk down to find his office dark. I flip on the light switch. I know Larry relies heavily on his memory palace to retain facts, believing file organization is for lesser beings. As I search without success, I feel a surge of irritation. If Larry can't be bothered with arranging the files, he shouldn't be surprised when people come into his office and sift through his desk.

I open the file cabinets, finding nothing. I scan the shelves behind the desk. Finally, steeling myself, I search Larry's desk. The top drawer is stuffed with half-used notepads, menus for several local restaurants, and paper-clipped stubs of his paychecks. Bundles of rubber bands, more paper clips, and ballpoint pens litter the bottom of the drawer.

Turning next to the large desk drawer on the right, I find an old copy of the Texas Bar directory. Beneath the book, a towel hides a half-finished bottle of Jim Beam. Knowing Larry's first question will be why I've been in the drawer in the first place, my irritation flares into frank anger.

I'm about to close the drawer, abandoning the search for the file, when the glint of metal catches my eye. Behind a stack of checkbooks, I see the dull metallic sheen of a

SW9 Smith and Wesson Sigma 9mm semi-automatic pistol. A firearm on-site is strictly off-limits to non-detective staff.

Several years ago, I was assigned a junior officer who, although his heart was in the right place, was incompetent. Reports went unfinished or were misfiled. Phone calls to potential witnesses went unmade. After several weeks I went to Delahunt and asked to have the officer reassigned.

Delahunt's response stayed with me.

"Tom," he'd said, shaking his head, "this guy's a project. You don't ever want to become somebody's project."

Three weeks later, Delahunt reassigned him process-serving detail.

I turn out the light and close the door. Larry Welk is officially a project.

■ ■ ■

On the way to my apartment, I stop at the 7-11 to buy a box of Redi-Made Pizzas. I stick a frozen pie in the oven and sort several days of mail, mostly trash like brochures for dental implants and windshield repair offers, before I discover a letter from Trina. The return address, in her neat, curved handwriting, is her sister's house in Naperville. It has been over three months since we separated. I'm surprised at feeling both happy and fearful she's chosen to write.

As I read the letter, I feel my pulse quicken.

Dear Tom,

I know you've called and left messages, but I haven't felt prepared to talk to you. I'm writing now, more for myself than for you. I don't want to rehash the cat or the fights. I want to understand why two people who've loved each other, and I think we have, can do so much damage.

I've come to some realizations about myself. I realize there's a part of me that's unfinished. I had Sophie early, and it seems like I've been living for someone else ever since. The job I had when I met you was only a short-time gig, yet I'm still there.

I also realize I've spent time being a peacemaker. The episode with the cat happened because I didn't want to disappoint Sophie because her father was a jerk, and I didn't want to confront you—I was in a bind. So I tried to play you while I bought time to fix things. I'm sorry because I don't think that was right.

I think we both need to recognize that having a blended family is more difficult than either of us thought. We both carry a lot of baggage about our kids. You are resentful a lot about the time I have with Sophie, and I think you favor Liam. I'm defensive of Sophie and probably not as supportive of you about your custody situation as I should be. I think there's truth in all of that.

Right now, I think it's pretty clear we're at a place where there's no coming back. I just wanted to say that I do love you, and I'm sorry.

T.

I put the letter back into the envelope and dial her number again. The same female voice tells me the subscriber has turned the number off.

CHAPTER FOURTEEN

WITH THE STUFF I'VE GATHERED IN THE back of Edwards' car, I have the core of an operating theory, rooted in the progressive deterioration of Edwards' relationship with his daughter, who's lived under her grandmother's spell. It was clear in my conversation with Emma that Faith Wesley administered a daily poisoning, waging a limited ground war against Emma's father. Lent's divorce from Linda Wesley happened years ago, but PAS is a progressive disease, and clearly Emma is in the middle to late stages of it. I call that motive.

As far as means and opportunity, Edwards has the military training and the strength to climb the wall, lie in wait, and garrote the old woman. From what I can see, he seems to have the disposition. He's become the prime suspect.

Work remains to follow up on witness interviews, follow up with forensic evidence, and to nail down Edwards' alibi.

I drive into Chicago to Carnahan's to see what I can find out about the woman Edwards said he was with the night before the murder. The manager, a tall blond bodybuilder who's wearing a tight T-shirt and too much Gaultier Le Male, stands behind the bar. He surveys me for a few seconds and then pleads ignorance. Certain he's lying, I ask to use the restroom. He directs me to the back of the pub, where I notice the fire door is locked with a chain. Making my way back to the bar, I tell Le Male that if his memory doesn't improve the fire door is going to be problem. He shrugs and says a woman who fits the description comes in as a regular. He remembers her, mostly because she isn't a pro and is a poor tipper. She nurses a beer or two, he says, and usually leaves alone. After more prodding, he's persuaded to fish out old credit card receipts, finally producing a name: Stacey Turner. I go to the car, call the credit card company, and get a phone number associated with the card. I run a Reverse Directory search and get an address.

Later that afternoon, as I wait at the steps to her apartment, I see her. In dim light, after a few beers, Stacey Turner might seem appealing. In the light of a summer afternoon, the attraction is less clear. She's in a knit sleeveless sweater and short pants, the top stretched against enormous breasts. Etched lines frame her lids and spread in a corona from her eyes. When I approach her, badge extended, she eyes me like a five-and-dime cashier being asked to make change for a hundred.

She's been shopping and is carrying two large brown bags, which she instinctively grips closer to her chest. "Can I help you?" she asks.

"I need to ask you some questions about a friend of

yours, Lent Edwards."

"Who's that?" she asks, her mouth drawing tight.

"He says the two of you spent the night together a few weeks back. Tall guy."

Bewildered, she shakes her head. "Don't know who you're talking about." She shifts the groceries around her chest.

"You met him at Carnahan's. You need some help with those?" I say, moving to help her.

She shakes her head again, pulling the bags tighter. "I gotta lot of friends at Carnahan's."

I'm sure she does, but whether she can remember them is another story.

"This guy would be kind of stiff, well dressed."

The well-dressed comment seems to jar something in her memory. "This guy a lawyer?"

"Yup."

"Yeah, I remember him," she says and starts to laugh. "No lead." She chuckles.

I suppress a smile. "What do you mean?"

She looks at me as if to see if I'm for real. She searches for a place to put her bag of groceries. "Really? You need me to spell it out? He looked good to start with, I'll give him that. Stood me to a couple of drinks and we talked for some time, maybe an hour or so. Then he asked if I'd like to come and see the view from his apartment. By the time we got there, he was so drunk, he couldn't—" She pauses and then laughs. "Figures," she mutters, still looking for a place to put the groceries down. She bends to place the bags on the stoop, revealing the Grand Canyon. Satisfied I'm not a threat, she pulls out a vape. She takes a long drag. "I called myself a cab and left him passed out on the bed." She takes

THE DEAD BELL   157

another long pull. "I'm glad he was asleep."

"Why?"

"He was really drunk, but when he couldn't get his pencil to work, he seemed a little edgy. Angry. I can laugh now, but it wasn't funny then. I wanted to get the fuck outta there," she says, shrugging.

"Do have any idea where he was the next day?"

She shrugs again, putting the vape in her purse. "After I left, I never heard from him. Probably felt like shit in the morning. I know I did." She smiles thinly at me, searching for some understanding. When I offer none, she reaches for her bags and starts up the steps to her apartment.

■ ■ ■

It's a Thursday evening in August and the heat sticks to everything. The air conditioner, still unrepaired and un-replaced, has me hoping each hot night will be the last. I just can't bring myself to lay out the cash for a new unit when there's only a few weeks left of summer. Balancing thrift and discomfort, thrift wins.

The door buzzes. I get up to answer. "Who's there?"

"It's Nora."

I've continued over the weeks to see Nora, despite the issues with Larry and the warnings from Delahunt. We seem to have arrived at the proverbial watershed. I've rejected Nora's requests to see my place, not wanting her to see my diminished circumstances. Truth be told, I haven't rearranged the apartment since Trina took her belongings and it sets empty, with spaces remaining where her furniture was.

Nora hasn't pressed the issue, and as the days turn to

weeks, and the weeks into months, I've discovered she is a bundle of surprises: an accomplished pianist, cook, and a voracious reader. She holds strong opinions on everything from the Middle East to campaign finance reform and, under the veneer of her upbringing, holds social convictions just left of Trotsky. When engaged, her sadness and reserve seem to vanish and her eyes come alive. Despite the voice in my head telling me what I'm doing is nuts, I'm becoming stuck to her.

But, whether because of lingering regret at the loss of Trina, or a deeper sense of inadequacy, I've held onto this last boundary to protect myself from Nora's judgment— good or bad. I've resisted inviting her here, fearing the sparse box will reveal some inadequacy, certain she will find me deficient. Her house, I've insisted, is far more comfortable because of the air conditioning, and spending time in my cramped, stuffy cell makes no sense when we have her place.

I buzz her up, scrambling to find a T-shirt and cleaning the place quickly. Aside from the remnants of the pizza, it's clean enough.

I wait for her at the door, wondering how she found my address. I haven't given it to her and, because I'm a detective, it's unlisted.

The doorbell rings and I open it to find Nora in a sheer silk shirt, blue jeans, and designer shoes. She isn't wearing makeup and looks as though she's been crying.

"Tom, I'm really sorry." She stands at the door, looking beyond me. "Are you alone?"

Gesturing inside the apartment, I say, "I am." Whether it's the heat, or the fact she isn't wearing makeup, her skin is the color of chalk and her eyes are rimmed with dark circles. I ask her if she wants something to drink, and she asks for a glass of sparkling water.

"Are you okay?" I ask, handing her the drink. Several weeks earlier, I explained to her that I don't drink, which didn't seem to bother her much. Taking the glass in her hand, she runs her fingers through the condensation.

"You mean what am I doing here?" she says, managing a small smile. "Strange as it may seem, Tom, I was feeling lonely. I felt it was time I should come see you."

"You could have called," I say brightly, hoping I haven't sounded defensive.

Nora inhales sharply. "I can go, if you want."

I shake my head. "I'm just a little surprised to see you here. How'd you get the address? I'm unlisted and, as far as I know, I haven't shared the address with you," I say, wanting to make it clear I'm making a concession.

Nora's expression turns into a grin. "You haven't been awake every minute you've been at my place."

"So?"

"So, I looked in your wallet and found your driver's license." She laughs.

Unsure how to feel about this confession of such a clear breach of boundaries, I waver, feeling flattered at her obvious curiosity, yet bridling at the violation. Settling on feeling flattered, I say, "I guess I should be happy you took enough interest to pull a trick like that."

"I'm definitely interested, Tom," she says, her expression growing soft. She places the glass on the counter. "Since you're too cheap to buy a new air conditioner, there is only one way to deal with the heat." Her skin has a fine sheen of perspiration and the silk shirt has small dark spots. She undoes the buttons. A trickle of sweat runs between her breasts. She strips to only her underpants.

I pull her to the bed and enter her in the heat of the apartment. Caught in the close air of my bedroom with the window open and the sounds of the baking summer night drifting in, I feel something in her surrender, although she didn't say as much. It seems our relationship has shifted. She's accepted the apartment and said nothing about its grim décor.

As we lie drifting between awareness and sleep, I run my hand over the smooth skin of her stomach. In the half-light, I notice a dark area around her navel, the unmistakable sign of a bruise.

"What's this? " I say, touching the area. Nora shifts quickly, wincing.

"Nothing. I tried to get something out of my closet, and it fell down on me. I caught it at a funny angle. Go to sleep."

Later, in the early hours of morning, Nora reaches to me in her sleep, throwing her arm over my neck, as pure and intimate a gesture as any between us. Awake, I stare at the streetlamp outside the window and listen to a light breeze that's arisen to rustle the leaves. I hear the tiny peeps of the first morning birds. The quiet is broken by the dull groan of thunder several miles away. Within a few minutes the air thickens and is stirred to a quick gust, and fat pelts of summer rain hit the windowpanes. The gray light of day is just beginning to show when I fall back asleep.

I awake after the rain to the cool breeze of an early summer morning. The bed is empty. I find Nora in the living room, staring out the window, her face pale and thin in the early light of day. She sits, transfixed by the rising sun. She looks at me once, smiles, goes back to silently watching the sunrise and doesn't move again for an hour.

CHAPTER FIFTEEN

I TAKE A BREAK FROM THE WESLEY CASE TO SPEND A day and a half interviewing witnesses to a string of arsons around the Armory Terrace housing project. Early in the week, we pinch a local kid for stealing tires and when we search the car, we find rags, a can of gas, and phosphorous leads. After some questioning, we find out he lives ten blocks from A T, as it's known. We tell him about the dead night watchman and sweat him overnight in general population When he finally understands he's looking at a felony murder rap, he pisses himself right there in the interview room. He gives up three of his pals who were hired for three grand to torch the stores around the project. Sniveling, he says he had no idea there was a night watchman in the last store. I put together a warrant for a wire. With any luck, they'll hook the kid up in a couple of days.

I'm still waiting on the lab. Steinman calls twice to check up on Edwards. I answer truthfully that I'm moving on the divorce angle and working to get in to see Stark.

Larry shows up in my doorway, and I fight the urge to wince. Leaning against the door lintel, the sclera of his eyes are tinged dark amber, his face dinged and nicked, framed by hair sticking out at a right angle from his left ear.

He plops himself in the ancient chair in the corner of my office.

"I got you in to see Dr. Stark. More like gaining audience with the Pope," he says, pulling at the loose strings of upholstery dangling from the chair. "What a piece of work."

"Larry, I need to talk to you about something import—"

"Yeah, well, let me finish telling you about Stark," he interrupts, barely able to suppress his irritation. Larry is stripped and raw, like road rash. Given the direction the conversation is likely to take, I decide to cede the floor, hoping to cool his temper before his inevitable angry exit.

"Guy's had a silver spoon in his mouth his whole life. His family in Ohio founded a publicly traded urgent care empire." He pauses for effect. "Which was shut down in the eighties for stock fraud. They ended paying two billion dollars in fines, and his father was removed from the board. Stark went to Princeton undergrad and Harvard Med School. Even with all that, he managed to get himself elected to the Ohio state senate on a public health platform, promising to clean up the state's Medicaid system."

"Larry, that's great, but—"

Larry pulls a particularly long string from the upholstery. "He goes through a nasty divorce and his ex-wife goes public with the story that when he was a med student he went to animal shelters, adopted dogs and cats, and did vivisection—cut 'em open alive."

I hand Larry a pair of scissors to cut the thread to prevent the fabric from completely unraveling. Larry cuts the string, handing me a balled-up length of thread.

I think Larry may sense a reprimand coming and is burning up the clock. Pointing to my desk top, I interrupt. "We really need to get to this other thing."

His face flushes. "Look, I'm trying to tell you about this guy. You interested?"

"Sure, I'm interested," I say, feigning interest.

He leans back. "It gets some traction in the local press, but before it blows up, the shelter records disappear. The shelter employees develop amnesia and it's dropped. During his race for the House of Representatives, it comes up again, but doesn't get any traction."

I have to say, I'm appalled. "Nasty piece of work."

Larry nods. "Yeah, well, he loses his seat in the state legislature, anyway. Guy goes into private practice as a psychiatrist. Somewhere along the line he moves to Illinois and starts consulting with the State Department of Corrections, getting on their mental health advisory board. He also starts doing divorce custody evaluations. He's apparently done hundreds of them."

Sensing Larry is finished, I brace myself.

"Other thing is," he continues, "CODIS finally came back negative on the blood sample from the fence. No match. Nada. Zip."

I feel my face flush. "I get the point. How wide did you run it?"

Larry's face drops, sensing a change in the weather "They ran it for State, Corrections, and Midwest."

"Can't you run it wider?"

"I'll go federal and military. It may take more time." He

grabs the arms of the destroyed armchair, pushing himself up.

"Oh yeah, ballistics came back on the Morales' gun. Nine mil with hollow-point rounds."

"We should follow up on ammo sales," I say tightly. I consider referring the whole mess—gun, Jim Beam, insubordination—to Delahunt, who'll can Larry on the spot. I hesitate only because I know Larry has run out of options. Despite myself, I feel responsible for the self-destructive, abrasive shit-kicker. There's also the matter of how much Larry knows about Nora.

I take a deep breath. He's almost to the door when I say, "Larry, stop. Really, let's stop the bullshit."

I can see him tense, sensing the Good Will Train is leaving town.

"I found whiskey and a gun in your desk."

He turns back towards my desk and leans forward, his shoulders rising on his not inconsiderable size. He looks me straight in the eye. "What the fuck were you doing in there?"

"Looking for the file you misplaced." I can feel the heat under my shirt and strain to keep my temper. "You've been MIA for three days. I figured you might have put it in your desk."

"You had no right. I had an expectancy of privacy and you—"

"Cut the lawyer shit, Larry." I take a deep breath. "Delahunt will can you for the booze alone, forget the unregistered gun. Sit down."

"It's registered in Texas," he says weakly, taking the seat in front of my desk.

I lean in, trying, as Larry himself might say, to reason

with a rattler. "You've got a problem. I can't protect you much longer. Get some help. I can put you in touch with some people I know."

He inhales sharply, sighs, and seems to shrink several sizes in the armchair. Slumping, he searches for the lost end of the twine and, finding it, begins to twist it around his finger. I resist the urge to tell him to stop. The room falls silent until he finally looks up. "Okay, I get it. I'll start runnin' with the antelope."

I nod.

Larry's face is sad and closed. He rises and walks to the door, where he stops. "You don't need to tell me I'm a shitbag. My daughter already did."

Suddenly, I understand. He hasn't been jabbering nonstop to avoid talking to me, he's been worried I'll ask him about the wedding.

"Your daughter's getting married, right?"

He nods slowly, gutshot. "Yeah, she's getting married. She just did me the courtesy of flying up here to tell me in person she doesn't want me at the wedding." He's flailing like a wounded bear. "I suppose I should be happy she didn't text me."

"I'm so sorry, Larry," I say, struggling for something else to say.

"I'll manage okay. I'll get in line," he says as he starts to step through the door.

I can still feel the tight coil of frustration in my chest. "It's more than falling in line, Larry, it's about getting some help."

"I'll do it my way," he says, walking slowly down the hall. I get up and walk to the door in time to catch him turning into his small inner office.

"Larry?"

He turns at the door to look at me.

I point to his office. "Lose the gun, even if it is registered."

That night, after struggling unsuccessfully to surrender myself to sleep, I watch the last film in a Kirk Douglas marathon on the classics' channel. Earlier, during dinner out with Nora, she excused herself four times, claiming the food upset her stomach. After dinner we attempted sex, and again she told me she was feeling sick. I left her house. The evening has not been a success.

■ ■ ■

In late August the days are hot, but the nights bring cool air off the lake. Waiting for sleep to take me, I'm reminded of summer nights in Springfield when, as a teenager, I lay awake listening to the crickets in the hot, still air.

I turn off the TV, staring into the dark, seeing Springfield spread before me, its streets teeming with ghosts. Returning to the archives has awakened my memory, which until now I've been able to review only from a great distance. The memories tantalize and terrify me like rediscovering faded nudes of an unfaithful lover. When I feel brave enough, I risk a sly peek, knowing fully the images can, in a moment, shift and break me.

From an early age, my brother Ben looked significantly older, which enabled him to sample the darker part of life earlier. He scored an illegal switchblade when he was twelve and, during the summer of the raft, procured several hazy, dog-eared black-and-white pictures of two women having sex.

The summer following my encounter with the accountant-cum-chaplain, Ben and I avoided the annual family trip to the Upper Peninsula where we'd be shoehorned into my aunt's double-wide for several days with my cousins. After my parents left, Ben vanished. I was watching late night TV in our living room when Ben appeared at the screen door with his friend, Billy Gerson. Ben swayed unevenly on the porch, shaking the door, which was locked. Billy's face was smudged with an untrimmed goatee, strings of long greasy hair falling to his shoulders. He always grunted and rarely smiled, except when grinning to no one in particular, amused by some creepy private joke. Like the darkening of Midwest skies before a tornado, I was sure Billy was a harbinger of nothing but bad for Ben.

"Tommy, what the fuck? Lemme come in. You can't have it all to yourself," Ben yelled, tugging at the screen door.

Whatever "it" was, I was sure I didn't want to let Ben and Billy into the house.

I surveyed Ben and his feral pal through the screen. Billy leered through the mesh, producing a whiskey bottle from the recesses of his leather jacket, which he wore despite the fact the Springfield summer night was still in the mid-eighties.

"You gonna let us in?" Billy asked, his smile cryptic.

"Yeah, he is," Ben said, pulling the door again, stressing it against the hinges.

To allow my brother and Billy the Thug into the house carried risks large enough to merit something in return. "What're you gonna give me?" I asked through the mesh.

Ben shook the screen door again, and I could hear the hinges singing with the strain.

"I won't give you a beating," Ben muttered, an empty threat if ever there was one. Although older, Ben was smaller than me. He seemed to have stopped growing. Leaving the question unanswered, I unhooked the door and let the two of them into the living room, the yellow shag rug and fake plywood-veneer paneling glowing in the light of the TV.

Once inside, Ben slapped me on the arm in mock imitation of a fight, wrapping his arm around my shoulders, pulling me into an alcohol-soaked bear hug reeking of cigarettes and sweat. Billy sat down in my father's chair and, unscrewing the top of the fifth of Dewar's White Label scotch, took a pull. He offered me the glistening mouth.

"Want some?" he asked, smirking at me.

Waving my hand as I sat down on the couch, I replied, "No thanks," content to watch Ben and his friend.

Possessed of a need to prove himself, Ben pointed to me. "You're a little faggot, Tommy." Grabbing the bottle from Gerson, wiping the lip with his sleeve and taking a long pull, he thrust the bottle at me. Stifling a cough, he shook it. "Come on, you little faggot," he repeated.

I took the bottle, more to silence Ben than through any desire to impress Gerson. Putting it to my mouth, the warm liquid slid easily down my throat, followed by a rush of vapor which caught me by surprise, choking me. I stopped gagging long enough to whisper, "Smooth."

I finished the night on the living room floor, having vomited several times, once in Ben's closet. Billy passed out in my father's recliner in his leather jacket, a sneer on his face. Ben stumbled down to the basement, where he mistook the dog's bed for a couch.

Three years later, when I was eighteen, Billy was

killed just outside Shawnee, Oklahoma on Interstate 40. According to Ben, Billy left a bar having drunk twice the legal limit and smashed his Ford Escort into the back of a tilt-bed trailer, ripping the top of the car off, which decapitated him.

About a year later, Ben completed his diesel mechanic's cert while living in his childhood room, pretending it wasn't demeaning to be living at home.

Unlike Ben, I excelled in school and was accepted to Northwestern University on a partial scholarship. Once there, I made short study of the hard facts of privilege. I quickly learned if you possessed talent, even if you didn't come from money, like the mockingbird singing other birds' songs, you could become accepted, if not indistinguishable. My talent was wit, and after a short time I'd developed razor-sharp irony into an art form.

One Saturday while I was at school, my mother's heart finally collapsed. Ben, who'd apparently passed out after coming home at five in the morning, didn't hear her as she fell to the floor in her room. My father, who was a carpenter and on a project when she died, took her death with something like stoic resignation. I never mistook his quiet grief for anything like indifference. But, at some point in the weeks that followed, I'm sure Ben must have thought to himself, "Difference does it make?"

I came home for the funeral, stayed two days and, pleading a busy schedule, fled Springfield back to Evanston.

∎ ∎ ∎

The phone startles me awake, and as I struggle to reach it, it rings again. I search the call register. "Blocked number."

I look over at the clock. 2:47 AM.

Turning on the light, I growl, "Who's this?"

The phone clicks, dead.

Fully awake, I sit up. After several seconds, I conclude the call could only have been from Trina. Her number is blocked, and my efforts to reach her have proven fruitless. I pull my address book to me. Scrolling through, I search for the one number I've avoided for weeks. I press the call button, reasoning if Trina is calling at this hour, it must be an emergency.

The call rings five times before a male voice, thick with sleep, grunts an unintelligible oath into the phone. I spend several seconds explaining to Trina's brother-in-law, the long-suffering Trevor, why I've made the call. Trevor grunts again and hands the phone to Dawn, Trina's sister.

Trevor tries, even in the middle of the night, to be courteous. But Dawn comes straight to the point. "Tom, what do you mean by calling here at three in the morning?"

"Dawn, I got an unidentified call on my cellphone. I'm worried it might've been Trina."

Dawn snorts. "Why you think it's from Trina?" she says. "Look, this is ridicu—"

"Can you just put her on the phone?" I growl, sensing she's about to hang up. "Just humor me."

She exhales heavily to make sure I know she's outraged and inconvenienced. The phone drops, and I wait patiently. After three minutes, I'm about to hang up when I hear her whisper to Trina as she hands her the phone.

"Tom?" Trina's voice is soft and tentative, despite the fact I'm calling at an ungodly hour. She sounds almost pleased to hear from me.

"Trina, did you just call me?"

"Absolutely not," she says, her voice suddenly distant.

"Someone called, and I thought it might be you." As soon as I say it, I realize how presumptuous it sounds. "I was extremely worried," I add quickly.

There's silence for several beats, then, without inflection, she finally offers, "I'm fine."

"What a freaky thing," I mutter, relieved and puzzled.

"Never a dull moment," she says, laughing lightly. I can hear Dawn's stage whisper, urging her to hang up.

Trina puts her hand over the receiver and says something sharp, after which Dawn's voice is gone.

"Trina?"

"Yeah?"

"I miss you," I say, realizing, as I speak them, how true the words are.

"I miss you too, Tom. I have to go to sleep. Sophie's got camp tomorrow and I've got to drive her over there early. It's good to hear your voice."

"You too. Goodnight."

"Goodnight." The phone goes dead.

CHAPTER SIXTEEN

I HAVE TO AGREE WITH LARRY, WAITING FOR STARK sixty-eight floors up in the Sears Tower is something like what I imagine being part of a Papal Audience is like. I've been waiting ten minutes when a stunning brunette emerges from a door hidden in the paneling. She escorts me down a long hall into a corner office that commands a view of the lake and Wacker Drive. Dr. Bill Stark gets up to meet me. He easily stands six-foot four. He motions for me to take a seat across the desk from him. I survey the office and see what I believe is a study by Piet Mondrian of *View From the Dunes*. In the corner is what looks like an original Lichtenstein. A telephone, an antique silver inkwell, and a small crystal clock are the only objects on an otherwise pristine desk. Following my glance around the room, Stark asks, "Do you like art, Detective?"

"Well, I had enough art history in college to appreciate it. But I don't know that I like it all."

Stark chuckles. "Well said. And where did you go to

school?"

"Northwestern," I answer without thinking. I know as I say it, the answer is not completely true.

"Fine school. Frank Amundsen is a friend of mine," Stark says, referring to the school's recently retired president. The wall behind him is hung with photographs of the Chicago mayor, a former Illinois Speaker of the House, dozens of golfing foursomes, and several celebrities.

I shift forward. "I'd like to talk to you about the Edwards' divorce case."

He frowns and then holds up his hands up in resignation. "I'll try to be helpful," he says, smiling, "but I've got to protect patient privilege."

I shake my head. "Doctor, you don't have doctor-patient privilege; you're an advisor to the court."

"True enough," he says as he brushes a piece of lint off his desk.

"So, as you know, we're investigating the murder of Faith Wesley and we have some questions about Lent Edwards."

"Yes, I heard about the murder. Terrible. I remember the case well. It was awful—so much misfortune," he says. "Very difficult indeed. The family dynamic was complex and the child . . . was her name Emma? She was a fragile kiddo."

I reach into my briefcase and extract a copy of the report, which I hand to him. "You favored Linda Edwards in your report. Why?"

Stark's face betrays a brief twitch of surprise. He picks up the report and starts to leaf through it. "May I ask how you got this?"

"Court order," I answer, feeling a small frisson of

satisfaction for catching him off guard. "We got the file unsealed."

He pauses again as he scans the report. He nods slowly as he reads the last several pages. "I believed—well I was pretty sure—Lent Edwards was a dangerous man."

"That's just it. We know Linda Wesley had a conviction for assaulting her mom. Did you know about that?"

He blinks again, surprised. "No, I hadn't heard that. Are you quite sure about that?"

"Yes, I'm sure." I reach into my briefcase and pull out a copy of the IJIN printout, which I proffer to the doctor.

Stark looks at the sheet. He glances quickly at his watch. "You seem to have discounted the testing for both parents. You say Lent's normal findings aren't worth anything."

Leaning forward, Stark places the papers on the desk in front of him. He folds his hands. "The Minnesota Multiphasic Personality Inventory, or MMPI, is a valuable tool, but just that—a tool. It doesn't substitute for professional judgment."

"Did you ever consider PAS?"

Stark nods. "Yes, I did. Parental Alienation Syndrome is something we must always consider in custody evaluations. Mr. Edwards was certain it was going on, but I saw no evidence of it."

"So you were sure the Wesleys, and in particular Faith Wesley, weren't doing anything to alienate Emma from her father?"

"Absolutely. Of course, it's common for parents in a divorce to be hypercritical of each other. Entire families are often factionalized. However, PAS is a different matter altogether. We learn to separate the wheat from the chaff, so to speak." He checks his watch again.

Oliver Wendell Holmes famously said even a dog knows the difference between being stumbled over and kicked. I can feel my skin starting to get warm.

Stark is around the desk in three steps. "I think we're done, Tom. I graciously agreed to offer you my insights regarding Mr. Edwards, but you seem intent on arguing medical and clinical standards with me." He gestures towards the door.

I remain seated. "You haven't answered my question. What made you say Lent is a dangerous man, other than three hours of interviews and some letters?"

"I've answered your questions," he says, putting a hand on my shoulder. "If you don't mind, I think my next appointment is here. You'll need to be going now."

I get up to face Stark, shrugging his hand off my shoulder.

"Thank you, doctor, for your time," I say, moving to one side.

He opens the door, ushering me out. "*Quaecumque sunt vera*," he says, pointing the way out. The door closes.

When I get back to my office, I Google what I think Stark said. After several tries I get, *Quaecumque sunt vera*. It's the Northwestern motto, derived from the Epistle of St. Paul to the Philippians, and I wasn't even swift enough to recognize it:

Whatsoever things are true, whatsoever things are honest, whatsoever things are lovely, whatsoever things are of good report; if there be any virtue, and if there be any praise, think on these things.

Stark told me in so many words to mind my own business.

■ ■ ■

Two days later, I'm with Liam at Cirque du Soleil.

I'm always anxious seeing Liam after a few days have passed. Every reunion is a reminder of lost time. A child's universe is defined by immediacy and proximity. When events occur, Liam experiences them in the present, sharing them with those nearest to him. When I see him days later, the boy's impatient efforts to recount his life, even brimming with enthusiasm, are a rushed mishmash of facts. In the process, there are lost details and connections, a disjointed narrative.

Now, I'm sitting next to Liam as he takes in the spectacular sights of the arena. I try, without much success, to coax a few sentences from him about what he's been doing for the last few days. He's distracted as he scans the dome, lit with bright greens, reds, and yellows. White, pink, yellow, and orange banners hang from the ceiling, which is touched with fluorescent light, and trapezes dangle from neon-colored ropes draped with electric fringe. We take our seats and the lights dim. From the darkness, a single organ pipe melody plays as lime green light dances in the center ring. High above, an exotic dragonfly—a woman in red and purple—soars through the light and dark, sweeping in circles over the crowd. With each turn, the arc grows, and finally the arena explodes in light, spotlighting the trampolines on the floor. Three birds of paradise, in bright green leotards and feathered tiaras, vault into the air. As each trapeze dancer swings out into the ether, the trampoliners jump higher. Reaching in the darkness, a trapeze dancer catches one of the small birds, whisking her into space and into the higher darkness where she disappears. The crowd goes wild.

Well into the event, I feel a tap on my back and turn to see Nora's face looking down at us.

"Nor—Ms. Summers, what a surprise."

When she'd offered the tickets, my first concern was explaining Nora to Liam. She solved the problem by telling me she was going to be sitting in one of the skyboxes. It never occurred to me she'd actually seek us out. I haven't seen her since her surprise visit to my apartment days ago, owing in part to the arson investigation. Part of my reluctance is the fact our relationship is forbidden as long as the Wesley investigation is pending.

Now, standing in front of me, she smiles at Liam. "You guys enjoying yourselves?"

"Yeah!" Liam answers, enthralled with the show.

Nora kneels next to Liam. "My pleasure," she says. She spends the next few minutes whispering to him. Although he keeps his attention on the show, he seems to warm to her. As I watch her talking to Liam, I'm struck by how tired she looks. I can't be certain, but it seems she's acquired hardness in her eyes and around her mouth, which could be the result of fatigue or stress. She pats Liam on the shoulder and turns to face me, her expression suddenly dark.

"We need to talk."

"Something wrong?"

"Now's not the time," she says, looking over at Liam. "There's just some stuff we need to talk about."

She turns quickly and beams at Liam, which gives me an uneasy feeling.

I feel a surge of frustration jump to my throat. It—the invitation to the circus, the visit with Liam—suddenly seems contrived.

"Thanks for the tickets, Nora."

As if sensing my thoughts, Nora reaches out and touches me on the arm.

"Tom, please, I . . ." Her breathing is fast and shallow. She tightens her grip on my arm, her eyes averted. It seems she might cry. The rapid emotional cycling catches me off guard and I have an involuntary reflex to protect Liam. I look down at my son, captivated by the glowing spectacle in front of him.

I turn to look for Nora, seeing her just as she disappears into the stairwell.

■ ■ ■

Judge Harold Wardman's chambers are at the end of a brightly lit hallway in the Lake County Courthouse. Tony Shahbaz and I sit, watching as the judge finishes reading the last of the submissions. On the opposite side of the room, the weasel dicks whisper to each other. Walking to the judge's chambers, Shahbaz explains making partner at STEW. The process is known to associates grinding away their youth as "getting stewed." Several state senators, many judges, and a number of in-house lawyers to the country's most prestigious companies were stewed at one time or another.

In chambers, Wardman's balding head shines in the overhead fluorescent light. His crumpled seersucker suit is marked with a constellation of small burn holes. After twenty-three years as a public defender, he ran for the bench on a law-and-order ticket, which had appealed to Lake County voters. He has never been stewed. Shahbaz told me Wardman dislikes pretense and is a hard worker.

When we're seated, Wardman begins slowly. "Folks, I've reviewed the production from the accountants." His watery eyes are shaded by heavy lids, folded into thick dark pouches. His breath whistles heavily through his nose. "This procedure is highly irregular. Typically, you can get a grand jury subpoena issued for this kind of information. I can see how the finances of the Wesley family might have bearing on the case." He pauses. "That being said, the Wesleys are certainly entitled to privacy. They've gotten involved early in this process."

I shift in my chair.

As if sensing my frustration, the judge leans further forward over his desk. "I'm going to release the accounting records, the bank records, and the credit accounts." The weasel dicks move to the edges of their chairs, ready to spring. Wardman eyes them darkly. "But on two conditions. They'll be produced under a protective order and they won't be used in evidence without a prior hearing in front of me.

The head weasel dick gets to his feet. "That's my order," the judge adds quickly.

"Your honor, David Satterman from Stanhope—"

Wardman's jaw tightens. "Mr. Satterman, I've given my ruling." He reaches into a humidor setting next to his desk, fishing out a large cigar. Despite the Illinois law, Wardman is known to fire up a stogie in his chambers.

Satterman clears his throat. "Your Honor, we don't see any reason to be going through these records."

Peeling the paper band off the cigar, the judge shakes his head. "You people. I don't get it. I've read the briefing and I've limited their use, yet you're still complaining? If this were in front of a grand jury, you wouldn't have any say."

Satterman shifts, leaning further forward. His stiff shoes creak. "We just feel there shouldn't be access at all."

"Sit down, counsel," Wardman barks. He reaches into his desk, produces a steel cigar clipper, and briskly snips the end of the Maduro in his hand. "Call me naïve," he says, checking the cigar end, "but I'd think your clients would want to help Major Crimes. Am I missing something?" he says, clicking the cigar clipper and eyeing Satterman in a way that makes it clear he's not expecting an answer.

Showing obvious reluctance, Satterman sits down. Wardman turns to Shahbaz who, up to this point, has said nothing.

"Mr. Shahbaz, will you prepare the order for my signature? Show it to Mr. Satterman first." He opens another drawer and secures an Avo Grand Corona, forgetting the Maduro next to him. "That will be all," he says, flicking the lighter and toasting the end of the cigar.

When we reach the bottom of the stairwell, Tony turns to me and smiles. "A good day at the races."

"I'll take it," I say.

Tony snorts. "The Wesleys probably paid twenty-five grand for the privilege of that walkover," he says, patting me on the back. "I'll give you a call as soon as we get the records." He turns and heads towards the States Attorneys' office.

Halfway to the exit, Nora intercepts me on the steps. "What are you doing here?" I say, scanning to see if anyone I know is walking by. "How'd you know I was here?"

She smiles brightly. She's wearing sunglasses and makeup, which is a first since I've known her. "I went to your office and your assistant, Larry, told me you were here at the courthouse for a hearing. I found out where it was and waited until you came out."

An icy drop tingles down my spine as I wonder how much she's shared with Larry. Larry is a talented observer, and he's now on high alert, given our recent conflict. Earlier this morning, I went so far as to recheck his drawers, confirming the booze and the gun are gone, the desk stripped clean. I tell myself I have nothing to hide other than the fact I'm freshly separated from Trina. But even as the thought crosses my mind, I know I'm whistling in the dark.

Pulling Nora into an alcove, I face her. "What did you tell Larry?"

"Just that I was a family friend and I wanted to talk to you about your brother."

"Did you tell him your name?"

She laughs. "Relax. Do you take me for an idiot? I told him I was here from Springfield, that I'd heard you'd been there recently and I wanted to see if we could have lunch. He didn't seem to care, really."

"I wish you hadn't done that, Nora. I've got issues with Larry."

She brings her face close to mine, and I have to admit, even with the makeup, she looks good. She's tanned and, although she looks thin, her arms and legs are smooth and brown. She whispers into my ear. "I wanted to make it up to you."

"Make up for what?"

"I owe you an apology. I've been moody recently." She begins to pull me down a side corridor.

"Where are we going?" I ask, letting her lead me.

"Be quiet and follow me," she says, laughing as she pulls me down the hallway until we stand outside an empty room reserved for client conferences. Then I understand what she has in mind. The door is unlocked. She drags me inside the darkened room and turns the sign which says "reserved."

"Nora?"

"Don't you like this?" she asks, locking the door. Her hand tugs at my pants.

"Jesus. We could get caught."

"Here," she says, pulling the shade over the frosted glass. I can still hear the busy voices of the court staff and attorneys.

"Shut up and enjoy this." She puts word to action by pulling my penis out and putting me in her mouth.

■ ■ ■

I'm back at my desk when Larry comes in an hour later. I fully expect to be cross-examined about Nora.

Larry puts the sheet on my desk. "The blood work came back from the Morales' autopsies."

"Really? I thought the investigation was closed."

Seeing the cloth armchair piled high with files which I strategically placed there to keep him off, Larry plops himself into the leather chair shoehorned into the other corner. "They're still murders, so they get autopsies, and I simply asked the lab to shoot me a copy when they were done. Pretty interesting stuff. You ready for this?"

"Let's have it."

Larry rattles a sheaf of papers at me. "The toxicology screen came up positive for ethchlorvynol."

"What's that?"

"Jelly babies. Placidyl. Schedule 2 psychotropic sedatives. You can barely still get them on the black market and they're no longer used clinically. They're like Quaaludes—nostalgia drugs. C'mon Tom, I had you pegged for a swinging kind of guy."

"Very funny," I say. "It doesn't fit. Valued domestic staff by day, zonked junkies by night?"

Larry tugs at a small flap of leather on the chair. "How would you get something like that into 'em?"

"Do you mind?" I say, pointing to the flap in his hand. "I'd like to have some office left at the end of the day. You pulled the other one apart."

He releases the strip of leather. "What's the motive?"

"Beats me." I shrug. "Why would someone sedate them and then whack 'em?"

"Easier to handle," Larry says, as a small piece of leather comes off in his hand. He gets up, bruised feelings apparently smoothed over. I brace myself for a comment about Nora. Larry even looks clean-shaven and wrinkle-free.

He saunters down the hall. Just as he turns into his office, he says in a loud voice, "Really enjoyed meeting your pretty cousin from Springfield." His face breaks into a knowing grin. Waving his hand in a mock salute, he walks into his office.

■　■　■

Several hours later, the receptionist comes in with a slip for a FedEx package and asks me to sign. In a few minutes she comes back with a hefty package. There's a handwritten cover letter.

Tom, I hope you'll forgive the presumption of this package, but I fear we got off to a bad start," Stark starts off amiably.

In reconsidering the substance of our conversation, I thought I might be able to help, as you seemed skeptical when we last spoke. I've done a lot of work in divorce-related psychosis. It's called Brief Reactive Dissociative Psychosis, BRDP, and is a reaction to severe emotional trauma, a precursor to serial family violence. It happens when, in layman's terms, things occur to awaken 'old ghosts.' Divorce can spark psychotic behavior in otherwise sane people.

I would refer you to the well-known Whitely case. Don Whitely was a supervisor at an ice cream factory in New Jersey. During his divorce, his ex-wife alleged child molestation. As you might expect, the report was extremely critical of the father, who came unglued, called the psychiatric board, and made allegations the custody evaluator was paid off. Mr. Edwards has alleged much the same thing here.

You seem very interested in PAS. In the Whitely case, there was solid evidence of alienation by mom. The kid's story was too pat and there was no depth to the reporting. Unfortunately, custody went to mother with supervised visitation to father, and an investigation by Child Services into the allegations of sexual misconduct. This was a bad result, I'll grant you. And even worse later. The custody evaluator was part of a group that met every month over lunch to 'roundtable' cases.

Putting aside the ethics of having such a meeting, Mr. Whitely found out and he shotgunned all of them over dim sum. He then turned the gun on himself.

As you know, I discounted PAS in the Edwards' case. That is because I don't believe Linda alienated the child. But I am sure Lent Edwards thought it was happening and that made him dangerous.

I've enclosed clippings from some cases around the country where parents who view themselves as 'crossed' can become extremely dangerous.

I look at the articles in my hand. Every one of them involves a murder of a child or an ex by an estranged spouse pushed to the limit by the system. I remember what Larry told me about Bill Stark in medical school. Despite his gesture of false bonhomie, Stark is a manipulative politician. He is a part of the system that creates the tragedies. He likes playing God.

I put the articles back in the envelope and throw it in the trash.

CHAPTER SEVENTEEN

———

W HEN I ARRIVE AT THE OFFICE THE NEXT day, Larry tells me the chief wants to see me. I head straight to Delahunt's office. He gestures for me to close the door and have a seat. "Tom, how are you moving on Edwards?"

"Well, Chief, I've got the financials and the psych stuff. All of it. If he killed her, he did it himself, but his alibi is pretty solid." I recount my conversation with the Carnahan's cutie, including her comment about Edwards' condition when she left him. "From what she told me, he wasn't in any shape to get up two hours later, climb over a fifteen-foot spiked wall, and brutally execute Faith Wesley."

Delahunt looks tired. He keeps a large bowl of mints on his desk. Reaching over and unwrapping one, he offers the bowl to me. The meeting looks to me like it's over, and I'm getting ready to get out of my chair when he clears his throat.

"Tom, there's something else we need to talk about. I've

gotten reports you're involved with the Summers woman. Is that true?"

The seat under me turns into a carnival ride, and I'm whipping up and backward. As I scramble to answer the question, I quickly calculate the variables—that Delahunt is asking for confirmation at all means he doubts the source. Running through potential informants, the list is short: Larry, Linda, and Nora herself. I'm not sure what Linda would gain from reporting, other than to have me removed and as retribution for our conflicts. It seems like a long shot.

As reckless as her recent behavior has been, I can't believe Nora would actually report our relationship to my office. Which leaves Larry. Between Larry and Linda, I'm certain I've been betrayed as payback for the booze in the desk. If it's Larry, Delahunt is unlikely to give what he's said much credence.

"No, sir," I say. "That's ridiculous."

He eyes me like risky shellfish, leaning forward. "You know, Tom, its disaster to fuck a witness."

I check myself—Delahunt's an intuitive and perceptive investigator. I shake my head. "Ms. Summers isn't a witness, sir. She's a family friend."

Popping another mint into his mouth, Delahunt frowns. "Those 'family friends' are busting our balls pretty good right now, wouldn't you say?" He reaches into his desk again. After several seconds, he extracts a small rubber troll. Gripping it in his fist, he rhythmically strangles the troll, watching its eyes bug out. "Look, Tom, I've always trusted your judgment. If something's going on, it's got to stop." He punctuates the point with two strong squeezes.

"It's not, sir. You have my word." I've now added lying

to Delahunt to the list of sins, which makes me feel about an inch high. I vow to myself I'm going to end it with Nora.

Delahunt closes the drawer, stowing the troll in the darkness of the desk.

I'm certain Larry is Delahunt's source. I decide that if Delahunt harbors any doubts I've got to land a preemptive strike. "There's something I want to talk to you about, Chief," I say, pausing until Delahunt looks up from the desk. "Larry."

"I was wondering about him," he says, going for another mint.

"I'm worried about him." I have to be sure. I fight the sour revulsion in my chest and say, "I found liquor in his desk." I decide not to mention the gun, wanting to walk the fine line between giving Delahunt enough to discredit Larry, but not enough to get him fired on the spot. It is my weak attempt at telling myself I'm still holding the moral high ground.

"Drunk on the job?" he asks. It looks like I've just made Larry a project.

I shake my head. "No sir, he hasn't been drunk on the job," a statement I know isn't true, "but I called him on the booze in the drawer and he got angry." If Larry was the source, I want the chief to see he might have a motive to burn me.

Delahunt rubs his eyes, sagging with ennui and fatigue. "D'you want to can him?"

I suspect the chief is to the point where he doubts everyone's motives, including his own.

"I think he's good at what he does," I answer truthfully, "but I'm worried about his personal habits."

Delahunt allows a thin smile. "If the personal habits of

everyone in this office counted for discipline, there'd be no one left to turn the lights out. Larry's not the only one to keep something in a drawer. Frankly, it's not the liquor that bothers me; the man's lousy with insubordination."

"I'll keep an eye on him. He's performed well. I'll tell him to clean it up."

Delahunt shrugs. I get to my feet, satisfied I've countered Larry's betrayal and raised enough doubt in Delahunt's mind to deflect the issue.

I'm almost to the door when Delahunt looks up. "Tom, the piece of ass doesn't exist that's worth your career. Take my word for it." He looks back down at his desk.

■ ■ ■

It's been sixteen weeks since Faith Wesley was found dead on her lawn. I'm still busy working the arson investigation. Chicago PD closed the Morales killings, filing them as drug murders. Working the arson-for-hire ring, I finally get a wire for the kid. With surprising cool, the kid persuades his buddies to set up another fire for one of the stores. It's just dumb luck when my CI brings up the dead guy in the last fire, and one of the skells says, "Don't worry, the crispy critter was just collateral damage." I'm sure we'll have enough to indict and send at least two of them to Menard for years. The kid tells them to meet him at the store later that night. Five minutes after he drops the wire with us, he pukes on his shoes.

After Delahunt's comment, I try calling Nora. I'm going to explain we should take it slow, keep some distance, at least until the Wesley case is a wrap. I get no answer and become increasingly concerned. Nora is not, as Delahunt said, simply a "piece of ass." She is, however, a liability, and as much as I dislike myself for it I've weighed my future career against my implicated and quirky relationship with her. The decision is clear. Three days later, I finally stop by her house, surprised to find it dark. The enclosed day-porch is sadly empty without the spread of books, newspapers, and coffee cups, the signs of life which usually trail around the room. Instead, I can see the tables are straightened and the couch is clear. There's no car in the driveway. It looks like she's gone and the house is empty. As I leave, I peer in the living room window. Across the room on the shelf sets the Dead Bell, its pocked sides glowing in the half-light.

Nora belongs to the privileged few who are not bound by jobs and obligations to routine or convention. She can, if she chooses, book a flight to Paris with the same ease as the rest of us order an Uber. On the spur of the moment, she can live there for months, simply renting a flat. After a couple more weeks without any sign of her, I've finally accepted a very real possibility: she's gone entirely.

■　■　■

Linda Wesley, as she's started calling herself, calls and asks me to meet her at the college. I'm genuinely surprised and wonder if there's a catch—a trap. I tell her I can't meet with her without running it by the weasel dicks. She tells me to keep my shirt on; she wants to talk about Nora. I try to sound casual.

"What is there to talk about Nora?" I ask.

"I think you would know that better than me," she says, and gives me the address to Holt Chapel at Lake Forest College before she hangs up.

Holt Chapel boasts a solid granite exterior with stained-glass windows framed in white wood adorning the walls. Inside, sunlight pours through red, green, yellow, and blue glass, illuminating scenes of miracles and redemption. Wood carvings adorn the chancel and sacristy, and pews are upholstered in deep red velvet. I haven't been to church since my stint as an altar boy with Father R., and despite the Sousa mass and the sherry-stealing altar boys, the place puts me at ease. As I enter, I hear the clear melodic sounds that I would bet are a Beethoven trio.

As soon as my eyes adjust to the light, I see Linda with her cello, flanked on the right by a striking blonde woman playing the piano, and on her left by a man in his mid-twenties who's drawing a bow quickly across the strings of a violin. The music soars, pulsing ascending triplets, finally reaching an exquisite note which the violin holds until it softens into a sustained lament. The movement comes to a close as the restated theme is played in unison. After a moment of silence, Linda looks over at me, rises from her chair, and signals the other two she has to talk.

"That was beautiful," I say, surprised to hear myself say it.

"Beethoven, Trio number six," she says, still holding her cello by the neck.

She gestures to a waiting area in the back of the chapel with several benches. Her cello case sets on the bench closest to the door. Opening it, she wipes down the instrument, its amber sheen glowing in the light of the stained glass. She picks up the bow, and adjusts it, running her fingers lightly along the horsehair. She clips the bow into the lid, stuffs the cloth into the compartment, and gently puts the instrument into its case and closes it.

Satisfied she's taken care of the cello, she motions to a door at the back of the chapel where I can see a large tree standing next to a stone bench. Once outside, I take in the open quads, encircled with tall pin oaks and maples, deep dusty green, their tops a burnt yellow in the heat. The brick and granite buildings frame the landscape in regular, rectangular spaces, monuments to order, privilege, and civilization.

Fall is just a week away, the red-throated loons and pie-billed grebes, their annual pilgrimage across the lake still ahead of them. Soon enough though, the paths will be alive with students streaming like ants in a trail, forging ahead in single-minded lines towards their destinies. Sitting on the bench next to Linda, I relax in the serenity of the end of summer.

She points to a palatial Tudor building on the far side of the quad. The structure boasts a sweeping lawn and a two-story enclosed glass porch. "That," she says, "belonged to my great-grandfather and was a gift to the college." Her expression softens, her mouth expanding into a smile. "The crazy Wesley history. My great-grandmother found the old man screwing one of the chambermaids there and peppered his ass with birdshot." She laughs. "If you know where to look, you can still see the pellet marks in the paneling." Her tone verges almost on intimacy. "It wasn't fatal," she adds quickly, laughing again.

Recognizing she's ventured too much, in a beat she retreats, becoming remote and formal. She fishes in her pocket for a cigarette. As she lights it, there's an awkward silence. She looks away.

"You wanted to talk to me about Nora," I say after a few moments.

"I would think you'd want to talk more than I do." The smile reemerges, now armed and knowing. I'm startled by the sudden shift, like finding out the garden snake I've been toying with for five minutes is in fact a black mambo.

"Do you know where she is?" I ask, trying to gauge how much she knows.

She pauses long enough to wave at the man and woman who are leaving the chapel before she says, "Yes." She takes a drag and shifts on the bench, turning towards me, exhaling. "She's taken a few days to go to the East Coast. Didn't she tell you?"

"Why would she tell me?"

Linda frowns, and takes a draw. "You know, you seem to dislike me for some reason. But, I like you." She gives my arm a gentle pat. "Really, I do." She chuckles lightly. "Because you actually seem to have a pair of balls. To be honest, I was surprised you would have the guts to reach for someone like Nora. I was even more surprised when she told me how much she liked you." She seems to genuinely enjoy needling me.

I can feel the color rising to my face. "What are you getting at, Linda?"

"Really, Tom? Don't you think Nora and I share everything?" She uncrosses her legs and re-crosses them. In the process, her skirt rises up. Despite myself, I glance at her thighs. She shakes her head. "Oh no, don't get that in your head. Naked Sexy Time with one of us is enough, don't you think?" She's toying with me like a yard cat casually gutting a vole. "Nora said you were—how did she say it? 'Sincere and gentle.' Not bad praise if you ask me."

"I don't know what you want," I reply honestly. She summoned me, so I figure she must have an agenda.

"I warned Nora about you, but she didn't listen. She's never listened, really." Linda gets up and starts towards the chapel. The sun has reached the tops of the buildings to the west, casting long shadows like skyscrapers across the expanse of the lawn. The sky is crystal blue. The auditorium is empty. Linda reopens the cello case and retrieves a small rosin can out of her pocket. "Nora and I have a lot of shared history. As children, we had fun. My mother hated her and tried to get rid of her. But my father wouldn't hear of it. It was one of the few things I ever saw them fight about in public."

"Why did your mother hate her?"

She reaches into the case and opens a compartment under the neck of the cello. She pulls out a box with several sets of cello strings and places the rosin at the bottom, replacing the strings on top. She closes the lid and gently shuts the case. "Dozens of reasons. Nora went through a political phase, a girl phase, and she introduced me to my independence. Mother couldn't stand it. Nora represented everything foreign to my mother's sense of order. My mother was from a small farm in Iowa and built herself into the very image of The Four Hundred. You know, Tessie Oelrichs was the daughter of a California hardscrabble miner. My mother disliked Nora because Nora was born into all that and then threw it away. She was a traitor to her class."

Linda picks up the case and starts to walk out. As she nears the exit, she walks back towards me. "You know, Tom, in your boy scout excitement to impress Nora, you managed to unearth the one thing she's worked for decades to bury." Her face is dark with menace.

"Nora's gone," I say. "She left without a word."

"She's gone to New York on some business. She'll be back. I need to know you'll leave her alone. She's—" She pauses. "She's not herself these days. You must have seen it. I would think you, of all people, would see what you are both doing is utter foolishness."

I debate whether to tell her I've come to the same conclusion myself, but at that moment Linda looks like a living, breathing Faith Wesley, her face implacable with galvanized disdain. She comes close to me, her breath warm on my cheek. "You're going to forget that mechanic's report and what it did or did not say. You're going to drop all of that and you're going to leave Nora alone." She steps back, her eyes shining with anger. "If you don't, I'll see you working a tollbooth." She puts the strap of the carrying case over her shoulder, pushing the heavy door on her way out.

As I make my way towards where I parked, a blue sedan pulls out of a space on the far side of the lot. I drive several blocks towards the freeway until I'm pretty sure the sedan is following me. I circle the block, and the car drops back. Suddenly, I put the Beast in reverse and spin. The sedan fishtails as it speeds towards the freeway. Hitting the ramp at seventy miles an hour, I make it out onto the road. I search the flow of traffic for the sedan. The car is gone.

CHAPTER EIGHTEEN

I DRIVE STRAIGHT TO THE HEALTH CLUB, WAVE HELLO to Tyler, the manager, and make my way down to the locker room. It's late enough to have the pool to myself. Fluorescent lights hum as I stand at the end of the pool watching the gentle undulations of the water. I brace myself and jump in. I swim thirty laps, finishing at the deep end. Checking again to see if the room is empty, I take several quick breaths and let myself fall to the bottom. I sit, transfixed, repeating my ritual. Images play in my mind like an endless film loop. I hope the numbing ache will slow the spinning in my head, but the water brings no solace, no peace.

Linda Wesley warned me off Nora, and her threat is real. I also risk losing my job if Delahunt finds out I'm still working on the Summers' case. But something about the way the case was handled and the fact Delahunt doesn't want to discuss Strauss makes me want to find out what happened, even if Nora and I aren't together anymore.

Back at the office, I decide I have to start with Dirty Pete Strauss. Delahunt said Strauss had an ex-wife. I figure if anyone knows about Dirty Pete Strauss, it will be his ex-wife. I close the door to my office and begin calling women in the Chicago area with the last name of Strauss. After several directory assistance failures and exploratory calls, I'm at a dead-end. I decided to try my luck with Verna.

Verna McNeil was crowned Miss Lake Michigan, 1977. Despite the years, and three children, she still retains the foundation of the profile that earned her the crown. If anything, the years have given her face character and the fine laugh lines around her mouth and eyes lend interest.

Senior Administrative Assistant, Personnel Services is Verna's official title. It's general knowledge she's assistant to no one—she runs the department. Over the years, she's helped me with garnishments, child support payments, paycheck adjustments, and employee benefits. She knows the minute workings of everyone's lives. When I started on the force, our relationship always contained a question mark, never really serious, which was fueled by Verna's double entendres and repartee. She liked the attention, but over the years our friendship has mellowed into a genuine affection. I'm torn about lying to her, but she's company through and through and I'll get nowhere if I don't.

When I arrive, she's on the phone, deep in conversation. She gestures for me to wait by the door. She turns to one side, embroiled in a heated argument with someone I suspect is one of her daughters. Several seconds into the conversation I've heard enough to infer Verna found a box of condoms under the girl's bed, which, she loudly announces, is disgusting.

"Goddam kids," she says, hanging up as she waves me

in. "I suppose I should be happy she's using birth control. Let me tell you, nobody ever says 'darlin' let's have another teenager.'"

I laugh.

"You laugh, Tom Edison, but you don't know. All you have to deal with is Liam."

Verna leans back in her chair, crossing her legs. I avert my eyes, trying to avoid an embarrassing moment. "I need a favor from you," I say. "The less you ask, the less I'll have to lie to you."

Verna's face darkens.

"Nothing illegal, right?" she asks, bringing her knees up, coming forward at the desk.

"No, nothing illegal." I falter, as I consider whether what I've just said is strictly true. "I need info on . . . someone . . . something I've been asked to lay cool on."

"Why would I know about it?" she asks, her eyes narrowing.

I can feel the moisture rise under my arms and a warm current running up the back of my neck. "Because it's someone who used to work here."

"Who?" she folds her arms, her expression tightly sealed. So far, I doubt Verna is going to cooperate.

I resist the urge to push, figuring that will piss her off even more. After a pause, I tell her. "Pete Strauss."

She bolts upright, shaking her head. "Jesus, Tom, I can't."

"Why?" I think I've misjudged Verna.

"If you've been looking into Dirty Pete, you know why every bit as much as I do." She looks straight at me. "Files of retired personnel are off limits."

"All I need is some old information."

"What kind?"

"The name of his ex-wife and a social for her if you have it."

She considers the request. "What're you planning to do with it?" She leans forward, unfolding her arms. "Dirty Pete was as nasty a piece of work as ever came through here," she adds.

"Just a name and a social. I wouldn't ask if it wasn't important. I'll deny ever getting it from you."

Her face grows shaded, troubled, and confused. She seems to reach for another time and place, like trying to recall an old phone number. As quickly as she left she's returned, but somehow changed; any doubt or confusion is settled.

"Wait here a sec," she says, and walks back towards the filing area.

■ ■ ■

I wouldn't know for several months, until she told me herself, why Verna McNeil chose to leave the post she guarded as zealously as her daughter's precious virtue.

As a young woman, Verna never considered herself a religious person, placing her faith instead in the potency of her dreams. Winning the Miss Lake Michigan title was less the answer to her prayers than tangible proof of the infallibility of her plans. For a girl from Wauwatosa, Wisconsin, winning the contest was the passport to an acting career and a ticket out of the double-wide she shared with her mother, her stepfather, and her four siblings. The blueprint for this plan was simple and linear and featured a small but crucial part in a movie leading, naturally, to bigger parts. Although her looks had caused as much trouble as benefit—her stepfather kept 'accidentally' interrupting her in the bathroom—she understood at an early age her looks were the one asset on which she could depend to breathe life into an idea which would otherwise have been nothing more than childish fantasy.

But, as the philosopher Jagger once observed, you can't always get what you want. After several months of false starts, unsigned contracts, and an agent whose services were conditioned on her performing acts of oral gratification on him, she decided to become her own agent, sure of her own perfect intentions. More months passed and her desperation grew, just as surely as her faith in her exit strategy began to wane. At home, scanning the pages of the trades in the corner of her Lilliputian bedroom, she finally spotted an ad which offered a thousand dollars for "modeling." Back then, a thousand dollars was enough to buy you a plane ticket somewhere far away and first month's rent if you weren't too picky. If you really scrimped, you might even squeeze groceries for a month or two out of it.

She rationalized the money was good, even as she reached the dingy entrance to the "agency" offices located above an auto parts store. She told herself the modeling was likely for underwear or wigs and, however unglamorous, would be the springboard she needed to get to New York or LA to start the next phase of her stalled life.

The door to the agency bore a hand-painted sign, "Global Products." She rang a buzzer and was greeted by a fat middle-aged man with large wet lips and an improbable toupee jutting from his forehead like the prow of a steamship. When she asked about the modeling job, his face broke into a smile, revealing several gold teeth in the front. Fighting the impulse to turn and run into the street, her conviction in herself, coupled with a new sensation— fear of failure—kept her feet in place.

The man explained the one-thousand-dollar modeling fee was actually on a sliding scale and was contingent on what she was willing to do. She began to understand the terms of the proposed agreement, and the combined weight of her aspirations and her growing desperation landed on her.

Telling herself the path to stardom frequently began on the casting couch, and even great stars made sacrifices, she told the gold-toothed man she was willing to do what it took for the thousand dollars, insisting on payment of half upfront. She complimented herself for her financial acumen, a sign of her worldly maturity and toughness. The toupee procured a wad of grey bills, counted twenty-five of them, and handed them to her. He pointed to a dingy curtain at the back of the front room, which led into a smaller windowless room furnished with a couch, a chair, and a large armoire covered by a large rug. Two klieg lights, trained on the couch, were suspended from the ceiling. Sitting on the divan was a man she guessed was in his thirties, his long blond hair tumbling over the collar of an untucked chamois shirt. His long legs stretched in front of him and were encased by tight blue jeans. He was barefoot. He smiled at her, introducing himself as Richard Large, saying she could call him Dick.

Verna was not a virgin and, having experienced enough of the male of the species to be familiar with what would be required of her, she undressed in silence without preliminaries. She hadn't gotten beyond taking her shirt off before the man with the gold teeth reached into a drawer and extracted a camera. He began taking pictures. She reminded herself she was going to New York or LA as each piece of clothing came off, praying the pictures would be swallowed in the bottomless sea of anonymous smut.

It took a half-hour. Dick was indeed large and paid no attention to her stifled requests for gentleness, thrusting away with the finesse of a steam turbine. She'd objected to doing it without protection, to which the toupee replied she would lose two-hundred-and-fifty dollars for such niceties. She reluctantly assented but managed to extract a promise from Dick he would withdraw before consummation, avoiding the potential consequences. Dick got to work until, apparently satisfied he'd fulfilled his part of the bargain, he loudly announced he was climaxing and, despite his earlier assurances, managed to finish in her and halfheartedly withdraw before depositing the remainder of his genetic material on her back.

She got to her feet, cleaned herself off, put on her clothes, and demanded the rest of her money. The toupee produced the wad of cash and peeled off another twenty-five bills, holding on when she reached for them. For an instant she felt a hot poker of fear in her innards until he released the money, laughing, telling her he'd enjoyed working with her. She ran down the stairs and into the sunlight. She walked to the bus, certain everyone she passed knew what she'd done and was judging her. When she reached the double-wide, she ran to the bathroom, locked herself in for two hours, and scrubbed her skin raw in the hot shower as her brothers pounded on the door telling her to get out.

What she didn't know, and was to find out two years later, was her brief acrobatic and entirely unsatisfying encounter with Dick Large was caught on film and circulated in theaters, frat houses, and porno stores around Chicago.

She held on to the money, hoarding it, keeping it a secret—no small feat when she shared a room with her two sisters. She kept waiting for a time when, with a flourish, she'd announce her departure, leaving on the next flight for LA. But as the days turned into weeks, she began to feel sick, and she knew her body enough to understand what had happened to her.

The dreams of Grauman's Chinese Theater, TV interviews, and a life away from the grey tomb of the double-wide gave way like rotten timbers and, trapped under the rubble, her broken innocence smashed like crystal on the concrete floor beneath.

Her choices were stark, real, and far different from her fantasies of life in Hollywood. In a perverse twist of luck, it turned out the money she'd socked away was just enough to get the problem safely solved. She swore her sister Ingrid to silence, telling her mother she was spending a few days with friends. She left, not for LA or New York, but for Chicago to get the problem fixed.

After that weekend, she gave up her dream, settling instead into a steady job at the Lake County Sherriff's Office as an administrative assistant. She might never have given the toupee or the weekend in Chicago a second thought, other than to have an occasional twinge of regret. She believed she was an anonymous set of tits, one set in thousands of anonymous sets of tits. It might have been entirely true if the movie and pictures hadn't found their way into the inventory of a grimy storefront in Waukegan and the head of the Morals Squad at the time hadn't been Pete Strauss.

These ugly facts came to light in the ladies' room one evening as she was preparing to go home. She'd finally left the double-wide, recently marrying a guy she'd met at a Kiwanis party. Her husband, Darryl, had just started off in an insurance firm in Milwaukee, and they'd barely managed to save a down payment on a tiny home in Union Grove, halfway between Waukegan and Milwaukee. Tuesday nights, Darryl met clients in Wisconsin, so she stayed after work to catalog files and send them to archives. The empty admin offices were dark, but she could hear the hum of activity in the station below.

Standing at the mirror, she was putting on her makeup and getting ready for the ride home when the door to the ladies' room opened. At first, she didn't look to see who'd come in, considering it rude to inventory coworkers using the facilities, however late. The figure at the door didn't move for several seconds. Sensing something strange in the absence of movement, she looked up to see Pete Strauss.

Up to that point, her interaction with Strauss had been limited to processing health insurance and pension papers. She'd been warned by several women to steer clear of Strauss. She was told he was better known by the moniker, Dirty Pete. It was never clear if he'd acquired the name because of his time in the Morals Squad, or because of his reputation as a cop on the take.

Strauss stood by the door, blocking the exit. He was a thin man whose short, steel grey hair was slicked back on his head. His face had deep-set eyes separated by a large flat nose, bent slightly to the left, likely the result of a poorly repaired break. Under his eyes, sharp cheeks dropped to his chin, which sported a prominent white scar. He stared at her with dull animal cunning, his wide mouth finally drawing into a grin, heavy with knowledge and intent.

Clearly there was no good reason for Strauss to be in the ladies' room with her after hours, and a reflexive spike of fear pierced her stomach. She tried to be calm. "Detective, what are you doing in the ladies' room?" she asked, trying, without much success, to sound indignant and in control.

Ignoring the question, Strauss moved to the center of the small room and leaned on the counter.

"You a movie fan, Verna?" he asked, his voice low and quiet.

"I don't have time for the movies. I'm married," she said, mistaking his question for an invitation to a date.

"I see a lot of movies in my line of work," he said, making it sound as if he did the work of ten men. He shook his head. "Lots of 'em. They're not the kind of movies you'd take your kids to though." The grin morphed into a leer, and she understood the reference to movies was not casual. Strauss was toying with her. He walked towards her, covering the distance between them in three steps. Standing next to her, she could smell his scent—sweat mixed with aftershave—and feel his heat. She took a step back and braced herself against the sink.

"I have to watch these movies as part of my job. It makes me sick," he said, running his tongue over his lips and shaking his head. He took a step closer to her, whispering, "disgusting."

"I was watching a movie we grabbed when we popped a joint downtown." He placed a hand next to hers on the bathroom counter. "I don't usually recognize anybody I know in these movies. Imagine my surprise when I see somebody I know."

The terms were simple: Dirty Pete's silence, Darryl's

blissful ignorance, and Verna's continued employment in exchange for her unwilling consent to his brief, unsatisfactory sexual advances. The logistics were equally simple, usually a motel several miles from the office, always arranged by Strauss. She explained her occasional absences to Darryl as work problems, which the young insurance broker seemed content to believe. The exchange lasted several months, and it seemed as though he'd actually come to believe Verna was happy with it. Several times, after taking his payment, Strauss became talkative, adopting a tone which might have passed for tenderness or halfhearted geniality. Strauss might have convinced himself the attraction was mutual, but Verna never lost the tight knot of hatred in her chest.

It might have gone on indefinitely, or until she finally gave in to the urge to shoot him in the pecker, the legs, the feet, and finally, the head. But as suddenly as he'd come into her life, like an ebbing grey tide of filth, he receded, leaving little more than the memory of his sour breath and the stink of his rancid sweat. The last time in the dark, dirty motel room, he'd told her he was leaving, that he'd "put together a deal" and would be gone within two days. He'd searched her face, as if looking for a sign she was sorry he was going. She stared at him as she put her bra on as quickly as she could.

"Pity," he said. "I thought you might actually learn to like me." When she didn't answer, he said, "Don't worry," his dull animal leer crossing his face, "I'll destroy the movie before I go. Now that I've had the real thing," he said, swatting her behind, "I don't need no movie."

Of course she didn't trust him. After he was gone, she ran to check the mail each day before Darryl got home, looking for a small, unmarked envelope or parcel. She waited for weeks to be called into Delahunt's office. After almost five years, she heard Strauss had died of a heart attack in Las Vegas. She buried him, along with her violation, deep in the vault of her memory and, until I asked for the file, it hadn't been opened for over twenty years.

· · ·

After what seems like an eternity, Verna comes back with a small yellow sticky on which she's written the name Tammy Strauss, followed by a social security number.

Taking the paper, I lean over and give Verna a friendly buss on the cheek.

"I don't want to know anything more about it. This conversation never happened," she says, sitting down at the desk. "Please close the door on your way out."

Returning to my office, I run the social through the system and come up with a Tamara Strauss aka Tammy or Tammy Uhler who lived at several Midwest addresses in the eighties, then moved to El Segundo, California, a suburb of Los Angeles. The reverse directory has a number and, given the time difference, I figure it's just after eight o'clock in the morning. After several rings, a thick female voice answers.

"Tammy, Tammy Strauss?"

"Who's this?" she says.

"This is Tom with Lake County—"

My voice is interrupted as she yells, "What do you want?"

"Are you Tammy Strauss?"

There's a pause. Finally she says, "I ain't gone by that name for twenty-five years."

I know with someone like Tammy, I have one shot to get what I need. I figure money's a good angle. "Right, Tammy Uhler. I'm with admin and we went through the files and it appears Detective Peter Strauss left behind a pension benefit naming you. I need you to sign some paperwork."

She drops the receiver which, from the sound of it, bangs against the floor. I don't hear anything for several seconds, and I'm about to hang up when she picks up the phone and I can hear her breathing heavily. Finally, she says, "Pete didn't leave me no freakin' money. Who are you?"

I decide it's better to come clean and tell her I'm a detective investigating one of Pete's old files and that I have some questions about what Strauss was doing in the last few months before he left.

She says something indistinguishable, which sounds like a growl. "Why don't you ask your asshole buddies? Ask Verna Mc—whateverthefuck her name is. They knew Pete was tapping me regular and didn't do nothin' about it. Fuck 'em. Fuck you," she barks, hanging up.

CHAPTER NINETEEN

WHEN STEW PRODUCES EIGHTEEN banker's boxes of accountants' records, Larry almost strokes out. He tells me we've received what in the legal business is known as a "boxcar" response. The game is to produce absolutely everything, burying the relevant stuff in among pounds of junk, although he says it's typically reserved for high-conflict litigation. Working against the clock, the more stuff there is, the less chance you have to find what you're looking for. Larry spends the first day and a half culling the junk in an attempt to find the annual bank summaries, cursing the skinny pencil-necked weasel dicks as he goes. With only seven days left on Wardman's order, we finally pull in two interns from Shahbaz's office, but not before Steinman scolds us for burning up valuable county assets.

For Charles, Faith, Linda, and Emma, the wealth is sealed and structured, institutionalized by their sharp and watchful ancestors. Charles, the sole remaining heir to what was Great Plains Steel Works, has the dubious task of preserving the financial legacy. Truth be told, he doesn't even have to do that, thanks to the small army of financial advisors and money managers who toil daily on the funds.

Charles, however, has an additional privilege granted to the wealthy: unorthodoxy. To some, this privilege means nothing more than eccentricity—weird hats, unusual eating habits, and an overarching disdain for anyone else. Linda Wesley, and it certainly appears the same had been true for Faith Wesley, shares a common belief in the absolute certainty of her family's superiority.

If, as they say, money talks, then the Wesley's money speaks volumes.

The accounts are organized into several designated funds, each a separate part of the business. There are operating accounts, including a legal services' fund set aside for the weasel dicks. The vast majority of the assets are held in several different trusts. Individual trusts have been established for each member of the family. There are Revocable Living Trusts, Charitable Remainder Trusts, Generation-Skipping Trusts, Tax Credit Trusts, and Intentionally Defective Grantor Trusts known as IDGTS. Thirty-eight in total. The Charitable Trusts fund everything from music schools to AIDS research. We find one account with two-million-eight-hundred-thousand dollars at North American Savings and Trust, a small bank with headquarters in New Mexico. The NAST account consists of cash stowed in money market funds and certificates of deposit. It has one signer: Faith Wesley. I mark the number for Larry to follow up on.

■　■　■

While Larry and the interns deal with the banking stuff, I finally make it through the pile of father's rights stuff from Edwards' trunk. I come across several highlighted references to Parents and Children Together, PACT, an advocacy group. Larry manages to find their address.

PACT is located in a storefront in Englewood. At the bottom of a set of stairs, a solid steel door holds a single pane of glass through which I can barely make out a fluorescent light and the shadowy movement of someone inside. I knock tentatively on the metal door, waiting several seconds before pounding again. A large, bearded face peers through the dirty pane, followed by the solid clack of a deadlock. The door opens to reveal a heavyset man with dark features whose face is framed with a bush of black whiskers sprouting from his jowls. On his head is the neat white turban of a Sikh. Set deep into the face, his eyes, black as olives, assess me.

"Can I help you?" the man asks, blocking the view of the interior. I show my ID. "Kapur Singh," he says, stepping into the room behind him. He wears a long-sleeved chamois shirt with the arms rolled up to his elbows. His arms are covered in tattoos and his loose dungarees are cinched with a large black belt. "We can't be too careful," he says, stepping to one side, escorting me into a dimly lit room. He offers me a cup of coffee, which I politely decline. I explain I've been unable to reach him by phone and have come to ask him about the materials I found in Lent Edwards' car. He begins by telling me about the organization, unleashing an explosive torrent of statistics: divorce rates, custody biases, child abuse, child neglect, unfounded allegations of child molestation during divorce, each one tethered to the next.

Finally, I interrupt. "So, how is PACT different from the nuts?" I ask, struggling to hide my exasperation.

"Numbers and statistics. They tell the story." Singh glances over at the dusty bank of computers glowing in the corner of the room. "We keep data on evaluators. We try to get the custody reports. A lot of them are marked confidential, but if at least one of the parents wants to share them, we can look at them. We aren't interested in the testing and the negative stuff. We're looking at the results. Which evaluators, which courts, and who gets custody. The fact all of this stuff is done confidentially means there's an entire culture of secrecy. We're trying to shed a little light. What we've found is compelling."

"You must see a lot of angry men in here. What did you give Lent Edwards?"

Singh nods. "We deal mostly by email and the internet and avoid the Dark Web. You're right, the process turns a lot of people, especially men, into animals. You think having your children ripped from you wouldn't affect your personality?"

I have to concede the point. "Did Lent Edwards seem to you like he was bent on revenge? Did he ask for anything out of the ordinary?"

"We don't do that. The Dark Web has sites and links if that is what you are interested in. We just gather data."

"So, all you did is give Edwards stuff on Stark?"

"Absolutely. We gave him statistical stuff on Bill Stark. Cases and results. That's all." Gesturing towards the computers, he says, "I'll give you what we have on Stark. We have updated since the Edward's case." He goes to one of the computers and, after several keystrokes, the printer in the corner leaps to life. He hands me a sheaf of paper.

"We've been following Bill Stark for years. He's turned custody evaluations into a cottage industry. If you get something on him, please let me know."

"I'll think about it," I say, taking the paper as I head towards the door and the light.

■   ■   ■

I review the summaries. Stark's testified in dozens of cases, almost invariably recommending supervised visitation or psychological evaluation for the unsuccessful parent. His evaluations never recommend shared custody, and it is always a zero-sum game—all or nothing. More often than not, his recommendations are adopted wholesale by the judges, who often take language from his report word for word. He has the power to change families and destinies forever.

Reviewing the PACT summary, I come to *Ainsworth v. Ainsworth*. Michael Ainsworth is the chief family law judge in Lake County, Illinois. His own divorce was public and messy. Ainsworth's wife, Ellen, said he was abusive, an alcoholic, and a serial cheater. The case was specially assigned to Judge Craig Morlan, a close friend and fellow judge on the Lake County bench. When Ellen Ainsworth's lawyer, Sam Farinelli, filed a motion to remove Morlan, he refused. Judge Ainsworth's lawyer, Lori Tralich, proposed Stark. Farinelli objected, and Stark recommended custody to Mike Ainsworth, with supervised visitation going to Ellen, his former wife and the mother of his children.

Since the divorce, Ainsworth has appointed Stark in twenty-three cases, including the Edwards' custody dispute. Lori Tralich represented Linda Edwards in her divorce.

■ ■ ■

That night, once I've finished my laps, I swim slowly to the deep end, sinking to the bottom. Enveloped in water, I hear the beating of my heart—nothing else.

With my eyes closed, I can see Jimmy Newsome, face down in the lake, and smell the green slime on the bottom of the raft. My lungs begin to ache, and I clench my diaphragm. Then I recall the sound of breaking branches and the smell of hackberry, black crowberry, buttonbush, and then damp underbrush.

Finally, exhaling a column of depleted air, I let my body gently float to the surface. I sit on the bench, looking at the water which, several minutes later, is still undulating. It wasn't until almost ten years later, in tears, and choking with rage, that I could finally say the name out loud: Paulie.

■ ■ ■

With fall finally upon us, Liam starts school at Westinghouse Middle School. With our new schedule, I'm down to pick him up on Fridays. At the stroke of three, the doors fly open, releasing children into the parking lot. Looking at them, I wonder sadly how many kids like Liam are the product of separate homes and blended families. I've read recently that in a single year, for every two million marriages, half will end in divorce. Seven million Americans are paying forty-billion dollars in child and spousal support every year.

Liam runs to the car, jumping in the back. "Missoula

Theater's coming and Mom put me in. I've got to go every day until the show and I get to play the big troll in *Jack in the Beanstalk!*" he shouts.

"What about camping?" I ask, referring to our long-planned trip at the end of September.

Liam's face falls, struggling with an answer to the question. He eyes me, looking for a trap. I quickly sort my options: the first is to insist Liam go on the trip, missing several rehearsals, and maybe setting up Liam to lose the part. The second is sacrifice the fishing trip and hope to make it up later.

In all of it, I can smell the telltale scent of betrayal. Liam, pushed, perhaps sensing my lack of enthusiasm, says, "Dad, it's really important to be in *Jack and the Beanstalk*."

"Don't you want to go fishing?" I ask, justifying the question as a lesson in natural consequences. As soon as I ask it, I feel petty for emotionally leveraging my eleven-year-old.

"Maybe we can go later this fall," Liam offers hopefully. His attempt to craft a solution frustrates me even more, highlighting the fact we're trapped in a situation that Liam neither created, nor possesses, the skills to broker a solution.

The best I can offer is, "We'll deal with it later."

Liam doesn't like that answer as it leaves *Jack in the Beanstalk* in play. But I know I've already lost and am just buying time before calling Katie and letting her have it.

The car makes its way slowly out of the parking lot, following the line of vehicles pumping exhaust into the air. We've almost made it to the front gate when the school pick-up coordinator, a volunteer named Alexa, comes over to Liam's window. She's smiling and shaking her head as she approaches.

"Has there been a mix-up?" she asks, bending into the open window. "The office got a call this morning, and we were told Liam was to wait by the curb."

"Do you know who it was?" I ask Alexa.

"I'm sorry, I'm sure I don't," she replies, shrugging.

"Man or woman, do you know?" I press.

Rather than take me on, Alexa withdraws quickly, her face suddenly hard for a young woman. "I really don't know. You can check in the office for the message," she says, walking quickly to another car. So much for safety.

I decide to take it up with Katie later.

"Hey, Dad?"

"Yessir."

"Are we gonna see Trina and Sophia again soon?"

Liam's hitting a thousand so far, each new topic a minefield. I'm drowning in bedevilments. More than three months have elapsed since Liam has seen Trina, and I've put off telling him the stark truth, telling him instead that Trina went to visit her sister—a half-truth. If Liam notices the missing photographs and the empty spaces in Trina's closet and on the bookshelves, he hasn't said anything about it. But it's clear he isn't going to be put off. I also suspect he may've been tipped to something by his mother.

"Well, they decided they're going to stay with Trina's sister for a little longer."

"How long, Dad?" he presses, which I take as an implied accusation of dishonesty. In fact, I *am* being dishonest and Liam has caught me at it.

Liam continues to push. "Dad, did Sophie's cat go with them?"

I explode. "Goddammit, Liam, the cat went with

them—and I don't know when they're coming back." I slam my hand on the steering wheel, quickly looking out the window to check if the other parents, and maybe Alexa, saw me. I'm ashamed and implicated.

Liam falls silent. I know he doesn't understand that field trips, school plays, and sleepovers are the hard currency of non-custodial parents. I feel cheated and hate myself for yelling, which feels like burning hundred-dollar bills.

As we leave the lot, I look in what Liam calls the "review" mirror . . . and see a blue sedan pull out behind us. The car follows for two blocks and as I slow to turn at the next left, the car stops, does a K turn, and speeds in the other direction.

"Liam?"

"Yup," the boy replies without enthusiasm.

"Look, I'm sorry, but I'm sad about the fishing trip." I try to be honest without putting the whole load on it. "Will you accept my apology, son?"

Liam nods, glad for the tacit permission he can be in the theater program.

"Okay, sure," he says. A few minutes later, as we get out of the car and start up the stairs to the apartment, Liam takes my hand, a gesture I understand for a boy of his age comes at a high cost.

We spend the evening eating Fat Boy Pizza and watching movies. Liam insists on watching *The Incredibles* for the ninth time. At nine o'clock, he starts to fight the first signs of fatigue as I pull out *Hidalgo*, a true story about a man who raced a horse across the Arabian Desert. He falls asleep in my lap as Frank Hopkins and Hidalgo face doom in the desert. Gently brushing the boy's hair, I pick him up and carry him to bed. He smells faintly of Fat Boy

Garlic Surprise.

Later, I start awake. I've fallen asleep on the couch. My cell phone buzzes. 1:45 AM. The call is from a blocked line.

"Hello?"

Nothing, except for what sounds like the soundtrack from a dance movie.

CHAPTER TWENTY

I'VE SEEN NORA ONLY ONCE SINCE MY ENCOUNTER with Linda. By chance, I run into Nora as she is leaving a spray tan boutique on the outskirts of Lake Forest. I'd reconciled myself to the fact she left without saying anything and had apparently decided our relationship was over. As we stand awkwardly in front of the spray tan place, I'm struck by the lines in her face that seem etched deeper. Her eyes are bright and distracted. I attempt a nonchalance I know neither of us feels and say I'm glad to see her. I ask her where she's been, to which she answers she had to take care of some family business in New York. As she edges toward the parking lot, it's clear she isn't going to volunteer anything more.

I shift and stand in front of her. I'm surprised by what I'm feeling: I've over-committed and underestimated my connection to her. If the truth were told, while she's been gone I've kept a vigil of sorts in her garden. Now, as we face each other outside the tanning salon I'm too proud to tell her I stopped by her house every day on some pretext of already being in Lake Forest just to see if the lights in the house were on, to check the door, to get a sense of when she'd be back, if at all. What makes it worse is I'm still conflicted about Trina and I've been warned off Nora, not just by Linda, but also by the chief. Despite my behavior, I'm still self-aware enough to know my motives for chasing Nora are unhealthy.

I settle for a commonplace, casually tossed invitation for coffee. She replies she'll call me, but I doubt it will ever be arranged. Given what Linda said about keeping my distance, it's just as well. I make my goodbyes without unloading my prepared speech.

Later, I'm sitting at my desk, the last afternoon autumn light streaming through the window, when the phone rings. The caller ID blinks several times: Trina. My chest tightens as I pick up the call.

"Hello?"

"Tom?"

I recognize the young female voice on the other end at once—Sophie.

"It's me, honey. How're you?"

Sophie's voice is shaky. "Tom, Bumpers died." She bursts into tears, her breathing broken with deep, silent sobs.

"I'm so sorry, honey. When did it happen?"

I can hear her taking large gulps of air. "She got sick last night. We took her to the vet . . ." Her voice trails off into something unintelligible as the receiver moves away from her mouth. I can make out "kidney problems", between sobs.

"Sophie, honey?" I say, although she doesn't appear to hear me. "Sophie, honey?" I say a little louder.

She gulps again. This time her breathing slows, her sobs replaced by several short bursts of air into the phone.

"Sophie?" I ask gently.

"Yeah."

"You know Bumpers was a great cat, and he was lucky to have you to take care of him." This seems to calm her down. "Is your mom there?"

There's a shuffle and bump as Sophie carries the phone, followed by a brief conversation.

"Hello?" Trina's voice is clear and strong.

"Trina, Sophie seems—"

"I'm sorry for the phone call, Tom. When Bumpers died, you're the first person she wanted to call. She wouldn't leave me alone until I gave her the number."

"That's okay, I really don't—"

"Honestly, she was as upset about not talking to you as she was about Bumpers. I didn't want to compound the situation by refusing to let her talk to you."

In the months she's been gone, I've thought often about what brought us to the edge, what had taken what we'd had and finally broken its back.

"I'm sorry, Trina. It must be difficult for Sophie."

"It's been difficult for everyone, Tom," she says simply. There's a pause.

I realize then the free-floating anxiety over the previous weeks, which I've blamed on the case, Nora, work, has actually been adjusting to life without Trina and Sophie. I'm suddenly very tired.

"It has," I say, sighing.

After a couple of seconds, she asks, "How's your case going?" Her voice is open and soft. "You still working that Lake Forest thing?"

I laugh, despite myself. "I'm wading through a river of shit, Trina. The politics are making the whole thing difficult."

"You'll get through this, Tom, you always do. French dogshit, right?"

I laugh again. "Dogshit it is. I'm afraid if I don't arrest Edwards soon, I'm gonna lose my job. They want to close this thing before winter, if not sooner."

"Well, that gives you just over three weeks."

"Thanks for the reminder." There's another pause. I find myself searching for things to talk about just to keep her on the phone. I'm afraid she'll turn her phone off again.

After what seems like an eternity goes by, Trina says, "Dawn wants us out. I didn't like living with her as kids, and she isn't any better now."

"Do you have any plans?"

"I'm—" She falters for a second. "Well, I'm thinking about going to New York. There's a program in criminology at John Jay City University."

"You should follow up on that, Trina. You're too smart to be where you are."

"Thanks for the support," she says, flatly. I scramble, realizing she's misinterpreted what I said by trying to be supportive. I recognize she's been floating her departure to see how I'd react. In encouraging her, I've unintentionally rejected her. She's angry.

"Good luck with the case, Tom. I'll keep you posted," she says, trying to extricate as quickly as she can.

"Are you going to replace Bumpers?" I ask, grasping for a couple more minutes.

"Not right away. Getting pets in my life seems to come at a high price," she says, sighing deeply before hanging up.

. . .

I was never clear whether my mother died in her sleep, or if she called out and Ben was too drunk or hungover to respond. My father was out of the house on a job, and I was gone. Her autopsy showed she died of a massive myocardial infarction—heart attack.

After she was gone, if Ben had any grief over her passing, her death didn't seem to change anything. He fixed cars during the day and went out with the same four guys, to the same two bars, night after night. He made a brief run at engagement to a Polish girl in Chicago. After a few months, she simply disappeared and my brother refused to talk about it.

At Northwestern, confident with my new personality, I put my family far behind me, spending every nickel I had on clothes and, trying to look the part, went so far as to get a small signet ring. In the summer of my junior year, I landed an internship with an advertising agency in Chicago and looked forward to respectable employment once I graduated.

But as much as I'd worked to create myself, I couldn't rid myself of what I'd been, what I was. I could feel a growing dissonance between my two selves. My psyche, sounding like a minor second, refused to resolve. I knew I was, at some level, an imposter. At the beginning of my senior year my mood darkened further as I sought to quiet the discord and, withdrawing farther, resisted the efforts of friends, and even my girlfriend, Phoebe, to reach me. By that point, my academic record, which at first looked promising, amounted to a collection of incompletes and pass/no passes. I'd simply stopped caring.

There was a Christmas party at one of the fraternity houses, and, likely from a vestigial sense of obligation, Phoebe asked me to go. I'd agreed to meet her at her apartment at eight, but on some pretext I'd stopped by The Oaks Bar and Tavern, a cavernous warren of tables and chairs, its beer-logged floors rotted soft from decades of spillage. Over the previous months, I'd taken to spending afternoons, which turned into evenings, wedged into the dark corners of the bar.

I sat in a smoky corner, sifting through my petty grievances, among which were Phoebe's concerns about the time I spent in the bar. I viewed my time at The Oaks as entirely my own business. The minutes turned to hours, and I took notice of the time only when I saw the streetlights on my way back from the men's room.

I arrived at Phoebe's room at 9:00 to find she'd left for the party without me. As I started up the front steps to Phi Tau Epsilon, I saw her inside, talking to a cluster of her friends, surrounded by several frat brothers. I made my way through the front hall, my mouth dry and numb. Despite the time of year, my clothes felt hot and tight. The house, a beautiful Georgian manor, was carefully decorated in seasonal greens and large red bows. In the main parlor to the left, several dozen people jostled and laughed, cocktails in hand, under the twinkling, colored lights. Pushing my way over to where Phoebe stood, I saw the wide smile on her face deflate. She took three steps forward to intercept me.

"You're drunk and you're late," she whispered in my ear. I looked at her, mourning the loss of the smile which, just seconds earlier, lit up her face. She eyed me with a mixture of fear and what looked to me like pity.

"Tom, I think you should go home," she said, glancing behind me, where several frat brothers were watching.

The lurking feeling I was an outsider made me certain they were judging me. Scanning the room, what I saw confirmed my expectations until everything had only one interpretation. I grabbed Phoebe's arm, trying to pull her out of the room where we could talk alone, feeling a sudden need to connect with her.

"Tom, let go of my arm. You're hurting me," she said, pulling her arm away, her face hard and distant, a reasonable reaction given the circumstances. In the space of a second, Phoebe became one of them.

Her face softened after a second. "Please, Tom," she pleaded, and had I not been drunk, I might have detected the trace of remorse and sorrow in her face. Instead, I pulled harder at her.

"Let's get the fuck out of here." I yanked her arm.

This was enough for the three closest frat brothers to grab me by the arms. But I was quicker and angrier. Wrestling an arm free, I grabbed one by the hair and drove his face into a bookshelf three times. I kicked the other in the groin and dove on top of the third before six men got a hold on me and beat me unconscious.

■ ■ ■

The incident at Northwestern left me with a broken rib, two missing teeth, and statements from seventeen frat brothers that established me as the aggressor. One frat brother had surgery on his cheekbone and part of his jaw. Clear and decisive in its actions, the college sent a summary of its findings, as brief and elegant as haiku:

"Witnesses in support of Respondent Tom Edison: None."
I was summarily expelled one quarter short of attaining my
degree.

For reasons I never fully understood, the college
brokered a deal under which no criminal charges would be
brought. It may have been because two of the frat brothers
were on academic probation and weren't supposed to be
serving alcohol.

One condition of the agreement to forgo criminal
charges was my agreement to participate in what they
euphemistically called personal development counseling,
which was really county-run anger management.

The group sessions were held in a small grey office
building in downtown Springfield, where I'd come home
to stay. Twice weekly, I drove downtown to Fifth Street to
a tall building where I'd sit in a small airless room as I and
my fellow inductees exposed our bruised souls.

After sitting an hour and a half in a stiff steel chair,
I felt the unmistakable urge to urinate. The fluorescent
lights emitted a dull buzz, bathing the conference room in
light the color of dishwater. The walls of the windowless
room were hung with posters extolling simple commands:
"Accountability", "Denial", "Victimhood", "Rationalize."
In the center of the wall, the largest poster portrayed a
circle, bisected by arrows, in dark bold letters: "Break the
cycle of violence."

Across from me sat a man sporting four-day facial hair.
He wore a Detroit Tigers' cap with darkened edges at the
bill. Catching my eye, he lifted his right leg, emitting the
telltale squeak of escaping intestinal gas loud enough to
draw the attention of several other men.

To avoid any mistaken perception that I saw humor in

the gesture, I looked away. My gaze landed on a man in his late thirties with a dirty red beard, disintegrating blue jeans, and a greasy gray T-shirt. He stared furiously at the floor. His head was shaved, and one meaty bicep was tattooed with gothic numbers 88 in dull blue-grey ink. The numbers, the eighth letter of the alphabet—HH, or Heil Hitler—were supported by a swastika placed strategically below them. Armed with a sixth sense, or simply overactive paranoia, the Nazi's head sprung up and, like a Komodo dragon, he eyed me with dull, carnivorous interest.

At the other end of the room sat a balding man, his shining skull marked by red splotches. His heavy face was deeply cragged with dark lines, and he stared ahead, arms folded on his stomach, which jutted in front of him, scanning the room. Finally, his eyes fell on a thin dark-haired man in his forties who wore a yellow sports coat and shiny patent-leather shoes.

"Hector, what can you tell us about accountability?"

The man called Hector looked up, his expression somewhere between a smile and a sneer. He opened his black notebook and pulled out a single piece of paper with dense writing on both sides. From where I sat, the sentences appeared to join like wavy strings from the center, spokes on a wheel, in no particular order.

"Accountability is being sorry for what you done," he said, staring defiantly around the room to gauge the reception to this pearl of wisdom.

The balding man shook his head slowly. "Not just that, Hector. It's understanding we live in a male-dominated world and that we have to be responsible for male power." This comment was received by a discontented Greek chorus of groans and sighs of disbelief. Two chairs to his left, a guy muttered "fuckin' bullshit" under his breath. Hector put the single sheet in his notebook and waited for another salvo. The balding man pursed his lips and exhaled loudly.

"I'm not getting the sense you guys understand about the dynamics of male power. We're gonna have to do some more work on that."

The insistent pressure in my bladder reminded me I had to pee. I motioned to the bald man, pointing to the door, indicating the need to relieve myself. The man nodded, and I walked down the hall to the fetid men's room. Even three months after the night at Phi Tau, my mouth was still sore, my tongue snaking to explore the empty gaps which had been my bicuspids. I moved towards the line of urinals, my side still tender, my mouth tasting like burnt toast, bitter and full of charcoal. A strong surge of nausea rose in my throat, and I extended a hand against the cool tile to balance myself, fighting the urge to gag at the dank odor of cigarettes and stale, dried pee.

As I relieved myself, I considered my current situation and the fact I'd refused to plan for, or even acknowledge, the disaster which confronted me. I'd always seen myself as responsible for the successes in my life and studiously avoided the fact my actions, arrogance, and drunkenness had actually been the cause of heartache, especially with Phoebe. Standing at the urinal, I saw my denial clearly. I'd refused, like some intrepid homesteader, even as the air thickened with dust, to believe the volcano was erupting.

The warm glow of relief seeped through me as I finally understood fighting the volcano was futile, that life was a matter of dodging lava rivers or, sooner or later, I'd be reduced to cinders.

But even then, I held on to my secrets. The group was

hardly a safe setting and like the camp pastor, Father R., and any of a number of people I might have come clean with, I held fast to my belief the only person I could trust with who I really was, was me.

My career at Northwestern was over. I never heard from Phoebe again.

I went back to my parent's house, to the room next to Ben's, down the hall from my father. Phoebe was gone, just as the Polish girl vanished from Ben's life.

Lying in the same bed I'd occupied since I was five, I understood why Ben refused to talk about it.

CHAPTER TWENTY-ONE

I WEIGH LETTING THE AFFAIR WITH NORA SIMPLY DIE against my need for closure. The answer leads me back to the tanning salon, hoping to catch her there. The streetlights have just come on in the parking lot as I pull in front of Maui Tan Salon. The dusk casts light the color of clarified butter on the cars in the lot. A breeze, loaded with sesame oil and garlic from the Chinese takeout across the way, pushes leaves along the pavement.

Peering in the window, I can see Nora seated in a row of chairs at the back of the store, waiting for the next available booth. In the blue fluorescent light she looks drawn and grey, the shadows under her eyes purple and brown. Her wrists and ankles jut out of her robe, as knobby and prominent as hawthorn burls.

When I push the door open, she looks up, betraying her surprise. As I look around me, I have to admit I'm conflicted. I know fully well if I was asked to explain my presence to anyone wanting a serious accounting of me,

I would be at a loss. I've given into impulse, acting on a whim, with little consideration of the consequences. My decision to confront Nora is, at a minimum, poorly conceived and inappropriate.

A thin girl, hair dyed brassy chrome and silver, stands at the front counter, her skin an improbable mahogany and orange. She flips through a magazine. She watches, her eyes glassy and bright, as I walk back to take a seat next to Nora. With the skittish energy of a chipmunk, the girl scurries from behind the counter. I manage to reach Nora before she can intercept me. The girl utters a tenuous, "Can I help you?" just as I sit down. When I don't answer, she takes the silence as confirmation everything is okay, and trots back to her magazine.

I've just turned to face Nora when a second tanorexic, her skin the color of burnt sienna, emerges, towel in hand, fresh from wiping down the tanning beds. She looks older than the chipmunk, and her tank top hangs loosely on her frame. Her shorts, which are one size too small, cling to bony hips.

"You want to tan?" she asks me, eyeing my street clothes.

"I'm just here to talk to my friend." I smile, leaning towards Nora. The girl looks to Nora and starts to wipe down a tanning booth to her right. The smile drops from my face, and I lean in to whisper in Nora's ear, "I think you owe me an explanation."

Looking straight ahead, Nora says, "I can't talk to you, Tom." The girl with the towel watches from a distance.

Wanting to avoid a scene, I wink at the girl with the towel and say, "We're just talking." She nods and returns to lovingly cleaning the tanning bed.

"I need to talk to you about what's happened here."

The girl finishes wiping the tanning bed, signaling to Nora her bed is ready.

"You left without a word and disappeared for weeks. I just don't understand."

Nora remains silent. Her loose-fitting robe falls open to reveal the smooth plate of her chest and the dark outline of a purple bruise. She's fragile and exposed and as demure as a Renaissance Madonna. She pulls the robe together.

"How'd you get that?" I ask, pointing at her chest.

"I think, Tom, it would be best if you leave," she says, gesturing towards the front of the store. I'm sure Linda told you we shouldn't be seeing each other. I thought you were something different. I thought we had something different."

Her face is set, and she's withdrawn, defiant, and shuttered.

The girl with the towel pauses, trying unsuccessfully to look like she isn't eavesdropping.

Nettled, I decide to share the fact I was going to end it with her. "You should know I was going to tell you we need to cool things down. I'm getting a lot of heat at work. I just want to know why you disappeared."

She gets up from her chair, holding the lapel of her robe, seemingly oblivious to her surroundings, the lids of her eyes low and shaded. She pauses, considering my question. "Douala, Tom." She sidles past me and toward the front door.

I reach for her as she passes, catching her arm. Through the terrycloth, I feel thin tendons and bones. She winces and pulls her arm away.

"Douala? What kind of answer is that?"

She grabs her purse and throws twenty dollars on the counter, gathering her shoes and clothes in a small pile. Still in her robe, she opens the door and walks out.

She makes her way to her car and tosses the bundle onto the front seat, then climbs in. The engine roars to life and I watch as she speeds out of the parking lot.

■ ■ ■

That night, I awake suddenly from a dream. In the dream, I'm in the Caribbean. Sitting alone on a resort bus, thundering down the coast road, the open windows rattle, and the salty wind whips my face. Dressed in a blazer and slacks, I'm barefoot. Outside the windows, the edge plunges to an electric green-and-blue sea below, sharp and brilliant as a knife's edge. The bus stops at a hotel, where I'm greeted at the desk by a woman who could be Trina, Nora, or Katie—I'm not sure. The woman asks me for my passport. Reaching into my jacket, with a shot of fear I realize I've left the passport home. I look down and see I've come with nothing. I reach into my pants pocket and find a debit card. The woman at the desk assures me arrangements can be made at the consulate. I'm shoeless and without clothes or cash in a foreign country. The woman simply watches me from the desk.

At the back of the lobby, a pager sounds. The woman turns to answer, but it keeps sounding. She turns, pointing to a group of children sitting on a bench. The pager sounds again, and I wander over to the bench. Waiting for the bus to the consulate with the children, the windows to the hotel seem to have changed to aquarium glass. Tropical fish swim past in colorful schools. The sound of the pager at the reception desk is getting louder and more persistent.

I start awake, my heart racing. I check the time: 2:37 a.m. My cellphone is buzzing and I realize the pager in the dream is the phone. I can't tell how many times it has rung. I answer, but it's dead.

Sleep eludes me. Half an hour later, fatigue takes me, but syrupy thick sleep only comes in the early morning as light begins to show in the windows. There is no more blue sea.

■ ■ ■

After Northwestern and the anger management, I went into what therapists call "deep situational depression." Ben welcomed me home, a fallen Icarus, knowing I'd flown too close to the sun. I never sensed he felt any satisfaction in my circumstances, just confirmation of his belief that anything or anyone reaching for the heights will inevitably fail.

Two months later, I got a job working in an engineering firm, processing blueprints. The work was tedious and low-paying, but it got me around the city. I delivered plans for projects to various construction companies in greater Chicago. One day, after about a year, I delivered a set to an architect's office on East Van Buren. The project manager's assistant was a pretty auburn-haired woman in her mid-twenties. The promise of a six-pack to the company's plans' clerk got me three more visits to the firm, which was enough. Although still recovering from Northwestern, something about Katie's blunt delivery and frank sexuality attracted me. Over dinner, I told her I was attending community college, which wasn't even half true because, while I intended to go, I hadn't applied. We ended up drunk in the apartment she shared with three other girls, and we fooled around on her bed. We dated for a year. I applied to the community college, eventually enrolling in the police academy—in Springfield of all places. Katie was my drinking pal and my cheerleading section. We got engaged, married, and quietly, without discussion, I got sober, figuring I owed it to her if we were going to work. What no one told me is that when you get sober and your wife is your drinking buddy, you've changed all the rules. I never asked Katie if she understood I wasn't changing much—just everything.

■ ■ ■

I've been at the office several hours when Larry's broad, sullen face, his eyes lidded and red, peers into my office. He tosses a sheaf of paper on the desk.

"What's this?" I ask, irritated.

"We got a CODIS hit on the blood from the fence. I cross-referenced again with Corrections and Armed Services. We ran it before, but for some reason, Corrections didn't have it on their primary index. This time, they did. Eduardo Rivera. What's strange is that Rivera's been in Menard for the last six years for aggravated assault."

At last, Larry's getting some vindication for the elusive DNA results, yet he seems distracted and somewhere distant. He's found excuses to miss the weekly pilgrimage to Buddy's Barbecue which, even after our run-in, trumped all other differences. We'd sit there, our fingers dripping with Buddy's Three Strikes Sauce, and make small talk. Recently, Larry's been pleading a prior obligation and opting out.

"Everything okay, Larry? We good?"

"Uh-huh," he grunts, flopping into the chair in front of me.

I can see plainly everything is not okay. His face is smudged with a two-day beard, and he looks like he hasn't slept in a couple of days.

As if he can hear me silently inventorying him, Larry looks at his shirt cuffs and strokes his face. A proud, even arrogant man, he seems to take a perverse pride in his bad behavior, which I think he sees as independence of spirit—a latter-day Shane. Yet he's definitely struggling, with scant reserves of bravado, to look good.

"C'mon, Larry, don't bullshit me."

He looks up, his eyes narrowing in defiance, staring for several seconds, before finally slumping in the chair. "Do you know what tomorrow is, Tom?"

I search my memory. It will be a Saturday in late September, one of the last fine-weather weekends. Several weeks earlier, I'd made plans with Nora to travel up to the lake for that weekend, which is now as irrelevant and vestigial as last week's sports' section. Suddenly, it hits me. This is the weekend Larry's daughter is getting married.

"I'm so sorry, Larry." I consider inviting him to do something with my newly destroyed weekend, imagining Larry sitting in his apartment alone, picturing his daughter's wedding a thousand miles away. I think about what two days straight with Larry would look like and check myself from making the offer, but not without feeling conflicted.

Larry looks at me. "It's alright, Tom. I'm sure I'll get a phone call." He looks away, starting again for the hallway, and stopping at the door. "Rivera's out—released on probation last spring. His P.O. hasn't seen him in weeks."

Grateful for the change in subject, I say, "He was reporting to a P.O.?"

"He was on some kind of medical probation, psych-care thing."

"Was he working?"

"At the Cook County Sanitary Transfer Station in a garbage line."

"Put him in the system and let's see if we can find him."

Stumbling to find words, we let silence fall. After a few seconds I say, "Larry, if you need to talk, you know where to find me."

He nods and turns, padding to his office and closing the door.

■ ■ ■

As we enter October, we complete interviews of all the acquaintances, vendors, and staff of the Wesleys, which gives us little, other than confirming Faith Wesley was a woman who kept people at arm's length and who could alternately be charming or a bitch. I have Larry follow up with Satterman about Frances Reynolds, the housekeeper, who was in England when Faith was killed. I calendared her return in early September. With the murder, the Wesleys allowed her an extra month in England before returning. She's been back a few weeks, and it's clear she's been avoiding me. Finally, after Larry pushed Satterman, Frances calls, making it clear the meeting is a great inconvenience. As a concession, I agree to meet her at a local Starbucks. Her interview is largely a formality, although I want to ask her about the night Linda attacked

Faith. The report said Frances was the one who called the assault in.

I recognize her immediately: a sturdy woman in her early sixties, steel-gray hair pulled back and pinned in a tight bun. She bears a strong resemblance to Agnes Moorhead. Her cold blue eyes are framed by horn-rimmed glasses. She wears an immaculate white blouse framed by a deep blue cardigan and a grey flannel skirt.

She's seated at a corner table, and as I approach, rises briefly. I gesture for her to sit, and she returns to slowly stirring a large cup of hot water, a tea bag dangling from the side. I go over the preliminaries and apologize for inconveniencing her.

"I've been attending to the hoose since ah got back," she says in an accent as thick as Yorkshire pudding.

"Mrs. Reynolds, I—"

"Miss Reynolds," she says quickly.

Over the loudspeaker, the barista announces a double decaf soy latte. Miss Reynolds winces at the noise. "You were in England when Mrs. Wesley was killed."

"Ah was," she says, frowning.

Picking a piece of blue lint off the sleeve of her cardigan, she then continues to stir the tea with precise, circular movements. After a few more turns, she places the spoon on the napkin setting next to the cup.

"You were there the night Linda assaulted Faith Wesley."

She inhales sharply, as if stuck with a hatpin, and looks around, possibly searching for an exit. "How dreadful," she says after a few seconds, picking up the cup.

"You called in the assault."

She nods, craning her head forward in a slow droop

to take a careful sip. She stares for several seconds out to the sidewalk, lost in a different time and place. Gently, she places the cup on the table and picks up her napkin and begins to fold it. "Ah told the police everything, I—"

The outside door flies open like a rodeo chute, and three teenage girls and two boys spill into the store. As a group, they rush to the counter, placing their orders, barking and hooting. I notice, despite the fall weather, the girls' tank tops cling to their slender bodies. One of the boys playfully slaps a girl on the behind, making her howl with laughter. Frances catches me watching the teenagers, pursing her lips in disapproval.

"Those two were like that, you know," she says.

"Those two?"

"Linda and Nora."

"Like that?" I say, nodding towards the girls.

Taking another sip of her tea, she pauses. "Loud, out of control," she says. She eyes me, waiting for my next question. It's clear she's remained employed with the Wesleys for thirty years more for her deep feudal sense of loyalty than for any ability to polish the silver. I ask her about her time with the Wesleys and if she noticed anything unusual about Faith Wesley before she left.

Frances glares at the kids, who by now have managed to completely bar access to the cashier. Finally, they leave as suddenly as they arrived, landing at a table outside. The store returns to a low friendly hum of conversation, comforting and narcotic.

"Was there anyone at the house at the time? Living there, I mean."

Her face darkens, her mouth drawing into a tight sneer. "The Hispanics," she hisses.

"You mean the Moraleses?"

"Alma, Jesus, and her brother—I can't remember his name . . ." She pauses. "I don't remember much of anything. I told your man," she sighs with exasperation, "that I made the report because I found Mrs. Wesley on the floor."

"Was Linda in the house when you got to Faith Wesley?"

"Yes, but I got her to leave. She'd been out with the other one. She was pissed."

"You mean she was angry?"

"No, she was drunk—pissed," she says, resorting to English slang. I'm surprised to hear her use vulgarity.

"Do you know what the fight was about?"

She brings the cup to her lips and stares at me, finishing the last of the tea. She carefully wraps the tea bag in the napkin and puts the folded package into the cup. "I remember two things about that night. Linda was drunker than I'd ever seen her." She stops, as if considering whether to share the next part.

"And?"

Frances' lip curls, summoning the last vestiges of goodwill she can muster. "Linda kept yelling at her mother about some man. I'd always assumed they were fighting about a college boyfriend."

"Do you remember the name?"

"Strang or Stratz or something"

"Strauss?"

"Something like that. It wasn't my business."

"Did you ever ask Faith or Linda about it?"

She glares at me, her expression shifting from distaste to frank disbelief. "As I said, it wasn't my business."

The genial buzz is shattered by the sound of glass and stainless steel hitting the floor, causing Frances to jump. A server bends quickly behind the counter to gather the dishes she's dropped.

Frances rises quickly to leave. "I'm afraid I don't know anything more," she says, picking up her cup.

"Did Faith Wesley ever talk about the fight with you?"

She takes a deep breath and, appearing as if she's struggling to hold on to her temper, says, "I'm not sure how many times I can say this, detective. It wasn't my business." Sensing I'm not going to be put off, she says, just above a whisper. "A few days later, Mrs. Wesley thanked me for calling the police and asked if I would please not discuss the incident with anyone. I've honored her request. She's gone, and you are the police."

She places the paper cup into a plastic bin as she walks out, narrowly missing two of the teenagers cavorting outside.

CHAPTER TWENTY-TWO

L ARRY AND THE INTERNS MANAGE TO GET THROUGH all the records, which are copied, the account numbers marked and traced. I ask Shahbaz to set up a meeting with Charles Wesley to discuss the accounts. Satterman balks until Tony threatens to bring the whole mess back to Wardman again.

We rise to the seventy-fifth floor in the Standard Oil Building, and I can feel the air pressure change as the fine wood veneer and etched steelwork whisks us skyward. The doors open to deposit us at STEW. We are greeted by the smiling face of a stunning blonde woman.

A few minutes later, we're in an oak-paneled conference room, dominated by portraits of Thomas Fleers Stanhope and Lamar Thornton. As we wait, Tony tells me about the firm's history. Stanhope's face, a ruddy mitt of imperious determination, glares from one end of the room. A century ago, before the age of forty-five, Stanhope brokered deals in transportation, textiles, steel, and meat. His grit, along with legendary sangfroid and a preternatural ability to ride the political tide, got him appointed to the newly created Federal Trade Commission. In making the appointment, Woodrow Wilson famously observed he'd rather have the biggest rascal alive writing the rules than breaking them. With the resulting regulations, Stanhope got his clients huge profits, while everyone else was three steps behind, figuring out the loopholes.

Lamar Thornton stares from the other end, frozen in a look of remote disdain. Thornton made his reputation, and the firm's real fortune, as an unapologetic union buster. Thornton's fights with labor began with the 1927 Columbine Mine Massacre and ran through Truman's seizure of the steel mills in the 1950s. Lamar's contribution is described on the firm's website as having "a distinguished history of supporting the corporate community."

The next generation who's keeping the balance sheet tilted to the right, enters the conference room, accompanied by Charles Wesley. Satterman extends a manicured hand and offers us coffee and water. I feel like I've been admitted to an exclusive men's club, but only as a guest, and only for a short while. I decline the beverages and immediately pull out the summaries.

I push the stack across the table. "Strange as this may sound, Mr. Wesley, I'm actually trying to figure out the motive for your wife's murder. The deeper I've gone into this, the more resistance I'm getting from you."

As soon as Charles starts to speak, hands folded in front of him on the table, Satterman tries to stop him, raising a hand. Glaring at his lawyer, Wesley pushes the hand to one side and takes a breath. "I'm exhausted, Tom. My household is a fortress. My wife was brutally murdered and two members of my house staff have been savagely shot and killed, yet here we are, months later . . ."

Satterman exhales, clearly upset his client has chosen to ignore him. He turns the summaries so Wesley can see them. I run through the Charitable Remainder Trusts and then through several Credit Shelter Trusts and the Economic Benefit Trust. We turn finally to the Wesley Family Trusts.

"These trusts," explains Satterman, "allow assets for the benefit of the Wesleys, accessible to the family, but without tax implications.

"What's the purpose?"

"Essentially, living expenses, education, housing, transportation, clothing, medical care," explains Satterman.

"Who decides? "

"The trustee."

"And who's that?"

"Our firm—Mr. Webb."

"So, any expense—a new house, a new car, or clothing—anything defined as a necessity is proper under the trust as long as it is paid to the beneficiaries?"

"Correct," says Satterman.

"That could include vacations, second homes, yachts, as long as they are deemed a necessity?"

Satterman shifts. "Let's say it substantially avoids taxation on a major part of the assets."

"Who are the beneficiaries?" I ask.

"The beneficiaries are, or should I say were, Faith and Charles Wesley. Linda and Emma are successor trustees and beneficiaries."

"What does that mean?"

Satterman looks at Charles, rolling his eyes as if to

say he could have anticipated questions like this. "When Charles—Mr. Wesley—dies, the funds and property are disbursed, according to the terms of the trust, to Linda and Emma. There's no probate. It's never in court," he adds, as if I don't know what avoiding probate means.

Wesley reviews the list while we talk.

I point to a line on the summary. "Take a look at NAST. It seems crazy to have money like that in a non-interest-bearing account." The account has over two-and-half-million dollars, liquid, in it. "Not even in a money market fund. Do you have any idea who set it up?"

Wesley says, "The only person who could have done that was Faith." He places the sheaf on the table.

"Do you have any idea why she might have set this up?" Tony asks. Up to this point, he's been largely silent.

"None." I can see Charles is either a good actor, or he's genuinely perplexed by the account.

"Would you excuse us for a minute?" Satterman asks. I nod and Satterman and Charles leave the room.

Several minutes later, they reappear. Satterman doesn't bother to sit.

"We'll call the bank this afternoon."

"Will you represent to us we've received all the outstanding accounts?" Tony asks.

Satterman shrugs. "We don't know anything about this account. We can't promise what we don't know."

I'm getting tired of the runaround, and I think it may be time to go back to Wardman. "Will you represent to us there aren't any other accounts like this one?" I say, pointing at the NAST statement. "I really don't want to go back to the judge again."

Satterman appears to consider what another visit to the

judge might look like. He sits back in his chair. He looks at Charles, who nods. "That's the only one."

"If you get the account statements to us by this afternoon, we've got a deal."

■ ■ ■

After the CODIS hit, forensically at least, Rivera is the prime suspect.

Rivera certainly fits. He has a history of violence and was just released from Menard on probation. With Rivera placed at the scene, the case now consists mostly of finding him, which could be a matter of hours or days.

One Edwards' loose end is Sam Farinelli, the lawyer in Ainsworth's divorce case. To me, it's entirely a waste of time, but Delahunt says until we find Rivera, Edwards remains a Person of Interest. According to the Illinois State Bar Association, Farinelli is inactive and has no forwarding address. After some digging, Larry manages to find an S. Farinelli operating a tour boat on the lake.

I dial the number and a voice answers, thick with sleep and cigarettes. I identify myself, asking if he's the guy who represented Judy Ainsworth in a divorce proceeding. In the background I hear repeating high-pitched beeps, like a truck backing up.

"I'm retired. That case was years go. I can't talk to you because of the attorney client privilege." I can hear the truck stop.

"I want to know about Stark. He's part of a case I'm working, and I think he's got a lot to answer for."

Farinelli tells me to meet him at the Waukegan Municipal Marina in an hour.

The Waukegan Marina parking lot is mostly empty, and in the early fall, strangely quiet. A cold breeze carries fried onions, diesel, and cigarettes. The asphalt is scarred from decades of boat trailers missing the ramp. A grimy sign advertising Dockside Dogs swings loosely over a man in his late fifties with a large handlebar mustache. I have to think this is Farinelli.

Seeing me, he folds a newspaper and rises to meet me. Even though it is fall, Sam wears a Hawaiian shirt. He crumples a paper bag, all that remains of his hot dog, and extends a hand. He's easily seven inches taller than I am. I take the proffered hand, and I can feel the hot dog grease in my palm.

"You know, I buried this thing when I left the practice," he says, shaking his head.

"I only want to know about Stark."

He gestures to a long building at the other end of the lot. "Look, I gotta get some stuff in there," he says, signaling for me to walk with him. "I've got a charter leaving in an hour and I need to provision."

"Why are you running out on the lake this late in the season?"

We enter a long single-story building at the edge of the lot. A faded sign lists a series of businesses: Northern Marine, First Mate Yacht Detailing, S&J Boats, and Augie's Bait and Tackle.

Sam shakes his head. "The second lake trout and fall steelhead season runs from now to late November. Great fishing, but not for the faint of heart."

We reach Augie's, where Sam opens the door, unleashing an oily waft of fish roe and stinkbait. Sitting at the counter, a heavy man in a greasy sweatshirt leafs through a magazine, a wet nub of half-smoked cigar stuck in his face. Over his head, large stuffed pike and muskies are mounted on wooden boards. The guy greets Sam by name. Sam asks for three boxes of cut bait and a dozen spinning spoons. The man disappears behind the sheet nailed over the doorframe behind him.

With the man gone, Sam turns to me, removing his sunglasses. His eyes are bloodshot and sad. "I should've known better than to take that case in the first place."

"Why did you?"

"Because Ellen was a friend of my wife's and no one else would take it because Ainsworth was a sitting judge."

The man returns with three large Chinese food containers and a handful of shiny silver spinners. Sam takes out a wad of cash and throws several bills on the counter, gathers the merchandise, and heads towards the door.

Outside in the corridor, he motions again to walk in the other direction towards a bench in a deserted area of the dimly-lit hall. The fluorescent lights pulse unevenly, lighting the hall with a brief surge, and then just as quickly die.

Sam sits on the bench, extracts a small flask, and offers me a pull, which I decline.

He's quiet as he allows the liquor to smooth the edges. Suddenly, he leans in, his breath heavy and sweet with the smell of alcohol. "Ainsworth is a jerk. He's an angry, controlling jerk. But that's as far as it went. Bill Stark is the reason I even agreed to talk to you."

He takes another long pull from the flask. "You know, I went to John Marshall at night for four years, got my law degree, and supported my family. I thought what I was doing was actually serving the families I represented. The system would take care of the problems because that's what it is designed to do, right?" He shrugs, pulling another slug.

"I guess."

"You a reader, Tom?" The alcohol smell is stronger, and Farinelli is drunk enough that his charter passengers will notice.

"I like to read."

"Ever read *Billy Budd*?"

"Melville. Sure, in school."

"Claggart, the master at arms, 'rabies of the heart', that's Stark."

"That's a little harsh, don't you think?"

He takes another pull. "Not at all. I had over twenty cases in the last fifteen years where Stark was involved. The thing I loathe in him is that he's deeply corrupt—I don't mean simply cash-register corrupt—I can't prove that, but I suspect it. I mean he's gamed the system. Christ, he *is* the system. He runs the merry-go-round—custody cases, jail cases, state boards, committees, all like some croupier taking chips as the roulette wheel turns."

Looking at his flask, Sam seems to realize he's visibly intoxicated. He screws the top on the flask and stows it in his vest. "I know for a fact he ran field tests on inmates at DOC. He oversaw pharmaceutical trials comparing atypical antipsychotics on inmates. At least one inmate committed suicide. Turns out the inmate was forced to choose between enrolling in the study or being involuntarily committed indefinitely to a state mental institution. Later, during the investigation, it turned out Stark was paid as a 'consultant' to the drug company for overseeing the study. That's Stark—he makes money and people end up dead."

He shifts on the bench. "I don't know what you're

looking into that involves him, but you can be sure Stark's dirty. On Ellen's case, I tried to get him removed because he'd handled prior evaluations on Ainsworth's cases. I was told if I ever filed a motion against Stark again, I'd see myself disbarred." I remember what Lent's lawyer, Schumer, told me about his experience trying to get Stark removed.

Sam glances at his watch. "I gotta go." He grabs the bag with the spoons and dons his sunglasses in the dark hallway. Out in the lot, he heads over to an aging Ford pickup with Sam's Guided Charters painted on the side in faded white. He gives the truck four turns of the starter before a cloud of oily exhaust signals the engine has been throttled back to life.

■ ■ ■

I'm headed back towards the office when my phone rings. The caller ID says Chicago North.

"We got another piñata for ya." Manny Gorak's voice blares from the earpiece.

"Piñata?"

"You were running CODIS on the same skell as us."

"Who?"

"Eddie Rivera. It took us a while to make him. I pulled it because of the Morales' connection."

"What? Where did you find him?"

"Southside. Fuller Park. He's a gasper."

"What?"

"A freak. Looks like he was wasted. We found him naked in a meth bando with his pecker in his hand, rope tied to the bed and a plastic bag over his head. Looks like he tapped off before the big show, though." Manny starts to laugh.

"Manny, is something funny?" I ask him, not really expecting an answer. I ask if they've moved the body. He tells me Rivera's at Cook County, and he certainly isn't going anywhere.

He lowers his voice, and says, "Listen, I figure we got some kind of weird drug connection between the Moraleses and this Rivera guy."

"I thought you said you figured it for a drug deal gone bad? Is there any connection at all?"

Manny chuckles. "Well, you know, Moraleses working in Lake Forest, Rivera breaking in and whacking somebody. I figure he whacked them after he screwed the robbery."

Much as I hate to admit it, Manny's theory almost has legs. I can imagine some kind of "weird drug thing" where Rivera goes up to Lake Forest for a B and E, runs into Faith and kills her because she's out looking at her roses and spots him.

"So, you think Eddie knows about Lake Forest and Faith Wesley because somehow he knows the Moraleses?"

Manny considers this for a moment. "Seems that way. You know, them people settle things their own way. Rivera goes up there to kill them for whatever reason. He kills Faith Wesley instead."

"Later he kills the Moraleses and now he's a gasper?"

"Looks like it. I don't know." Manny really doesn't seem to care. I can tell he isn't going to expend a lot of effort getting to the bottom of this.

"Where'd you find him again?"

"Fuller Park. In a dive near the corner of Root and Wells."

■ ■ ■

With Nora gone, and Trina headed for parts unknown, I'm adrift. In my search for an identity, I've tried to find myself in others—usually women—catalyzing my emotions, memories, and history into a new psyche. I've sought to lose myself in each new lover. The things they loved, I loved, their pasts became my past, the places they lived became sacred spaces imbued with meaning. With the current objects of desire lost, I am left with nothing, like grasping a handful of water. Being alone terrifies me.

I'm confronted with the process of looking at myself, of acquiring in middle age that elusive quarry: self-knowledge. Between waves of regret and self-pity, I can see I may be gaining some self-awareness.

Returning to my apartment, I'm greeted by the unmistakable smell of paella, a heady Spanish seafood stew. One of my favorites. The shellfish, lobster, and scallops, cooked in a broth of saffron, wine, and tomatoes, are served over a bed of flavored rice. There's only one person I know who makes a paella like this.

Trina stands at the kitchen door. I look at her for several beats, saying nothing, tangled in non-comprehension. She waves a kitchen spoon at me. "You didn't change the locks."

"Where's Sophie?"

"With my sister."

"Trina—"

She takes me by the arm and leads me to the dining room table, which is set for two. "Let's just have dinner tonight. Eat and stop talking."

After she serves up a bowl of paella, I spend the rest of

the evening relearning what I've forgotten about Trina.

Later, in the middle of the night, I lie awake, engrossed in relationship calculus. My father liked Trina and said she brought out the good parts in me. Four years ago, the old man was diagnosed with lung cancer. Just before he died, he asked why I didn't marry Trina. At the time, I gave a flip answer about how I was done with marriage.

Sitting in the dim living room, attached to green oxygen tanks and plastic tubing, my father told me that in the sixties he'd had a girlfriend who loved to go to the movies. One night, they'd gone to see an art-house movie. The plot was simple: a man and woman fall in love. The problem is, they're married to other people. They have no money and no future together. Love can only exist if they commit mutual suicide. They do. End of movie.

Coming out of the movie, my father's date dabbed her eyes, asking whether he thought the movie was great. Lying, he said it was, thinking to himself it was the biggest piece of sentimental crap he'd ever seen.

Several months later, Donna, or whatever her name was, was gone. Shortly after, he had a dinner date with another girl. He gave her the test, and asked if she'd seen the movie. "It's the biggest piece of garbage I've ever seen," she said. He told me that's when he knew he'd found his soulmate. The dinner date was my mother.

By the time my father died in hospice, I still hadn't proposed to Trina. Now, lying in bed next to her, I realize what I lost—and I let her go over a cat.

CHAPTER TWENTY-THREE

I WAKE TO THE SOUND OF TRINA WASHING DISHES. The clock says six-thirty. I move down the hall, where early morning sunlight filters through the blinds, painting the kitchen in golds and yellows. Other than the sound of the water in the sink, the room is quiet and suspended in serenity. As I sit down at the table to a glass of juice, Trina turns from the kitchen sink to face me. Her expression is soft, and briefly she smiles, but then settles into something less. I watch her struggling and get up from my seat to hold her by the shoulders.

She starts to cry and mumbles, "I want to keep last night separate." She looks at me, her features a pastiche of hope and regret. "I'm trying to see what's right for me." She takes several breaths, stammering, "I got—I got accepted to the criminal justice program in New York."

I flinch, feeling sick, and suddenly at sea.

"Is this your way of getting back at me? Coming here and then hitting me with this the first thing in the morning?"

She sits down at the table, folding her arms. "I wanted to see if I had what it takes to get in." She smiles, and in that moment I understand and feel a surge of love and affection for her.

I sit next to her, reaching for my glass, swirling what is left of the juice. "I can't figure you out. I'm about to tell you I've missed you, that I've made a mistake, and now you're here telling me you're going to New York."

Her eyes darken, as her face folds into a frown. "I feel closer to you after all of this," she says, waving her hand at the kitchen, "than I've felt in months. Being with you like this is great. It's doing the business of life; it's the other stuff that's impossible."

I have to agree with her. Dealing with the business of life is like sand in the gears of our relationship. She shifts in her seat and leans closer. "I don't want to put Sophie through something like this again. I'm sure you agree it's not in Liam's best interests either."

I start to talk, drawing breath in—and then stop. I can see Trina bracing for a speech. I shake my head. "You know, you're right. It wouldn't be fair to either of the kids to get them involved while everything's up in the air. Have you made the decision to go?"

For a few seconds, the room is completely quiet, the small ticking of the quartz clock over the stove beating in the stillness. "I'm going to New York next week to scout out schools for Sophie."

"What's this about then?" I ask, gesturing to the two of us. "Was this just one for old time's sake?"

Trina shakes her head, rising from her seat, then kneels next to me. "Since I've been up with my sister, I've gotten

some clarity. I see we're good for each other, but we both
have a lot of work to do. I'm going to work on myself.
This," she says taking hold of my hand, "is about having
a door open and letting you know I'm going through it. If
I didn't care about you—didn't love you—I'd simply walk
out. I'm walking in a different direction and it's up to you
to decide if you want to follow."

■ ■ ■

She stays another day. As she leaves, standing at the open
door of her car, she hands me a small book: "It's Rilke.
One of your favorites. Read the page I've marked. He says
it better than I ever could."

I watch the taillights disappear into the late summer
evening and can't recall having ever felt so lonely.

Back in the apartment, I open the book to the place
she's marked with a yellow sticky.

Do you know, I would quietly
slip from the loud circle,
when first I know the pale
stars above the oaks
are blooming.
Ways will I elect
that seldom any tread
in pale evening meadows—
and no dream but this:
You come too.

■ ■ ■

The envelope is hand-delivered from Satterman's office with the accounts from North American Savings and Trust. I've just ripped the edge of the envelope when a tall, thin, blond-haired man steps into my office.

"Detective Edison?" he says, flashing a badge. "I'm Gerry Novak with IAD. Do you have a few minutes?" I'm sure Novak is used to seeing people flinch when he shows up and probably even enjoys it. I'm sure he's here to see me about Nora.

"What can I do for you?" I motion for him to sit, trying not to betray my fear. "Normally we go through formal channels, don't we?"

Novak shakes his head, and remains standing. "Larry Welk work for you?"

My first instinct is that Larry has settled our beef by going to IAD. I push back. "You know he does, or you wouldn't be here. What's wrong?" I swallow twice, waiting for Novak to drop me.

"Larry's over at Vista Medical Center in ICU. Wrapped his car around a phone pole early Sunday morning. His BAC was point two three, just short of severe alcohol poisoning."

"So why are you here?" I ask, settling back into my chair.

"We heard something about a gun and booze in his drawer. You know anything about that?"

Larry is lying broken in the hospital, and I sit there knowing I dodged the simple task of being available when he needed someone to talk to.

"Did he do it intentionally, or was it a mistake?"

"Too early to tell. We just know he's had a number of problems and I'm following up."

I wonder how Novak learned about Larry's gun, when I didn't tell Delahunt. It's possible someone else in the office has been snooping around in Larry's desk. He hasn't won any popularity contests in Major Crimes. "Does his family know about the accident?"

"We called his daughter yesterday afternoon. Son-in-law called last night. Some kind of family gathering. Someone's coming up day after tomorrow."

"Did you know about booze or a gun?" he asks again, pressing the question.

"Nope." I know if Novak asked Delahunt, he's denied it as well.

"He ever threaten to take himself out?"

"Not at all."

"Uh-huh." Novak nods slowly. He pauses, letting the sound of the radio in the next office fill the dead air. Finally, he asks me to call if I remember anything. He turns quickly and walks down the hall towards the elevator like a man used to having people happy to see him go.

Watching him leave, I suddenly feel the full weight of my culpability for Nora. With that clarity, I fully understand that in pursuing Nora I've been blinded by my own appetites. I've sifted out only things I wanted to believe; that Larry was disloyal, for one. Now, it looks as though Larry was not only loyal, but reached out for help, and, finding it too awkward, I simply walked way.

I reach for the NAST envelope that lies open on the desk. I notice two stapled sheets, partially hidden by the NAST envelope, written in Larry's distinctive handwriting.

Friday September 30th

Tom. Stuff came in on Rivera from the Mexican

consulate. I know you were scheduled to talk to Gorak yesterday. This should shed some light on who Eddie Rivera was.

The consulate request was for the Moraleses and I pause, puzzled. As soon as I finish the first sentence, I understand. Alma's maiden name was Rivera. Her brother or brothers would have been named Rivera . . . one of whom was Eduardo Rivera.

The consulate called Friday afternoon about Alma and Jesus Morales. It turns out Alma Morales' full name was Alma Morales Rivera. Not being from parts south, you probably don't know Mexicans use a Spanish naming convention. To everyone, she was known as Alma Morales Rivera. In the1970s she came up to the States on a temporary visa in search of her younger brother who left Mexico a couple of years earlier.

According to Miguel Rivera, Alma's brother in Guadalajara, Eddie was the youngest of three children. Alma was the oldest. The father abandoned the family when Eddie was about two. They were living dirt-poor in Chiapas. The cops were called in multiple times for assaults which involved the step-dad and, in particular, Eddie. Eddie was arrested for beating his stepfather unconscious. When he was released he took off and ended up in San Diego working in the shipyards. According to Miguel, he was living in an abandoned shipping container and strung out on heroin. Alma and Jesus travelled to the states on a tourist visa, found Eddie in San Diego, and tried to

*bring him back. By the early eighties the three of them
ended up in Chicago, where Jesus had a line on a job.
Alma and Jesus start working for a family, which I'll
bet are the Wesleys.*

*About ten years later, Eddie was arrested again for
assault, this time on a coworker. He does time in
Menard. By the time Eddie returns from Menard
in 1999, he's strung out on heroin, delusional, and
paranoid. He drops below the radar for more than a
decade until 2008 when he almost kills a guy in a
bar on the South Side and is charged with attempted
murder. He pleads to Ag Assault and, because of his
record, gets fifteen to life, with the possibility of parole
after ten years.*

*Eddie was released at the end of last year on a
conditional probation program through DOC and was
able to find work at the sanitation transfer yard.*

*Tom, I'm not sure if we'll get a chance to talk about
this stuff personally. My mother used to say the worm
is the only animal which can't fall down. I'm feeling
pretty low right now, and I think she might have
been wrong. I wanted you to know I've really enjoyed
working with you.*

Good luck.
Larry

I place the NAST envelope on the desk and leave the
office.

. . .

It's a study in contrast: shining aluminum, bright lighting reflecting off stainless steel, white plastic and bleached cotton, disposable paper, and bandages, all set off against the dark purples, browns, and reds of Larry's bruised face. He's lying on his back, and I can see his right eye is swollen completely shut. Under the tape on his right cheek, I can make out the dark outline of stitches where his face was sliced open.

The room is bisected by a white, half-drawn curtain. The other half of the room sets in darkness, punctuated by the sound of a TV. The low squawks of the intercom, the whisper of the ventilator in the next bed, and talk out in the hall all blend into a low ambient roar like the seaside. Against this, the ascending tones of the LCD beat a syncopated rhythm over the hum.

A thin white crust of dried saliva coats Larry's mouth and cracked lips. He's awake, and tries to sit up, grimacing in pain, stiff with ungainly intention like a bad mummy movie.

I stick my hand out. "Larry, please don't try to get up."

He ignores me, eventually propping himself on his elbow, struggling without much success to leverage his body against the rail guards. I move to help him, but Larry raises his hand and, after several seconds, he's succeeded only in rolling himself against the rail. Flailing, he throws his bruised arm over the edge like a man trying to hoist himself into a lifeboat. He gives up struggling and gestures to a chair next to the bed so I'll sit down.

I survey the small area, seeing no sign anyone besides me has visited. Larry, drained by the effort to prop himself up, motions me to come closer.

"I'm sorry," he says, his breath close and sour.

I draw away. "Nothing to be sorry about. I'm sorry I didn't remember about this weekend."

Clinging to the metal rail, Larry points to a long plastic tube snaking out of the blankets. It's filled with dark amber fluid: urine. Connected and dependent, he looks haunted and old.

"Careful," he whispers, his voice dry as chalk, "to drain the fluid." He leans back on the pillow and breathes deeply. "I used to be a lawyer in Texas," he says, as much as a question as a fact. "Ever wonder why I'm not practicing anymore?"

I look at him, pilloried on the railing.

"Not now Larry, really—enough."

He draws a thin smile. "Tom, no time like the present. That shit back in Austin ain't why I left Texas. The judge's wife and all that was more for show than anything else. I needed a reason to go. Call it assisted suicide," he says.

The room smells strongly of piss and disinfectant. Larry shifts again and takes another deep breath.

"One day in '14 I got a call from a guy I'd represented several times on possession charges. He'd never had more than a few grams and they never managed to make it stick . . . thought I was a fucking genius. But this time he wasn't calling for himself. He had a cousin who'd gotten pinched down in Dryden on a murder rap. I tried to put him off. I didn't want to bother driving four-hundred miles to pick up a case for the scumbag relative of a small-time dealer."

A tall dark-skinned woman carrying a clipboard and tray strides into the room and, without comment, lowers the rail. She eyes me like I'm a disobedient kindergartner. She lifts Larry by his good arm and pushes him back onto the bed. With stunning efficiency, she checks the line running out of the blankets, disentangles IV bags and the LCD, then writes briskly on the clipboard.

"Please don't tire him out," she says, leaving as quickly as she came.

Larry tries to lift himself again, but whatever reserves he once possessed to overcome the pain are now depleted. He collapses like a stuffed doll, staring at the ceiling.

"Larry, please don't. She said you shouldn't tire yourself."

He winces, and takes a long breath, making it clear he doesn't intend to stop. "I took the job down in Dryden because the client had something to make me change my mind. He had a greasy grocery bag that contained one-hundred-thousand dollars in small, unmarked bills. He told me it was a one-third down payment for taking the case."

I feel a creeping sense of unease, worried Larry is going to confess to something he might regret later. "Larry, I'm a cop . . ."

"Business was slow," he says, ignoring me, "and Dawn was on my case about getting a kitchen remodel. I conveniently ignored the fact that in my twenty years as a defense attorney, I'd never received a down payment one-tenth the size to cover a case, much less in cash. The following day, I drove down to Sanderson, the county seat, which is where they were keeping my client's cousin, and which is about as far from anyplace else as you could ever be."

Larry pauses, staring at the ceiling. Somewhere under the sheets in the dark space under the bed, something gurgles. I shift in my chair.

I look up at the IV drips and can see one clearly says

Duramorph—morphine. "Look, you're in no shape to be talking."

He shakes his head. "Doing criminal defense, you meet your share of deviants. I'd always soothed my conscience with the belief I was helping people with the deck stacked against them. You can get by if you don't look too closely."

There's a ring of applause from the TV in the next bed. Larry's face has gone grey and solemn. He blinks several times then closes his eyes. I'm pretty sure he's nodded off, and I can leave without being rude. But I'm still feeling bad for not being there for him and want to be sure he's really out before going.

Suddenly Larry catches his breath and comes to. He coughs for a second and then continues. "You never expect to run into a monster. When I met the guy in lockup, I should have known right there this was something different." He coughs again a couple of times and his breathing seems to shorten.

"The charges were assault with a deadly weapon, rape, and first-degree murder." Larry's breathing gets shorter. He looks up at the ceiling, refusing to look at me.

"You know what the deadly weapon was, Tom?" he asks, beginning to rock his head.

I don't reply.

"It was his dick. This animal was called Burro—not because he was strong as a donkey, which he was—but because he was hung like one. Mr. Burro was what they call a coyote down in Terrell County. He trafficked in human flesh, taking them across the border for money. When they couldn't pay well, Burro, being an enterprising guy, found ways for them to work off their debt.

"Apparently my client, Mr. Burro, took a shine to a

pretty young thing of thirteen whose family couldn't make the payments to get them up to Dallas."

The red, rough surfaces of Larry's cheeks are streaked as the wells of his eyes fill with tears. "Seems she didn't like Burro and she fought him. So he did it to her until she died."

He shifts again, turning to face me. "Course the police don't know all this when they find the girl's body in an arroyo, beaten beyond recognition. The police get an anonymous tip about Burro and the ranch where he's staying. They bust the place. Ol' Burro protests his innocence and says he wasn't there, that he doesn't know anything about what happened to the girl, who's 'just like a niece' to him."

Larry coughs, turning to search for a water container. Unable to locate it, he rolls onto his back. "Even for one-hundred K, I have my limits. I told Burro I was going to decline the case."

Larry raises up, finally finding a cup on the bedside and gestures for me to pour some water. I get up to look for a pitcher, finding one under the sink. I run the water until it's cool, fill the cup, and hand it to him. He drinks slowly and deeply and then lies back on the bed, his breathing loud and shallow. I'm getting concerned.

"Larry, really, I think you should rest now."

"Fuck, Tom, can't a guy make a confession around here? What kind of cop are you?" He smiles through his swollen, dry, cracked lips.

"I called the guy in Amarillo to tell him to get another lawyer for his cousin. But you know when a rattler's most dangerous, Tom? When it's up against a rock. Burro could tell the cops were stalling and wanted him dead. If the situation worked out just right, ol' Burro might be found hanging from a bedsheet in his cell. Maybe he might take an unlucky fall down the jailhouse steps while handcuffed. I found out later the deputy who found that little girl in the arroyo surrendered his badge the next day. Burro knew if he waited too much longer, he wasn't going to make it to trial."

He took another sip of water. "My small-time client, the petty thief, neglected to tell me his 'cousin' Burro was a lieutenant in a cartel out of Sinaloa, with connections running all the way from Galveston to Amarillo. He was an enforcer for one of the largest meth operations in northern Mexico. Burro worked the old-fashioned way. When he thought two of his guys were snitches, he made one of them dig the hole, then buried both of them up to their necks in the desert and let the sun and the ants do the dirty work. When they were dead, he had their heads put on posts as examples. His cousin told him I was a great lawyer, and Burro wasn't going to be deprived of a great defense, especially when they were measuring the rope down the hall. Burro's network didn't reach as far as Sanderson, so he knew that if he couldn't get off legally, he wasn't going to leave Terrell County vertical."

Larry gestures for me to pour another glass of water. He takes a long, slow drink and puts the glass on the table next to him. He rolls back again. "Sitting across from me, staring at me with the dull reptile eyes of a Gila monster, Burro told me that if I didn't take his case he was going to have me, my wife, and my two kids killed in front of each other. To make his point, he gave me my address and their names."

Larry takes another drink from the cup. I notice his

hand that's clinging to the railing is shaking, and a fine sheen of sweat covers his forehead.

"Larry, you can tell me the rest later. I get the picture. Please stop."

His face darkens.

"The worst part was Burro got lucky. The cops had fucked up the chain of evidence on the sex-kit swab from the girl. Some rookie cop named Lesmeister, with less than three months on the job, was charged with taking the evidence to the lab up in Midland. Well, the kid stopped by his girlfriend's house for a little afternoon delight and left the swab in his car in the summer afternoon in the Texas sun, where it cooked.

The TV blares with another round of applause through the curtain. Larry reaches for the cup again and, finding it empty, gestures for me to fill it again. I run some cool water in the sink and refill the pitcher, then the cup, and sit down next to him.

"Larry, I know this is important, but I am seriously worried you are going to wear yourself out."

"Shut up, Tom," he says. "I filed a motion to have the evidence excluded. When the judge heard about the DNA setting in the car, and about Lesmeisters' pit stop, he threw out the evidence. With no DNA and no direct evidence placing Burro at the scene, they had to throw out the case."

He rolls over on his back. I hear the gurgling under the blanket again. "Don't worry, they're just draining me." He smiles, enjoying my discomfort. "Well, Burro, he was ecstatic. Called me 'El Milagro', miracle worker, said I must've made a deal with the devil or something—asked if I did black magic. He handed me another grocery bag with the rest of my money . . . two-hundred K. He put his arm around me and told me we were going to celebrate, kept calling me Señor Milagro. He and his friends took me for a night in Juarez that turned into three days. With my brain half fried on tequila and meth, I didn't look too closely at what I was doing, and I didn't want to piss off my best client. Towards the end of day two, me being his savior and all, ol' Burro figured he could trust me. He pulled me to him, all sweaty and stinking of tequila, sex, and excess, and asked me if the attorney-client privilege extended after the trial. Like an idiot, I told him it did. He grinned like an evil clown and told me he had a shipping container sixteen miles south side of Juarez where he kept his stable. He said, 'I tell you what, Milagro, I deed the chica and wasn't satisfied till she was done. That's how business gets done here in Juarez.'

"I realized Burro just told me he also took part in Las muertas de Juárez. Where nearly four-hundred girls and women were tortured, raped, killed, and left in a ditch."

Larry's face turns the color of river silt, and a fine sheen of sweat beads over his eyebrows. He closes his eyes.

Over the years, I've visited Victory Memorial well over a hundred times. Transporting the mangled remains of bar fights, taking reports of domestic abuse, watching the frenetic ballet of the emergency room. I've witnessed all life's pivotal crossings—births, deaths, transitions from health to disability. I've become inured to the side effects of trauma and have arrived at the point where I can see a quadriplegic after a collision with a phone pole and tell myself it's just a part of life.

I'm astounded at my reaction then, when Larry starts sobbing, great rocking, silent gasps. My first reflex is shame, which makes me feel more shame at my inability to handle what's happening in front of me. My shame leads to descending cascades of regret and I want nothing so much as to look away from Larry's bruised, red face, streaked by bright moist stains and snot. Except for the steady beep and the low roar of the TV in the next bed, the room turns silent.

Then Larry coughs and reaches for a tissue, turning his head to look at me. "I had to do something to protect myself. I knew I was only safe until Burro decided I wasn't useful or to be trusted. When that happened, and it surely would, I was dead, and so was my family. I either had to disappear, or make it look like I'd lost it and I wasn't a threat . . . make it look like the wheels came off. I knew it was a gamble. If he thought I was gonna talk, he'd kill me and anyone who he thought I'd talked to. I had to become literally unbelievable. Given the choices, it was a desperate move."

"Why didn't you go to the Rangers, or the sheriff's office?" I ask.

"I thought about that. After more than twenty years in criminal defense, I didn't have a lot of friends on the other side, and I knew, especially after that mess with Henry Lee Lucas, I couldn't really trust anyone. I didn't know who was dirty on the other side. Besides, if they believed me, Burro would still find a way to kill my family."

Larry pushes the electric button to bring the head of the bed up so he can see me. "So, I had to gamble. If Burro thought I was a liability, I was dead. The trick was to make him think my family thought I was crazy too—then he might leave them alone. Killing me would be bad, but at least he would stay away from my family. It really wasn't too hard to start. I returned to Houston, where Dawn and I had been coming apart for months. I knew she was fooling around with Rob, the house painter, so I started drinking openly and excessively. That was nothing exceptional. Plenty of criminal defense lawyers drink to excess. Then I had a brief, indiscreet affair with the wife of a senior Appeals Court judge who'd flirted with me over years." He chuckles darkly. "The stroke of genius was the Governor's dinner. That got me disbarred."

"What did your family think you were doing?"

He coughs again, this time harder and longer. His face is twisted with pain. "I couldn't tell them about Burro. I knew Burro would track me down and put my head on a post if he thought I'd betrayed him. But they couldn't know about him. If he thought they knew, he'd do them, too. To remind me, he'd call and leave friendly messages every other week, asking how the family was, and telling me we had to get together for another trip to Juarez. I still had no guarantee that simply proving I was a crazy drunk would put Burro off." Larry's face darkens. "I didn't count on losing my kids, though. They watched, like horrified rubberneckers, seeing the smoking wreck my life became." He takes another sip of water and slumps back on the bed, his breathing hard and quick. "You know, God has a sense of humor, Tom. The delicious irony was after I'd set my life on fire, lost everything, and they truly believed I was nuts, Burro wasn't a problem anymore. A buddy of mine in Amarillo told me ol' Burro was stabbed in the ear with an icepick. Whoever did it pithed him like a frog—a real pro job. The best part is when they found him. His famous appendage had been removed and nailed above the bed. Probably a rival drug cartel."

Larry begins to cough, unable to stop, and his face is

stained an unnatural grey. Alarmed, I lean closer. Larry's eyes are staring at the ceiling. When Larry doesn't respond, I run down to the nursing station where I manage, after several desperate seconds, to get the attention of the nurse, whose attention is riveted to her computer screen. She sounds an alarm and runs to where Larry is staring at the ceiling.

Once she sees him, she whips out a stethoscope, planting it on his chest. She listens and then directs me into the hall. Seconds later, the room is crowded with staff, detaching Larry and speeding him down the corridor.

Managing to keep pace with the nurse, who clearly blames me for Larry's condition, I follow the gurney down the hall.

"What's going on?" I ask, as they push the gurney through the swinging doors to the ER.

"Congestive heart failure," she spits at me. "He's got fluid in his heart cavity," she says, and the emergency doors swing back at me, leaving me to stand at the entrance to the restricted area.

CHAPTER TWENTY-FOUR

I REMAIN AT THE HOSPITAL FOR SEVERAL HOURS, finally leaving at midnight when the nurse tells me Larry's in stable but guarded condition. She asks if Larry has any close family, and I admit all I know is the family is in Texas and was contacted. I'm not even sure if they're coming to see Larry.

As I sit waiting, I turn to the NAST envelope. The documents reflect transactions from a single account. The starting balance seven years ago was seven million dollars, and for first five years two-hundred-fifty thousand a quarter was disbursed, each transfer corresponding to a wire to Credit Zurich, Switzerland.

I calculate five-million-two-hundred-thousand dollars withdrawn. No activity this entire spring. The only name on the account: Faith Wesley.

I dial Dan Hagen in the Economic Office at the State's Attorney's office, known in Major Crimes as The Propeller Heads.

Dan got his degree in economics from University of Illinois, did a stint in banking in Chicago, attended law school at night, and, forsaking private practice, joined the Economic Crimes Unit. We've worked several cases together.

"Tom, how're you doing?"

In a few minutes I summarize the case, the problems with the records, and the pressure to arrest Edwards. I also share we've recently gotten a hit for Rivera. After a short lull, I get to the reason for my call. "Swiss accounts. You know about 'em, right?"

Dan clears his throat. "Yup. They're not as secret as everyone thinks. Swiss Banks used to be impossible to get into. They guarded their clients' information like their mother's honor. Then the stuff came out about the Holocaust and the Nazis, and they had to clean up their act. Now people go to the Caymans and Singapore. After the HSBC mess and the money laundering scandals, it's gotten even easier to track the money. No more nameless numbered accounts. If the account is owned by a company, however, they still don't look too hard at the stockholders. So, you have a lot more anonymous holding companies. You know about the Panama files, right?

"Yeah, a huge database of offshore accounts. How do I find out who owns an account?"

"A 'lifting order.'"

"How long does that take?"

"It can be expedited. A couple of days."

"I need it yesterday," I reply, hoping Dan won't push further.

"I can get it done. Get me the account information and I can get it to the embassy today."

"Tony knows, but Steinman doesn't need to know." I figure I don't need to drag Dan into the politics. There's nothing sinister about the accounts, but Steinman has resisted everything to do with the banking.

Hagen chuckles. "I get it."

Like me, Dan's divorced. He's helping to raise a boy with autism who's just a little older than Liam. He's actually Dan's nephew, as Dan's brother was killed in a car accident. Over the years, we've developed a friendship, which at one point included racquetball and lunch. I came to find the lunches tedious, as they had a Groundhog Day quality about them with Dan going on about fighting the schools for services or rehashing his insistence his kid's condition was caused by childhood vaccines containing thimerosal, a form of mercury.

Eventually, I gave Dan a wide berth, and the lunches and racquetball became infrequent.

Perhaps sensing the change, Dan stopped mentioning the issues, and the conversations tended to be about football scores and Trina, the new admin in Special Victims. Forgetting myself, I casually mentioned Liam was set to get his five-year booster shots. As soon as I said it, I regretted it, as Dan exploded into facts and statistics about vaccines. I asked him to mind his own business, telling him there was no connection between autism and vaccines— any connection had been disproven. Dan got up abruptly and left the table. I doubted we would ever hang out again.

Two days later, he came to my office holding a binder containing three-hundred-and-fifty pages of a transcript of a secret meeting in June of 2000 at the Simpsonwood Meeting Center in Georgia, attended by every major drug company in the world, the FDA, and the Centers for

Disease Control. Dan told me he obtained the transcript from the CDC with a Freedom of Information request. Excerpts were tabbed and highlighted. Dan told me to read the transcript before putting a needle in my kid. I spent three hours looking through it, and to my horror, the CDC doctors admitted a causal connection between vaccines, specifically thimerosal, the mercury preservative, and what they called "outcomes", a fancy term for autism, ADHD, ADD, speech delays, and ticks. Then at the end of the meeting they agreed to bury the whole thing. Since that time, they've consistently denied the meeting ever happened or the study was ever done.

Over Katie's objections and the pediatrician's surly resistance, I'd had Liam tested for residual immunity, and found that none of the boosters were needed.

I didn't think Dan was a kook after that.

He tells me he will get right on it. I email him the Credite Zurich information.

When I hang up, I quickly call Manny Gorak, telling him I need to see where they found Rivera. He gives me the address in South Chicago and hangs up.

■ ■ ■

Several hours later, I pull up in the Beast in Fuller Park, cursing myself for not thinking to bring a station unit. Across the street, several men lounge outside the Root Inn Liquor store, eyeing me as I sit in the car. They are drinking beer. One of them puts a can on the ground and as he stares at me steps on it and crushes it into a small circle under his foot. In a gamble, I flash my police identification, placing it prominently in the windshield. I figure it will either incite the vandals or deter them. I give it even odds.

I open the car door and feel the cool fall breeze pushing leaves and light trash down the street. The root-bound trees wedged in the concrete walkways are turning color; that and the shifting autumn light are both signs of change. The blue sky, hard as a diamond, carries the optimism of a new season. Even here in Fuller Park, with the changing sky and sun, someone might fall prey to hope.

I walk twenty feet when Manny Gorak pulls up in his late-model dark blue Bonneville. As he heaves his weight to get out, I can see his telltale short-sleeved white shirt and, despite the cool breeze, the sweat stains at the armpits and on the back of his neck. Manny glares at me through a pair of cheap sunglasses.

"Let's keep this short," he says, kicking a soda can into the gutter.

I can't resist needling him. "I'll try not to interrupt your busy schedule."

"Fuck you," he replies dryly.

They found Rivera in what's known in the business as a "bando"—an abandoned drug house. Often houses in tax foreclosure, bandos' owners are long since gone. The corner of Root and Wells is pockmarked with empty lots where homes previously stood and were either burned down or condemned. Ravaged by arson or neglect, abandoned buildings are free, and there's no paper trail. When there are documented landlords, they've got anonymous names like XYZ Enterprises and are registered to other companies out of state. If there are tenants, the game is to collect the Section Eight rents and let the building rot. When it's too far gone, you burn it to the ground and collect the insurance.

The house matching the address Manny gave me sits in the middle of a block lined with one- and two-story prewar houses. The empty lots between are piled high with garbage. A few of the houses are fronted with small pots of flowers or a plant or two placed in a desultory effort at curb appeal. Manny starts toward the one-story house with a front porch piled high with trash and rubber tires. One side of it is scorched, and a large blue tarp hangs off the roof to shield the side of the building from the elements.

"Home sweet home," Manny says as he ascends the three steps to the front door. The front door is sealed with police tape. Manny pulls the tape off and searches for the key. He turns the lock and pushes the door open, waving me inside. I'm accosted by the acrid odor of vomit. Manny follows me inside. Surveying the front room, he shakes his head. "Fucking animals."

The front room, if you can call it that, is piled high with mattresses, and littered with wax paper, tin foil balls, wrappers, empty cans, and other garbage. The tin foil is the telltale sign of someone having smoked meth here. The stench is overpowering. I fight the urge to wretch.

"Place has been used for years as a bando-traphouse," Manny says. "They bust it regular, but the skells always come back. Neighbors set fire to the place a few months ago. It's owned by some holding company. Been in and out of tax foreclosure a few times. We even got the health guys in here. They tried putting a tag on it, but someone in the city bypassed that. We found Eddie on an anonymous tip. Somebody called and told us some guy tapped it in here."

"Where was he?" I scan the place. Parts of the walls have been ripped away, and the floors are stained and burned.

"In there on a mattress," he says, pointing to the back of the house. "Had a plastic bag over his head. Noose around his neck, tied it to the doorknob. Naked. Gasper."

"Anyone else here?"

"As far as we can tell, Rivera was the only skell crashing here in the last few weeks. The john's there," he says, pointing again towards the back of the house.

"How long was he here before you found him?"

Manny shrugs. "Hard to say. It looked like a couple of days. No telling where he'd been."

I walk to the back of the house. There's an open door. Taking care not to touch the walls, I step into a small bathroom where the toilet, or what's left of it, consists of a cracked bowl with no seat, ringed with decades of brown rust. There's no water in the tank, probably because service was shut off ages ago. Not to be deterred, it's clear the toilet's been used.

I pull open the medicine cabinet. A couple of robust roaches scurry to the back of the shelf before disappearing into the wall. I'm about to leave when I see three empty prescription bottles. Marked Dispensary State of Illinois Department of Corrections, they are lying under the sink in a pile of garbage. They have Rivera's name and are about six months old.

"You missed the prescriptions," I shout into the next room.

Manny comes to the bathroom door and grimaces. "We didn't think personal stuff needed to be inventoried."

I pick up the bottles. "Prozac, Invega, and Paliperidone. You have any idea what this stuff is for?"

Manny's face falls to an uncertain grin.

"What's it for?"

"Invega's for schizophrenia."

Manny shrugs.

"I'll leave that to you, Mr. Pharmacist," he says, walking back to the other room. "You ready to leave?"

"What else did you find in here?"

"We found his works, and a couple of jelly babies—"

"Placidyl?"

"Yeah, if you say so. Exotic, like I said—the ME said he had it in him, so we figured he was sampling his own stuff."

"That's the same stuff they found in the Moraleses."

"Yeah. So?"

"So, it hasn't been made in years. Where did he get it?"

"Fuck if I know. He's dead."

Manny hands me the crime scene photos. We move out of the bathroom and into the room where they found Eddie. Now, it's empty, with only a solitary mattress. The bedroom floor, like the other rooms, is littered with garbage.

The photos show Eddie on the bed, kneeling forward, a plastic bag over his head and rope around his neck.

"Porn, laundry rope, plastic bag," Manny observes.

"Laundry rope and plastic bag—both?"

"Yeah, sure. Belt and suspenders." Manny chuckles.

"Manny, you made another funny."

He stares at me, then gestures towards the door. "We done?"

We make our way outside, and as Manny locks the door and replaces the tape, he shakes his head in disbelief. "You think there's some connection between this and that shit up in Lake Forest?"

"You thought so, too."

"I said I thought Rivera had some plan to kill the Moraleses and killed Faith Wesley on accident. Whatever it was, we ain't gonna find out, so it don't matter."

"Rivera's been linked to Faith's murder by DNA. The Moraleses worked for Faith Wesley. It's more than coincidence."

We've reached the street. Manny heads off to his Bonneville, which is untouched. He glares at the guys across the street, climbs in, and starts the engine. I walk over to the Beast, which has somehow also miraculously survived intact. I'm about to get into the car when I notice the small circular beer can placed neatly on the roof of the car. I look over to the storefront. The guys are gone.

As I make my way to the Cook County ME's office, I push the pieces together. Rivera had a link to Faith's murder, and now has the same stuff in him as Alma and Jesus, who were also murdered. Alma and Jesus worked for Faith. But, if he's a junkie, as Manny thinks, nothing's been taken from the Wesley house. If theft was the motive, Rivera could've done an inside job. Charles' Masamune katana could've been fenced for enough junk to last two years.

Housed in a modern labyrinth of labs and examining rooms, the Cook County Medical Examiner's office is responsible for half the population of the State of Illinois.

I'm escorted to Examining Room Six, which is occupied by a man in his late forties with a shaved bald head and glasses, accompanied by a short woman who, like the man, is dressed in green surgical gear. They are both leaning over a table. Instinctively, I look away.

The man looks up and introduces himself as Ismael Bielmans, Chief Assistant ME. I tell him I've come to see Eduardo Rivera. He instructs the woman to continue without him and motions me towards a steel door marked Storage Room 2, which opens into a room lined with MOPAC coolers. Noisy ventilators circulate air.

"Welcome to the Big Chill," he says, smiling. Walking to the end of the room he checks a notebook hanging from the wall. "Mr. Rivera originally came in as a suspected suicide or accidental death. We ran CODIS and it took a few days." Bielmans reaches down and gives a sharp pull on the latch, which opens with a distinctive *thunk*, followed by the low quiet sound of rollers as the tray extends.

"Tell me about it," I say. "We had a sample for weeks and no hit."

"The problem isn't CODIS," Bielmans says. "It's the data entered to match the medical data. It's matching CODIS with NCIC, the National Crime Information Center. What's even stranger is that Eddie wasn't picked up in the Illinois DOC database, even though he's been in Menard for years."

He gestures for me to step forward. I brace myself.

"You ready?" Bielmans asks, nodding towards the table.

"Yes sir."

He pulls back the sheet.

Eddie's emaciated body, especially his arms, are covered in colorful snakes and exotic flowers. His eyes are open and his face is contorted in a rictus.

Bielmans sighs. "Autoerotic asphyxia—gaspers some people call them. It's a particularly complicated paraphilia. They found him leaning forward on his bed with a ligature tied to the headboard and a plastic bag over his head."

"Gorak called it belt and suspenders."

Bielmans chuckles. "Manny does have colorful way

of expressing himself. It does seem a little like overkill, if you'll forgive the pun. But seventy to eighty percent of autoerotic deaths are caused by hanging, while ten to thirty percent are caused by plastic bags or drugs. Some people even use electrocution, coupled with foreign body insertion, overdressing, and body wrapping. I've seen amyl nitrite, GHB, or nitrous oxide, and props and tools such as knives, oversized dildos, ligatures or bags for asphyxiation, duct tape, electrical apparatus for shocks. Here there's no paraphernalia and only magazines. He doesn't seem to have reached climax either. As far as this went, it was a fail."

"Meaning?"

"Part of the attraction, the kink if you will, is the ritual—the tools and such. This seems almost amateurish. Either Eddie was new to this, or he didn't know what he was doing. The more elaborate the setting, the more complicated the ritual, the bigger the charge. We had a guy in here earlier this summer, tried this in a swimming pool by self-immersion. Drowned before he could reach climax. Whatever turns you on . . ."

I look away.

"Male victims are much more likely to use a variety of devices during autoerotic behavior than female victims. The other thing is he was so drugged. That seems completely out of place. As I said, poppers, amyl nitrate, uppers, even nitrous, but not sedation. No way was he going to get the job done when he was drugged like that."

"Sedated?"

"Yes, very interesting," he says, opening the folder in his hand. "We found Placidyl in the tox screen."

"There was a double homicide a few weeks ago and—"

"Yeah—the Morales case. I did the post on that too."

"How often do you see that stuff?"

"Never. They stopped making it more than twenty years ago. On the street, it's like an '82 Chateau Lafitte."

"How long does it take to work?"

"With booze, a couple of minutes."

"Did you find any other cuts, lacerations, or puncture wounds?" I ask, thinking of the wicked spikes on the wall at the Wesley place. If he slipped and caught one of the spikes, it's going to show.

Bielmans shrugs. "You know, a guy like this, his body is a mass of tattoos, scars, piercings."

"Anything fresh, like within the last several months?"

Bielmans shakes his head. "Nope. One other interesting thing in the blood work—we found traces of the psychotropic Invega."

I nod. "He was on antipsychotics at one point." I tell him about the bottles, including the Paliperidone.

Bielmans shoots me a skeptical look. "Well, if he was, they weren't doing anything for him."

Bielmans gives Rivera's leg a friendly pat and begins to roll the body back toward the cooler.

"Weaning off antipsychotics has to be done carefully," he says as he slides Eddie back into storage and shuts the latch.

"Why's that?"

"Sudden withdrawal causes reemergence of pathology, panic, aggression, you name it."

"Any next of kin?"

"I haven't gotten any notification. I'm prepared to release the body. We can keep them at below-freezing temperatures for extended periods, but we try and get them placed out at Homewood Gardens within six months, latest, if no one comes to claim them.

"Has anybody claimed Alma and Jesus Morales?"

Bielmans nods.

"Who?"

"Charles Wesley."

. . .

Early the next morning, as the sun rises over the lake turning its surface first purple, then gold, and finally slate green, the sky breaks into a new day. Dan Hagen insists on meeting at the Deer Creek Racquet Club. I haven't lifted a racquet for a couple of years.

The Deer Creek Club is thirty minutes south in Highland Park.

Hagen sits on a bench at the end of the reception area. He's a large man, and although physically well built, carries the signs of a sedentary lifestyle. He holds his racquet in his hand. "You're late," he says. "I'll be on Court 3."

A few minutes later, I enter number three, one of two racquetball courts enclosed by a glass wall. I feel self-conscious. Dan has already broken a sweat and, judging by his demeanor, there's no doubt he'll put his heart into our game.

We volley for several minutes, and I begin to feel limber, sending the blue ball quickly back. We say nothing, testing the other's residual ability.

After a few minutes of warm-up, Dan suggests we play best of five. He wins the first volley. He opens the point with a blazing backhand serve, glancing off the far wall. Anticipating it, I fire it back off the back wall, only to be met with Dan's return, which wins him the point.

As he prepares to serve again, I'm nettled, wondering if the game is worth the effort, especially now that the forensics all point away from Edwards to Rivera. The accounts hardly seem to matter anymore. Aside from making me feel out of shape, I owe Dan the courtesy of a game, especially when he's expedited the request for me. I'm resigned to the game and steel myself for the next serve.

Before he serves, Dan pauses. He places a hand against the wall to support himself, catching his breath. After several seconds he says, "I got the records. I told them there's an ongoing investigation involving this account."

He hits another serve, this time directly to me. I quickly return it, low and off the far corner, winning the point. I can see Dan's starting to feel the effects of running around. Before I serve, I bounce the ball against the floor. "It's that easy?"

He stands upright, sufficiently recovered to signal me to serve. Before I hit the ball, he says, "I think you'll be interested in the results." I lob a high ball off the front wall, which lands in the back right corner. With surprising speed, Dan reaches it and, with a flick of the wrist, scoops it out, sending it back down the left wall. I scramble to get it, misjudging the distance, watching as it bounces twice and drops dead in the back corner. Dan's point.

He gestures again to hold up, breathing heavily. His T-shirt is now soaked through with sweat. He bends to catch his breath. "What're you dealing with Tom? That account has millions in it. What is it—drugs?"

"I'm not sure," I say truthfully, "but I think it may be buying and selling families."

"You're messing with big players. You know that, right?" Hagan says, nodding for me to serve. I respond by hitting the ball, effectively bringing an end to the conversation about the account.

We continue to play for another forty-five minutes, by which time I've beaten Dan soundly. Although Dan is technically superior, he's not up to my endurance. I'm in far better shape. As we change in the locker room, he hands me a gray envelope. "Don't say I never did you any favors. I'll deny knowing about this if there's blowback. Okay?"

"Who owns the account, Dan? Why the drama?"

Hagan just shakes his head. "Look for yourself."

I nod and look in the envelope at the account information, my suspicions confirmed.

Dan finishes dressing. As he prepares to leave the locker room, he approaches me, extending a beefy hand.

He eyes me, evidently judging from my expression not to press further. "Just watch out, okay? I'll call you for lunch sometime soon."

CHAPTER TWENTY-FIVE

I RETURN TO WORK TO FIND A DISHEVELED PILE OF phone messages waiting for me. With Larry gone, I'm forced to share support staff with several other detectives who've let me know they're unhappy with what they view as poaching. The office staff follows suit, feeling free to approach my work with something less than neglect.

I'm surprised when Delahunt denies my request for a replacement. From what I can figure, the chief is paying me back for my decision to hire Larry in the first place. Earlier in the week, I walked by Larry's darkened office and was struck by regret. I call Victory Memorial again to check his status. The desk nurse tells me Larry regained consciousness, but he's restricted visitors—no one outside of family members. I push, telling her I'm a detective. Apparently satisfied my intentions are good, she confides Larry was transferred to rehab, and they don't know what the prognosis is.

Leafing through a thick sheaf of phone slips Larry left me, I see one of the pink slips contains a scribbled name of a contact at the Department of Corrections. The note says simply, "not going to comply with subpoena re Rivera—HIPPA." Fighting to suppress my rising tide of frustration, I pick up the phone and dial Tony, who instructs me to keep my shirt on. He says he'll call over to DOC's lawyers and find out what the problem is.

"The guy is dead, for Chrissakes, Tony. What's the problem?"

"HIPPA protects dead folks, too. Everybody needs protection. I'll get back to you."

The staff has also taken to dumping my mail in a pile in Larry's empty office. Setting at the top of the pile is a large gray envelope: Abbott Laboratories. The results have come back in for the Placidyl. I rip open the heavy gray envelope, extracting 134 pages of serial lots for Placidyl. From 1991 through 2001: shipment dates, destinations, lot numbers, and fulfillment codes. There are only three entries in 2001. After that, Abbott stopped distributing altogether.

After three hours, I finally find what I'm looking for: December 2000, three full lot shipments of Placidyl were made to the Illinois State Department of Corrections' dispensary.

I call Abbott's customer service line in Chicago and, after wading through several service reps, I'm finally transferred to the regional distribution manager. The manager explains a lot represents a thousand trade packs, or four to five thousand units or capsules in each lot. From 1992 through 2000 DOC, requested a total of one-hundred-and-fifty lot shipments, or four-hundred-and-fifty thousand pills. Even for a corrections' population of thirty-eight thousand, that's enough jelly babies for every man and woman incarcerated in the Illinois system and then some. I mark the invoice number and the billing receipt. DOC will have invoices for every dollar it ever spent. I ask the rep why the company stopped making the drug.

I can hear him shuffling papers. After I push him, he says, "Basically, the drug got a lot of bad publicity and was no longer profitable."

On my way out, Delahunt motions through the glass door to have a seat. Since Larry's accident, I've avoided the chief, fearing Delahunt would take Larry's crash, if you could call it that, as the best evidence he should go. I take a seat.

"I just got off the phone with Steinman, Tom. It seems you've been stirring things up at Corrections. They're some very unhappy people. I don't—"

Relieved the first item on the agenda isn't firing Larry, I interrupt. "I'm trying to get records for Rivera, sir. He was doped with the same stuff the Moraleses had in their system. He also had prescriptions for Invega and Prozac from the State dispensary."

As Delahunt begins to shake his head, I press on. "Someone made the decision to take him off meds, and I'd like to know who and why."

Delahunt picks up the troll toy setting on his desk, squeezing several times. The rubber doll's eyes bug out. He leans across the desk, clearly piqued. "You found Faith Wesley's killer. The family's satisfied. That should be enough. I would've thought with Rivera dead and the DNA results back, you'd be pleased to close this file."

Rising from his chair, he moves over to the window, and sighs audibly.

"Steinman also told me he's getting blowback from Chicago PD because you interfered with Gorak's handling of the file. Killings involving illegals, I might add."

"Gorak's just looking for an excuse to close the cases."

"Just as we should," Delahunt growls from the window. He turns to face me, his expression tight and set. "Look, I stood behind you when they wanted to hang Edwards. Your instincts proved right. Now, we've got Faith Wesley's killer, and he's dead. No need to waste taxpayer money, right?" he says, returning to his desk. "The case doesn't need solving, Tom, and for once the family's satisfied with the work we did."

I lean across the desk. "I get it. But why would Rivera murder Faith Wesley for nothing? The only missing money is in a Swiss bank account. Looks like more than two million. Why were Jesus and Alma Morales shot in the head?"

"Look, Tom," he says, adopting a tone I've heard him use with new rookies. "You were assigned a murder in one of the most esteemed families in our community. You've got my grateful thanks, as well as the department's, so please move your caseload. That's an order."

He leans back in his chair, then looks down at his desk, leafing through a stack of reports. The interview is over.

I start to walk out of the office when I hear Delahunt behind me. "Tom?"

I turn. "Yes, sir."

"Trust you've also dealt with the Summers issue."

"Handled," I say as Delahunt selects a report and begins reading.

"Good."

As I enter the parking lot, my phone vibrates—Katie.

"Tom, did you arrange a pick up for Liam this afternoon?" Her voice is sharp and quick.

With the coming of fall, our lives shift to meet Liam's new schedule, which includes a performance of the middle school play, *Jack in the Beanstalk*, where he's secured a significant role as one of the giant's elves. I check my watch, remembering Liam is supposed to be at the school at 6:00 that evening. It's four o'clock.

I'm vexed. "No, you're supposed to do that, aren't you?"

"I'm at the school, Tom. They say some woman picked up Liam. He seemed to know her. Do you know who that is?"

A small current of frustration runs down my back as I consider the list of people who'd pick up Liam. "I thought we agreed he wasn't to be released to anyone except you and me." I'm tempted to mention Ronald Erland but think better of it.

"Tom, we have to find Liam. Oh my God . . ." I can hear Katie start to descend into panic, her breathing fast and short.

I hover somewhere between irritation and confusion, refusing to believe there's an issue, and am about to tell Katie to relax, when a second call comes through.

I abruptly hang up and answer the second call.

"Hello?"

A short breath, and then simply, "Tom, Liam and I are together."

Nora's voice is quiet, just above a whisper, her diction slurred. She sounds drunk. As I think of the two of them driving together, a cold ice pick of fear jabs my insides.

"Nora, what have you—"

"Liam and I are doing great, right champ?" I can hear traffic and an echo of music in the background.

"Where are you? Put him on the phone."

Nora grunts a simple "uh-huh" into the phone, slow and heavy. "I need to talk to you, Tom. I need to meet you . . ."

"Where are you? Where's Liam?" My mind is racing, as I begin to understand my son is in danger.

I can hear Nora's breath on the phone.

"Put Liam on the phone, Nora," I say, struggling to check the anxiety creeping into my voice.

I hear a bump and shuffle as the phone passes, followed by the clear high sound of Liam's voice. "Hi, Dad. Are you going to meet me and Nora?" Liam sounds bewildered, not scared.

"I'm working on it, chief. Where are—"

I can hear the quick echo of Liam's voice as the phone is taken from him. "Meet me at Illinois Beach Park off of Patomos . . . down by the benches . . . at six. The bench by parking lot B." She coughs twice. "I just need to talk to you. You owe it to me."

The phone goes dead.

There's a little over an hour and forty-five minutes until Liam's show, when this thing will blow up. Running through my options, I briefly consider an AMBER alert, which would certainly result in embarrassing questions. Tracking them down myself, I may be able to catch Nora off guard. Just for a second, I feel a sharp tug of regret, knowing that if Larry were here, he might help. Instead, I am on my own.

Most of all, I know I can't trust Katie to keep out of the way. Wanting more than anything else to avoid the scandal, I settle on buying myself time and dealing with Nora directly, trying to convince myself there's no reason to believe Liam is in any real danger. Once I have him, I'll get a restraining order and shut the whole mess down.

I dial Katie, telling her I've spoken to Liam and he's with Nora Summers.

She gasps. "Is she that woman you and Liam went to the concert with?"

"We didn't go there with her," I say, putting the best spin on what, in hindsight, seems a profound lapse of judgment.

"What the fuck is she doing with Liam, Tom?"

"She picked him up after school and they're having something to eat."

"Where, Tom? Where the fuck are they?"

"They're in Waukegan. I'm going to meet them."

"Where? What are they doing up there?"

I pause for a second, as the school bell rings into the phone. Katie's still in Vernon Hills, probably forty-five minutes away.

"I'm going to meet them at the school at six o'clock."

"Jesus, Tom, his performance is at seven. He's supposed to be at the theater at five—in an hour."

"I know."

I hang up. My phone rings several times as she tries to call back. Finally, after five tries, she gives up. I know she'll call Central Command and maybe start an Amber Alert. I have at most an hour before the whole mess comes down around my ankles.

■   ■   ■

Half an hour later, I make it to Illinois Beach Park ahead of schedule. During the summer months the park is crowded, and the parking lots fill to overflowing. South of here, the beach is less crowded and a mile of shoreline extends to an inlet, then into a wetland. Depending on weather, this inlet can be blocked by a berm from the lake waters, and the water inside the berm can be significantly warmer than Lake Michigan, which is rather cold until August. The park also includes dunes, wetlands, a prairie, and a black oak savanna. The area at the far southern end of the park is a designated nature preserve.

By now, it's mid-fall, and migrating canvasbacks, like ghosts against the water, skim just above the lake, and the sun sets just several degrees above the horizon in the west, painting their feathers deep crimson. The wind whistles through the trees and pushes dead leaves in rolling waves along the path. I'm growing more anxious as the light dims, coloring the clouds out on the lake in lilacs, roses, blues, and creamy whites, which stretch like a veil across the face of the sky. Night is falling.

I find Nora sitting on a bench looking out on the lake with Liam sitting next to her. Even at a distance, I'm shocked at how much she's changed physically in the few weeks since I saw her at the tanning salon. Emaciated, her cheeks stretch over the sharp contours of her face, her eyes sink deep into her skull, her skin is a chrome yellow, and the irises of her eyes, once clear and bright, are dull and the color of aged cream.

Liam catches sight of me, shifting quickly on the bench to greet me, his face lighting up. Nora, alerted, turns to watch me approach. Wearing only the sweatshirt he'd worn to school, I can see Liam is cold and carrying the same expression I saw the day he assayed the high diving board ladder at the local pool: fear and a strong determination not to show it. Gauging whether he's in trouble, Liam glances quickly at Nora, then back at me.

I make the distance to the bench in seconds, reaching the two of them quickly. Nora stands with Liam, with her arms around him.

"Hi, buddy," I say as Nora steps back. "Nora, what a surprise you picked up Liam at school," I add, trying to sound casual for Liam. I remember the mystery call to Westinghouse Middle School. "Did you call the school the other day, and ask them about picking up Liam?"

"I did," she says, smiling and giving Liam a little squeeze. Her expression reminds me of the night she admitted going through my wallet for my address. "Liam, say hi to your dad."

"Hi, Dad," he says, attempting to join me, but Nora holds him fast in her arms.

Nora retreats a couple of steps. "I trusted you, Tom." Her voice is thick in her throat and I can see her eyes are swollen. She's visibly unsteady on her shoeless feet. She runs her fingers through her tangled hair.

I stop, watching her closely. "I know. I trusted you, too. Then it all went bad." I'm trying to speak generally in front of Liam. "When we talked at the salon, you acted like you never wanted to talk to me again." Venturing a little more, I tell her, "Linda told me I shouldn't talk to you anymore. That was it for me."

I take a step closer and as she moves back again, this time I see the Glock-9 in her hand. I feel cold panic grip me by the groin. Liam, sensing my alarm, squirms in her arms.

The sunset has faded to an opaque sheen in the sky, and the lights lining the path come on. The park is deserted.

"Nora, why?" I say slowly as I take another step. Nora raises the dull black pistol level to my stomach. Even a glancing shot at this distance would shred my intestines.

I put my hands at my sides. When she doesn't answer, I steal a look at my watch in the light of the streetlamp and see it's almost six o'clock.

Liam's resolve begins to give way as he struggles to make sense of the surreal. "Dad, I gotta go to *Jack in the Beanstalk*."

Nora seems not to have heard him. Her body sways as she bolsters herself unsteadily on the back of the bench and licks her lips several times.

"*Jack and the Beanstalk*," Liam says, reciting his mantra in an ascending whine.

Nora shakes him by the shoulders. "Shut up!"

I see I have no choice but to disarm Nora, or take her out, if necessary. I can feel my sidearm holstered tightly to my side. "Nora, give me the gun."

She kicks a pebble on the ground, watching it roll away. I inch nearer. "Eddie called me . . ." she says, pulling Liam closer to her.

"Eddie Rivera?"

She nods.

The darkness has come fully on, and the breeze freshens to a cold October wind off the lake. Dancing from one foot to another, Liam shivers, staring at me. He pleads, almost in a whisper, "I have to pee." I desperately will him to be quiet and calm.

"Why would Eddie call you?" I ask, trying to divert her attention away from Liam.

"To come clean," she says, staring out at the lake, apparently oblivious to Liam's gyrations.

"Nora, can he pee?" I ask, hoping to prevail on Nora's tenderness for Liam.

She stands still, staring to where the lake disappears, a dark line where the horizon is pulled into dusk. Finally, she comes back, as if summoned to answer an insoluble math problem.

"You know, from the time we're in grade school, they tell us about justice. They tell us we're citizens in a country founded on justice. We've got a right to believe in it, to expect it. And then things happen that make us doubt. Some innocent gets the needle, or a cold-blooded killer goes free. Then, because of DNA, someone gets freed after seventeen years in prison, or some decrepit war criminal stands trial for killing people in Auschwitz, and we congratulate ourselves, saying the wheels of justice may grind slowly, but they're inevitable."

I hate to see Liam suffer. He's only eleven, and I know although he senses this is weird, I doubt he knows how dangerous it is. "He needs to pee, Nora," I say, taking another step towards her. Nora fires the gun at my feet. The blast whips sand and dirt into my face, stinging my ankles. The sound echoes off the trees.

"Stay where you are, Tom."

Liam begins to keen quietly, looking at me to help him.

I watch Nora, appalled at her transformation. Five months earlier, we'd chartered a sailboat, venturing out onto the lake. Nora was an able sailor, and I was elated as we left the confines of the cove, heading out onto the open water. The waves smacked loud against the hull. Nora let out the jib, which ballooned into an expanse of white cloth, pulling against the painter. I crawled the length of the deck, narrowly missing the boom, and reached her in time to kiss her deeply, touching her cheek. She'd smiled at me, telling me to take her place by the ropes as she steered the boat into deeper waters, the lake bottom falling fathoms below. Bathed in clear light, Nora's face was rosy with sun and wind, and her hair blew back like a flag.

Just then, as she's waving the Glock, I hope to reach to some vestige of reason, gesturing towards restrooms just visible in the dim half-light. She's either ignoring Liam or simply hasn't heard.

"What about people who never get justice?" she asks, her voice coarse with indignation. "What about kids who die at the hands of their parents because Protective Services didn't act in time? What about people who die in fiery wrecks because some car giant won't spend fifty cents on a piece of plastic to make the thing safer?"

"What does this have to do with Eddie Rivera?" I ask, taking the measure of the distance between us, hoping I can overtake her.

She glares at me, disbelief and rage darkening her face. "The night my parents were in the car, I was supposed to go to town to stay overnight with my cousins. I should have been in that car. All three of us . . ." She's yelling at me, and as she turns to face me, I can see lines from her tears reflected in the white glare of the halogen park lights; her nose streams in the cold air. "But I stayed home, and they left. Too late, Tom, always too late . . . too fucking late." She begins waving the gun in the air.

"It couldn't be helped—"

"Really, Tom?" she asks, her expression twisting into a sneer as she pulls Liam closer, caressing the back of his ear with the point of the Glock.

"Really, Tom?" she asks, her expression pulling into a sneer as she pulls Liam closer, caressing the back of his ear with the point of the Glock. "It couldn't be helped? My mother was pregnant when she died. They never did an autopsy, thanks to Strauss, but she told me just before they went to the party that I was going to have a baby brother."

I weigh this information with what I know about her baby brother and her parents dying, and I'm overwhelmed by the amount of personal tragedy she's had in her life. It dawns on me what she said.

"You know about Pete Strauss?" she asks.

"Who?" I lie, trying to hide my surprise but falling short. Although I shared what I found in Springfield with her, I never mentioned the mechanic's report or Dirty Pete.

Nora clenches Liam's shoulders, shaking him. "Don't lie to me. You know all about him, and what he did."

"I know he was an animal, and he didn't complete the investigation into your parents' death. That's all I know."

Looking at Liam, she pauses for a few seconds, brushing her fingers through his hair. Talking more to Liam than to me, she says, "You know, the lake's almost a thousand feet deep." She looks up at me, the expression gone, replaced with sadness and fatigue. "Liam and I talked about the fish in the lake, down where it's dark and cold. Right, Liam?" She gives his arm a little shake.

Liam, sensing an opportunity, looks at her and says, "I have to go."

"Nora, put the gun down and we can talk about it."

Something in her changes again, and she starts to breathe heavy and fast. "Bitch-fucking bitch." Her breath is broken by sobs; her arm waves the gun in the air, sweeping the horizon. "Evil bitch." She stops waving the gun. "Eddie knew everything. He called me and told me to meet him downtown. Before I could talk to him, he was dead. They killed him."

"Knew everything about what, Nora? Who killed him?"

"My parents, about Dirty Pete, the accident. He wanted to talk."

Liam begins whining and dancing, and finally I see the unmistakable stream of yellow fluid trickling down his leg, steaming in the cold air. Liam starts to cry.

Nora glances down, following my eyes, pursing her lips. She shakes her head slowly. "Too bad. Sorry, champ." She gives my son a gentle pat on the shoulder. Nora lets her hand fall to her side. "Then, Douala."

"What about Douala? You mean the capitol of Cameroon?"

It's Nora's turn to cry.

"What, Nora?"

She takes a deep breath, turning with Liam to her right, her eyes filled with wet tears. "They kept me out, and I paid the price. I'm still paying the price."

She staggers, teetering, and I reach to grab her just as she puts the gun in her mouth and pulls the trigger.

The report is deafening as she tumbles back. I grab Liam, pulling him into my chest. "Don't look," I say, holding him, walking him to the park entrance. The first responders arrive at the site within minutes. I call Katie, telling her Liam is safe.

Walking back to where Nora lies on the ground, I avert my eyes from her head, and pick up her Glock. I drop the gun into a plastic evidence bag and tag it for ballistics.

. . .

It's three in the morning when I return home. Between processing the scene, and the IAD interview with Novak, who's done nothing to hide his disgusted disbelief, I've spent six hours at Central. As the IAD interview grinds on, Novak works to pry out inconsistencies, asking me repeatedly how I happened to be at Illinois Beach Park after dark. In the end, he tells me to go home, assuring me they'll get the truth one way or another.

Earlier in the evening, Katie took Liam in her arms, calmly hugging him, asked if he was okay, and instructed him to get into her waiting car. I braced myself for a replay of the scene at the pool in Mexico and stood to face her.

She looked at me, searching my eyes. "Tom, I want to believe you didn't intentionally send me on a goose chase when you knew where the bitch was."

Struggling to produce a rational explanation, I say, "I thought if you came to the scene she might go crazy."

"Crazier than she was?" Katie shakes her head.

Before I can answer, she pivots on her heels, walking briskly to her car, where Long-Suffering Len sits waiting at the wheel. He averts his glance.

At home, I stand in the dim light of the refrigerator, leaning in to find two small cartons of Chinese takeout alone in the cavernous expanse of the empty fridge. Prying opening the cartons, I hesitantly taste the food, satisfying myself the contents are at least marginally safe. I pop the containers into the microwave. I sit on the couch, carefully spooning the stale remnants of moo goo gai pan into my mouth, when, overcome, I put the cardboard box down, put my head in my hands, and weep.

I wake on the couch two hours later, exhausted. Checking my watch, I retrieve the gym bag, arriving early enough to find the pool empty. I change and swim twenty laps before finally coming to rest at the deep end. As always, I inhale and drop to the bottom. I force air from my lungs. I'm overtaken by a black electric surge coursing through my head as I begin to choke for air. Reaching for something to hold on the bottom, I find a small drain outlet on the floor of the pool and pull myself down, feeling water enter my sinuses and a sharp pain stabbing behind my eyes. I hear a deep thump. My fingers grip the small metal grate as the pounding in my ears beats to the rhythm of my heart. I open my mouth, drawing water into my lungs, until blackness surrounds me.

CHAPTER TWENTY-SIX

I AVOID A PSYCH SUSPENSION ONLY BECAUSE I'M ABLE to convince Tyler, the club associate, the whole blackout episode is a mistake.

Coming to on the pool deck, I'm covered in puke. Tyler's kneeling next to me. His clothes are wet and, I can see, also covered in vomit. He leans me against the tile wall and puts a towel behind my head.

"Jesus man, what are you trying to do? Kill yourself?"

Through the haze, I know anything I try to tell Tyler is probably not going to convince him. I scramble to come up with a rational explanation for why I basically tried to drown myself.

I take a deep breath. "I'm really sorry, Tyler. I was training for a field certification for underwater rescue. I've got to be able to hold my breath for two minutes straight, or I won't pass the test."

He stares at me in disbelief. "I don't know Mr. Edison; maybe I should call the club owner and get you some medical attention."

I sit up, removing the towel from behind my head. "Please don't bother. I'm fine, really."

"I know you've had a couple of incidents before," he says, shaking his head. "If this is some kind of test, maybe you should train for it elsewhere." He glances at the exit door, as if he expects his boss and a full squad of emergency personnel to barge through the door at any second. "You can't be doing this again—ever," he says, getting to his feet. He looks at his uniform with disgust. "I think you're done."

I get up and slowly walk to the locker room. I wash myself and put on my street clothes. On my way out, I stop by the front desk where Tyler, changed into fresh clothes, looks at me again with concern. "You've got to promise me, Mr. Edison, that you won't try anything like that again." I nod and reach in my pocket, pulling out three twenties, which is all the cash I have. I awkwardly push it at him.

"This is for your trouble. I'd appreciate it if you wouldn't let anyone know about this evening. I know a bunch of the guys from my office come in to work out, and I would never hear the end of it."

Tyler looks at the money in his palm and hands it back. "That won't be necessary, Mr. Edison. Please, just no more stunts like that."

I nod and walk out.

Pending the IAD investigation into Nora's death, I'm placed on administrative leave.

Novak smugly assures me the leave will be at least five weeks, maybe more, and with a growing smirk tells me I'll have to negotiate paid time through my union rep, as my entitlement to pay is up in the air. Tallying potential witnesses, I feel a clammy sweat as I wonder what Linda

Edwards would say if asked about my handling of the case and, in particular, my relationship with Nora. I'm certain Novak will try to track down Larry. I'm in the uncomfortable position of having to rely on others to do the right thing and to hope for the best.

I also have some unfinished business to take care of.

It was late April the first time I drove up the drive to the Wesley house and the final traces of winter were still on the ground. Scanning the grounds as I approach the locked gate, it's obvious in late fall the garden has gone to seed, the bushes and flower beds dead or overgrown. It seems as though Charles and Linda have decided not to replace Jesus, at least for the time being.

I called ahead, asking to see Linda, and she relented only after I assured her the purpose of my visit is administrative. I told her it is policy for the investigating detective to turn over sensitive documents personally. The front gate slides open and I park along the drive, walking the last twenty yards to the front door. As I approach the steps, the door opens and Linda stands like a sentry in the threshold.

"Detective. I'd heard you were on leave," she says, scanning the walk behind me to see if I'm alone, carefully holding the door ajar. I hand her several forms releasing documents we've recovered and items which were processed for DNA and fingerprints. "Don't you have better things to do in your time off?" She accepts the paperwork, takes the pen I offer her, and balances the clipboard on her knee.

"I wanted to come and personally let you know we've closed our case. The department is satisfied the DNA evidence collected from the blood places Mr. Rivera at the scene at the time of your mother's death. The Chicago

Police Department is investigating the deaths of Alma, Jesus, and Mr. Rivera separately. "

She finishes signing without looking at the forms and smiles thinly. "You needn't have come all the way here. It's fine to deal with Satterman." She starts to close the door. I lean in, wedging my foot into the space between us. "Out there on the lake, she—Nora—was talking all about Eddie Rivera and Douala. You know what that's about?"

"Regrettably, no. I don't." She pulls the door against my foot.

Taking the measure of me, she's clearly at a loss about what to do. She's loathe to slam the door in my face, and I'm pleased to watch her squirm. She's trying with false bonhomie to get me to leave, like getting the staff to leave after a cup of grog at Christmas.

"Nora was an unhappy woman," she says, finally discarding decorum and pulling in earnest to close the door. When it's almost closed, I manage to push a second sheaf of papers through the crack. The door shuts with a bang.

I start down the steps and, after a few seconds, Linda reopens the door and I watch her quickly scanning the pages. Her face is pulled into a tight knot.

I know I've got her, and I feel the warm glow of satisfaction run down my spine like a piss shiver. There's a moment past which there's no reason for manners. We've just arrived.

She steps through the threshold, loosening her grip on the door. I stroll back to the door and lean against the lintel. Linda holds the sheaf like a soiled napkin.

"I thought you would want those personally delivered. I didn't want them falling into the wrong hands."

Glancing behind her to see if anyone can hear, she gestures for me to come inside.

Waving the papers, she says, "I can explain this." She shepherds me further into the house, pointing to a door at the back of the central hall. Once inside the small, well-lit room, she nods to a blue brocade settee and begins searching for something on one of the bookshelves. After a few fruitless seconds, she decides that whatever it is can wait, and sits down on the settee, and starts sifting through the highlighted entries on the Credite Zurich printout from Dan Hagen with the name of the account: William Stark.

"I just thought you'd want to know we had this information. I thought maybe we could come to an understanding," I say, moving to a seat across from her.

Nodding, she says, "What do you want? Money?"

"I want the truth and some discretion."

Waving the bundle of paper at me, she's breathing quickly. "I told mother not to do it . . . I told her not to pay Stark." Tears gather in her eyes.

"What was she paying him for?"

"Isn't it obvious?" she replies sharply. "To . . . to," she stammers, tossing the papers on the couch next to her. She pauses for several seconds. "To get the right result," she adds finally.

"Did you tell her you wouldn't go along?"

"It's pretty obvious no one—least of all me—stood up to my mother. I mean, I was living here after the divorce because 'Faith wouldn't have it any other way.'" Sitting on the couch, the facade of ice broken, her battlements breached, she's a scared twelve-year-old girl.

"How'd you find out?"

Linda shrugs. "She'd had a few cocktails, and she just

said she had everything sewn up. When Stark's report came out, it was so one-sided, I knew. She told me not to worry, that everything was taken care of."

"That didn't stop you from giving the false report to the court. You committed perjury."

Linda's up again, moving to the bookcase, pushing aside books and a stack of magazines on the shelf. Turning to me, she says, "What did you expect I'd say? 'I know you're judging my fitness as a mother, but you should know I suspect, but can't prove, my crazy mother's bribing the custody evaluator.'" She snorts, trying unsuccessfully to be indignant.

"So, what, you just went along because it was easier?"

Her search of the bookcase fails to yield results, and she moves to a credenza at the far end of the room, opening the small drawers of the piece in rapid succession. "You wouldn't understand."

"Try me."

"For mother, the Wesley image was a crusade. She was almost feudal about it. I know she resented the fact I was a girl. She wanted a boy to carry on the Wesley name. Any threat to that name was eradicated, like weeds in the garden. What's laughable is that what or who she thought the Wesleys were was a myth, a creation for *Town and Country* magazine."

"So?"

"I told mother I thought it was disgraceful and threatened to tell Lent. I told her if she didn't do something to make it right, I'd expose them both."

"But the report was never changed, was it?"

"She said there was no going back."

"Why?" I ask, surprised.

"She said she'd done it for me, for us, and Stark had a piece of insurance—a guarantee." She moves to a second bookcase on the far wall, finally producing a box of cigarettes. "Mind if I smoke?"

I remain still.

"I keep a stash in here, but Daddy doesn't know." She fumbles with the pack, extracting a single cigarette to light it.

"The insurance policy?" I push, watching her exhale.

"Eddie Rivera got out of jail . . ." she pauses, quickly stubbing the cigarette, looking to the door behind me.

Charles walks in, shaking his head. He makes it to the center of the room and stands next to Linda. He doesn't seem particularly surprised to see me, or to see Linda smoking, for that matter. "I suppose it's too late to ask you what brings you here, Tom," he motions to Linda to sit, then seats himself on the settee next to his daughter. Turning to her, he says, "You really should cut back on those filthy things. You'll look like Delia van Ostergaard."

I chuckle, despite myself. "I think you know why I'm here, Mr. Wesley."

He nods in slow assent, and I wonder whether he's going to summon Webb or Satterman. "Regrettably, I do. I wasn't a party to Faith's stupid attempt to make sure everything went her way. I was, however, part of the effort to get it cleaned up."

Waving the account summaries, Linda turns to him. "You knew about this?"

"Only after the fact," he says, taking them from her.

I turn to Charles. "You and Satterman put us through hell getting this stuff. I should charge you with obstruction of justice. When we met at the law firm, you seemed surprised by the NAST account. Either you're a great actor, or this is really news to you."

"It was news. I knew Faith worked out something with Stark, because, like Linda, she'd told me she had everything arranged." He puts down the account summary and reaches down to the coffee table to adjust three porcelain Japanese figures. "I told her it was a bad idea, but she was intent on making sure everything went her way."

Charles takes one of the figurines in his hand and shrugs. "I was pretty sure he was extorting her, just didn't know how or for how much. Faith wouldn't have told me if I'd asked. Of course, I didn't ask Satterman or the accountants for an audit because I didn't want people asking questions. I've spent a good part of my life cleaning up the messes my late wife left behind her." He glares at Linda, who's now on her fourth cigarette. "I didn't—and don't—want this kind of garbage floating around."

Looking directly at me, he says, "We found my wife's killer—that's enough for me."

"So, I've heard," I say. "We can prosecute Stark for extortion. We can still consider whether your efforts to hide this stuff are something to discuss with Judges Ainsworth and Wardman."

Charles shakes his head. "That won't be necessary," he says, with the kind of expression you have when you know the time has come to do something you've been avoiding for a long time.

He walks to a desk at the far end of the room and opens the side drawer. "When I found out about Faith's failed deal, I hired some . . ." he says, pausing to find a word, "fixers, if you will. They looked into Bill Stark. They found some interesting things. Here," he says, pulling out a thick manila envelope that he hands to me. The envelope contains dozens of pages of Illinois Department of Corrections letterhead with hundreds of entries for orders at the dispensary. I flip through the documents. Each order made by WHS is highlighted. There are dozens of orders through the dispensary. I'm sure if I compare the Abbott Lab orders, it will show they were placed by WHS.

"I told Faith not to pay him another dime," Charles says, picking up the Japanese figurine again, tapping it on the bottom several times as if to make sure it's authentic. "After that, I assumed we were done with him. Until this, it was closed business as far as I was concerned."

"Did you know Eddie Rivera?"

Glancing over at Linda, he nods. "I knew Mr. Rivera was Alma's brother."

"You never mentioned him when we were interviewing you."

Charles sighs. "Eddie Rivera came over here several times a long time ago when he was a young man. He had some tough times and then disappeared. I hadn't seen him for decades and had no reason to suspect he was involved in this mess."

"Why would he want to kill Mrs. Wesley?"

"In retrospect, I can only surmise something Faith said to Alma or Jesus got back to him and he was angry or crazy enough to kill her. Faith threatened to fire and deport them both several times, over one pretext or another. As you know, her opinions got her into trouble more than once."

I reach over and pick up the bank printouts on the couch, rising to leave. I look at Linda. "As far as I'm concerned, Mrs. Wesley's case is closed. If I were you, though, I'd build bridges with Lent Edwards. I'd see if you can arrive at an arrangement that works for everyone—informally."

I turn to face Charles. "As for me, Nora's suicide means Internal Affairs may be asking some questions about my investigation. Just like the custody case, the less said the better."

I pause by the door. "Otherwise," I add, "you'll have to explain this stuff to the court and retry the custody case with all of this other stuff out in the open. That can't be good for anyone."

Charles and Linda get to their feet. Charles looks over at Linda to see if she understands. She sighs and nods in assent, her face pinched in sour determination.

"Good, then. I'll let myself out."

■ ■ ■

On my way home, I head to the nearest Desk Max store, fill out a fax cover sheet, and address it to Lent. The note on the fax sheet reads:

Lent,

These are accounts kept by Bill Stark. I figure you'll know how to use the information.

Tom

I ponder the grimy machine and the sheaf of forty pages fanned out, waiting to be fed through. I recall Nora's description of justice: The need to set things right. As much as I dislike Lent Edwards, I can't help feeling he's been wronged.

I push the send button and the pages started to feed.

■ ■ ■

The next day, I spend another full day with Novak, reiterating the circumstances of Nora's call and her relationship to Liam, especially how she knew Liam at all. In the process, I admit going to the concert at Cirque du Soleil.

Novak shakes his head. "You went to a concert with a witness in a murder investigation?"

"I accepted the offer of tickets from a person peripherally connected to a family involved in a murder investigation," I answer carefully.

"That didn't cloud your judgment?" Novak says, pulling up a chair.

"Not at all." For the moment, I figure I'm safe about the rest of it. Assuming he's even in any shape to do it, Larry won't talk to Novak out of principle. Linda and Charles have too much to lose by outing me.

My questions about Nora are rubbing me as raw as a wet sneaker. When I arrive, the house is dark and empty, and I narrowly miss falling on my face, stumbling through the brush in the shadows. Nora died without a will or next of kin, so the house waits empty until a court-appointed executor can settle her estate.

Although Nora and I never discussed it, I assumed by the way she lived she was what my mother always referred to as "independently wealthy." She had enough so she could live as she pleased and travel as she liked. What I learn after she's gone is that she has an estate approaching thirty-million dollars. Her father's family had money, and when her parents died, it was held in trust for her until she reached majority. Her financial advisor after her parents' deaths was, of course, Charles.

I stand still by the back corner of the house, hearing sadness in the sound of the few leaves in the November wind in the empty tree boughs. I kneel next to the back porch, reaching under until my hand feels the cold stone foundation and my fingers locate the key. The back door opens easily into the unheated porch, strangely quiet.

I make my way from room to room by the light of the streetlights shining through the curtained windows. The wood floors moan under my feet until I reach the living room, where I see the Dead Bell, solid and black, setting on the shelf. I reach for it, feeling its heft. I run my hand over the cold, smooth surface, feeling the raised detail, like braille, in the metal. The bell makes a solitary low hum as I put it into the bag I've brought with me.

On the way out, I walk to Nora's desk, cluttered with bills, several small notebooks, and lists—lists of vitamins, list of prescriptions, lists of events, lists of doctors. In the top drawer, several letters are clipped together. On the top, a white envelope, with a large purple stamp from Spain, is directed to Nora. The postmark is dated two years ago, the return address: *Grupo Hospitalario Quirónsalud* in Madrid.

I reach into the envelope and retrieve a cover letter written in Spanish:

Querida Sra. Summers, siguiendo nuestra conversación telefónica de ayer aquí están los resultados de sus pruebas. Lamento informarle que son positivos para cáncer de páncreas.

Le imploro a su regreso a los Estados Unidos que contacte a un especialista en oncolgia lo más posible.

Te deseo la mejor de las suertes.

Dr. Umberto Campos

I don't speak Spanish, but I'm able to decipher the worst: Nora's tests are positive for pancreatic cancer. Suddenly, I understand. Nora came home to die. What we had together was a final gesture of defiance, a beacon in the shadows that eventually overcame her.

I've overlooked the clear signs of her illness: the jaundice, weight loss, and bruising. Her sudden disappearance and the trip to New York was part of her treatment. I also now understand she faced her impending end with purpose and order and, until the end, detachment.

She sought to summarize, to understand, the complex collected events making up her life. Her parents' death was a breach in the hull, and over time she'd taken on water, listing unnaturally against the tide. Finally, she'd come to believe that single event was the original cause of the misfortunes which followed.

Behind the letter from Dr. Campos is a second envelope from the Clinique Central de Douala. Enclosed within is a grey photocopy with a letter attached in broken English. The letter says, "After diligent search, the enclosed was all that could be found for Thurston Kimball Summers (Kip)." Gently unfolding the brittle photocopy, I find a medical report from the Clinique Central de Douala in the Cameroon, dated November 4th, 1966, for Thurston Kimball Summers (Kip), DOB 1944. In the bottom right corner in bold: Discharge diagnostic: TB (tuberculose).

I train the flashlight in the drawer, sifting through receipts, parking tickets, and check stubs, until finally my eye catches another sheaf of papers neatly folded on the left-hand side, to which is attached an undated, handwritten note:

Dear Nora,

*It was good talking with you the other day. It was
a surprise to hear from someone interested in one of
Gary's old cases. He wasn't in the habit of keeping old
reports, but I know this one bothered him a lot. I found
a copy of this in the attic.*

Best,
Adele Burdell

I point the flashlight at the first brittle, yellowed page, bearing the seal of the State of Illinois, offset against the seal of the Lake County Sherriff's Office. At the top of the page is the header for the Lake County Sheriff's office. The document, dated March 1969, is signed *Gary Burdell, Lead Mechanic.*

The report contains an exhaustive inspection of the 1964 Cadillac Deville, concluding with the recommendation:

*Inspection of the braking systems revealed three
incisions in the rubber hosing leading into the brake
master cylinder. Close inspection of the hose shows
traces of paraffin or a waxy substance covering the
area of the incision. With the operation of the vehicle
for a period of over twenty minutes, the ambient engine
heat would melt the paraffin, resulting in failure of
the pressurized brake system. Report was delivered to
investigating officer P. Strauss with recommendation to
open homicide investigation.*

I put the report into my pocket and quickly make for the back porch. As I open the screen door, I see the framed photograph of the Summers family: mother, father, and daughter.

. . .

The only way I'm going to get a straight answer about Dirty Pete is to apply direct pressure on Tammy Strauss. With Nora dead, and the revelations about the payments to Stark, Linda's threats are empty. With my newfound freedom during my suspension, I book a flight to LAX. At Los Angeles airport, I hand the cabbie the address in El Segundo that I got from the reverse directory months earlier. I tell the cabbie to wait down the block, pitching him a twenty to keep the meter running.

Tammy Uhler, the former Mrs. Strauss, lives in a small hospital-green bungalow at the end of a numbered street. I ring the doorbell several times until the door opens halfway to reveal a thin woman in her late sixties wearing a stained bathrobe and tattered slippers. The skin around her eyes and mouth are etched. In her right hand she holds a beer can; the other shields her eyes against the morning light. I check my watch: 9:17 AM. She would be more welcoming to a burning bag of shit left at her front door.

Dispensing with the niceties, I identify myself. She stands, unmoving, making no effort to open the door further, ready to slam it shut.

"I told you on the phone, Pete's none of my business."

I was hoping by surprising her to catch her off guard and leverage her. I'm out of my jurisdiction, suspended, and the subject of an investigation. I've also underestimated her. She's as hard as fire-treated ironwood and has an animal cunning possessed by people who've lived most of their lives on the hard edge. "I need to find out why Pete closed the investigation and the report."

She's having none of it. I suspect she's refused meaner

than me. She looks at me, shaking her head. "He's dead. Leave me alone." She starts to withdraw behind the door.

"It'll only take a few minutes, and I've got a cab waiting. I'll pay you for your time."

The last offer is a gamble. If the former Mrs. Strauss is proud, she'll slam the door in my face. As it is, the money talk seems to melt whatever resolve she has. She gestures for me to come inside. The house reeks of overpowering deodorizer and kitty litter. Beer cans cover what passes for a coffee table.

Moved by some vestigial sense of decorum, she grabs a handful of cans, spiriting them away. On the TV, the volume down, improbably happy contestants jump ecstatically as a peroxide blonde in a tight dress flashes numbers on a screen.

Tammy returns, apparently satisfied with her efforts at tidying up. Scanning the room, I notice a faded photo: a younger and less sour Tammy with two boys who could not have been more than ten or twelve at the time.

"Your boys?" I ask, as she sits across from me.

She nods. "Got pregnant when I was sixteen. They're Pete's, but he always said he could never be sure." On the right corner of the mantle sets a picture of a young man in army uniform. Draped over the frame is a ribboned medal. I glance at Tammy, who nods. "Grenada Invasion. Only nineteen soldiers killed. He was one of them. Nineteen years old."

"What about your other boy?"

"Lives in New York with his husband. We don't talk." She pushes aside a pile of magazines and an old throw blanket and sits down. She picks up a beer can on the table and checks to see if it's full. "You wanna beer?" she asks, waving the can at me. I shake my head. She leans back, looking out the window, her eyes someplace distant. I reach into my pocket and pull out five twenties and lay them on the table. She eyes them, then reaches to take them and deposits them in the breast pocket of her shirt.

"I don't know about no report, but about three months before he left, Pete told me he pinned some Mexican cholo kid for tampering with someone's car. Said it was gonna be a good deal for him. I didn't make it my business to ask Pete about what he did. He didn't say nothing about it until a couple of months later when he turned into some kind of fuckin' big shot . . . new clothes, new car, you name it."

"Did you know where the money was coming from?"

"Like I said, I didn't mind his business." She pauses and takes a pull off the beer can. "I was stupid enough once to tell him I knew he was doing that Verna McNeil bitch," she says, frowning.

"And . . .?" I ask, trying to hide my surprise.

"Got me six stitches and fuckin' black eye," she says, depositing the can on the table.

After a couple of seconds, she gets up and clears several of the remaining beer cans, placing them on a side table. She picks up another one that is apparently still full and takes a pull. "Pete left me and the boys and disappeared. Just like that. I heard he moved to Las Vegas and opened a card parlor, but I suspect it was a whorehouse. Not so much as a fucking Christmas card. Then, five years after that, he's dead—a stroke—the fuck," she says, waving the beer can as if brushing away her complicated, brutish, ugly life.

"Why didn't the department investigate him?"

She leans tenuously against an old brown bookshelf for support. "I know internal affairs looked at it and tried to jerk Pete's junior partner."

"Do you know who that was?"

"Same guy for the last five years of Pete's time there— Ed Delahunt. He started as an investigator with Pete. They hated each other. Ed Delahunt asked three times to be transferred, but the chief turned him down every time. After Pete was gone, IAD turned the heat up on Ed, but Ed's a real 'honor among brothers' type."

"I know," I say, trying to hide my surprise.

"They tried to hook Pete after he landed in Vegas, but Nevada refused to cooperate. I guess some of Pete's new customers owed him a thing or two." She takes another pull at the beer in her hand, gulping loudly. "Then he was dead."

I get up, careful to avoid touching the fabric on the couch. Making my way to the front door, I worry the cabbie has left, stranding me with Tammy in a maze of brown lawns and windshield glare. Leaving the safety of the bookcase, she follows me to the tiny atrium.

Whether out of charity, or just to make sure I've gotten everything she knows, I extend a hand with two more bills in it, which she seizes in her hand, hard and dry as a claw.

"I appreciate your willingness to talk to me, Tammy."

She sways unsteadily, her eyes glassy. She mashes the new bills into her shirt pocket.

Clearly eager to show the money has been well earned, as she opens the door, she says, "There's been a lot of interest in that case recently."

I stop, facing her in the shadows of the front hall, as I hold the screen door on the small landing outside. "What do you mean?"

"Well, about a year ago I got a visit from a woman wanting to know, just like you, about Pete and the accident."

"What was her name?"

Tammy shrugs. "Dunno. Tried to put her off, just like you. She said she was a relative tying up some loose ends."

"What did you tell her?"

"Pretty much everything I just told you," she says, struggling through the beer to recall.

"Including the bit about pinching the cholo kid?"

"Yeah, I told her that."

"You demand money from her?"

She shifts. "Nope. Should have," she says, patting the wad in her shirt pocket. "She came to find me, like you, but she was stuck up, a real bitch." Tammy gives me what might be intended as a smile, pitches the can into a bin by the front door, and shrugs. The screen door slams behind me.

I turn and walk down the path to the waiting cab, avoiding a pile of dogshit.

The cholo kid Strauss pinched was Eddie Rivera. I'm willing to bet my badge Tammy's stuck-up bitch was Linda. I went to archives for Nora, but Linda already knew about the investigation and Dirty Pete. She'd been to see Tammy months before her mother was murdered. Linda threatened me away from investigating Nora's parents, because she knew Pete Strauss pinched Rivera for killing them. As the cab makes its way back to the airport, I have to wonder how a guy like Strauss could die, rich and out of harm's way, of a heart attack. If there's some larger system of justice, as Nora thought, I have to admit a lot of the time it doesn't seem to be working.

. . .

After I land in Chicago, Katie calls. I debate whether to pick up but, opting to face the onslaught, brace myself for the barrage of renewed accusations. We haven't spoken since the confrontation after Nora's suicide.

"I want to have you make up the time after the mix-up with *Jack in Beanstalk* and your fishing trip with Liam," she says, her voice bright and loud in the earpiece. I suspect a trap and look for a catch.

Negotiating the on-ramp, I ask, "What do you want in exchange?"

"No, Tom. No strings. I talked to Liam, and he told me Nora convinced the counselors she was an aunt. When they asked Liam, he said she was 'kind of like an aunt.' He said she was really nice to him at Cirque du Soleil. Liam's okay, and we should just put it behind us."

I'm not sure what's prompted the change in Katie, but I'm not about to ask. Maybe, true to her word, she just wants the conflict to end. "Thanks, Katie. Is Liam there?"

"No, actually, he's outside playing with his friend Robbie. Do you want me to get him?"

"No, but thanks for the offer."

"I should be going, Tom. I'll talk to you soon."

"Is everything okay? You sound a little tired."

She hesitates, then sighs. "Everything is fine, Tom. I just wish things had worked out differently, that's all."

She hangs up. We've arrived at a watershed moment in our relationship. I don't expect it to be conflict-free moving forward, but we've managed to work out a system of exchange without custody evaluators, judges, or mediators. I know I owe it as much to Katie as to anything I've done. I take a deep breath. Smiling to myself, I pull into the office parking lot.

CHAPTER TWENTY-SEVEN

TWO WEEKS LATER I'M SITTING IN DANI'S, across from Tony Shahbaz, who's invited me to lunch. The restaurant is two blocks from Tony's office, and it hasn't changed its décor or menu since Nixon was President, a time whose virtues the owner, Daniel Testaverde, can frequently be heard extolling. Autographed photographs line the walls in rows of dingy frames. Pictures of anchormen; politicians; minor celebrities; some living, some dead, all make homage to Danny and pay tribute to simpler times. It's always busy and, whatever time of year, always too warm.

Tony asked me to lunch, ostensibly to see how my suspension is going. Given my status as *persona non grata* in the office, I think the choice of Dani's is curious. I can see several people glare at me as I walk to the back. A couple of assistants wave a half-hearted hello and get back to their pasta.

I share as much with Tony as I think wise, keeping

to generalities. I tell him it's taking a long time, there's nothing to find, Novak's on a mission and out to get me, etc. I don't tell Tony that, as expected, Novak interviewed Linda Wesley, which she told me when she called to see if I planned to attend Nora's funeral. I told her under the circumstances I thought that would be a bad idea.

"Well, I guess you got what you needed, didn't you?" she said.

Linda's turning into a stereotypical man-hater. She doesn't dislike me because I'm a cop. She seems to hold a special disdain for me simply because I am a man.

"Do I need to remind you about the NAST account, Linda?"

I can hear her exhale with exasperation. "No, Tom. I didn't tell him anything."

"Good." She might hate me, but I think she's smart enough to keep her mouth shut.

With Larry released from the hospital and MIA, unlike Linda, he remains an open question. I try to reach him, but his cellphone doesn't answer. Unlike Linda and Charles, I have no idea whether Novak is going to track him down. He's in enough trouble in his own right to be wary of talking to IAD. It's also possible Novak might offer him a deal if he rolls on me.

Tony and I are seated at a back table usually reserved for local politicians which, judging from the reception Dani gives Tony, might easily include him in the near future. Tony reaches into his briefcase, extracting a yellow manila envelope about an inch thick. The return address is the now familiar Illinois Department of Corrections.

"Look, I know you're suspended and all, but I got these from the AG's office after you closed the Wesley case. Remember when you called and yelled at me about treatment records for Eddie Rivera and HIPAA?"

"I'm sorry about that. Those records were something Larry was supposed to be tracking. I called you when I found the response in a pile on his desk, and I was angry."

Tony laughs. "No worries. To be honest, I didn't bother looking at them until about a week ago."

"What does this have to do with anything? We closed that file."

"Rivera was under the care of your buddy Dr. Stark."

"What?"

"Yeah, released early under some special dispensation from Menard."

"So?"

"The thing is, the records were being held at DOJ by Stark."

"Why would he do that, I wonder?"

"I don't know. You closed the case, but I thought, well, you have some time on your hands so you might want to look at these. You figure it out."

■ ■ ■

Once I'm at my apartment, I fix myself a strong pot of coffee and spread the folders on the empty couch.

There's an intake summary cataloging Eddie's medical history, followed by notes from his treating physician and, after his release, a discharge summary. Attached to the back of the folder is the medication chart.

I scan the summary sheet. Stamped on the top in bright red is the word HOLD and the handwritten words: Per W.S., M.D.

I begin to read the summary.

The treating doctor, Eugene Walker, provided a description of Eddie at his initial psychiatric evaluation in 2003 at Menard. He was undernourished, with uneven thought processes and erratic speech, and had reports of paranoid behavior.

Walker gave Eddie a diagnosis of paranoid psychosis and delusional behavior and started him on antipsychotics. An entry catches my eye:

May 14th,

Patient presents this morning following a visit yesterday afternoon with his sister, Alma. He's extremely agitated and is expressing hostile ideation. He asked about the doctor-patient privilege and I confirmed it was in place. He reported his sister and her husband are living in the Chicago area and that they are undocumented. He has expressed deep love and affection for his sister, whom he describes as his "savior." He reports his sister told him about a confrontation she had with her employer, a Mrs. Wesley, calling his sister and her husband "lazy wetbacks."

He reported he has done "very bad things" in the past for Mrs. Wesley and that he is concerned she will, in his words, "bury his sister and her husband." He would not elaborate on what he's done in the past. This clinician questions whether these confessions are a paranoid ideation or are legitimate statements of past crimes. Given Eddie's current status, I believe this is largely academic.

Recommendation: Increase antianxiety meds Lexapro
20mg/day for short term. Continue on Invega.

Eugene R. Walker M.D.
Clinical Director Menard Psych Facility.

I leaf through the notes until I find.

December 2nd

Received transfer request for patient Eduardo Rivera
today from DOC admin offices. Transfer case will
be made to Dr. William Stark, a clinician who is a
psychiatrist at Cook County Central Services through
DOC. At his request, Eddie will be sent for evaluation
for transfer to a pilot outpatient support program run
by Dr. Stark. I've voiced my strong objections to this
plan and don't believe it is indicated or that subject is
ready to transfer out of this facility.

Dr. Charles Walker, M.D.

I call Joyce Hong at the Lake County ME's office. Hoping to avoid one of Joyce's patented lectures, I get straight to the point.

"What can you tell me about antipsychotic drugs in patients?"

Joyce puts her hand over the receiver and shouts briefly to someone to transfer the lab data. Removing her palm, she says, "What do you want to know? They're complicated, and there's not a lot we know about why some of them work."

"What about pulling someone off of them?"

"Any first-year resident knows it's insane to pull a patient off antipsychotics cold turkey."

"Why? What happens?"

"Aside from horrible physical side effects—dizziness, nausea, and headaches—the patient will spiral. You'll get a resurgence of pathology."

"So, a patient who's paranoid, or prone to violence, and obsessive-compulsive, would—"

"Become a time bomb—delusional, hyperactive, prone to suicide and maybe even homicidal ideation. It takes months to change a medication mix." Joyce pauses and adds, "If you're going to go after some doc, count me out as an expert, okay?"

■　■　■

The next day is Nora's funeral, and as I sit gazing out the window, I recall our time on her back porch in the summer sun. The winds of November sweep through the streets, and soon the snow will bury the streets in white. I haven't been back to the pool since the stunt in front of Tyler, and I'm feeling the urge to get some exercise, maybe go for a run, when my phone rings. It's Delahunt. He orders me to come to the office immediately. When I arrive, he's standing at the window, waiting. A tall, thin woman in a gray suit sits in a chair. Gesturing at the other chair setting in front of his desk, Delahunt says, "Tom, this is Marsha Camden, the department's lawyer." The woman does not rise.

I do a double take. Several years ago, Marsha Camden was known as Mort Camden before she transitioned. She's been a leader in the LGBT community and a frequent spokesperson on issues of diversity and equity. I nod briefly at Marsha, but she chooses to ignore me.

I'm about to sit down when I notice Novak in the back corner of the room, his hands in his pockets, shaking his head. Glancing at Novak, Delahunt says, "You already know Detective Novak, I assume."

Without preliminaries, Camden produces a stack of paper, placing it on the desk in front of me. "We got served with this lawsuit this afternoon. It seeks an emergency injunction and asks for damages of twenty-three million dollars. It's from Dr. Stark. You know anything about this?"

"No, I don't," I answer truthfully.

Camden adjusts her reading glasses. "It's alleging you've violated his privacy, defamed him, and put his bank information out on the Internet on a website run by a group called PACT. The website says Dr. Stark accepted bribes as part of custody evaluations."

Delahunt leans forward. "You didn't do something stupid like give bank account data to a bunch of wackos, did you Tom?" he says, picking up a pen and tapping the pad in front of him. "Well?"

Searching for an appropriate answer, I wonder what possessed me to send the Credite Zurich account stuff to Edwards. I feel a tight, quick beat of panic in my chest.

I figure it's useless to lie and after several beats nod my head. "I gave Edwards some information on Stark, but I—"

Delahunt slams his hand on the desk, running the fingers of his other hand through his sparse hair. "Goddamit, Tom," he says, reaching into his desk and pulling out the rubber troll.

I try to shore up my case, insisting, "PACT is keeping statistics on custody evaluators across the country. There's no criminal investigation involved. Edwards probably gave it to them for research."

Novak shakes his head, moving over to a spare chair at the conference room table. He turns it around, sitting on it in reverse. "That's the problem, Tom," Novak says, gloating, "you're on administrative leave."

Camden adjusts her glasses again. "If there wasn't a criminal investigation—which we know there wasn't, because you shut it down—you don't have privilege."

Delahunt leans back in his chair and runs his fingers through his hair. "As it is, we've got to take some pretty drastic action. We told the Wesleys the investigation was closed, so we can't suddenly reopen it. Sharing the banking stuff was a plain invasion of privacy. Do you understand what this means?"

"I expect to continue on leave."

Novak chuckles darkly. "No, Tom. I'm sorry." I doubt very much he's sorry. "The best defense the Department has at this point is to show you're a rogue cop. You'll need to surrender your badge now. As of this moment, you're done. We'll just add this to the mess we're investigating now."

In shock, I reach mechanically for my badge, carefully placing it on Delahunt's desk, in front of him.

"This is a tragedy, Tom," he says. He leaves the badge setting in front of him, as if he doesn't want to touch it. "I thought better of you. You should've taken a vacation with your kid like I told you." Camden looks away.

Novak stands up, surveying me like the remnants of a car wreck. "It was your choice and you're gonna live with it. The union rep will call you later today about getting you a lawyer when you get served." He points to the door, signaling me it's time to leave.

The last thing I see as Novak closes the door is Delahunt staring at his desk at the badge. It takes me a few minutes to pack my desk, passing Larry's darkened office as I leave.

■ ■ ■

The lot under my apartment building is full, so I park the car in a spot down the street and walk to my apartment, carrying the box filled with the contents of my work life. As I approach the building, the door to a black Cadillac Escalade opens, and a large man with a shaved, bald head steps out. He's sporting a pair of sunglasses despite the fact dusk has already fallen.

He stands easily four inches taller than me, his hands loose at his sides. "You Tom Edison?" he asks. Remembering I'm not armed and I'm carrying a forty-pound carton, I stall for time.

"Who wants to know?" I ask, noticing for the first time the man carries a yellow envelope in his right hand.

The man's face expands slowly into a smirk of grim amusement, as if he's just been challenged to a playground game.

"You Tom Edison?" he asks again, his voice laced with menace. I'm preparing to drop the carton and hit the guy in the abdomen when he reaches into his jacket and produces a plastic cardholder, which he waves at me. It says, "Anthony Holder, Process Server."

"Yeah," I answer simply.

Holder tosses the envelope into the carton. "Consider yourself served, asshole," he says, walking to the Escalade. He speeds away to a chorus of screeching tires.

I put down the box, staring at the envelope, which I open to extract a complaint filed in Lake County Circuit Court with the caption:

William Stark M.D. PsyD
V.
Lake County, Illinois,
Waukegan Police Department,
Lake County Major Crimes Task Force

And Thomas Edison, aka Tom Edison, an individual,

Parent and Children Together, an Illinois Not For
Profit corporation

and John Does 1-10 representing certain
administrative personnel of the Police Department of
Lake County

The complaint asks for twenty-three million dollars, claiming defamation, fraud, and civil rights violations.

The injunction calls for me to appear in court within a week.

I pick up the box, carrying it up to my apartment.

Reaching into my pockets, I locate several ten-dollar bills folded up in a neat roll. I start towards the door, but pause, extracting my telephone, and hit Trina's speed dial, which rings through immediately:

The subscriber at this number has temporarily
suspended service.

The machine beeps.

I throw the phone on the bed, pause to tuck the bills back in my pocket, then put on my jacket and walk down the street to a small storefront topped with a bright sign:

Mark's Fine Spirits.

The clerk stands behind a Plexiglas wall on which the entire liquor-consuming public appears to have vented its spleen in one form or another. Etched into the plastic, the scrawl ranges from obscenities to imaginative depictions of human copulation, all framed by stickers, and gooey dried smears. The clerk stares at me with the dull interest of an iguana as I fish the money out of my pocket.

"A quart of Dewar's White Label."

He stares at the ten-dollar bill I hand him through the Plexiglas.

"Gonna cost a lot more than that," he says. I fish out another two tens and push them through the divider. He places the bottle in the secure dispenser, followed by my change. The bottle is heavy and warm and makes a cheerful clink as the fluid gurgles and bubbles inside. When I arrive at the apartment, I carefully place the bottle on the coffee table. It stands there like a silent totem, gleaming with warm amber liquid and the promise of forgetfulness.

■ ■ ■

Because we never talked to anyone about it, least of all to each other, we never shared the fact there were other reasons the boat came gunning for us that afternoon. The identities of the thugs in the boat were never officially determined, but I knew who at least one of them was. I knew the thug with the long cigarette dangling from his mouth was known simply as "Paulie." I knew he was seventeen and a regular at the bar and grill known as Günters that sat at the other end of the lake.

The Summer of the Raft, we started going to Günters,

riding bikes the two miles down the lake to the restaurant. Camped at the picnic tables at the lakeside, we never ventured around the corner to the back. There, in a secluded area, bordered by a laurel hedge on one side and dark brush of bog willow, hackberry, black alder, and buttonbush, Paulie and his friends transacted business.

One day early that summer, business was especially busy, and we'd waited over twenty minutes for our food. Restless and hungry, I left the table, heading for nowhere in particular. I turned the corner just in time to see Paulie smash a boy in the face with his fist. Two other guys leaned against the building, watching as the kid fell to the ground, blood spewing from his nose. Paulie looked up, grinning, in time to see me back away.

"Hey, you little shit," he said. "Get over here."

I froze. Measuring the distance for a run, I saw I was close enough for Paulie and the others to overtake me. If they did, I'd end up like the kid clutching his face. Paulie, as if to make his point, kicked the kid in the ribs for good measure.

The kid with the broken nose, taking advantage of Paulie's diverted interest, ran towards the road, the two others watching with their eyes, but glued in place.

"Get the fuck over here," the man-boy repeated.

I went over to him. As I approached, I could smell his stained T-shirt, sour with sweat, cigarettes, and fried food. I could smell alcohol on his breath. He loomed eight inches taller and outweighed me by seventy pounds.

"You know what? You're a nosey little prick," he said, with a grin like a slit, assessing me. His face finally broke into a smile.

The ground behind Günters sloped down to a line of

hackberry tangle to form a solid wall, after which the grade sloped several yards away to a gully and disappeared into the muddy overgrowth and, eventually, the lake. Paulie grabbed me by the arm, putting me in a headlock, yanking me towards the gully.

"Come on," he said, as we descended into the thicket. "Let's teach this little fucker."

The other two followed, looking back to see if anyone from the restaurant or the other side of the area could see.

"I'm going to teach you good, you nosey little fuck. I'm gonna make you bleed," he said, dragging me into the undergrowth.

Forty minutes later, walking dazed towards Günters, I checked myself over. Aside from a red mark on my neck where the monster held me, there was nothing outward to show what had happened. I walked over to a stand of buttonbush and disgorged the contents of my stomach. I retched several times because there wasn't much in there. I stood, dazed, in the parking lot for several minutes, until Ben, Dolan, Jimmy, and Kraut came around the corner, asking where I'd been. Lying, I told them I'd simply gone for a walk. I lied and never stopped lying because Paulie told me that if I ever snitched, he'd gut me like a pig.

Two days later, the speedboat racing towards the raft had nothing to do with Ben's vain act of stupidity and everything to do with me keeping my mouth shut. For years, Ben believed Jimmy Newsome was his fault, but I knew the real reason Paulie the Monster came looking: to make sure his secret was safe.

That day, I emerged from the underbrush deeply changed—marked. In the weeks that followed, I came to view Paulie as a catastrophe as senseless and random as Stalingrad or the bubonic plague. Like Ben, I became infected with a fatalism that asked how a God with any sense of order or compassion could visit someone or something like Paulie on me. But where Ben chose apathy and withdrawal, I chose to endure, isolating myself from pain, and trusting no one. At thirteen, the only thing I could be certain of was my own innate ability to survive.

The next summer, the camp accountant-cum-chaplain interrogated me and I held onto the secret, as hard and dark as onyx.

The days and weeks following the accident passed, and I waited and watched, planning for Paulie's reemergence, when he would rise like a protean monster from the lake to claim me. I promised myself that, rather than suffer again, I'd fight, and take whatever he could dole out, and if the chance presented itself, I'd jam my fourteen-inch Bowie knife into his guts, disemboweling him. But, as fate would have it, Paulie's departure was as inexplicable and sudden as his arrival. Days became weeks, weeks became months, and months turned into years. Like a freak storm, the only trace of his presence was a dark stinking slick of retreating water and the marshy smell of the mud, buttonbush, black willow, and bog birch that stuck to my hair and clothes in frequent, haunted half-sleep.

■ ■ ■

Staring at the court papers in my hands, I rise after several seconds, moving the Dewar's bottle carefully to the kitchen counter, twisting the cap, which, once free, releases a dark peaty waft. Selecting a shot glass from the cabinet, I pour myself three fingers, swirling the amber liquid in the bottom as I turn the small tumbler several times on the counter. I feel the heft of the liquid and glass dense and warm in my hand. After several seconds, I grab the bottle by the neck and go to the sink to deliver its contents into the sewer system of greater Waukegan. I rinse the bottle to make sure there is no residue and reach for the garbage can under the sink and pitch the bottle in.

The apartment air is still. I feel a dull ache behind my eyes, and my temples throb, but for at least today, I decide I will endure the dogshit.

I go to the club and swim a mile, careful to avoid the watchful eyes of Tyler. Reaching my favorite corner, I take several breaths and slowly drift to the bottom. The pump and high whisper of the water soothes me as I realize I can never rid myself of the scar Paulie left, that it's a part of me, something which, instead of destroying me, makes me stronger.

Emerging into the late afternoon, the November light falls in the west and tints the clouds a pale blue and rose. I feel the sharp clean sensation of hunger and stop by Fat Boy's to order a Garlic Supreme pizza. After I have a couple of slices, I may reek of garlic, but there's no one besides myself to offend.

As I negotiate the door to my apartment, carefully cradling the remainder of the pie, I realize I've managed to finally settle into what might pass for acceptance. I've just gotten the door open when my phone rings. I search my pockets, hoping to answer before the next ring. In the process, I lose my grip on the carton, sending it spiraling to the ground. I stare at the carton on the floor, snatching the ringing phone out of my pocket. The caller ID says the number is blocked. It rings twice more, and before I can answer, it stops.

Bending to lift the pizza box, I steel myself for the carnage inside. I consider myself a modern man, firmly rooted in reason, but gripping the sagging cardboard, I revert to a cosmology as atavistic, primitive, and immediate as an aboriginal witch doctor. In that universe, the God of my childhood, far too busy and important to visit small misfortune on humans, cedes this work instead to a pantheon of lesser deities. Opening the lid and seeing the misshapen folds of bread and dangling webs of melted cheese, roasted garlic bits and spattered tomato sauce, I curse the lesser gods: the god of idiots, the god of bad drivers, the god of Internet Technical Assistance, who all gleefully mete out retribution on those whose offerings are deemed insufficient. I mentally shake my fist in the air: "Why, God? Why?"

Rearranging the pie into an abstract semblance of what it might have looked like as it came out of the oven, I search for a paper towel. The phone rings again. I press the answer button, ready to unload on the unlucky caller.

"Tom?" Lent Edwards asks, his voice clear and deliberate.

"How'd you get this number?" I demand, carefully replacing the top on the pizza box, hoping to preserve some of the heat. I lift the sagging box to put it on the kitchen table.

I think I can hear the sound of music in the background. "Shut the fuck up and listen."

Staring at the Fat Boy logo on the box, I want to get rid of him. "The case is closed, and I'm on leave."

Edwards gives me an address in Highland Park. "I'm here getting answers, which is more than you seem able to do," he says. He hangs up.

I stop tinkering with the box, scribbling the address just above the well-fed face of the eponymous Fat Boy.

It's half an hour south from Waukegan to Highland Park in light traffic. I hope to make it in twenty minutes.

CHAPTER TWENTY-EIGHT

T HE DIVIDER LINES FLASH TO STROBOSCOPIC effect, making the road appear motionless. Two cold slices of Garlic Supreme droop on a sagging paper plate next to me. My once urgent hunger has now receded to background noise.

I run a reverse directory on the address Lent gave me. As I expect, it comes back to Stark. I wonder why, instead of simply killing him, Lent has chosen to call me. In my head I tally a list of potential reasons, each equally plausible. The first is that, like Nora, Lent has a deeply rooted sense of justice. He's likely also looking for vindication. I'm not sure what makes him think I can give him either one. As I race to Highland Park, something drawn taut and thin inside me finally snaps. On the seat beside me, next to the greasy paper plate, a large Redweld folder holds the closest thing I can offer Lent to vindication. I'm compelled by an angry need to settle accounts, and my visceral drive to be right drowns any voice counseling reason.

I begin by trivializing the possible consequences of following Lent up to Stark's house. Like a smoker telling myself it's not bad for me, I convince myself I'm a good cop going to intercede in a bad situation. I also try to avoid personal responsibility for my lack of self-control. Like an alcoholic protesting that I only drink socially, I ignore the fact I'm unarmed and on suspension. I begin racing endlessly through a cycle of regression, asking myself why, and for each answer, I get "yes, but why?"

I'm on the verge of losing it when I glance in my rearview mirror and catch a glimpse of a green SUV moving into the lane behind me. I'm pretty sure it's been following me for a mile or two. The fleet of unmarked vehicles at Major Crimes consists of several black late model sedans and two white Econoline vans. I've passed my time in purgatory in some of them, doing surveillance. I figure IAD probably keeps their own fleet of disintegrating rolling stock in the unlikely event they need to take them on the road. If it's Novak, I'm going to dust his sorry ass.

I put the Beast into high gear and watch the odometer hit one-hundred-ten miles per hour, quickly putting the SUV more than a quarter of a mile behind me. The pizza on the plate has gelled to the dull sheen of latex. I reach the next exit, roll down the window, and pitch the slices onto the road, watching them vaporize. I pull into a deserted parking lot of an auto glass shop and wait. I sort through the Redweld file, the hot knot in my chest dominating me. By the time I'm back on the road, any doubt I have about confronting Stark is gone.

Eglandale Drive is in a gated community. I try several default emergency codes. After four tries, the steel gates quietly swing open. I follow the GPS, finally stopping in front of a large colonial house overlooking the lake. The driveway ends in a circular drive where I see Lent's BMW. A hunter green Aston Martin D89 coupe sets in the open garage. The trimmed lawn slopes to a path running parallel to the lakeshore and, finally, the lake itself.

I walk through the open garage, glancing at the security camera over the door. After several seconds, I turn the doorknob to the house and enter the kitchen, finding my way to the Great Hall. I can hear music drifting from the far end of the house. The kitchen and dining room are empty, and in the great room hangs a huge Lichtenstein and three paintings by what appears to be Chagall.

I follow the music down the hall, peering around the door, where I see Stark sitting upright in a chair, his lower lip swollen to the size of a walnut. Blood seeps, dark and slow, from a gash on his forehead. Stark sees me and nods toward the other side of the room, where Lent sits on a leather ottoman facing the desk. A Colt Defender .45 lies next to him. He holds the Credite Zurich accounts in his hand.

"Hello, Tom," Lent says, motioning to an armchair next to the sofa. He looks over towards Stark and chuckles. "I got started without you. I wasn't sure you were coming."

"I'm unarmed," I say, scanning the room. "Is anybody else here?"

"Just us," Edwards says.

"Why did you bring me here?" I ask, as Stark moves in the chair. I can see he's bound with several courses of duct tape.

Edwards gets up, making his way to a table on the other side of the room. He unravels a black bundle containing a set of steel tools. He looks over at me. "Your presence here is entirely voluntary; you came because you wanted to. But, if you stay," he says, as he lays out the tools, "we're going to get some answers."

Stark clears his throat, his voice just about a whisper. "Tom, prevail on Lent to show some sense and let me go. We can work out this misunderstanding."

I look at Stark, and then over at Lent. I start to chuckle. "*Veritas*."

"What's that?" Stark's eyes narrow in confusion.

"You remember our first meeting when you sent me packing with that *Quaecumque* bullshit? You went to Harvard, didn't you, doc? *Veritas*." I turn to Lent. "It's Harvard's motto—it means 'truth.'"

I walk over towards Stark.

"Easy there, Tom," Lent warns, touching the gun.

"Dr. Stark and I had a little talk about college mottos," I say, inventorying Lent's tools, which include vice grips and an ice pick.

"This is going too far," Stark says, as he tugs at the duct tape.

Lent moves quickly and hits Stark across the face with the back of his hand. "Silence!" he shouts.

He turns to his tools, which he's arranged neatly in a row. "There was this guy in my Ranger unit from Oklahoma. We called him Comanche." He runs his finger across the gleaming edge of a carpet cutter. "When we did black ops in Iraq, he took trophies. They don't talk about that stuff on CNN, but let me tell you, it's not as easy as it looks." Stark draws his breath sharply as Lent tests the point of the cutter on the table. "You've got to get the skin clean off." He chuckles, pointing at a roll of tape setting on the table. "That's what duct tape is for.

"*Veritas.*" Lent shakes his head, scraping the cutter over the veneer of the side table again. "We're gonna get us some *veritas.*"

Fear jabs my gut like a thin sliver of glass as I realize Lent means to scalp Stark in front of me. Whatever the reason for my being there, I doubt he's going to let me live.

Reaching for the manila envelope I placed on a side table, I wave it at Lent.

"Lent, wait," I say as I begin pulling documents out of the file. "We've got proof." They both stare at me like I've lost it.

Lent tickles Stark's ear with the point of the cutter. "This isn't about proof, Tom, it's about—"

"Vindication," I say. "It's about being right, getting to the truth."

"The truth doesn't matter, Tom. He'll just go free. Look at him. He's been buying and selling children to the highest bidder for years. No one's ever caught him."

I point to the Mondrian and the Klee setting in place of pride on the study wall. "Do you wonder how he can afford all this art? How he can live the life of a rock star? He's a doctor, a celebrated one, but look around you. He lives like a king."

I toss the printout on the coffee table. I reach into my bag and take out two other envelopes and pile them on top. "Credite Zurich and NAST accounts," I say. "DOC records."

Lent stares at me, his face set with icy impatience. "So? What's all that got to do with throwing custody cases?"

I sit down on the ottoman, leafing through the DOC dispensary records. Locating a page with the corner turned down, I look at Stark. "Bill's been ordering drugs out of the dispensary for years. Nothing unusual about that. He's a doctor and has privileges at Corrections."

Lent arranges the tools in a neat row, lining them up. "Get to the point."

"You ever heard of Placidyl, Lent?"

"No," he answers, taking the icepick in his hand, stabbing the leather ottoman next to him.

"Jelly babies. The ME said they're like an 82 Chateau Laffite on the street."

"So?"

"We did three autopsies, Alma and Jesus Morales and Eddie Rivera. This stuff shows up on their tox screens. Two shootings and strangulation."

I can tell I've gotten Lent's interest. "So, I follow up to see who's ordering the stuff at the dispensary. A unit, in pharma speak, is a thousand pills. Ten units in a lot. Bill here, ordered over fifty lots for DOC over the last decade. Do the math. Fifty lots, ten units each, equals five-hundred thousand pills, with a conservative street value of twenty dollars apiece, and you have ten million bucks."

I pick up the other envelope. I start to leaf through the DOC orders. "Then I searched the entire DOC database. There are dozens of orders over ten years."

Stark shakes his head. "You can't prove I did any of that."

"Oh, but you're wrong," I say, turning to Lent. "Bill thinks because every tracking number for these shipments was deleted, he's in the clear. But . . ." I look at Stark. "To remove a tracking order, you have to have an individual access code. The first three shipments were made by Jim Bain, head procurement officer at DOC. Mr. Bain died in a tragic car accident eight years ago. The transfers were deleted using an access code issued to Dr. Bill Stark."

The smirk on Stark's face drops.

"Jesus," Edwards says.

I sift through the DOC summaries. "Two-hundred shipments, including Dilaudid and Fiorinal, MDMA—Ecstasy. Once the lots are broken down into individual units, it becomes impossible to trace the pills. Each shipment is 4500 units, a total of 900,000 capsules. At a street value of twenty bucks a cap, that's thirty-six million over ten years."

"Holy shit," Lent says, moving closer to Stark.

"The custody stuff is a lucrative sideline, but it got complicated."

"Complicated?" Lent says.

I stare at Stark. "The custody work was part of the cover. Bill needs his connections with DOC and the county. A private practice with affluent clients, high-profile domestic relations cases, committees, boards—it's all part of that. But the Wesley case was a steaming hot mess from the start."

Stark shifts in his chair again. His right eye is almost closed. His lip's purple and hard. I recall Larry's comment about Burro, that a rattler is most dangerous when cornered. I'm caught between Scylla and Charybdis. Either Stark or Lent will kill me. My money's on Lent killing Stark in front of me, shooting me, and turning the gun on himself.

"Faith paid you to make sure things went her way," I say to Stark. "While doing your workup, you found out about the Moraleses. Then you stumble on Eddie. You find out he's doing time in Menard and he hates the Wesleys. You pull some strings and get him on a release program.

Somewhere in there, he comes clean about the Summers' murders. You told Faith you knew Eddie cut the hoses on the Cadillac for her. So, you made her pay, and pay she did—millions. Eddie was your insurance policy."

Lent walks over to the sideboard and pours four fingers of scotch. He throws the drink back and pours himself another four fingers.

"Go on," he says, gesturing to me.

I figure the longer I talk, the more time I have to try to figure a way out and the more Lent will have had to drink.

"Then, when Linda threatened to reveal everything, and Charles came at you with his fixers, you couldn't have that. Eddie was perfect: damaged, suggestible, and grateful to you, and, most of all, he blamed Faith Wesley for destroying his life. You dropped his meds. You wanted Eddie Rivera to become an angry guard dog."

Lent moves towards Stark again.

"Enough of this bullshit, Tom. I want to hear Bill talk."

Stark's cellphone chimes and we stand still, letting it ring four times before it stops. Stark shifts in his chair. "I'm supposed to be in Chicago at a benefit honoring the APA person of the year. I'm certain to be missed."

I look at my watch: eight-forty.

Stark tries to sound indignant. "I'm pretty sure they must be wondering where I am."

"Let 'em wonder," Lent says, taking another pull from the glass of whiskey.

I stare at Stark. "And then Eddie made the biggest mistake of his life. He tells you he's talked to Alma and Jesus and told them everything he did for Faith Wesley. You couldn't risk any of that, so you had to act quickly."

Lent peels a bacon strip-sized piece off one side of the

Chippendale end table.

"You go to the Morales' house. You're his case doctor from DOC. You've come to talk to them about Eddie. You put them at ease. Alma's been sick for years, so you give them both something to settle them down, and they take the jelly babies right in front of you. When they're sedated, you execute them—bad blood among Mexicans, and Chicago PD's following your line to the end."

"Complete and utter crap, Tom," Stark says, shaking his head.

"After Alma and Jesus are dead, you convince him it's the work of the Wesleys. Eddie kills Faith. You visit him up in a bando in Fuller and slip Placidyl in his booze. When he's down, you tie a bag around his head and make it look like he's a crazy gasper who offed himself. You make an anonymous tip and CPD finds him. Just another junkie freak. It's all clean. No loose ends."

Stark's cellphone leaps to life. Lent looks at the screen. "Winston," he says.

"Doctor Winston, the chair of the nominating committee," Stark volunteers. "They're calling to see where I am." The phone rings five times and then the voicemail notification sounds.

The cell springs to life again. It rings four more times and again goes to voicemail.

"Winston will keep calling until he gets me. He's OCD and is obviously getting anxious. I can guarantee he'll send the police if I don't talk to him in the next couple of minutes, if he hasn't already."

The phone sounds again. "Lent, let him answer the phone."

Lent looks tired and a little drunk. He's helped himself

to a third pass at the tumbler of whiskey. Grunting, he takes out the carpet cutter and releases one of Stark's hands.

Stark reaches for the phone, answering. "Hello? Oh, I'm so sorry Terry, I've been caught up unexpectedly," he says, eyeing Edwards, who stands next to him with the carpet cutter at his throat. "I'll try to get there by the awards ceremony. Yes, I understand, please don't worry. Thanks for your concern." He pushes the end button and puts the cell down.

Lent starts to refasten his arm to the chair.

"Listen," Stark says, before you tie me up again, I've got to pee. I've been sitting here for three hours. The bathroom is right over there. He points to the corner of the study, where there's a small vanity bathroom.

I'm not sure whether Edwards, who a few minutes ago was intent on scalping Stark, really cares whether he pisses himself. Recalling the episode with Liam in the park, I nod to Edwards. "Give him a shot." I figure it will buy more time. Lent seems to be moving slower, as the alcohol takes effect and the adrenaline and novelty wear off.

He grunts as Stark hobbles over to the door of the small powder room. Standing at the toilet, Stark reaches down to his underpants, stopping short.

"Do you mind?" he says, pointing to the bathroom door.

"Yes, I mind," Lent says, holding the open door.

Stark laboriously extracts his penis, and in a reflex as old as grammar school, Edwards averts his eyes just long enough to enable Stark to smash the solid wood door onto his hand. The gun discharges in the small bathroom with a deafening thud. They wrestle to recover the gun. Despite his injuries, Stark gets to it first, takes aim and shoots

Lent in the left shoulder. Blood splatters the back of the bathroom wall. Sprawled on the floor, Lent writhes in pain. Stark moves out of the powder room. I'd hit the ground with the first shot, waiting for Stark to move out into the open. I'm unarmed and there's nothing I can do but wait.

"Now," he says, loose like an angry cobra, and as coolly menacing as a high-voltage wire.

Lent rolls on the floor, moaning.

Stark moves back towards Lent, who's on his back in the powder room. He leans over Lent, his swollen face twisted with the shadow of a grin. "In Illinois, if you shoot in self-defense, it has to be necessary to prevent imminent death or great bodily harm."

Lent doesn't answer. Gouts of dark blood flow between his fingers as he tries to get up.

"When you both broke in, I had to defend myself. Lent's armed and came to kill me. I got a couple of shots off." He cocks the gun. "Obviously, one hit you in the shoulder, and the other—"

He shoots Lent in the head, blowing the top off.

"Was on target."

Stark isn't going to let me live after what I've just seen. My heart races as I scramble for cover behind a chair at the far end of the den. Stark aims and hits the top of the chair. It explodes in a cloud of splinters and matting. Moving the gun to where I am on the floor, his purple, swollen face sports the same condescending smile he had when we first met at his office.

"Regrettably, the recently disgraced Detective Edison chose to accompany Mr. Edwards as an accomplice, enraged by the recent lawsuit I had to file as a result of his rash actions. I had to defend myself against him as well."

He fires.

A searing flash of pain surges through my leg as the round shatters my shin. The blow is followed by a hot, electric pulsing, and I feel the urge to vomit. Stark chuckles, now staring down at me.

"So smart, aren't you, Tom?" I stare up at him as he wipes a blood clot on his forehead. "You carry your trauma around like a badge. Never good enough, was it? Northwestern. Failed marriage. Failed relationship with your kid. You fucked up the Wesley investigation and had an affair with Nora Summers. No discipline. A drunk." The handgun makes a solid metallic click as Stark cocks the chamber again. "A failure," he says, shaking his head.

He fires—this time into my arm. The pain is excruciating. I begin to lose consciousness.

"Not just yet, Tom," he says, kicking me. "I didn't hit any major arteries. Nothing fatal."

Reaching for the tumbler of scotch, he pours two fingers and waves the gun. "I can review court custody files." He swirls the drink in the glass. "I read your file several months ago. No evaluator. Curious. I wonder why." He's toying with me, the way you might poke at a dying rat before putting it out of its misery.

He moves to the table where I put the manila envelope. Picking it up and feeling its heft, he points the gun at my head.

"Good work, Tom. You had most of it right, but unfortunately . . ." He puts the envelope back on the table and pulls the hammer back on the gun.

I brace myself, sure this will be my last light. A deafening sound shatters the room, followed by a howl from Stark. His face is twisted in a grimace of agony. He grabs his right arm and spins, firing wildly at the door, blowing a piece the size of a coffee cup off the desk. A second gunshot blows a hole in the ceiling above Stark, raining down a fine snowfall of plaster. A third shot hits Stark in the left knee, bringing him to the floor.

Stark writhes in pain, and I can hear shuffling as someone moves across the room. Pulling myself up with my good arm on the desk, I wretch as the lights spin. My sight grows dim and muddy, and I'm about to fade to black when the distinctive outline of Larry's road-worn face comes into view.

Larry limps over to Stark and leans down. "What's up, doc?" he says, kicking the Colt Defender out of reach.

I only hear Stark's labored breathing, then the distant sounds of sirens as I slip into darkness.

WINTER

CHAPTER TWENTY-NINE

STEELY WINTER WINDS BLOW ACROSS MILES OF frozen lake, punching into the empty trees lining the shore. A dull sky, the color of tarnished silver, gives the streets a graphite gray sheen like faded black-and-white photographs. Snow and ice gather in corners and gullies and harden into dirty blocks.

The months that follow see the investigation into the murders of Eduardo Rivera and Alma and Jesus Morales reopened after Chicago P.D. acknowledges the cases were prematurely closed.

An exhaustive search of Stark's house, spearheaded by Shahbaz, turns up a Glock 9-millimeter handgun which, along with two boxes of Black Talon in the potting shed, are matched to the weapon used to kill the Moraleses. The search of the Eglandale house turns up receipts for a storage unit in Naperville. When they cut the lock on the unit, they find a stash of prescription drugs large enough to stock a large infirmary for years. Dozens of cartons, floor to ceiling, filled with schedule 2 drugs: Oxy, Dilaudid, Adderall, Vicodin, and MDMA. Included in the inventory are several thousand jelly babies and thousands of Quaaludes. In the corner are six steamer trunks filled with packets of one-hundred-dollar bills, each trunk easily worth two million dollars.

■ ■ ■

According to my doctor, the gunshots will probably leave me with a permanent limp and limited range of motion in my right arm. The bullet shattered my tibia, and it will be months before I can walk without a cane. The radius was partially fractured, but the shot missed most of the nerves. The arm works okay, but I have a large scar on my forearm to match the one over my eye. I'm not going to be doing any hand modeling anytime soon, so I'm not too worried about it.

I'm in my hospital bed, watching *Antiques Roadshow* as the host cheerfully delivers the news to an eager collector that a prized Lou Gehrig autographed baseball is a phony. The next segment promises a shred of bloodstained cloth purportedly taken from Lincoln's chair the night he was shot at the Ford Theater. I resign myself to counting the minutes until the next round of painkillers, as my arm and leg begin to hum as the pain medication wears off. My view of the television is suddenly obstructed by the large, crooked smile of Lawrence Welk, framed by an outsized Stetson hat.

I shift in my bed. "Larry, you need to lose that hat," I say, clicking off the television just as a square of red plaid stained the color of dark chocolate comes up for evaluation.

"Well, just like the rebel boys said," he announces, as he drapes his overcoat over the arm of the chair next to my bed, "'they kilt us, but they ain't whupped us.'" His face is clean and open, and for the first time I can remember, his eyes are clear and alert. Removing the cowboy hat, he folds a newspaper he's been carrying, placing both on the tray table that still holds the remains of my uneaten breakfast.

"Well, they ain't kilt us neither, thanks to you." I laugh, then adjust the level of the bed. "Seems odd, but the last time I remember seeing you," I say, touching the bed frame, "you were in one of these, on your way out."

"Felt the wind of the wings of the Angel of Death, Tom," he says, shaking his head, the smile on his face momentarily shaded by a frown. "Very close."

"Your family had you in lockdown."

He smirks darkly. "They tried, and so did IAD." He thumps a boot up on the bed frame, making me wince. "I was weak and bedridden and Novak thought he had me where he wanted me, but I got better." He points to his side. "Took a couple of weeks, but finally all the bleeding stopped, the swelling went down, and I got mobile." His face clouds again. "Then I talked to my daughter, and we agreed to give it a new start."

"That's great to hear."

"I didn't say shit to IAD, and I wanted to thank you personally for stopping me from making a terrible mistake. I could've thrown it all away," he says, staring out into the hallway, as if to consider right then how close he'd come. "It all just got out of hand. Novak even offered me immunity if I'd turn on you and say you'd compromised the Wesley investigation because of Nora Summers . . . sonofabitch."

"It happened, and it's over," I say, letting the sentence

drift into silence, and for several seconds the only sound is the descending beat of the LCD.

Larry thumps the side rail, sending another tremor through the bed frame. "Why'd you send that paperwork to Edwards? You must've known there'd be consequences."

I stop to consider the question for a minute.

"A lonely impulse of delight," I say, for the lack of any better explanation.

He snorts. "Yeats. Very clever. A whole poem about copping out." He taps the railing of the bed again. "'In balance with this life, this death'—isn't that it? Seemed like a good idea at the time, is what I take that to mean."

Despite the increasingly angry thrumming in my arm and shin, I laugh. "You know what, Larry? For a guy who likes to come off as a cornpone shit-kicker from Amarillo, you're pretty literate." I adjust my leg, temporarily quieting the current of pain. I move my arm so it's supported by a pillow, which seems to help. The room's quiet again, the LCD beep marking time until, finally, turning to face Larry head on, I ask, "What kind of car do you drive?"

"Well, until I got in the accident I drove a junker. Something I bought from my brother-in-law."

"White Ford sedan, wasn't it?"

"Well," he touches his brow, mimicking someone in deep thought. "I think it was. Yeah."

"Did you get another car after you totaled the sedan?"

His face expands into a bemused smile.

"I did. Another junker."

"Green Explorer?"

"Think so. Why?"

"Why?" I ask simply, moving my leg again. I reach for the ringer and push twice. The duty nurse persists in calling what's going on in my arm and leg 'discomfort', which to my way of thinking is like calling a triple fatality car crash a 'traffic incident.'

The smile on Larry's face falls. "Paranoia?"

"You thought I was out to get you?"

"After the incident with the gun and the booze in my drawer, I figured you put Novak onto me and I was worried I was on my way out. Chalk it up to paranoia, but I thought following you was a good idea. As it turns out, I was right. It was as easy as getting a GPS unit."

I feel a hot surge rise in my chest, which blends with the pain in my leg. "You put a tracker on my car?"

Larry visibly withdraws, until finally, he shrugs. "Old habits die hard. I wouldn't be too critical, Tom. It saved your life," he says, clearly hoping to be judged by the outcome.

He's right, at least as far as being alive. "How long have you been watching me?" I ask, acutely aware he knows all about Nora.

He sighs, picking at a length of tape dangling from the bed. "Just after you found the booze, right up until I got into my accident. Don't worry, everything about Nora's safe." He stares at me, trying to gauge my reaction.

Unsure whether to take his reference to Nora as a challenge, or a genuine assurance of confidentiality, I reply, "I should punch you in the face. But I'm grateful you took out Stark. For what it's worth, I would never have put Novak onto you."

"I was coming to see you at your house when you started down to Highland Park. You caught my tail, so I had to find you the old-fashioned way." He pauses for several seconds. "How's the arm and leg?"

"Still getting therapy," I reply, pausing to ring the alert button. Like the insistent whine of a midnight mosquito, the pain in my leg has grown from a small irritation to the strident drone of a bagpipe. I can feel my pulse race at the prospect of facing the full fury of my injuries.

Pointing to his side, Larry chuckles. "Therapy's painful, but . . ." he seems to struggle for words. Clearing his throat, he says, "Thanks." The room falls into silence. We both know it is the closest either of us is going to get to making amends.

I nod and ask if he intends to return to work.

Leaning back in his chair, his face brightens. "If I still have a job. I've been cleared by IAD for shooting Stark. I even figured out who put them on to me in the first place."

"Who?"

"Remember that Texas Appeals Judge? The one with no sense of humor and a wife with loose morals?"

I laugh, which makes my leg throb. "That's one way of looking at it."

"Turns out he has a long memory and a taste for revenge to match. At least that's what Novak said."

"Novak cleared you?"

"Yup, but they haven't said if my job is still available."

I ring the alert button again. "You're lucky you're not in a cell. I'll call Delahunt and clear it. I may not be back for a while. If you don't hear from me, you should report next Monday." My shin's ringing clearly and more frequently. "Good thing I'm not throwing a clot or having a seizure."

"I'll just take that and call it good," he says and shrugs, mustering a halfhearted grin. He gets up, gathering his hat, overcoat, and a newspaper he's brought with him.

"Larry," I say, fighting the speed metal band thrashing

away in my leg. "You still haven't told me why you followed me to Stark's."

The door flies open, admitting the floor nurse. She makes it to the bed in three quick strides and takes the call switch from me. Surveying the outsized lid Larry carries in his hand, the Angel of Mercy eyes him like the inside of a Port-a-Potty. I choose not to mention she's late with the pain meds, knowing she could, on some pretext, leave me for another half an hour. Larry moves quickly towards the door. The nurse briskly hands me a paper cup with my pain killers and fills a plastic bottle with water, handing it to me. She watches as I swallow the pills and takes the crumpled cup from me. She deposits the cup in the trash and, narrowly missing Larry, walks out. Just as quickly as she arrived, she's gone.

Watching her disappear down the hall, Larry holds the door to leave. After a couple of seconds, he says, "Well, I'd been talking to your buddy Tyler down at the club. Seems like you'd been trying some pretty strange stuff in that pool. Tyler was pretty clear he thought you'd been trying to off yourself." He pauses and lets out a deep sigh. "I guess, Tom, I wasn't sure if you weren't trying some other method." He takes another step out into the hall, then leans back in. "I sure wish when I went down to Sanderson to see Burro someone'd been trailing me." He dons the Stetson, tipping it Texas-style, and lets the door close behind him.

■ ■ ■

My recovery is slow. After ten weeks on partial disability, I return to the office and my desk. Novak pushes for a reprimand, but after a few days, and I suspect some intervention by Delahunt, the IAD matter is dropped.

One of the first things I decide to do is ask Verna out to lunch. Tammy Strauss said Verna was involved with Pete Strauss. I recount my meeting with Tammy and, after some prodding, she tells me about her run-in with Dirty Pete. I also want to confront Delahunt about Strauss, but think better of it. At first, Delahunt is cool, but after the civil charges are dismissed by the trial judge, he warms up. No sense in rocking the boat, I tell myself.

Just before Valentine's Day, Delahunt summons me into his office. Setting on his desk, a bottle of Red Label Scotch stands lonely vigil. "Have a seat," he says, gesturing towards an open chair. I can't tell if it's the spirit of the season or the spirit of Johnny Walker, but for Ed Delahunt, he is positively jovial. Pouring himself two fingers, he says, "I'd offer you some, but I know you don't."

He grabs a single sheet of paper setting in front of him. "I thought you'd appreciate this," he says, handing me the paper. I scan the short memo until I come to the bottom of the page:

Therefore, due to job-related stress, I have decided to take early retirement and to spend more time with my family. Executive Assistant State's Attorney, Frank Steinman

"Job-related stress?" I ask.

Smiling, he places a solitary index finger to his lips. "Got this from a source inside the State's Attorney's Office—not to be shared."

"Any idea why?"

"Job-related stress might have something to do with getting caught in a bust of high-priced hookers."

"Circle of Ecstasy?"

"The very same," Delahunt replies, smirking. "Couldn't

have happened to a nicer guy."

Following two years of undercover investigation, Circle of Ecstasy, a ring of call girls run out of Chicago was busted by the Illinois Attorney General's Office. Dozens of prominent Illinois businessmen and several law enforcement officials, including Steinman, were caught in the net.

"Who's gonna run the bureau?"

"Word has it, your pal Tony," Delahunt says, smiling.

Delahunt's use of the term pal rankles, but I'm not going to argue with him. What I do know is Shahbaz's, perfect for the job, political and expedient—and hopefully possessing smaller appetites than Steinman.

Thinking the interview's over, I get up, preparing to leave. Delahunt becomes suddenly serious. "Steinman isn't the only one leaving, Tom."

I feel a cold jab of anxiety, wondering if Delahunt called me in to can me.

"Who's going, Chief?" I ask.

"I'm retiring at the end of this month," he says, handing me a short letter on Victory Memorial Medical Center letterhead. I skip to the bottom of the findings' section: *Amyotrophic Lateral Sclerosis.*

"Gehrig's Disease?" I say, staring at Delahunt.

Delahunt shifts in his seat. He takes a long sip from his glass. "It's funny," he says, pouring another two fingers. "I always figured myself as one of the guys who'd get shot in the line of duty—one of those big bagpipe deals."

"Jesus, Chief."

"Tom," Delahunt says, leaning forward, "for what it's worth, I've recommended to the brass that you be promoted to Chief Assistant." He nods slowly. "What you did took balls. You were insubordinate, but you followed your instincts and you weren't political. Some people might even call that leadership."

I decide to push my luck with him.

"Can I ask you a question?"

"Shoot," he says, taking another sip from the glass.

"Why didn't you tell me you were Strauss' partner for almost five years?"

Delahunt swirls the golden liquid in the glass, staring at me, his expression fixed and closed. "You do have a set of balls, Edison," he says, the smile erased from his face. Placing the glass on the desk, he turns to stare out the window at the darkening sky. Finally, he spins back and picks up the glass again. "Dorothy and I were married about eight months before I went into the Academy. She's from a town in Iowa so small it's not on most roadmaps. I met her through her brother, who was in the service with me. She was the most beautiful woman I'd ever seen."

He stares out the window again. Snow is falling in big lazy flakes, the sky the color of charcoal.

"You know, it took me three years before I tried for detective. When I passed, I was immediately assigned to Strauss. People warned me about Dirty Pete, and there were rumors he beat the shit out of his wife." The chief picks up the glass, and draws a long sip, shaking his head. "He may have been all that, but he was something else, too. Pete was a crack detective. Not in the polished badge and crisp blue formals sense. The man could swim in sewage to find the silver dollar. He'd bully anyone into giving him what he wanted. He was also very dangerous."

He stops, staring at me. "I don't know why I'm telling all of this to you." He tempers the comment by raising his glass to me.

"Any fucking how, during my first several years, I'd worked irregular hours and seen a lot of stuff that changed me. I wasn't very nice to be around. Dot and I were fighting. We tried to get pregnant but lost two of them. Things were pretty much shit."

He takes another drink. "Pete and I were on the lake, investigating a hijacking ring with a crazy bunch of Chicago micks smuggling guns up to Thunder Bay in Canada, presumably for the IRA. ATF passed on it, so we were working it ourselves. One of the Micks had a sister, everything Dorothy used to be, only wilder and much more dangerous."

Sensing we've come to a place where Delahunt might say something he'll regret later, I interrupt. "Chief, you don't have to tell me anything more if—"

Delahunt nods, raising his hand. "It's okay. I don't have to tell you about the birds and the bees Tom, but I can tell you I flew more and buzzed around faster than any bird or bee ever did. He smiles again, his eyes unfocused. But," he says, taking another pull at the glass, "there was a problem."

"Strauss."

Downing the last of the glass, he places the glass firmly on the table with a *thunk* and nods slowly. "Once Pete had a piece of you, he didn't let go. He squeezed you like a ripe grapefruit until there was nothing left, no pulp, no juice— nothing. I had to stand by and watch, or Pete was going to ruin everything I ever had with Dorothy, including the family I finally got when Dotty got pregnant."

"Is that why you took the heat?"

"That and the fact that, back then, things were a lot

different when it came to loyalty. They figured if you could blow the whistle on someone like Pete, you couldn't be trusted to keep a secret about anything. It was a career-ender. I asked to be transferred, but Pete got wind of it and said he'd ruin me. In a sick way, he liked and trusted me."

"Did you know about the Summers' accident, about Eddie Rivera?"

Delahunt shakes his head. "I knew he was working an automobile investigation in LF, and that he closed it and suddenly moved to Vegas."

"Can I ask another question?"

He pours two fingers, nodding. "Today's your lucky day." He raises his glass to toast me again.

"You asked me point blank if I was getting it on with Nora Summers."

He chuckles. "I did."

"Is that because Larry told you I was chasing after her?" I want to know if Larry is capable of that level of disloyalty.

Delahunt laughs out loud. "Is that what you think?" He smacks the top of the table. "Wow, you must like Larry a lot if you think he could do something like that to you and not throw him under the bus."

"I've had my doubts."

"Well, calm yourself, Tom. Steinman was getting calls from Linda Wesley, telling him to keep an eye on you with Nora Summers. It really doesn't matter at this point if you did or didn't. I'm pretty sure Linda Wesley was doing it to try to get you thrown off the case. She really hates you. So, I figured I'd ignore her and tell you to keep your nose clean."

I realize then that Delahunt's comment earlier that year, about a piece of ass not being worth a career, stemmed from bitter experience.

Delahunt puts his glass down, reaching into his desk drawer.

"This is for you," he says, handing me the rubber troll with the bug eyes. "You'll have projects, Tom, and this sure helps with them."

■ ■ ■

I arrive home to find a package from Trina, accompanied by a card: *I'm thinking of you. It's almost Valentine's Day. Sophie is visiting her dad and I've got some free time. Love, Trina.*

The note makes me want to call and tell her what happened. After ruminating on it, it's clear that explaining everything to her—Nora, the suicide—everything needs to be done in person. But that can wait until she returns from New York, if at all.

The package is from Argosy Book Dealers in New York, purveyors of fine and rare manuscripts. Containing a first edition translation of the poems of Li Po, this must've cost Trina a fortune.

The small, fragile book, which smells strongly of pine cones, has a scrap of paper that marks a poem. I already know which one it is.

Lifting my head
I watch the bright moon
Lowering my head
I dream that I'm home

After digesting the poem, I phone the number I tried so many times before. This time it rings through. Talking to Trina, I look at the window, marking the dark greens and blues in a small stained-glass collage of a sailboat Liam made for my birthday. The ocean, deep emerald, and the sky, an improbable sapphire blue, surrounds a small boat made of two triangular pieces of cream-white glass rescued from a bottle of coconut liqueur. I've never treasured any piece of jewelry or artwork more.

Talking on the phone, I flex my sore leg and feel a deep longing and sense of gratitude—recognition of the gifts in my life. I'm overcome with a feeling I haven't known since early childhood—joy.

An hour later, I end the call with Trina, redialing quickly to book a last-minute, expensive flight to New York.

When I get there, I intend to tell her everything, Nora, Paulie, everything—because I know if I'm to have peace, I'll need to trust, and maybe Trina is the only person I can trust. I run the risk when she learns about Nora she'll decide she's had enough of me. But she might also forgive me, and that will be a start.

∎ ∎ ∎

After Northwestern, I returned to live with my father and Ben. Sitting in the dark living room with the television on, I watched Ben, unconscious in the chair. I saw myself in a few years. It frightened me.

I continued the tradition of Saturday morning breakfasts with my father until shortly before he died. One morning over eggs, my father told me he was worried about Ben. Nodding toward the far corner of the dingy diner, he said, "Look over there." I saw three old men hunched over coffee, silent and waiting for something to take them away . . . from the corner and each other.

Ladling a spoonful of raspberry preserves onto a piece of bread, he said, "See them?"

I nodded slowly.

"That's what scares me about your brother." Putting the bread on his plate and turning his attention to spooning sugar into his coffee, he added, "You know what? There are two types of old people. One type—they're kind, with something like wisdom." Stirring for several seconds, he gestured at the corner. "Then, there's them. Rigid as concrete and afraid. That's what I think Ben's like now. Scares the shit out of me."

I chuckled. "Ben isn't even forty-five."

Picking up the toast, the Old Man looked at me, his eyes set deep in his skull. His gaze was framed by eyebrows sprouting like sawgrass, and a solitary hair extended from the end of his nose. He leaned forward. "You know what a crucible is?"

I nodded. "In chemistry. You use it to separate the metal from ore at very high temperatures."

My father smiled, biting off a large section of purple toast, which he washed down with coffee. "That good education coming through. The impurities burn off, the dross."

"Okay, so what's your point?"

"Life's a crucible," he said, taking another large bite of his toast. He reached across the table and took two more foil containers of raspberry jam, ladling the contents onto the bread. "After great heat, the pure metal—the gold—separates," he said, suiting words to action and pouring imaginary liquid into the air. "Once you go through the heat, you change chemically."

My father held out his hand as if holding a precious

ingot. "Hopefully, what comes out is purer than what went in. Less shit, more patience, flexibility, tolerance, charity, and yes, even love."

He turned his attention to the pork sausage, which we both knew was forbidden by his doctor. "Some people learn why we go on. Others don't, and them that don't," he said, his mouth not yet empty, nodding over at the men in the corner booth, "when they die, no one misses them." He took a long sip of his coffee and placed the cup carefully in the saucer. "And for all I know, they'll come back here and have to do it all over again."

My father died four months later. I wonder if the devoted mid-western agnostic carpenter experienced something like enlightenment as he passed to the other side.

Ben never rid himself of Jimmy Newsome or Billy Gerson. His simple refrain, "Difference does it make?" echoed his view that life was a perpetual wintry ordeal without the hope of spring. After our dad succumbed to cancer, Ben put a shotgun in his mouth and finally did what he'd been thinking about for decades. The old man's fears were justified.

I have yet to figure out why some can see spring coming, while others . . . well, they simply endure and then give up. I never told my father about Paulie, but I'm fairly sure the old man would simply tell me Paulie was my time in the crucible.

SPRING

CHAPTER THIRTY

A FTER SOME INTERNECINE WRANGLING WITH Cook County, Stark is indicted by a Lake County Grand Jury on three counts of first-degree murder, and an additional count for conspiracy to murder for Faith Wesley. Given the circumstances of his death, the States Attorney decides not to file charges or indict Stark for the murder of Lent Edwards. After a review of Gary Burdell's report, there is a movement to reopen the Summers' homicide case. After heated debate, it is decided that because Pete Strauss, Eddie Rivera, and Faith Wesley are all dead, there's no point in pursuing it.

Almost as an afterthought, Shahbaz includes a separate indictment for attempted murder and assault with a deadly weapon for Stark's attack on me.

Stark's indictment also includes seventy-four counts for violation of Article Four of the Illinois Controlled Substances Act, specifically Possession with Intent to

Distribute, and three counts of first-degree extortion. Word has it, the FBI is looking to take control of the drug cases under Title 21 of the Federal Drug Prevention Act.

Stark's highly compensated criminal defense lawyers promptly file motions to throw out the evidence found during the search of his house. The team argues the evidence is the product of an illegal search obtained by yours truly and my alleged coconspirator, Lent Edwards. The trial judge denies the motions, succinctly observing, "Mr. Edison could not have been engaged in an unlawful search and seizure because at the time of the entry he was no longer acting as a police officer as a result of the lawsuit filed by the criminal defendant here. Mr. Edison's motive to enter the house was to protect the defendant, rather than to carry out any official police action, an action for which the defendant here shot him."

Stark is convicted on all counts. He is promptly remanded to Menard Correctional Facility. Although his attorneys request placement in protective custody, he's placed in general population. Following the conviction, the State's Attorney's office announces it will seek consecutive life imprisonment sentences, as Illinois no longer imposes the death sentence. With Stark's conviction, the Illinois court dockets explode with parties demanding reconsideration in cases Stark handled. The Illinois Legislature pushes the Council on Court Procedures to start investigating the use of custody evaluators. Among the people called to testify before the committee is Kapur Singh.

■ ■ ■

Following a week with Trina in New York, we've agreed that when summer comes, she'll look at returning to Illinois. Until then, we've put off deciding what we are going to do about our lives together. I'm not sure what it will look like, but if we're together, we'll probably have a cat.

■ ■ ■

The road into Lake Forest Memorial Cemetery dips slightly into a narrow-paved drive. I glide quietly among the headstones, coasting past the founding fathers, the leaders of industry, and the Wesley plot, and stop finally at the back.

Although it's early June, as I get out of the car a cool gust hits me and I brace myself, making my way to the small cluster of three newly dug graves.

The three headstones, all in a line, bear identical scrolled markings.

The first: Alma Rivera Morales. *Et lux perpétua, luceat eis.* In English: Eternal Light Grant Them Oh Lord.

The next: Jesus Morales. *Quia erípuit ánimam meam de morte: óculos meos a lácrimis, pedes meos a lapsu:* Thou hast delivered my soul from death, mine eyes from tears, and my feet from falling. The inscriptions are from the Anglican Office of the Dead, the unmistakable hand of Charles Wesley.

The last is the one I've come to see, new, shiny, and unstained. The earth on the grave is not yet completely settled. The stone: Eduardo Rivera. *Wash me thoroughly from my wickedness, and forgive me all my sin. Psalm 51.*

I asked Bielmans to release Rivera to me after I reached

out to Charles and told him I wanted to put Eddie with the rest of his family. Charles agreed. Eddie was buried as soon as the ground softened up. The headstone took a few weeks and was a gift from Charles, apparently blind to the irony of burying the man who was your wife's killer. Or perhaps it was a backhanded way of getting back at Faith; a small but meaningful gesture.

Surveying the three gravestones, I'm struck by the instinct, as old as the human race itself, which compels us to mark our dead with narratives, as if by this act we might control Fate and, ultimately, our destiny in the Great Unknown. By etching the meager details of our lives on pyramids, caves, sarcophagi, and cathedrals, we, the living, defiantly bargain with Death, Time, and Memory. We etch the stone in the fervent hope that even if the granite erodes with the centuries, at least we tried. As Larry might say, we might've been kilt, but we ain't been whupped.

Standing at the foot of Eddie Rivera's grave, I have a moment of clarity. With time, the secrets of my innocence—love, sex, jealousy, regret—have all unfurled, one by one, until only Death remains as the Last Great Secret. My devils loom large and fierce.

I make my way over to the Wesley plot. Over the winter months, the earth has subsided into a darker, denser patch, topped with a granite slab on which is inscribed: Faith Wesley, Beloved Wife, and Devoted Mother. This inscription also marks the human urge to rewrite history. Faith, while alive, was driven by a single-minded need to rewrite herself. In her zeal to become more of a Wesley than Charles himself, she was neither beloved as a wife, nor devoted as a mother. Yet the inscription is as much a prayer that she might be remembered for those things, as it is a piece of posthumous propaganda.

I save the most fervent prayer for the other side. Away from Faith, next to the plot no doubt reserved for himself, Charles placed the stone for Nora which reads:

Nora Summers

Beloved Daughter and Sister

For now, we see through a glass darkly, but then face to face.

1st Corinthians 13:12

I walk over to the car, open the trunk, and retrieve a gray blanket. Standing in front of Nora's grave, I place the blanket on the ground and unwrap the heavy bell. Lifting it in my hands, it sounds a single note, sad, pure, and deep. I grip the handle and ring it several times more, its ancient voice echoing off the cool granite and trees.

The Dead Bell is rung, not for posterity, but to protect the newly dead, emerging like newborns, wet and screaming, into whatever awaits them on the Other Side. It also sounds for the living. The living—devout and frightened people—who cherish the last breath and the frail light passing through, and pray the bell shucks the demons gathered in life, which cling like leeches to the passing soul.

As I drive the winding path to the exit, I feel serene, easing down the window to smell the fresh breeze, watching the redstarts and warblers dancing in the trees as they make their way back north. The limbs on the bitternut hickories and sweetgums have softened into grey-green in anticipation of their late spring bloom.

■ ■ ■

After my trip to the cemetery, I reach out to Charles,

wanting to tell him I appreciate what he's done for Eddie, Nora, and the Moraleses. When I first called him about burying Eddie, given that our prior conversation ended with my threat to bury him and Linda, I didn't expect a warm response. Instead, he was gracious. When I call to report on my trip, I'm even more surprised when he invites me to come to the house for coffee.

Charles seems always to take a longer view. He's an eccentric who was tethered in a deeply complicated marriage. Eccentricity is the privilege of those lucky enough to be immune to the consequences of their actions. His agreement to bury Eddie on the hill, richly steeped in irony, is a calculated shot at the very people for whom stature is everything: Faith, Delia Ostergaard, maybe even Linda. The Wesley plot itself is less than fifty yards from where Alma, Jesus, and Eddie are interred, and when her time finally comes, Delia herself will lie a few hundred yards away.

We have coffee and studiously avoid discussing the case. He seems lonely and adrift. With Faith gone, he tells me he's considering putting the place up for sale. "Too much space," he tells me. Linda has no use for the place, he says, and Emma likely has bad memories. A curious decision for someone who has always lived in the family's ancestral home. Charles also says he's going to establish a scholarship in Jesus' and Alma's name for Hispanic students at the college.

I look over to the corner where the Masamune katana and shogun armor were once on display. The case is gone.

"What happened to the sword and armor?" I ask.

Charles extends a pensive lip. "They went to the Smithsonian. My father was comfortable with their questionable provenance. I'm not. They had bad karma."

As I'm leaving, I turn to him. "Why did Nora leave here? What happened that night between Linda and her mother?"

Charles frowns deeply. "Faith threw Nora out because she believed Nora was a bad influence on Linda. When Linda found out, she attacked her mother." His mouth folds into a sneer. "Faith was wrong, as she was wrong about a lot of things."

I shake my head. Linda was several years older than Nora, so I don't buy the bad influence narrative. "What about Africa, the Cameroon? Nora seemed fixated on Douala and her father's stay there. I found a letter from a clinic in Douala with her father's medical record. He had TB. Nora dug all that up."

Charles' face settles. He pulls at his cheek, as if to gauge his thoughts. "It was a tragedy. Kip and Mary Louise were two of our best friends. My father went to school with Kip's dad at Exeter. Faith was a maid of honor at their wedding."

"I know. Pete Strauss investigated it as a potential homicide but dropped it." I look at Charles to see whether he registers even a glimmer of recognition at the mention of Strauss. "Frances Reynolds said the night Faith and Linda were fighting, they were yelling about Strauss."

Charles shakes his head slowly, his eyes downcast and almost closed. "Nora had no one else in the world."

"You were Nora's second family."

A small wistful smile comes to his face. "Yes, well . . ." he pauses and stares at a family photograph on the bookshelf: himself, Faith, Linda, and Emma. "After Kip graduated from Yale, he went to Central Africa to the Cameroon to be in the Peace Corps, which had just started."

"Cameroon?"

Charles nods. "Yes, he was stationed in Douala. Unfortunately, when he returned, he was very sick. He'd contracted tuberculosis. He'd been away for two years, and he and Mary Lou got married very quickly. ML always wanted to have children. It took them a long time—years, and it looked like they might never have children. When Nora was born, they seemed happy. It was a shock to everyone when they died."

"I still don't understand why Faith had so much anger towards Nora. Nora must have become like her own child after a time."

We've reached the front hall.

Charles purses his lips, his shoulders fall, and he looks tired. "Well, it wasn't quite like that," he says, holding the door open. "After Linda was born, Faith was told she couldn't have any more children. Her pregnancy with Linda almost killed her—eclampsia. Linda was born by emergency C-section." He's quietly agitated, as if signaling an urgent need to relieve himself, but too delicate to say so. "Not having a boy was the great disappointment of her life. She'd have kept trying if she could have. She always wanted a male Wesley heir, you see."

"So Mary Lou got pregnant and had Nora. Everyone must have been happy. I'm not seeing the problem."

Charles rolls his eyes, and as if to a particularly dull child, he says slowly, "Among the things TB does is make its host sterile. Kip never told anyone except, of course, me." Charles closes his eyelids and sighs. "When ML got pregnant, everyone assumed the baby was Kip's."

"If Kip was sterile, who was Nora's father?"

Charles stares at me for several seconds and then nods.

"So, if ML is fertile, she might have another child—a boy—your boy."

Charles quickly extends a hand. "Thank you again for everything, Tom. And thank you for what you did for Alma and her family." He firmly grips my fist and turns quickly on his heel, vanishing into the depths of the house. The heavy door slides noiselessly shut, leaving me at the brass fixtures and the burnished wood.

As I sit in the car, I look around me at the lawn, bathed in the light of a June afternoon. I see the brick wall and the long wicked spikes at the top. The wall was built to deter even the most motivated intruder from climbing over. To scale it and get in or out, you'd have to be in good shape. An emaciated junkie would have a hell of a time climbing up and over. Any slip and you'd find yourself impaled on a five-inch spike.

I call Joyce Hong at the Medical Examiner's office. It takes several minutes, but eventually, she comes to the phone.

"Doc, did you ever do an autopsy on Nora Summers? She was a suicide. I was on administrative leave. The case closed, and I never got the results."

Joyce clears her throat. "Yup, we did. Normally we don't do autopsies on suicides, but Novak wanted one because the Summers woman was drunk and he was sure there was some connection to you. We got some resistance from the Wesleys, but we did one in the end."

"What'd you find?"

"She was on a bunch of cancer meds. There were some antidepressants too, but not enough in her system to make a difference. She'd been drinking. She shot herself in the head."

I flinch. "Any marks on her body?"

I can hear her roll her chair across the room. "Wait a minute," she says. The keyboard emits a telltale *clak clak clak*. A few seconds later, she answers. "Yes, there was a puncture wound on the left thigh below the gluteus. Healed, but it looked pretty substantial—I recorded ten centimeters, and stitches even. Look, I'm behind twenty-three cases, can I fax this later?" she asks, making it clear she doesn't care.

"No need. One last question. A few months ago you mentioned the garrote is used for execution in some countries."

She sighs. "Yes, in several countries it is the method of choice."

"Which ones?"

"It was used in Spain for centuries, why?"

"Thanks," I say, hanging up.

Seated in the TT, I finally understand. I take the steps two at a time, ringing the bell until after more than a minute Frances Reynolds opens the door, giving me an icy glare.

"I thought you were gone," she says, abandoning her customary decorum.

"Is Linda home?" I say, stepping across the threshold of the door and making it clear I'm not about to be dismissed.

Raising her brow in Saxon disdain, she hurries up the stairs, her planned interference failed.

Two minutes later, Linda appears at the door. Frances eyes me from where she stands, looking at me as if I'm a rupturing trash bag.

Moving to check my further ingress, Linda's feet move

in a boxer's bob and weave. "Hello, Tom, you're almost getting to be a fixture around here," she says through a thin smile.

"You play the cello," I say, pointing into the house.

"You know I do. You saw me playing."

"I want to see your cello case," I demand, pushing at the door.

Her uncertain smile fades. "Whatever for?" she says, pushing the door back at me.

"Get the case, or I'll get a warrant and the uniforms in here," I say, shoving on the door.

She takes the measure of me—a badger loose in the living room, gauging my potential to inflict injury. After several beats, she shrugs. "Just a minute." She goes up the stairs, where I can see her mumble something to Frances. Both of them melt into the house, leaving me to stand in the hallway. The antique clock on the wall beats time until Linda reappears, carrying a heavy black case, which I recognize from the recital at the college.

"Open it."

Nodding towards a door at the back of the hall, she says, "It's a Montagnana. Can't we open it in the tearoom?"

I nod, following her as she carries the cello into the tearoom, where she lays it on the sofa, then returns to the door, to ensure it's closed. She opens the case. The cello's amber body glows in the sunlight streaming through the window. She takes a seat next to the case.

Reaching into the case compartment, I extract four packages of Corelli 480 cello strings. The three closed packages contain complete sets, C, G, D, and A. One package is open and holds C, G, and D strings. The A string is missing.

"If I checked the strings on your instrument for wear, I know they'd be the same. You didn't have to replace an A string. It's all the same set." Linda can't charm or dissemble, and she stands speechless.

I finish the indictment. "Which means the A string is missing."

Linda seems adrift, waiting for a cue. I take a seat opposite her. I push. "Nora got cancer and returned home from Spain. She wanted to make sense of her life and started digging up ancient history. She reached out to the clinic in Douala to find out about her father. You started to look into the Summers' accident. You already knew about Pete Strauss. You found Tammy and linked Eddie Rivera to Nora's parents. Frances said you and your mother fought about Strauss the night you assaulted her.

"When Eddie called Nora, she thought she could finally get answers." I wait for Linda, letting the silence wear at her. I know she can shift at any moment and demand I leave the house. One call to the weasel dicks and it will all be over.

Linda's face drops. "I found the mechanical report and tracked down Tammy Strauss," she says, reaching for the open packet of strings. "I told Nora about my meeting with Tammy and we put the pieces together. She figured out what my mother and Eddie did, but she didn't know why. She always thought it was because Mother and Kip had something going. Some secret."

I debate sharing what Charles told me about TB with Linda. It's not clear if she knows.

I lean closer to Linda, my faces inches from hers. "After you went to the archives, you found out about Dirty Pete Strauss, which is why you didn't want me digging around out in Springfield. It's why you put Steinman on my ass. It's why you've been trying to get me off this case almost from the beginning."

Linda puts the open packet back into the case. She sits back and begins to sway back and forth, holding herself. The mantel clock chimes twice. Outside the window, I see a meadowlark bobbing on the raised ridge of a planting bed. Sun streaks spotlight floating dust motes as Linda sits in silence. Finally, she gets up, moves to the couch, and closes the cello case.

She shrugs. "Eddie killed my mother. The lab said so."

Watching her light a cigarette, which trembles in her fingers, I shake my head. "I don't think so. There's something that's been bothering me for months. I went to Eddie's autopsy and didn't see any marks on him. The blood on the spike on the wall came from a deep puncture, probably in the leg or groin. Eddie was a physical wreck, a junkie. There's no way he could have climbed that wall. Somebody in shape had to be able to do that—Eddie wasn't the killer."

"But the blood was his," she says, turning towards me, a large flake of cigarette ash drifting to the floor.

"I'm not sure about that."

"There was blood." She reaches for a large black marble ashtray and I tense for a second, wondering if she'd do something as stupid as trying to brain me. She places the ashtray on the table next to the ottoman, sitting again. Her resolve gives way like shifting sand, her shoulders falling as she exhales a long grey column into the air.

"Nora slipped trying to get back over the wall. But it wasn't a murder." She takes another deep draw on the cigarette, dropping more ash on the carpet. She turns to me, her eyes dark and angry. "Nora wanted justice. 'Let justice be done, though the heavens fall,' something like that, isn't it?" She glares at me, waiting for my reaction.

I shake my head in disbelief. "Really? Piso's justice? Justice must be done, whatever the consequences. Punishment, which is technically correct, but morally wrong."

I watch her stub the cigarette in the heavy ashtray and reach for another. "You erased the surveillance data. You were an accessory to murder. You obstructed justice."

She flicks the lighter five times before the flame touches the end of the cigarette.

"Why did Nora climb over the wall? She could have just as easily slipped out the front gate."

"We were worried Daddy would be awake. Alma and Jesus were scheduled to be there that morning, and Emma might be up. No one could see her at the house. With Frances gone, it was only a matter of waiting until Faith came out, just as she always did. I kept the lookout, and Nora did the rest."

I look at the door, figuring Frances hasn't called Webb or Charles after all. This is a private matter. This is something not even Charles knew about. Linda waits to see what I'm going to do.

"Why did Nora stay in Lake Forest?"

"You wouldn't understand," she says, shrugging.

"Stop jerking me around, Linda. There must be a reason."

Pushing the last of her cigarette into the ashtray, she folds her arms, her face now an impenetrable mask of defiance. Tapping the lighter several times on the coffee table, she says finally, "We were sisters. We were going to face whatever happened together. You must know she was very sick. She'd come home."

"You didn't kill your mother, but you helped Nora escape."

"After she hurt herself on the spike, I bandaged her and stemmed the bleeding. She got it stitched up at an urgent care later that morning."

I look out the window. The spot with the meadowlark is empty and the sunlight now floods the eastern part of the room. I think of Ben, wishing I'd dared to trust him with my secret. Rising to my feet, I startle Linda.

I move to the door and open it quickly, half expecting to catch Frances.

"As far as I'm concerned," I say, entering the empty hallway, now loud enough for the benefit of everyone in earshot, "Eddie Rivera murdered your mother. He's dead. His blood is in the lab and the case is officially closed."

I leave the door open, making my way down the corridor and out into the sunlight.

■ ■ ■

Driving towards the office, I consider whether, in the scheme of things, Nora and Stark are different. They both murdered in cold blood. What it finally comes down to, I decide, is humanity or lack of it. Both Stark and Nora were balancing an equation—they both saw the world in binary terms—what separated them was motive. For Nora, revenge was the motive; for Stark, it was greed.

I doubt Linda understood the reference to Piso's justice when she quoted him. Gnaeus Piso was a Roman governor who ordered the execution of a soldier who'd returned from leave without his buddy. Piso presumed because the man could not produce his friend, he'd killed him. As the condemned man was about to die, the very friend who was supposedly murdered showed up. The centurion overseeing the execution halted and led the condemned man back to Piso, expecting a reprieve. But Piso, mounting the tribunal in a rage, said, "let justice be done, though the heavens fall," and ordered all three soldiers executed. The first man, because the sentence had already been passed; the centurion for failing to perform his duty; and finally, the friend, because he'd been the cause of the death of two innocent men. Let justice be done, regardless of consequences or morality.

For Nora, killing Faith was a completely moral act. It was an outward sign of an inward and spiritual grace, like ringing the Dead Bell. Faith's murder was a ritual right down to the use of the garrote. Faith was executed. Nora killed to redress a wrong before succumbing to her own death sentence.

For Stark, murder is about removing obstacles. You remove an inconvenient person, a liability, like adjusting a ledger. It is an act devoid of morality. Stark chose to ignore the very truth Nora clung to until her death: that a human life is precious and must be avenged. Nora killed Faith because life is sacred and retribution essential. To Stark, killing is a means to accomplish a necessary end, nothing more, like pithing a frog or removing a tumor.

I wonder whether, in the eyes of whatever force runs the Universe, either will receive forgiveness. I hope that in judging Nora some measure will be given to the fact she believed she was sounding the Dead Bell for the parents she lost and the life she never had.

I wonder, too, whether I actually meant something to Nora, or whether she chose, with the singleness of purpose she'd given to carrying out Faith's execution, to simply savor the last morsels of carnal pleasure her wrecked body would allow.

■ ■ ■

I know, despite her confession, Linda's right about one thing: the labs contradict everything. Everything points to Eddie Rivera.

I go to the Illinois State Police Crime Lab. As Bielmans said, the lab has been under siege, its former director resigning under a cloud of falsified backlog numbers, which stand at 1,227 cases.

After signing in, I make my way to the DNA lab and ask to see the evidence registers for the previous year. Once the evidence is logged, the sample is placed in the system. The log is the only written documentation of the lodging. It is critical to the chain of title. It is also a pain in the ass to track it back. The receptionist eyes me warily until I explain, bracing myself on my good leg for effect, I'm looking into a closed case. Surveying my cane and the gimpy leg, she tells me to wait, reappearing several minutes later with two bound volumes. She points to a table by the counter.

It takes me almost twenty minutes to find entries from the previous summer. I finally find Lou Watson's notes, logging the blood sample with a corresponding lab number. Several pages later, in late July, the lab appears again, marked with the initials WLS, followed by a handwritten entry: *case review*. Apparently, no one thought to ask Dr.

Stark why he needed to review the sample.

I was right about Stark, but wrong about Eddie Rivera. Stark intended for Eddie to kill Faith. Eddie, in his bizarre order of things, believed Faith ruined his life, and that she killed Alma and Jesus. Nora got to Faith before Eddie. In Stark's simple math, Eddie became expendable, an untidy loose end. Because Stark couldn't risk what Eddie might have told the Moraleses, he killed them. When Eddie didn't get to Faith in time, Stark killed Eddie, too. Clean and complete.

But he forgot about one thing: Placidyl. He thought no one would be able to trace an ancient sedative. He had them, and they were as effective as an elephant gun in bringing down your quarry.

But why go to the trouble of holding up CODIS and substituting Eddie's blood in the lab? The answer is "belt and suspenders" as Manny Gorak says. The same reason Stark killed Eddie with both a plastic bag and a rope. Overkill, as Joyce Hong said. Because it's Bill Stark's nature to over-engineer. It wasn't enough to simply shoot the Moraleses, he had to drug them first. Bill Stark wanted Charles Wesley to know he could be reached. With Eddie's blood on the fence, Stark sent the message to Charles he was not safe. With Eddie dead, a crazed gasper suicide in Chicago, and the Moraleses' case closed, there's no messy loose ends. Hermetically sealed. Even Delahunt told me to close the case because there was no reason to keep it open—just what Stark wanted.

For Stark, the fact someone else killed Faith Wesley was just dumb luck.

■ ■ ■

My father said the crucible is about forgiveness. I never forgave Paulie, and it took me years to finally understand what happened in the underbrush next to Günther's restaurant. During one of my routine sex offender searches for Katie, I came across a serial rapist named Paul Mazernik, who'd been arrested in Wisconsin. Along with the record was a picture. Staring out at me was the older, corroded face of the monster in the speedboat. I ran his sheet. He had multiple convictions for aggravated assault, rape, sexual assault, and burglary. But his luck finally ran out. He died four years before my search. After a couple of phone calls, I found out Paulie the Monster was stabbed to death at Boscobel Supermax.

That said, forgiving someone who was once your friend is even more difficult. I've arrived at a place where I've forgiven Katie, and I'm learning to live alongside her as we raise our child. I'm grateful Katie didn't find or use a guy like Stark. Forgiveness is what tumbles out of the crucible, gold and hot, and missing it is to endure for no reason, to suffer for nothing.

I need to start by forgiving myself, for letting Ben believe the tragedy of Jimmy Newsome occurred because he gave Paulie the finger. If Ben had known the truth about Paulie, if I'd told Ben, my older brother, what happened to me, he might have threatened Paulie the Monster and, knowing the secret was out, Paulie might well have killed us all. Instead, we lived to endure.

■　■　■

In July, I drive to Springfield, taking the last exit off the highway. The county road takes me through small neat houses, past the Civil War memorial to the honored dead, until I finally arrive at the place I've come to see.

Günters was torn down decades ago, replaced by a row of townhouses overlooking the lake. Behind the development, the ground still slopes down to the underbrush at the far end of the lot. I stare at the lake for several minutes, finally leaving my car, carrying a folding spade with me. Opening the trunk, I extract the heavy blanket, carrying it under my arm. I check my pocket to make sure the cloth is still there.

The blue-winged warblers and waterthrushes gather in the bushes and along the shore. Their voices chirp loud and clear in the hot July sun as they bob and skitter in the tall grass. Carrying the folding shovel and the gray blanket, I make my way toward the thicket at the bottom of the slope, walking in the warm, fragrant wet mud, careful not to trip in the divots and holes.

The tangle of hackberry and buttonbush is smaller than I remember, but several feet in, I lose all sight of the lake and the townhouses. After pushing through the underbrush, I finally reach a small clearing. The scent of the prairie cordgrass under my feet transports me back in time. Closing my eyes, I recall the dark smell of the dirt and the sour odor of dirty jeans and cigarettes. I survey the clearing, reaching into my pocket and pulling out a wad of torn cloth, its bright orange faded by the years. I shake it until it dangles like a flag, waving gently in the breeze, which stirs the new growth on the bushes. Despite the years and the passage of time, the fabric still holds the same slightly metallic fragrance as the day I recovered it from the raft. Folded and tucked neatly in the back of my dresser, it has sat through the years, even as I've moved, married, divorced, and moved again.

I carefully map the clearing again, looking for landmarks. Secure in the belief I'm at the right place, I unfold the spade and dig a hole in the dark earth. When I finish, I fold the cloth, kiss it once, and drop it into the hole. I unfold the blanket and take the heavy bell in my hands, placing it next to the folded cloth. Grabbing the shovel, I cover them both with fresh dirt. I stand up, brush my hands, and wipe the tears from my cheeks.

One place remains before the trip is done. I follow the road, unthinking, until I reach the tree-lined street, pull the car to the curb, and turn off the engine. The inside of the car is silent except for the ticking of the hot motor.

The solitary pin oak in the front is larger, and the dusty junipers along the borders stretch farther in untamed waves towards the siding, but the house is the same. It still retains the shape and color I remember. The entrance is still guarded by the same aluminum screen door through which I taunted Ben and Bill. I can, without much effort, erase the years, washing away other families who have been there, other disappointments, sorrows, and other lives lived, to find my own.

The place transforms, suddenly filled with the sounds, smells, and memories of my past, marked like the pencil lines my father placed on the doorpost tallying the inches and years as Ben and I grew. I know the smudges and nicks in the paint, the broken doorknob, the tattered screen, and for each know its story. With the narrative force of a warrior, I can recount the losses and scars. I can hear the gravel of my mother's voice and smell the scent of hot, dry laundry spread on the couch for folding. I can hear the sound of my father's patient steps as he turned the lights off, ready for sleep. I can hear the tinny sound of the radio in Ben's room as he listens to Cubs games. Sitting in the car, I have no need to walk to the rear of the house, remembering the sensation of the deep loam, spongy and brown under the trees at the far end of the yard where I've lain transfixed by the sun through the tall trees. It is alive for me and I carry it all inside.

Across the street, the house stands as it has always stood, an inanimate skeleton of wood, glass, and steel. But it is a sacred space, a battlefield; solemn and consecrated. I've come here to bury my dead, and in this place have dutifully met its ghosts, sitting a long while with them, finally putting them to rest. I will not come back here again. They are gone, released, and there's no need to speak with them again, or fear their sudden appearance. Nor will I flee from them on the Last Day when it will inevitably come and I will join them.

POSTSCRIPT

STATE OF ILLINOIS
DEPARTMENT OF CORRECTIONS

MENARD CORRECTIONAL CENTER

Incident Report

Date April 7th
Ref: Inmate #259184 William Stark

At 10:45 AM on Tuesday, April 1st, inmate William Stark (#278184) was found by correctional staff (Withorn #2234, and Eggars #5579) with multiple stab wounds to the chest and stomach area. Inmate #278184 also sustained multiple facial contusions consistent with a severe assault immediately before the time of death.

Inmate #278184 was pronounced dead at the scene by correctional facility medical staff.

An investigation is ongoing.
Persons of interest:
Alfonso "Shiv" Gutierrez (inmate #258177)
Carlos "Puta" Lamasta (inmate #254121)

Both of the above are known past associates of Eduardo "Eddie" Rivera (formerly inmate #253238)

ACKNOWLEDGMENTS

I BEGAN WRITING THIS BOOK ALMOST EIGHTEEN YEARS ago. It has gone through several major changes, including narrative voice, tense, and structure. With each of these changes, people took the time to read, comment, and offer suggestions. I have had the gift of readers who were patient, engaged, and kind enough to offer criticism in a way that did not deflate me to the point where I simply abandoned the project.

Included in the group of earlier readers is my friend and colleague Gilion Dumas, my brother Malcolm, my friend and former law partner, Dave, and my sister Libby, all of whom have contributed to the process. To all of you a heartfelt thanks.

What you are reading is also the product of the tireless, insightful, and inspired work of my editor Linda Stirling, who helped turn the book into a polished novel. I am both thankful for your meticulous sense of phrasing, which helped me convey what I meant, and grateful for the fact you were willing to spend the time and resources to make this book a reality.

Finally, I am thankful for the love and support of my wife, Jane, who has been a reader, a skeptic, a cheering section, Supreme Allied Command, and a soulmate. Words are insufficient.

ABOUT THE AUTHOR

In a prior life, Reid Winslow was a prosecutor and trial attorney. A photographer and outdoorsman, he lives with his family in the beautiful Pacific Northwest.

If you enjoyed this book, would you leave a review? Reviews help the author and they help other readers find books they enjoy.

CPSIA information can be obtained
at www.ICGtesting.com
Printed in the USA
LVHW041945020123
736291LV00002B/220